THE SWANS AT CLEARLAKE

THE SWANS AT CLEARLAKE

RICHARD JOHN THORNTON

THIS STORY IS DEDICATED TO THE GENERATION GAP.

The Swan.
Halcyon symbol.
The epitome of grace.
The paragon of guardianship.
Exemplary to one and all.

PROLOGUE

It was a demand for attention. A signature of fearlessness borne out of a will for the world to stop and look. But it was nearly too late. The futile waving of a faltering flag. The intrusion of rusting metal into perfect flesh.

Yet nobody saw. Because nobody cared. Least of all the owner of that once perfect flesh. Desecration of what was naturally bestowed at birth; awarded in the earnest belief that it would always be cherished.

But that boy, he cherished little.

Especially his own, imperfect flesh.

I
DISSENSION

ONE

It was on the fourth kick that the jawbone finally gave way. The victim lay silently quivering as they set about his cowering, pathetic form. At first, Jonka Wilson suspected that the apparent suffering incurred was being fabricated as a desperate plea for mercy.

A futile claim for a concession. But it's obvious when someone's really hurt. When they are truly disabled. They go very quiet. The extreme pain induces shock, which paralyses most of the body's reactions.

The gang used to laugh at footballers, for instance. Players that screamed, jumped, and dived around throughout the match, but haven't really got as much as a scratch on them when the final whistle blows. It's easy to tell when someone's truly broken their leg. They lie still; silent; motionless. They get scared when the reality hits. They instinctively want to protect the part of them that has failed to withstand the impact.

Jonka knew his target was hurting alright. There was no blood. Just a familiar conveyance of numbness that only a practised assailant could detect in his victim.

A submissive air enshrouded the defenceless youth hunched at Jonka's feet.

Perhaps one more. In the face. Just to make sure. Just to finish the job off properly.

Then a stark order echoed along the alleyway.

'NO! ENOUGH. WE'RE DONE. MOVE IT!'

The command came from the shadows.

A tall, lean figure stood against the tarred, damp brickwork of the railway arch. His hooded face peered through the half-light as he assessed the progress of the latest Black Stars attack.

Jonka did not hear the order in time and once more proceeded to swing the toe of his leather training shoe into the indented, distorted face of the barely conscious quarry.

The adrenaline fuelled his desire to kick again and again. The next he knew, Jonka had himself received a solid punch on the back of the head.

'I SAID GO! SHIFT IT!'

This time the request was adhered to without delay. Jonka turned from the hapless casualty on the ground and began to sprint into the darkness after his friends. They ran for what seemed like hours.

Within twenty minutes the group had covered three miles and were back in the vicinity of Talworth town centre.

This was a well proven tactic for evasion. This was where they could be easily seen on the CCTV cameras as being present and correct at around the time of the mugging.

Not that the cameras proved anything. Either there would be no one manning them at the police station or there would be no recorded proof inside anyhow.

Avoiding the restricted arm of the law was easy these days.

Congregating in the small market square under the shadow of the large sycamore tree, the gang arranged themselves along a bench as the leader stood out front and addressed his troops. Breathless and perspiring, the group awaited their de-briefing.

'What the fuck was that about, Jonks? You don't half go over the top. He's gonna probably need surgery now. That's if he lives. I hope he didn't see your face. Cos if he comes looking for you in about a year when he's all healed up, I will stand back and let him have you. You understand me?'

The other two stared at their friend as he bowed his head before the self-appointed sergeant major of the Black Stars, Liam Warburton. Eventually, a low muttering could be heard from beneath a dark hood.

'Sorry, Liam. I was just enjoying myself, I guess.'

With hands remaining in the pockets of his own hooded top, Liam leaned forward and whispered.

'Don't worry, fool. I was joking. You did good. I'll protect you from evil should it come looking. As usual.'

With a knowing smirk Liam turned to the second member of the gang. Elson Stevens glanced around the square to check for passers-by, before relaying the contents of his coat pocket to an eager audience.

'An I-Phone and twenty-four quid. No cards though. Not bad, Liam. Not bad, man.'

'Right. I'm having the I-Phone.' sneered the third boy, Glendin Jones.

Liam's responsive glare soon made Glendin realise that the I-phone would only be destined for one person's possession.

'I can get a charger for this. So…I'd better take it.'

'Come on, Liam! That's not fair, man!' snapped Glendin.

There was a momentary pause as the leader of the gang drew closer to the objector.

Liam briefly scanned for witnesses as he slowly opened and closed his fists, caressing the brass knuckle-duster that adorned his right hand.

'Fair, Glenners? Fair? What's *fair* got to do with anything? Was it fair that we set about that guy and dragged him down the aqueduct to kick his head to bits? Was that fair? No...but you still did it...didn't you?'

Glendin looked across to the other two sitting in learned silence. It was a wise policy to avoid questioning the assumed authority of their commander. But wisdom wasn't Glendin's strong point.

'We *all* did it, Liam. We *all* had a go at him. We all took the risk. We should all share the spoils, man.'

The boys' attention was distracted by the distant siren of a police car.

Or of course, it could have been an ambulance.

'Correction, fool! *You* three kicked his head off his shoulders. I, as your chosen protector, stood guard for your safety and welfare.'

Glendin was not happy about the distribution of the stolen bounty and promptly stood face to face with Liam.

'That's cos you're chicken-shit, man! You're too scared to wade in!'

Liam looked around the square once more before rapidly grabbing his friend's windpipe between his thumb and forefinger. He began to squeeze...as Glendin rapidly began to wheeze.

'Leave it out, Liam.' ordered Jonka. 'He's just pullin' your leg, dude.'

Elson rose to his feet in concerned astonishment as the gasping Glendin collapsed to his knees.

'Liam...come on, man. Leave it!'

Liam crouched down to view the absolute, undiluted fear in his friend's eyes. He had total control over Glendin's life at that moment. It was the kind of situation that made Liam feel invincible to anyone or anything.

A sensation that he had begun to thrive on.

'Right, Glendin, my so unfairly treated colleague. I will let you survive on this occasion. But any more of this "chicken-shit" business from your mouth will greatly affect my attitude.'

With that, Liam released his prey, who then proceeded to writhe around on the floor, desperately gulping deep breaths to replenish his starving lungs.

Elson and Jonka watched in fearful silence, both baffled and afraid by the potential consequences of what they had just witnessed. However, to their inspirational leader, it was simply an expression in positive tutorage.

Liam addressed the gang once more.

'Okay…let's start again. I'm keeping the I-Phone. Okay? Any problems with that?'

Liam's grimace of superiority was enough to deter any further vocal objection to his claims.

'There's good boys. The money you can split between you. Get yourself some supper. You've deserved it.'

Liam stood aside as the other two helped Glendin unsteadily to his feet. Rubbing his throat whilst stemming the onset of tears, he glared at Liam's face for a flicker of sorrow.

There was nothing.

Not a glimmer of compassion in the eyes of the perpetrator.

Just a returning, cold stare emanated from the half-shadow of his hood.

Struggling for an exchange of words to alter the mood, the four were alerted to an unannounced presence across the other side of the road, concealed behind the thick trunk of the sycamore tree. The figure stood watching the boys at the bench for a few seconds before moving toward them. The silhouette was not difficult to identify as the uniform of a policeman.

A policeman that knew the boys all too well.

Liam took control of the situation with a sarcastic greeting as he secretly dropped the stolen goods into a dustbin close behind and covertly removing the brass wrapped around his knuckles.

'Ahh! Police Constable Philip Wainwright, no less! A pleasure to see you on this unseasonably warm evening, officer. Caught any offenders tonight?'

From the corner of his eye, the officer saw Liam's captive audience attempt to hide their smirks. Unbeknown to them, this was only a passing social enquiry from the local constabulary.

'Been out long have we, Liam?' enquired the officer.

'No…half hour, maybe less. Just left Jonka's house.'

Jonka attempted to authenticate Liam's lie with a feigned and hopeful expression of affirmation.

P.C. Philip Wainwright was not at all convinced but cared little for causing any undue disruption within the group at that particular moment.

'Oh…right. Okay, lads.'

The walkie-talkie on the policeman's shoulder hissed into life with an inaudible message, making Elson jump in his seat.

'You'd better answer that…might be important.' exclaimed Liam.

The officer eyed the gang for a few moments.

'No…not for me. For some of our lads north of the town. Some poor kid has had the living daylights kicked out of him…up by the aqueduct. Can't speak, apparently. Broken jaw. Someone made a right mess of him.'

The members of the Black Stars quickly glanced at one another before Liam resumed his chatter to quell their momentary discomfort. As he spoke, the knuckle duster was slipped into his hoody pocket.

'Jesus. There's always some innocent soul getting hurt, isn't there, officer?'

P.C. Wainwright took a few paces toward Liam and his friends and glanced around the floor area at their feet as Liam lit a cigarette.

'Does your mother know you smoke, Liam?'

Liam grinned from ear to ear as his reply burst from between his lips.

'No, sir. But she doesn't know I'm drinking lager or shagging birds either…sir!'

With that, the group exploded into laughter, including the policeman, who began to walk toward the junction of the high street.

'Bloody smart-arses. Take it easy, lads. See you around. Though…not too often I hope!'

Liam maintained the act of courtesy until the officer was out of earshot, before muttering a contemptuous farewell under his breath.

'Yes, sir. Thank you, sir. You useless…tosspot…sir.'

Retrieving the I-phone from the dustbin, Liam inserted it into his pocket before announcing his own departure.

'Look, lads. I'm off. It's boring tonight. See you at the prison tomorrow. If I can be bothered.'

'What's our first lesson?' asked Elson.

'God knows.' snorted Liam. 'See you at the gates. And it's *your* turn for ciggies, Els! So, make sure to bring some with you, yeah? My mum's sick of funding your filthy habit!'

'I thought you weren't pinching off her no more.'

Liam chuckled at the presumption of his friend.

'Don't be soft, Els. She's got that much dough she doesn't even notice.'

The three teenagers sat huddled on the bench watching their master depart into the night. They observed his practiced swagger merge into the distant murk without further utterance. Finally, when deciding that Liam was out of hearing range, Jonka turned to his partners in crime, yet maintained a careful whisper.

'I can't believe that shit he just pulled on you Glenners. Warburton is tapped. Slice short of a full loaf!'

Glendin said nothing as he stared vacantly upward into the early evening sky.

With a wary diversion of his gaze, he gratefully watched Liam vanish from sight as he nervously closed his grip around the twenty-four pounds in cash.

With his free hand, he began to gently rub his bruised throat.

The Black Stars were quietly thankful for their leader's exit.

In turn, Liam did not look back at his team as he strode onward without distraction.

He was almost strutting home as the adrenaline that had fuelled his veins a while earlier began to subside.

The water below the canal bridge lay motionless as Liam crossed by the locks.

Disturbing the peace of his march homeward, his pocket began to drone and vibrate. Retrieving the mobile phone, Liam threw down his cigarette butt and squinted at the azure display.

A cynical smirk dressed his lips as he proceeded to launch it over his shoulder and into the depths of the ebony cut.

Perhaps someone wanted to know the whereabouts of the true owner, who now lay in the back of an ambulance, fighting for his life.

The electronic ring tone fizzled into fused silence as it sank without trace.

TWO

'Yes. Well, it's a proposition that needs some serious thought, but not *too* much serious thought, mind.'

Richard Warburton laughed heartily as he glanced across the lounge to his wife, Stephanie.

'Well, we've been keeping our fingers crossed for weeks. This could be the making of SRW! We need this deal. It could set us up for life. Jesus, I'm excited just thinking about it!'

Stephanie watched her husband fondly as he exchanged enthusiasm on the phone with their foreign business solicitor, William Boyd.

'Listen Bill. You sort out the finer stuff. The decision is practically made anyway. The home market is packed out with competition. But Greece? It's a property developer's heaven!'

With a thumbs-up to his wife, Richard's smile grew ever larger amid his carefully trimmed beard as the good tidings were passed on from their lawyer.

'You reckon an interim period of two months? Yeah, okay. Just to get a feel for the locations we're considering. Yeah, sounds good. Just got to find somewhere to store the brat and we're sorted to get out there.'

Richard laughed once again as he winked at his wife.

Stephanie did not like to hear Liam's father refer to their son in such a way, but certainly sympathised with the motive. If this deal came off, there was no possibility she would let their only offspring come along and spoil the party. She rose from the settee and continued to listen avidly whilst inspecting her perfectly made-up features in the lounge mirror.

'No, shouldn't be a problem. Anyway, I can deal with that side. You worry about the legal arrangements and the accommodation. That's what I pay you for. Not bloody childcare.'

More laughter ensued before farewells were exchanged.

'You tie up ends over there, then. Great! Give me a call when we're clear to book our flights. Hopefully we'll be standing on the balcony with you by the end of July!'

Thoughts of a splendid retirement in paradise flooded Stephanie's mind as she studied the reflection of the man she loved whilst scrutinising her manicured eyebrows.

'Okay, Bill. Speak soon. Ta-ra for now. Bye!'

Richard joyously disconnected the handset before embracing his wife and pulling her on a merry waltz around the lounge floor.

'Rich, you are like a child at times! I take it all is looking good for our foreign venture?'

He kissed her full on the lips as a gesture of utmost confirmation.

'Never been better, love. Never…been…better!'

Stephanie's chuckles at Richard's impromptu clowning were suddenly eclipsed once more by thoughts of her son.

'So…what do you have in mind for Liam, then?'

Her husband instantly stood still and rested his hands on his hips.

'You have to go and spoil the mood don't you! I don't know. We could try the nearest kennels, couldn't we? Perhaps a couple of months in the Salvation Army wouldn't go amiss? Or even the Territorial Army!'

More giggles between man and wife detracted from the fact that Stephanie required a serious answer from her husband for once. Relocating Liam for the summer was not going to be easy. Options were limited.

'Well, I know where he's *not* going, Steph. With *us*! That's final. No ifs or buts.'

Stephanie was in total agreement.

'No, of course not. Not a chance. What about asking him if he'd like to stay with his friends?'

A look of earnest horror befell Richard's features.

'No way!'

'Why not?'

'Because he'd be back round here like a shot having house parties every bloody night with his scumbag mates. The conservatory would be like a pot den when we returned. And it would be a bloody miracle if the windows remained intact. Then there'd no doubt be police crawling all over, damage to our stuff…'

Stephanie raised her hand to call a cease to Richard's truthful tirade.

'Okay…okay…point taken. Liam staying here is not an option, then. So…I suppose the only solution is getting him away from Talworth?'

Richard offered a look of partial trepidation to his wife, who responded with the inevitable nod of the head.

'Yes, I know. I can't see another way around it, either.'

'What about your parents though, Steph? You haven't spoken to them for an age. It must be year or more?'

Richard admired his wife's slim figure as she retreated to the kitchen and flicked on the kettle.

'Well, that's *their* fault, isn't it? I'm not responsible for the fact that *they're* mad with *me*. Well, Dad, anyway. He was the one who always resented me wanting the city career. *He's* the one with the issue. Mum will be fine about it.'

Richard moved behind Stephanie and placed his arms around her waist. Nuzzling into her ear was a sure-fire way of placating her concerns.

'And I'd bet you'd have made a smashing farmer's wife, too!'

'Don't tease, Rich. It's been a serious rift. I never thought it would go on this long. They seem to have become angrier with me over the past fifteen years instead of more understanding.'

'Look, love. All you have to do is pick up the phone and talk to them.'

Stephanie turned to her husband in mock anger.

'And why, Richard Warburton, might I ask, do *I* have to make the first move?'

Richard withdrew from his clinch and pulled two mugs from the wooden tree on the worktop behind him.

'Because, my dear, they're *your* parents...not *mine*. Mine are dead, or I'd ring *them* instead.'

'I'm sorry. That's not a good enough reason. You're still a coward!'

'Okay, darling. You need to ring them to ask if we can deposit our delightful son for the summer so we can go and soak up some sun for a few weeks. If you put it like that, they'll welcome Liam with open arms!'

Stephanie tried not to look amused by her husband's cynicism.

'No, sorry. That's far too honest. Think of a plan B, hubby dear. Three strikes and you're out!'

Facing away from his wife, Richard poured hot water into the two mugs and stirred them loudly as he spoke.

'Okay. I can't ring your parents because...your father hates me for dragging you away from the boring country life he had mapped out for you since you were born. There...how's that?'

Stephanie smiled before planting a kiss on his lips.

'That's excellent, darling. By the way...my father also hates *me*...of course...you always forget that bit! Though, he's not overly keen on Liam, either!'

The pair reclined on the settee with their drinks. Richard observed the clock on the lounge wall.

'Jesus. The army life did nothing for your dad's approach to his family, did it? Which reminds me, where is the apple of my eye? I haven't seen him today. He can't still be out. It's getting late.'

Looking wide-eyed at her husband, Stephanie tutted and sipped her drink.

'That statement alone just shows how much interest you take in *our* family life as well! Liam's not been in bed before midnight for about the last two years. He'll be out with his mates somewhere.'

'Yes, creating havoc no doubt. Honestly, though, Steph. Do you think you could swing it for us to dump him with your folks?'

Stephanie continued to drink her coffee whilst pondering the future and its unpredictable premise.

'Well, Liam was a little bleeder last time we went. Can you remember? He filled my dad's Wellingtons with water. Glued the cutlery together! Set Dad's newspaper on fire as he was reading it…'

Richard's earnest guffaws delayed his response.

'Oh, come off it, Steph! Liam could only have been about ten years old then. He's a different person now.'

She watched her husband as he emptied the remains of his cup.

'Oh yes, he's bloody *worse* now! And Liam was twelve – not ten. Plus of course there's Dad's condition. He's in no state for shouting orders at unruly teenagers. He might have been decorated by the military but he's not the man he was. Not with his throat. Mum said in her last letter that he was struggling to eat some kinds of food because it hurt so bad.'

Richard leaned forward to place his empty mug on the coffee table.

'Why doesn't he go and get it sorted, then? He's always had a cough as long as I've known him.'

'He's ex-army, Rich. Soldiers act hard because they *are* hard. You won't see my dad in a doctor's surgery. He'd rather suffer in silence.'

'Huh! Bet it hasn't stopped him barking at Barbara. Nasty sod, your dad… when he wants to be.'

'Well, if anyone was likely to make things worse, it could only be Liam. He winds people up for pleasure these days.'

Richard yawned loudly and clasped his hands behind his back.

'Look…just *ring* them. I can't see them saying no, can you? It might heal this daft rift you're on about. But I think you make things far more dramatic than they need to be. A friendly word to your mum and it'll be all systems go.'

Stephanie was not convinced. Her knowing look made Richard yawn once more.

'Okay, so things weren't so hot when we last saw them. But this is a chance to make it all better, Steph. Everyone will benefit, love! Go on, ring them.'

'What…now?'

'Yes. Why not now?'

'Cos, it's half-past midnight! I can't believe Bill was still awake! Must be having one of his wild parties! Anyway, my parents will be fast asleep. That's why not now, dopey.'

Richard looked across to her and offered the smile that melted her heart every time.

'So…tomorrow then?'

'Yes, damn it! I'll ring them tomorrow. For now, let's get to bed. We've both got appointments in the morning you know!'

'Yes, love. I know. Come on.'

It was nearly two am when Stephanie heard Liam turn the key in the front door lock and let himself in. With her head remaining on the pillow, she instantly detected the aroma of dope wafting its way up the staircase followed by her son.

Richard had dropped straight to sleep and was snoring quietly as the teenager reached the landing to hear the whispered greeting of his mother.

'Liam? Liam?'

Stephanie waited for the reply from the other side of her bedroom door. Eventually, a slurred response was barely audible as Liam opened the door to his own bedroom.

'What, Mum? I'm knackered.'

'You alright, love?'

'Yeah…fine. Tired. Need to kip.'

'Where have you been 'til this time?'

'Well, I was coming home earlier, but got side-tracked.'

'Not your friend round the corner – him who sells you them funny fags?'

There was a slight hesitancy in his reply, which suggested that his mother had been correct in her assumption.

'No, Mum. Of course not!'

The pungent aroma began to irritate Stephanie's nostrils.

'Okay, love. Get to bed. See you in the morning.'

Shutting the bedroom door behind him, Liam reached into his pockets and retrieved three small polythene wallets containing brown weed. Placing them in the bottom of the wardrobe in the heel of a shoe, he then collapsed fully clothed onto the mattress.

Under the influence of a cheap but reliably effective stimulant, Liam Warburton drifted away into another, perhaps happier world.

THREE

'Get up to much last night, Liam?'

Richard observed his slouching son throw an expression of contempt as eggs and bacon were placed before him at the dining table.

'Liam…I'm speaking to you.'

Peeling his eyes open, the aroma of breakfast became slowly more amenable as the disapproving vision of his father came into partial focus. An image that prompted Liam to let his head drop to rest on the tabletop.

'Eh?'

'You're still out of it! Do you even know where you are, lad?'

The vague familiarity of his father's voice compelled another half-hearted response, although Liam did not remove his face from the darkened vicinity of his armpit. The reply was muffled, yet audible.

'Lay off, man. I'm hurting.'

Richard closed the newspaper and picked up his cutlery.

'I'm not "man". I'm not one of your scummy mates. I'm your father. Remember? You know? That bloke that allows you to live here in complete luxury for free?'

Liam continued to mumble into the tablecloth.

'Yeah, yeah…yadder yadder yadder…why don't you fill your mouth with food Pops and give my ears a rest!'

'Cheeky little shit! You're a waste of space! Going bloody nowhere!'

'Yeah, Dad. I'm the waste of space *you* made!'

Stephanie observed the ensuing battle between father and son but remained silent as she dished up the remaining breakfast.

'You are still going to school I take it?'

'Of course, Daddy, dear. Wouldn't miss it for the world! I'm loving it, aren't I!'

'Liam. You're a talented lad. You need to get your head out of your backside and get it back around schooling. I recall what your art teacher said about your work. He's very enthusiastic about your ability. He said so at the last parent's evening. Why don't you respond to his encouragement, instead of going out every night with your idiot friends?'

Finally, Liam reluctantly lifted his gaze and briefly observed the plate of cooling food under his nose.

'Dad…that was ages ago. I don't even talk to Smithy that much these days.'

'Well, you *should* go and talk to him. Get some sense into that doped up skull of yours! He said you could be a good artist. As far as I could see, he was the only teacher that ever said anything good about you.'

'I don't care, Dad. I don't want to hear it. Not now.'

Having listened to enough of the ritualistic morning quarrel herself, Stephanie turned from the blazing grill.

'Right, boys. Enough now. Eat your breakfast. Let's have quiet…or I'm going to put on some classical music.'

Tilting his scornful expression toward his mother, Liam placed a fork full of bacon into one cheek.

'I can't stand that shit, Mum. What about some Busta Rhymes? Proper music to learn from?'

Stephanie could not help but smile at her son's cockiness.

'Never mind busting rhymes, I'll bust your teeth if you don't shape up, Liam. Now, eat.'

Richard wearily eyed his oblivious son across the table before immersing himself back into the morning's headlines once again.

It seemed there was no sense in talking to the boy when he portrayed such an obstructive demeanour. But at least Liam had an appetite. His plate was emptied within two minutes before he exited the kitchen to get ready for the day ahead.

*****

The walk to school was accompanied by blurred vision and a thumping headache. His mother knew full well that Liam had come home smashed but opted to say nothing at breakfast. His father's criticisms seemed to play a daily part of Liam's life and she would readily stand back and let her husband take the reins.

Yet Stephanie often wondered whether her son would respond better to some positive commentary, but of late there was little to inspire two frustrated parents into appraisal. Only apathy. Liam was becoming a problem. Of that there was little doubt. His future was in the balance. Fifteen-years-old was a critical age to fall out of sync with peers.

Liam needed to aspire to something, but there was little in his life at that moment to divert his attention from the dubious activity he preferred to indulge himself in of an evening.

It would be true to say that Liam's eventual arrival that morning at St. Forsters Secondary School was nothing short of a miracle. He had followed the twenty-minute route on autopilot. Only when a familiar voice hurled itself across the playground did he begin to fully realise where he was.

Standing outside the school gates, Liam proudly lit his first cigarette of the day in an effort to revitalize numbed senses. The holler echoed toward him once again, as he gratifyingly continued to inhale the nicotine.

Robert Harris, Headmaster of St. Forsters, had other ideas on how to erode morning fatigue and on spotting Liam's ramshackle form he made a rapid approach.

'Warburton! Get rid of that! Put it out! What kind of example does it set to the younger pupils?'

Peering menacingly from under the shroud of his hood, Liam viewed the figure of the irate teacher. Content to retain the cigarette drooping from the corner of his mouth, he raised a mocking hand of greeting to Mr. Harris, much to the amusement of those around him.

'Warburton! Where is your uniform? You know you're on a final warning for this? Suspension is imminent, boy! Get that rubbish out of your mouth, lad!'

The daily repetition of the exchange was becoming extremely tiresome for Liam. Secretly, he hoped that the school would expel him for good and leave him in peace. The only downside of such a move would be that he would have nobody to antagonize first thing in a morning - an exercise that fuelled him into life far quicker than coffee or tobacco. Battle commenced in amusing fashion for those in proximity.

'Hey – Leader! How's tricks?'

Robert Harris' hand swiped the cigarette from between the lips of its owner, narrowly missing contact with Liam's mouth.

'Hey, man! In the street you'd have been downed for that move!'

'Don't try the heroics with me, Warburton. You're still a little boy who thinks he knows what it is to be a man. Well, listen up. I'm prepared to let you into school today being as you've obliged us by an appearance. But your parents will have to be informed about your dress.'

Again, Liam raised his open hands in mocking self-defence as the audience observed.

'My...dress? Look mighty Leader, I'll try a lot of things at school but not wearing dresses...no way, man!'

The mirthful response from those in the vicinity was quashed by Robert Harris' angered bark.

'You'll work outside my office today, boy. Where I can keep an eye on every move you make! You're pushing it, Warburton! Another little fact I will be telling your mother and father about. You're treading a fine line here at St. Forsters.'

Without further retort, Liam shrugged and retrieved the half full packet of cigarettes from his pocket before attempting to ignite another. With disbelieving rage, the Head snatched the packet from Liam's grasp and shoved him inside the school gates.

'Don't touch what you don't respect, man. Out of order, Mister Leader.'

'Come on, Warburton. Time to get your attendance registered. I'm sure Mister Smith is waiting for you in the form room.'

Further laughter from the incidental onlookers accompanied the pair as they argued their way into the main building of the school.

For a fleeting moment as he was ushered along the corridor, Liam thought about the earlier exchange with his father at the breakfast table and his comments about his form tutor.

Colin Smith had almost given up on Liam's evaporated will to address his own potential. Unbeknown to Liam's parents, he was still Liam's form teacher, but for some reason, the praise given to Liam over the last couple of years for his creative ability seemed to have a detrimental effect on his attitude.

He felt sad that a teacher should be somewhat obliged to observe a pupil with such natural talent let it all go to waste. Yes, Liam struggled academically, but his natural artistic flair still adorned the walls of the form room for all to admire.

The only person who had an aversion to acknowledging his own natural born gift for art and design…was Liam himself.

The classroom door burst open allowing the highly audible squabble between Headmaster and pupil to filter into the eardrums of the form tutor, who sat quietly behind his desk, scheduling the day ahead. He looked up from his diary and sighed with resignation at the sight paraded before him.

The now all too familiar vision of Liam Warburton…in strife once again.

'Sorry to disturb you, Colin.' proclaimed the Head.

Mr. Smith sat back in his chair and clasped his hands behind his head. Glancing to the wall clock, he was surprised to see that Liam had arrived five minutes before the registration bell was due to drone into life. Liam stood forlornly before his tutor as Mr. Harris explained events.

'Just to let you know, Colin. I want him outside my room all day. Set him up with his work. I'll see to it that he gets up to nothing. By the way, I've confiscated these.'

The Headteacher tossed the half packet of cigarettes onto the desk.

Liam stared into the eyes of Mr. Smith, whose thin yet caring smile expanded under his slightly hooked nose. Liam smirked knowingly back, being careful not to let the Head see his amusement.

'Thank you for the delivery, Mister Harris. Can you give us a little while? I'd like some time with Liam after registration. I haven't got a lesson until second period.'

'Best of luck, Colin. You know where I am should you need me.'

'Yes…thank you, Mr. Harris.'

Teacher and pupil watched in silence as the Headmaster departed and closed the door behind him. With the two of them now alone together, Colin Smith could begin.

'Take your usual seat, Liam. I'll do the register. Then we'll talk in private when I've got rid of the animals. As if I haven't got enough to do!'

Without further word, Liam obliged and slumped into a chair at the back of the room. Just as he did so, the registration bell sounded, barely encouraging a gradual flow of pupils through the door. The commotion was deafening as nearly thirty teenage boys and girls slowly took their positions amid the din of banging desks and scraping chairs, whilst exchanging details of their most intimate secrets.

Liam listened candidly to the array of commentary as he slouched unacknowledged. Nobody seemed to notice him sat at the back of the room, but Liam heard everything around him as differing voices offered varying opinions on every subject imaginable.

'Yeah, then she smacked her one!'

'Doesn't wear condoms!'

'We reckon she's up the duff!'

'Broke his nose!'

'Bought some pills for Friday!'

'She can't. She's got an ASBO!'

'Got any fags for break-time?'

The plethora of part-conversations enveloped Liam's mind as he continued to perch undisturbed. It also slightly annoyed him that the room was full of people, yet no one felt obliged to concede to his presence.

Aside, that is, from one particularly brazen young lady who as usual needed little encouragement to commence a conversation.

'What's up with you, Warbs? Here early, aren't you? Have you pissed the bed or something?'

The cackles of her close friends echoed around the ceiling of classroom as Liam idly responded by raising both his middle fingers. Typically, Carla Ferris was not perturbed by the gesture.

'Yes please, Liam. Bike sheds. Is home time alright for you?'

Liam now smiled under his hood. He secretly liked Carla. She was a good sport and could take comical and critical abuse as well as ably dish it out. Liam finally felt compelled to offer a vocal reply.

'No thanks Carls, old bean. I'm not going to stir half of St. Forsters' porridge, even with my fanny finger!'

More laughter abounded as Carla visibly struggled to disguise a smile of mild embarrassment.

'You're a cheeky bastard, Warburton! One of these days!'

'In your dreams, Carla. In your dreams.'

Liam simply offered a wink of victory as Mr. Smith rose from his desk, closed the door, and waited patiently for hush.

Seconds later, partial quiet was achieved, and the register was taken.

Then with a gesturing hand from the teacher back toward the door, the room was quickly cleared once again, leaving Liam alone with his thoughts. But not without the ritual parting shot from Carla.

'Don't strain yourself, Liam! See you later, babes.'

The face under the hood grinned once again and offered a nod of appreciation for the entertainment.

Now alone again at the back of the room, Liam centred attention on Mr. Smith. He watched as the teacher walked slowly around the classroom with his hands clasped behind his back. Not a word was uttered for seconds on end, as the art teacher scanned the walls, admiring the work of the young man sat before him.

Finally, the conversation opened.

'Great stuff this, Liam. Visionary. Mindful. Original. Can you still draw like this?'

Liam Warburton was becoming confused. There was no anticipated reprimand forthcoming from Colin Smith for the earlier issue with the Headmaster. There was no mention of the cigarettes. Or the plan to seat him outside Robert Harris' office for the duration of the day. It appeared that the art teacher wanted to talk properly to Liam. Then again, he was just about the only adult that ever did talk to him with any level of civility.

'How do you mean, sir?'

The teacher gestured toward the walls.

'I mean, can you still draw like this, Liam? This wonderful display that you produced a couple of years ago which I boasted as being some of the best artwork I had ever seen from a thirteen-year-old. Do you remember those days, Liam?'

Now looking to the floor, the youngster was stuck for an answer as Colin Smith stood directly before him with hands in pockets.

'Look at your work again, Liam. And take that bloody hood off. Look at your capability. Look at what you did.'

Liam's eyes widened as they peered upward to meet the teacher's gaze.

'You shouldn't swear at pupils, sir.'

'Never mind that. Anyway, *bloody* isn't swearing. Do as I ask. Lose the hood. Who are you hiding from? Look. Come here. Look!'

Liam stood to his full height of five feet ten inches. He liked his height. He dwarfed most of his peers. He was also a good three or four inches taller than his teacher, who placed an arm around Liam's shoulder and gave him a guided tour of forgotten talent.

'Could you do this again?'

'I don't get you, sir.'

'Do you still have the ability within yourself to produce work like this?'

Liam studied the various pictures in pencil, charcoal, paint, and pastel. Landscapes; still life; portraits. They seemed from another time.

When Liam was a seemingly different person.

'You are now in the most important period of your school life, Liam. But the path you are choosing could mean that this time next year you will be on the scrap heap. A sixteen-year-old loser. No qualifications. No ambition. No direction. Is that what you want? To waste what you've been blessed with?'

Liam felt anger burning within him.

He wanted to lash out but couldn't find a motive. He wanted to leave the room at that moment but couldn't justify doing so. The truth hurt badly. He was defenceless under the weight of such a proclamation.

'I'll never be a loser, sir.'

Mr. Smith pushed his face in front of Liam's and widened his gaze to breach the façade of bravery that had become Liam's protection over recent months.

'Yes…you…will…son. Trust me. Oh, yes you will. That's if you live long enough to be sixteen.'

Liam snapped under such perceived, imposing scrutiny.

'What the fuck is that supposed to mean?'

'You shouldn't swear at teachers, Liam.'

The teenager retreated under his cotton shroud and mumbled an apology as he stepped backward.

A time to pause; a time to think.

'No sir. Sorry sir.'

'That's alright, son. Now get that bloody hood back off.'

Liam broke into a fit of laughter that he felt obliged to contain but didn't really want to. Mr. Smith re-positioned his own kind smile and replaced the hand of concern on the pupil's shoulder.

'Now, lad. As I was saying. It's now the middle of June. In a year's time, it will be too late to save you. So, listen. I know you can't stand it here. Not many kids can. In that respect, you're quite normal. But I've seen and heard what people are saying about you, Liam. And I don't like the decisions you're making.'

Liam suddenly became angry and defensive at the prospect of being talked about behind his back. He squared up to Mr. Smith and spat a demand for expansion.

'What? Who's saying what? I'll kill them! I'll stick 'em…I'll…'

Mr. Smith simply stood and watched the continuing disintegration of promise before his eyes. A neurotic, paranoid talent.

'The word is that Liam Warburton is a bully. Violent. Nasty. Hateful. Disrespectful. Not a very nice person.'

Liam gestured with pointed fingers and fists of fury.

'Who's saying these things? Tell me! Tell me now! I'll rip their heads off!'

The teacher continued, totally unimpressed by Liam's display of savage contempt, yet very concerned by the immediate and unwarranted rage of a young boy.

'Judging by your reaction, you don't want to be seen as these things. I'm right though, aren't I?'

Silence resumed in the room once more. Liam looked guiltily to the wall beyond the teacher's desk, privately acknowledging Colin Smith's suspicions as being more than correct.

'So why don't you change back, Liam? Become the person you once were. Make me some beautiful pictures again. Become Liam the artist...instead of Liam, the mindless thug who everyone hates and fears.'

Liam's eyes lit up on hearing that word.

The word that drove him to distraction every breathing hour.

Fear.

Everybody *fears* him.

He loved the notoriety.

Yet he secretly hated himself for it.

'I shall not say another word. Off you go, lad. And think on.'

Liam was puzzled by Mr. Smith's calm approach to the morning's events.

'But, what about the Headmaster?'

'Liam. I'll sort it. But ask yourself this. Why should I care if you don't? I'm trying to tell you that you're worth far more than you think. I just need *you* to believe it again. That's all. Don't concern yourself with Mister Harris. Not that you are, anyway. Get off to your first lesson. We'll talk again soon.'

Liam moved tentatively toward the door of his tutor room and pulled down on the handle. He turned to Colin Smith, who had re-positioned himself back at his desk and into his diary.

'Sir?'

The teacher slowly turned to Liam and presented his familiar expression of friendship.

'Yes, Liam?'

'Can I have my fags back?'

The teacher laughed loudly and rocked back in his chair. Perceiving the answer as negative, Liam's thoughts turned to a more discerning issue as he stared at the art teacher.

'Do you *really* believe in me, sir?'

Mr. Smith nodded. His gaze never leaving the boy's.

'You bet, kid. More than you'll ever know.'

Liam felt slightly inflated.

And simultaneously almost confused by an unfamiliar sensation of inner pride. He pulled the door open as Colin Smith's voice carried after him.

'Oh, Liam. Just one more thing before you hop off.'

'Yes, sir?'

'You can collect your ciggies at home time. But don't let old Harris see you with them. Okay?'

'Okay. Sound. Thank you, sir.'

There was a momentary pause before the teacher spoke again.

'And Liam…'

'Sir?'

'Keep that bleeding hood off! You're a handsome young man. Let the world see your face awhile!'

Liam smiled as he closed the door behind him and stood in the empty assembly hall.

A boy alone with his mindless distractions.

Yet that same boy was now warmed by the voice of the one adult in the world he had true respect for.

FOUR

Richard watched his wife as she spoke softly on the lounge telephone. He could not ascertain the tone of the distant responses, having to rely on Stephanie's contribution to the dialogue to deduce the mood.

'Mum?'

'Mum? Yes. It's me. How are you?'

'Yes. I'm fine. We're all fine. It's been a while…I know.'

'Yes…he's okay. Growing up faster with each day, as teenagers unfortunately tend to do.'

'Yes. The business is doing very well.'

'Yes. Richard's good.'

'Actually…its Richard and I…we need a little favour, Mum.'

'Don't say it like that.'

'I wouldn't ring unless it was important.'

Man and wife stared knowingly at one another across the room, as though in resignation that the attempt at positive communication with Stephanie's parents had fallen at the first hurdle.

But Stephanie calmly persisted.

'Well, yes. It is to do with the business in a way.'

'No. I know you don't approve.'

'But you're the only person I can think of to ask.'

'It's pretty simple, really. We need you to have Liam stay with you and Dad for a while.'

'Well…for the whole summer, actually.'

'Yes…a business trip to Greece. No…July and August, perhaps.'

'Yes. The school holidays.'

'Yes, he is still at school, Mum.'

'No. There's nowhere else for him to go.'

'We need you to keep an eye on him for us.'

'No. He'll be fine.'

'Yes…I know, but he's grown out of all that nonsense now.'

'No. We don't want him here alone.'

'No. He needs still needs supervising.'

'Yes, even if he is fifteen.'

'Yes, I know he should be responsible at that age.'

'No. We can't take him with us.'

'Because this deal could be our big break.'

35

'Mum…don't be like that.'

'I know Dad won't approve.'

'But it is his only grandson for crying out loud!'

'Yes. I'm sorry, too.'

'I shouldn't have spoken to you like that.'

'I've a good friend who will watch the house for us.'

'Do you want to think about it?'

'Shouldn't you speak to Dad as well?'

'Well…he ought to be pre-warned that he'll be entertaining the monster for a while.'

'Well…if you think he'll be okay about it.'

'We'll know for definite within the next fortnight.'

'It'll give us a chance to make friends again.'

'I've missed you, Mum.'

'Yes. I'm sorry, too.'

'I'll speak to you again soon.'

'Okay, bye!'

Stephanie felt her heart beating like a bass drum as she replaced the receiver into its cradle and glanced toward her husband.

'That…was…bloody…painful!'

Richard embraced his wife as images of foreign climes presented themselves in his head.

'You did great, Steph! I told you things would be alright.'

*****

Two days passed before Liam was given details of his impending summer diversion. He sauntered into the kitchen one evening as his mother checked the contents of the oven.

'Roast chicken tonight. Alright, love?' smiled Stephanie.

Liam checked his recently acquired watch, removed forcibly from the wrist of a teenager from a rival school.

'No. It's half-seven. I'm going out soon.'

'Well, it's up to you. I've left your father at the office to come and prepare this. There's plenty. He'll be home for eight, he said.'

'I'll get chips, later.'

Stephanie folded the tea towel and placed it carefully on the stove before turning to her one and only son.

He shifted his weight from foot to foot, as though nervous of her imminent words.

'Liam...I'd like you to hang around at home for a while. Please. Your father and I would like to talk to you at some point this evening.'

'You can talk to me now, Ma. I'm out of here soon. Besides, why does he want to see me? Another whinge about my existence?'

'No. It's about the summer holidays.'

'What of it?'

Stephanie did not plan on making the announcement before Richard had come home. However, having now started the ball rolling, she found herself powerless to stop it. Especially as Liam's curiosity had now been roused. His silent glare was demanding her continuation. She became decidedly uncomfortable as her explanation ensued.

'Your father and I need to go away on business. For quite a while. For a few weeks, actually.'

Liam's instantaneous enthusiasm for his parents' potential absence was heavily disguised by feigned apathy.

'So? What's it to me? Go if you want. So long as I don't have to come.'

Stephanie was trying to handle things carefully, but the unavoidable bombshell was descending rapidly.

'Well. You won't be able to come with us anyway, Liam. We'll be working on setting up a contract for most of the time. Looking at locations...that type of thing.'

Liam continued to sway his form uneasily on the spot as he eyed her from beneath the shadow of his hood.

'Where?'

'Greece. Well, Crete, to be precise. Our lawyer Bill, you know Bill, well he is prepping some holdings for development. We get first refusal. But we have to get ourselves out there to see them first-hand.'

Liam gave little reaction to the revelation aside indifference. Pulling his hood further over his brow, he simply shrugged his shoulders and focused on the floor at his feet.

'Fine. Enjoy it. I won't miss you. I'm sure you won't miss me, either.'

Stephanie was becoming gradually more wary. She wished Richard would walk through the door at any moment to relieve her of the burden. 'Well. Your father and I...we need to discuss your position...with you.'

Liam was quickly becoming bored with the futile exchange with his mother.

'Come on, Ma. Spit it out I'm busy soon. Things to do!'

Swallowing a jagged pill of trepidation, Stephanie continued.

'Well, the thing is, Liam. We don't want to leave you here…on your own.'

Liam maintained a firm focus on the tiled kitchen floor and offered his mother a hand gesture of defiance as she quivered beside the oven.

'Don't tell me I'm having a babysitter for the summer! Please, Ma. I'm fifteen. It's no sweat. I'll be sound. Things will be all cool.'

Stephanie paused for breath. She observed her son's increasingly imposing physique and considered his unpredictable temperament.

'No, Liam. That's the point. *Nobody* will be staying here.'

Liam became visibly puzzled and could not resist engaging with his mother's gaze.

'What you talking about, Ma?'

'Your father and I could be away for nearly two months. We don't want you here for that length of time on your own.'

Stephanie could sense the fury erupting in her son as he twitched irritably in the kitchen doorway and began pointing angrily toward her.

'You don't trust me? You don't fucking trust me? Yeah? Is that it? You don't fucking trust me? This is Dad, isn't it? It's his fucking idea. He doesn't fucking trust me!'

A mother should never feel fearful of her offspring. It was an unwelcome sign of failed parenting. But at that precise moment, Stephanie was certainly cautious of her son's obvious displeasure.

Yet still she held her nerve to expand on the issue.

'That's just about the strength of it, Liam…yes. We need this deal to go through. It could let us make real money for once. We need to concentrate on getting things right over there. Without worrying about what's going on over here.'

The clatter of Liam's foot shunting the nearest convenient leg of the dining table dispersed the uneasy silence.

'Nothing's going to fucking happen, Ma! Jesus! I'll look after things!'

Stephanie shook her head at her fuming son as a chair crashed onto its back.

'No. Liam. It isn't going to happen.'

Liam thrust back his shoulders and advanced toward his mother, locking his glare into hers.

'You don't fucking trust your own fucking son? Some fucking mother you are!'

She could smell the malice on her son's breath as he hissed. He exuded menace. His fraying temperament was awry now.

'No. Liam. Please calm down. We don't want you to be mad. We can't leave you here alone. That's why we've made arrangements for you to stay elsewhere.'

Liam's eyes bored into his mother's with seeming contempt for her very existence at that moment.

'What the fuck do'ya mean...*elsewhere*? What is elsewhere? Who is elsewhere? This is all we fucking are.'

'Please stop swearing at me, Liam. I'm your mother.'

'Yes. The mother who doesn't fucking trust her own son! Whose fault is that then, eh?'

Stephanie contemplated her immediate predicament.

One final step away from total revelation.

Then Liam would hopefully be gone from the room. Gone from the house. Taking his anger with him. Easing her burden. Erasing her fears.

'I've spoken to my parents. Your grandparents.'

Liam hung his arms in a reaction of total disbelieving frustration.

'You mean...the oldies? The piss-bags? The coffin-testers? No way, Ma! No fucking way! You can't do this to me! They *hate* me!'

'No...they don't hate you, Liam. I've spoken to them earlier this week. It was difficult at first. But they've said you can stay with them during the summer holidays. Out at Clearlake. You liked it there last time. It's nice.'

Liam shunted the kitchen table once more, dislodging the China condiment set from its cradle. Salt spilled back toward him across the wooden surface. His voice became laced with a vicious rage.

'NO WAY. I'LL GO TO ELSON'S OR JONKA'S. BUT NOT THE DEAD PEOPLE. THEY HATE ME, MA! NO FUCKING WAY!'

As a mother tried to calm her irate son, his temper began to spiral beyond control. Throwing aside her oncoming gesture of consolation, Liam once more turned his attention to destruction. With the smashing of plates and the throwing of cutlery, Liam vacated the room, then in turn the house, just as his mother had silently, hopefully predicted.

Liam ran into the hazy summer evening as the setting sun advanced a steady descent toward the roofline. Lengthening shadows guided the boy as he deserted his estate.

The premise of a summer in the countryside.

It sounded like the ultimate penalty.

A total reprimand for all he had purveyed in recent times.

The oldies. They despised him. Or was it the other way around?

Those decrepit specimens.

Those finished articles.

Clearlake was hell on earth for a boy with a daring mind.

As Liam ran breathlessly toward the town centre, he forced his thoughts to concentrate on the next scheduled episode of the evening.

He had no money. He owed people. He had arranged to meet them to settle one or two scores.

It might be dangerous.

He also needed to buy from them. He would command the necessary arrangements to amend this problem. The money he had taken from his mother's purse that morning was not for spending liberally. It was for debt he had incurred. For filth he had swallowed. Yet his appetite had returned. He would need to pay one debt that evening before creating another.

And as he ran to his meeting place, a red sky slowly formed above.

*****

Fifteen minutes later he was in the market square and amidst two of his loyal gang members. Glendin looked nervously at the leader of the Black Stars as he approached with steel in his eyes. Jonka rose from the bench to address his friend's arrival.

'Yo, Warbs! What's up?'

'Gentlemen. No fucking about, tonight. You hear? I'm in the mood for business. Not fuck-ups. Shall we go?'

No further words were exchanged.

Meeting Elson in the park as darkness gradually prevailed over light meant that the gang was finally reunited.

The chosen destination was hidden under a canopy of trees near the cemetery. A place where the deceased could listen to the disturbing sound of wagers being made, favours being repaid…and feigned pledges being broken.

The evening was particularly mild as the four boys adorned their protective hoods and congregated in the wooded glade.

Yet the prospective meeting was not to go as planned.

Little did the Black Stars know that this meeting was not orthodox in nature. They were in fact the sitting target for an ambush.

Only Liam knew of the true motive of the business that evening.

He owed and would pay up.

And would owe all over again.

His friends were mere pawns. Unwitting soldiers in battle.

Liam alone knew what this summit was really about.

But it would not transpire in the way that had been foreseen by him.

Somebody from the opposition secretly wanted vengeance.

For a brother's shattered jaw.

A brother now residing in intensive care.

Left for dead under the aqueduct, some nights before.

As the group of loaded assailants appeared one by one from the murk, Liam quickly realised that they were outnumbered. His friends began to panic as they too realised that the odds were firmly against them.

The adrenalin that filled Liam's every pore since he left his mother in the kitchen was now numbing his senses to what was about to happen around him.

Figures emerged from the shadows to rightfully claim their payment, and to leave an indelible mark of receipt. Within seconds and without announcement, fists and feet rapidly flew all around in the semi-darkness.

Hardly anybody connected properly in the ensuing melee.

Aside one fortunate soul, whose knuckles caught Glendin Jones square in the temple, and grounded him cold.

As Liam, Elson and Jonka fought for their gang mates, Glendin became the subject of brief discussion by two of the opposing protagonists. As their oblivious subject, he knew very little as he lay purring amid the dry dirt, cradling his aching face.

Then a moment of decision from the enemy.

Nobody saw the flash of the blade.

But it was clearly visible.

Until it entered Glendin's heart, to be immediately withdrawn, sheathed in warm, pumping, hardening claret.

Then twice more that same heart was pierced.

Then, as metal withdrew from flesh for the final time, that heart unknowingly began to drain the very life from its host.

A vital organ; unwittingly robbed of function.

Deprived of its capacity to provide and sustain.

No longer able to maintain duty in a once able and youthful body.

No time to scream for help.

Glendin Jones was dead within seconds.

The conflict ensued, ignorant of the fatal sufferance in its nucleus.

Eventually, and without their intended bounty, the attackers retreated into the darkness with the knowledge that they were leaving death behind in their wake.

Only one of the bodies in the cemetery now lay above ground.

The body of Glendin Jones.

Standing in disbelief at their horrific discovery, the remaining members of the Black Stars lifted their heads and looked to each other.

Blood congealed into the dust as minds raced with their misfortune.

'JESUS, LIAM! HE'S FUCKING GONE! THOSE BASTARDS FINISHED GLENNERS! JESUS LIAM!'

Jonka's terrified cries of horror were accompanied by the tears of Elson as they crouched beside their lifeless friend.

For the first time, their position of apparent superiority had been placed in question.

For the first time, the gang could be made to answer for their actions.

Liam felt into his pocket.

His mother's money remained untouched.

Yet, so indelibly tarnished.

He removed a mobile phone - another trophy from another battle - and calmly dialled for an ambulance.

Under that leafy canopy in the cemetery, with their friend's corpse at their feet, three boys tasted loss, for the first time in their young lives.

And Liam secretly wished he was anywhere but there.

Amongst the decrepit; the ravaged; the dead.

FIVE

Glendin Jones' funeral took place only eight days after his murder.

As a mark of respect, Headmaster Robert Harris had ordered St Forsters to close for the day.

Elson and Jonka reluctantly attended the final farewell to their friend. As did scores of other pupils, most of which were obliged to congregate outside the chapel due to limited room inside.

Liam was notable by his absence.

Despite his dubious associations, Glendin Jones was relatively popular at school with real academic potential. A quiet, unassuming boy who had become mixed up with undesirable company.

A pattern of misguidance that always led him to the wrong places at the wrong times.

The story of Glendin's tragically short life.

This was the story that the police were happy to believe.

Case closed as soon as opened.

Death by misadventure. No witness. No weapon. No alibi.

Just three friends who apparently discovered his body by chance, supposedly unaware of any perpetrator.

Standing beside the corpse of their dead companion. Under the wooded canopy near the cemetery. Exactly where they had arranged to meet for undisclosed, now seemingly irrelevant reasons.

Paramedics pronounced him dead at the scene as three friends kept mouths firmly closed and watched in mournful disquiet.

And as two of those friends watched the coffin being covered in earth, they would opt to forever remain silent about the reasons for his demise for the rest of their lives, carrying the painful knowledge that one absent witness that day probably knew full well of the motives for their friend's murder.

Nonetheless, The Black Stars would remain firm in their policy.

Silent and unquestioned.

Unseen and unsuspected.

Apparently free from the shroud of blame.

*****

As Liam Warburton walked through the school gates the following morning, he felt little need to display any modicum of remorse for the departed.

Yet he secretly felt a searing agony in his soul.

A pain that would remain undetected by all and sundry.

He would make certain of that much.

Nodding to Elson and Jonka on his approach, the trio simply observed one another through their darkened hoods as they waited nervously for the registration bell.

Yet all around, eyes were watching them. From every corner of the school grounds. From every window. Through every door. They felt under surveillance.

The heat was too much…almost.

Liam's inner guilt was something he could never show his audience.

Vindication was his sole ambition, and this had seemingly been achieved without any particular effort on his part.

Yet such suppressed remorse finally compelled crass words to emit from the leader of the Black Stars.

'Come on boys. Smile a while. All is fine'

Elson and Jonka stared ahead in worried disbelief at their friend's unwarranted commentary. The eventual response was whispered and carried on the morning summer breeze.

'Me and Jonks aren't feeling too fine. If you hadn't…'

'Yeah? If what? If black was white? If morning was night? If nothin'! It's done. He's gone. No fault. No failure. Just life.'

Elson looked determinedly into the visage of the gang leader.

He saw no compassion.

No recognition of wrongdoing, even.

Just a sinister hardness.

A callous absence of any typically natural sensation.

There was no light in the eyes of Liam Warburton.

'How can you just accept it, Liam? How can you just stand and take it and say it's okay?'

Liam loomed closer to Elson causing him to step back against the wall. The voice hissed a toxic reply.

'We…have…no…choice. Right? What happened was not of our doing. It was bad luck. Pure as that.'

Jonka was not convinced by the philosophical attitude.

'No, Warbs! It was *your* meeting. *Your* enemy. *Your* instruction.'

The volume in Liam's voice increased with the need for a defence.

'How was I to fucking know that we'd attacked one of theirs under the aqueduct? He looked just like any other dude to us. We couldn't have known.'

'We shouldn't have been there.' claimed Elson.

'Where?'

'Anywhere near the fucking railway arch! Or anywhere near the cemetery. Then Glenners would still be here! Standing with us now. Talking with us.'

Liam was becoming angry at his friends' misplaced sensibilities.

'Yeah...probably talking about the next hit, you fucking pussies! He took the risks with all of us. He wanted it more than all of us!'

'Yeah...and now he's paid the ultimate price.' screamed Elson.

'Part of the job, boys. Part of the risk.'

Jonka squared up to the leader of the gang and swallowed his fears.

'It ain't part of my job to stand there and watch a mother cry as her son gets buried. That could have been *my* mother! And where the fuck *were* you yesterday, anyway? You've got thinking to do, Liam. Lots of thinking. The Black Stars are wanted men. The police are on us like dogs. They will want to hang us up for this when they get someone to squeal.'

Liam remained defiant as he walked toward the main door of the school.

'*I've* got thinking to do, you say? It seems to me that thinking does you no good, Jonks. And it seems like you two are doing far too much of this thinking business. You'd better think about where your loyalties lie. I can't wait for you forever. If you want out...then do it. No half-way with me. Think about *that*!'

*****

Mr. Smith closed the door to commence registration. He surveyed the silent throng before him. There was none of the incessant chatter that accompanied most mornings in the form room. He surveyed the scene before imparting a few choice words.

Deep, measured breaths preceded the monologue.

For once, the teacher had the full attention of everyone.

'A very sad day yesterday, boys and girls. Absolutely tragic. I'm sure you all agree. Mister and Mrs. Jones have passed on their thanks for those who attended Glendin's funeral. They were most appreciative of your presence.'

Carla Ferris turned to offer Liam a discerning glare as he sat with head bowed under his hood. Her whispers echoed around the walls and ceiling of the classroom for all present to hear.

'Those of us that could be bothered to turn up!'

Liam lifted his gaze to meet Carla's.

Her stern expression began to annoy him.

'Something to say to me, little woman?'

The attention of thirty pupils centred on the exchange in the corner.

'Yeah…plenty! Where the fuck was you yesterday, Warbs? He was supposed to be your *friend*. If only he knew how little you cared.'

Liam leaned forward to confront his antagonist, sensing immediately that all eyes and ears were fixed on the debate.

'None of your fucking business, bitch! Shut it!'

'It's not right, Warbs. Just not turning up. I think he'll know you weren't there to say goodbye.'

Mr. Smith interjected to avoid raised tempers.

'Erm, Carla. I don't think now is the time or the place, do you? Leave Mister Warburton with his thoughts and face front, please.'

Carla was not quite finished with the uninvited morality lecture.

'One day, Warbs, you might need somebody to wave *you* off for the last goodbye! Maybe *nobody* will come that day!'

The blue touch paper had been lit.

Liam rose to his feet and moving toward Carla, he grabbed her roughly by the lapels. Pulling her off her backside and up toward him, he looked into her eyes, which were now white with fear. Her pupils dilated to dark pools as her features crumpled with terror.

'Do you think I don't care, bitch? Of course I fucking care! It was because of me he fucking died! Now leave me alone! Every fucker in this room – just leave me the fuck alone!'

Throwing a now shocked and tearful Carla Ferris back onto her chair, Liam quickly made for the classroom door.

'Liam, where are you going?' barked a concerned Mr. Smith.

'For some fucking air! I'm sick of all this shit! I'm sick of people pointing the finger. Fuck the lot of you!'

Watching helplessly as Liam made his angered departure, Colin Smith closed the register on his desk.

'We'll assume everyone's here, shall we? Off to your lessons, you lot. Now! I'd better try and calm Warburton down before he flattens somebody!'

The class hurriedly filed past the front desk clutching their bags, more than a little shaken by Liam's exhibition. The form tutor watched each of the worried faces of the group disappear through the doorway, enquiring as to the welfare of one in particular.

'You okay, Carla?'

'Yes, sir. Fine. He doesn't bother me. He's a pussy cat!'

'Yes, well, thanks to you I've got to try and locate him now. Then try and talk to him.'

Carla's expression became thoughtful, even hopeful, as she stood in the doorway.

'Sir?'

'Yes, Carla?'

'You know when you catch up with Liam...'

'Yes?'

'...will you tell him...tell him...I'm sorry?'

Mr. Smith nodded without word as he observed the attractive young woman that Carla Ferris was becoming.

'Will you, sir? Will you do that for me?'

'You've a lot of time for Liam Warburton, haven't you, Miss Ferris? Lord knows why. He's nothing but bloody trouble.'

With her cheeks turning crimson, Carla merely offered her form tutor an uncomfortable nod and ventured to her first lesson.

*****

Having set tasks for his first class of the day, the art teacher excused himself and wandered beyond the building and into the playground. He quickly scanned the surrounding sports field, eventually noticing a distant figure hunched by the canal that flanked the school grounds.

On reaching the young man, Colin Smith did not announce his approach and simply sat a couple of yards away along the bank. Liam did not sense the teacher's presence as he gazed thoughtfully at the water, squinting at the glistening surface.

They both watched the tranquil scene without word for a couple of minutes before Colin Smith opted to open a conversation.

'You really shouldn't grab girls by the throat, Liam. It's regarded as most un-gentlemanly.'

Eventually, Liam turned his head, revealing a half-smirk. The teacher offered a smile in return.

'Aren't you hot under that hood, lad?'

Liam nodded but did not speak.

'Get the fucker off, then!'

Now the half-smile evolved quickly into a chuckle as Liam threw back his protection, exposing his closely shaved head to the ascending summer sun.

'You shouldn't swear at the pupils, sir.'

'What? You lot taught me how to do that! That's better! By the way, I've got a message to pass on. Carla says she's sorry for tormenting you.'

Liam looked back to the mirror-like water.

'Carla was *right*, sir. I *should* have been there yesterday. I let a friend down...badly. I deserve to be criticised.'

A gliding heron briefly distracted the pair from their exchange. Retrieving a fish from the water, it was gone again with a gracefully precise take-off that fully held the attentions of master and pupil.

'Impressive, aren't they?' claimed the teacher.

'Listen, Mister Smith, why are you here? Haven't you got a class to annoy?'

The teacher looked to his pupil with a gaze of bemusement.

'Yes, Liam. And you should be there as well. You seem to disappear during art lessons these days. It's such a waste. There's still time to turn things around.'

'But everyone thinks I'm a bad boy, sir. A drug-head. A good for nothing.'

The teacher rose to his feet and stared across the canal to the passing traffic on the main road.

'No, Liam. Not everybody.'

A pause ensued before the pupil stood and faced his teacher.

'I know you were close to Glendin Jones. Probably closer than anyone in the school. I know it's bound to have hit hard, Liam. You're just dealing with things differently to most others. That's all. There's nothing wrong in it. It's who you are.'

Mr. Smith studied Liam's chiselled, handsome face. It masked a thousand thoughts at that moment. Yet not one was uttered as he reluctantly joined his teacher on the stroll back to the main building.

But then Liam suddenly felt confident to speak as he noticed the heads of curiosity appearing at various classroom windows.

'Sir...'

'Yes, Liam.'

'I don't want people to hate me. I want them to like me. To trust me. But even my own parents don't trust me. It's difficult to accept that anyone here should feel different.'

Colin Smith placed an arm around his favourite art student.

'Like I said, Liam. I have faith in you...and your potential.'

Liam observed the sincerity in the voice of the one adult he felt he could accommodate in his life at that moment.

'You mean that, sir?'

'I've got time for you, lad. Yes. And I'll tell you something else you don't know, as well.'

'What?'

'I'm not the only one...'

Liam became puzzled by the comment but did not ponder further.

'Come on, son. Time to get back to class.'

*****

Dinner time arrived with the usual trawl across the road to the fish and chip shop. The regular congregation of pupils discussed the morning's events and exchanged nuggets of gossip along with nuggets of chicken.

Declining the opportunity to queue with his peers, Liam waited outside the shop whilst Elson and Jonka joined the line of hungry teenagers.

He stared vacantly into the distance, his eyes following the traffic and his mind whirring with thoughts of the impending summer arrangements.

And those who would not be witnessing another summer.

But Glendin Jones was a subject he had opted to place at the back of his mind. Discussion of the issue would resolve little.

'Do you want one?'

Liam slowly turned his head to be confronted by the smiling face of Carla Ferris.

49

He observed her warily before selecting a chip from the bag cradled in her palm.

'Cheers.'

He opted to revert to silence. A situation that Carla was not willing to tolerate.

'Liam…I didn't mean to upset you. I'm sorry.'

Again, he slanted his head to face her. Her words seemed genuine, but he cared little for her apology.

'Yeah…Smithy said so.'

Further quiet prevailed as Liam deliberated his position.

Time for him to soften a little, perhaps.

'I'm sorry too…for grabbing you…I hope I didn't hurt you…'

Carla giggled and offered another chip.

'Take more than you, Warbs. You'd have been flat on your back if I'd have meant it. Glad we're mates again.'

Re-joining her friends, she walked to the curbside. Liam shouted after her with a glint of humour in his eye.

'Hey…Ferris…we ain't mates. I don't like you *that* much!'

Crossing the road with a fit of giggles, she offered Liam a final glance before entering the school gates.

'Here you are, Warbs. Battered sausage and chips. Just like you ordered.'

Jonka placed the tray of food into Liam's grasp.

'We've been thinking, Liam. Me and Elson. About forgetting all this shit. At the end of term. A break. A night somewhere. Camping, yeah? A real laugh! Seaside perhaps. The three of us. To chill. Forget about stuff and get whammed. You game?'

Cramming some of his sausage into one cheek, Liam gave a muffled response.

'Yeah, great. Sounds neat.'

Elson watched as Liam grimaced at the contents of his mouth.

'What is it, man?'

The leader of the Black Stars turned on his friend and scowled.

'Where's the curry sauce? Where's my fucking curry, man?'

Elson adopted a reaction of genuine remorse.

'Shit, Liam. Sorry, man. Forgot. Jesus. Sorry! I'll get it, now.'

Liam laughed heartily as he chewed.

'It don't matter, Jonks. Forget it. It don't matter.'

SIX

'A word, Liam. Now, please. Downstairs.'

Liam barely acknowledged the request of his father as he lay on his bed. The I-Pod blasted into his ear drums, leaving his hearing rather impeded. However, the scornful expression on Richard Warburton's face suggested that perhaps it would be a wise idea to oblige the request without unnecessary delay.

Even more reason then, he figured, to ignore the command.

Ten minutes later, Liam's father burst back through his bedroom door and wrenched the ear plugs from their positions.

'What you fucking doing, man? That's my music you're tampering with!'

Liam's father was now in the grip of incessant rage.

'Get yourself down those stairs, now!'

With earnest reluctance and mostly feigned obedience, Liam followed. He trudged past his father and was formally ushered into the kitchen to meet his mother who sat at the table. Slouching into a chair, he barely acknowledged her presence.

'Right. I want an explanation for your attitude.'

'What about it, Pops? I can't remember any attitude. Jesus, man!'

'Your attitude to staying at Clearlake, with your grandparents.'

'Yeah? So? I ain't going. That's it.'

Richard struggled to contain his anger and perched across the table opposite his son in effort to refrain from throttling him there and then.

'We need you to cooperate with us, Liam. This is a big deal for your mother and me. It would help matters greatly if you would play along with the arrangement. See eye to eye with us for a change. Just this once.'

Liam stared intently from the shadow of his hood.

'I ain't going to stay with the oldies. They're dead, man. It would be a prison.'

Stephanie opted to contribute to the debate.

'But we need you to help us.'

'Even though you admit you don't trust me to stay here alone. Yes? That it? Thought so. Don't talk to me about help, Ma. You can't even spell the word. Your world is all about business. Not family. I'm a hindrance to your plans. Not a part of them.'

Richard looked to his wife for continued assistance.

Stephanie was reluctant to become further embroiled in another fruitless family row, leaving her husband to plough a lone furrow.

'Why do you get so annoyed when we ask you to toe the line now and again, Liam? We aren't asking the earth. Just two months of your life. You might even enjoy yourself up there?'

'Clearlake is a morgue. I'd go there to die. Fuck the oldies. They hate me and I hate them. Don't pass me on to them. I would just corpse. That's if they don't make me kill myself first!'

A temporary silence ensued before Liam made an announcement of his own.

'Anyway. I'm going camping with the gang.'

Husband and wife looked to one another for an answer to the vitriol expressed by their son. Richard's response to the teenager's declaration was automatic.

'No chance. No chance at all.'

'Yeah? Try and stop me. I'll break your necks - the pair of you!'

Richard looked at his only offspring in despairing disbelief.

'Why do you say these things, Liam? It's horrible to listen to. It's almost tragic to hear. Your grandparents are your family. They're looking forward to having you. Your mum has made the arrangements for your benefit.'

Without further warning, Liam stood to his feet and forced his chair across the kitchen to impact with the oak cabinets.

'Yeah! For *your* benefit, don't you mean? Made plans without even asking me! It's always the same. Business comes first. I come second. Every time!'

Richard's fury was now beginning to match that of his son, and he rose to meet the challenge as Stephanie fearfully observed the developing spectacle. Her husband opted to draw a line in the sand.

'You are a spoiled, nasty brat, Liam! You have been living in luxury for most of your life and abused the privilege. You *will* be going to Clearlake at the end of July. For two months. It's settled. Your grandfather can sit and suffer with you. I'm bloody sick of you and your attitude!'

Another chair flew from its position under the table and clattered into the oven door.

'Fuck you two as well, then! I'm sick of *everything*. Sick of this life. Being told what to do and what not to do. I want to be me. Do what I want to do! You're the pits. I hate the pair of you.'

Liam barged his way out of the kitchen and back up to his room. Reaching into his bedside drawer, he retrieved a small bottle of whiskey shop-lifted from a local store a few days earlier, and a Swiss army knife. Placing the items into the pockets of his hooded top, he descended the stairs and let himself out into the warmth of early dusk.

He had only one destination in mind.

The canal bridge.

He would not be disturbed.

He could think in peace.

*****

He liked to be alone. Liam could ably tolerate his own company. He seemed to struggle when somebody else invaded his space. He liked the solitude. He enjoyed the freedom to brood.

Yet all the time he was plagued by an untouchable sadness.

A lack of recognition for who he was.

For his role in life.

Always playing second fiddle to his parents' financial concerns.

Always the afterthought.

Liam swigged from the bottle of Scotch as he surveyed the steadily flowing water from the shadow of the bridge. Hardly ever used by pedestrians, the location had been of great use over the previous months.

A place to contemplate his worries.

A place to hide.

A place to exert perpetual distaste…on himself, as well as others.

The alcohol diluted his veins and began to make his head feel numb. He liked the growing sensation of deadness. The lack of feeling. If he could feel nothing, then nothing could harm him.

Nothing could get to him.

Except from within his own soul.

That was his weak spot. His betrayer.

The ultimate knowledge regarding most dealings in life was that his way was *not* the right way. But he would not openly concede to such instinct. Instead, he would try and eclipse it with pain.

To encourage the numbness; to detract from the blackness in his heart.

Liam lazily played with the penknife with his finger ends and thumb.

He placed pressure on the blade with his bare skin. Applying just enough force to allow the metal to penetrate the top layers, but not enough to draw blood.

Rolling up the sleeve of his top, he then traced the blade over the top of his arm, from elbow to wrist. He swigged more whiskey, fighting the desire to harm himself, yet simultaneously willing the pain that would come and ease his guilt.

Guilt that he had fought to bury deep.

Guilt over a dead friend and a grieving family.

Guilt that he could not, and would not, display as evidence to others.

Evidence of vulnerability.

Evidence of conscience.

Apply a little more pressure.

Fight the will. Will the pain.

Harder still he pressed the blade onto his forearm.

More whisky. More solace. More pain needed.

More whisky. More pressure.

Then, at last, warmth.

Soothing, congealing, healing warmth.

The blood ran from his arm, over the knuckles of the hand with the knife, and finally in droplets to the floor below.

He reached for the bottle and drained its contents.

Now he had achieved the ultimate result.

Solace and pain.

Together.

The dual emotion. All his own doing.

Without looking, he sensed the blade enter his flesh once more, further releasing the blockage in his soul.

Two rivers. Two outlets for his remorse to bleed from.

Two avenues for peace to travel and reign.

Finally, he looked down at the damage and the rivers flowing so freely.

The empty whiskey bottle was launched into the water beyond.

Liam sat, relieved; alone; contented as his wounds ebbed and stemmed.

But only for a moment, before reality hit.

It was not the first time he had wilfully shed his own blood.

The scars were well concealed from unwanted, prying eyes.

But this time, it was the blood of another that should be running unchecked.

The blood of a murderer. The blood of a killer.

A killer who had taken the life of a dear friend.

A killer who had laughed at the law and escaped free from the deed.

As the wounds desperately fought to knit themselves together in his opened limb, Liam thought of only one thing.

Somebody must serve a penance for Glendin.

He must exert retribution for a friend taken away.

The Black Stars would avenge their former member.

If it took a lifetime.

Yes.

However long it took.

*****

Eventually Liam returned home in the darkness, undetected by his slumbering parents. He cleaned himself in the bathroom and lain in the bedroom he had rendered his own since infancy.

Albeit temporarily, things had become clearer by the canal side.

Yet the demons of Liam Warburton's mindset were never vanquished.

They were always present.

Clouding his every thought. Spurring his every misguided whim.

The only respite from the perpetual torment was the sanctity of sleep, which encroached quickly, and took him away once more to a supposedly happier place.

SEVEN

School the following day was attended by Liam without word or incident. He hid the fresh scars under the sleeves of his hooded top. No one suspected. No one questioned.

Yet if they had cause to look at the damage he had so selfishly incurred, they would have cringed in repulsion. Healed, dark lines were now the base foundation for new, fresh tracks of pure crimson.

It was the legacy of personal anguish that Liam Warburton strived to hide from a watching world on a daily basis.

Under the shadow of the playground veranda, Liam held court with Elson and Jonka, away from scrutiny and the bright summer sun.

'It's a crazy idea, Liam. Someone else will get hurt. Or worse.'

'Listen Jonks, Glenners would want this. He would want this for himself and for us. It's a matter of honour. We owe it to him.'

Elson considered the issue of revenge.

'No, man. Besides, we have no idea who we're looking for. That gang at the cemetery was full of strangers. And everyone will know who's behind another attack if we do this.'

Liam stood to his impressive full height, a tactic he regularly employed when trying to make a point.

'*Somebody* knows who he is. The killer of our friend is still out there. Who knows? He could be watching us as we speak right now.'

Jonka was not convinced.

'You're paranoid, man. They settled their own score for what we did to *their* friend. The way I see it, you'll start a war. I don't want my parents burying me just yet, thank you.'

Liam surveyed his fellow pupils scattered around the vicinity. A few seconds of quiet resumed, giving Elson chance to change the subject.

'What about camping, Warbs? You coming? First week of the summer holidays?'

The hopeful enquirer was met with the familiar stare from the leader of the Black Stars. The expression was difficult to determine. Neither pleasure nor disapproval.

In fact, there was almost a wariness in Liam's eventual response.

'I...I ain't sure...the folks are on about packing me off for the summer. They're getting heavy about things. I could do with staying here though and sorting out our little bit of business.'

Jonka's tone was decidedly upbeat as he tried to steer Liam's concentration further from the subject of Glendin's killer.

'We thought the coast. Ilcombe...or maybe Wenstaple. Plenty of end of term hornies out there, man. Plenty plenty!'

Elson broke into a chuckle.

'Yeah...like *you'd* know how to play them, Jonka! Real man about town aren't you, yeah? What do you reckon, Liam? This dude cruising the strip with his kebab? Eyeing up the talent!'

A line resembling a smile formed under Liam's nose. He shook his head slowly as though in mocking distaste.

'I don't think either of you two goons would stand a chance. You're barely growing stubble. Barely out of nappies, boys! No women would be interested!'

Jonka was quick to retort.

'Oh yeah? You're track record ain't so refined, Warbs! When was the last time you even had a kiss? Never mind a feel?'

'I don't tell you fools everything you know. Some things are best kept private. For my own personal reflection.'

Now Liam's friends were holding their sides in hysterics, forcing their leader to laugh along with the joke.

'Okay...okay...so we've been a little short of female company so far. But things will improve. I've got a feeling in my stomach.'

Elson fought to splutter the last word on the issue.
'Yeah...so have most of the girls that look at Jonka!'

The bell signalled the end of break-time as several hundred pupils made their way slowly back into the school building. With the crowd bottlenecking in the cloak room, it gave Liam a chance to scan the surrounding faces. The crescendo of chatter emanated from all directions, yet Liam felt strangely compelled to look straight to his immediate left.

Elson and Jonka followed the eyes of their leader and saw the focus of attention. Carla Ferris stood in the corner of the cloakroom taking a last few draws on her cigarette. Her attention was centred firmly on the strapping young man in the hooded top that shuffled past only yards away.

Despite his unattractive traits, one thing Liam Warburton did manage with ease was to stand out in a crowd. Carla exchanged stares for a few moments until mild embarrassment got the better of her. She then threw a mocking V-sign with the cigarette butt wedged firmly between her fingers. The smile that followed was welcome, and somewhat intriguing.

Liam responded by sticking his tongue out in her direction, achieving the aim of making her smile even wider and much more pleasurable to behold.

Then, eclipsed by the throng of noisy students, both vanished from one another's view.

*****

Maths was not a favoured past time for Elson, Jonka or indeed Liam. It was deemed the subject everyone had to study as some kind of punishment. Elson wasn't totally against the use of numbers and found the lessons comparatively easy to his two counterparts. But his attention soon wavered if distracted from the desk or blackboard.

Jonka's lowered voice carried across the back wall to Liam, whose daydream was abruptly disturbed.

'So…what's this shit about your parents and summer?'

'Eh? Oh…they're going abroad…on business…so I'm being deported for the safety of the surrounding neighbourhood.'

'But you can come camping for a few days first, yeah?'

'I don't know, Jonks. Depends on when they fly. They'll fuck me up if they can, though. They've already laid the law down.'

The conversation's whispered tone had been detected by Miss Stock, the maths teacher, whose disparaging grimace located itself toward the rear of the classroom, and to Liam. She turned to the disinterested throng and placed her hands on her hips. Her acid bark then resonated around the room.

'What have I just been explaining to the class, Mister Warburton?'

Suddenly, all eyes fell on Liam. He had no idea what to say. He became distinctly uncomfortable at the attention from fellow pupils and annoyed at the sudden scrutiny from Miss Stock. The teacher peered determinedly through thick, square framed spectacles. Liam noticed that the line of fine dark hair above her upper lip looked particularly prominent that morning.

'Well, boy? Speak! What have I just been explaining to the class?'

Elson and Jonka could not help their friend without being detected.

Liam was completely alone in this unexpected battle of wits.

Or so he thought.

Miss Stock's line of enquiry now became mildly infuriated.

'Have you not been writing this down as I have explained it, Mister Warburton?'

Thirty pairs of eyes burned into him as he mentally fumbled for some response. He began to rock onto the back legs of his chair, trying to buy time. Perhaps even an offer of help.

Liam did not have to wait long for that help to present itself.

Without warning, the answer was covertly placed on his lap by an adjacent pupil, Scott Wilson.

Liam glanced at the open section of the exercise book. The handwriting was not Scott's. It was not even Scott's book. Thinking quickly, Liam relayed the words on the page, secretly hoping that the reply to the teacher's inquisition would appease her.

'Erm...angles, Miss. With our calculators, Miss.'

Miss Stock was not completely satisfied and continued to press for expansion.

'Yes...and?'

'And what, Miss?'

Liam could tell that his initial trepidation about being the centre of speculation was unfounded. He was now on the verge of entertaining his audience. They were silently willing him on into battle.

'And what are we going to look at today in particular?'

His eyes quickly scanned the neat writing on the page.

'Erm...sine and cosine, Miss.'

The teacher smiled and nodded her head.

'Thank you for listening, Mister Warburton. Now...is it alright with you if I carry on with the lesson...or would you like to continue your conversation with Mister Wilson?'

Liam became temporarily puzzled.

'I wasn't talking to Scott, Miss.'

The teacher narrowed her eyes.

'Are you sure, boy?'

'Yes, Miss.'

'Okay. My mistake.'

No sooner had Miss Stock returned to face the blackboard, Liam delivered his punchline to the class with practised timing that afforded all in the room a collective chance to laugh in appreciation.

'No, Miss. I was actually talking to Jonka about how many birds we're going to shag on holiday.'

The eruption of mirth echoed around the windows, walls and ceilings for what seemed like an age. When quiet composure eventually resumed, Miss Stock continued with her response.

'Well, Mister Warburton. Do you think you could save the fantasies until home-time, please? We've some mathematical reality to confront before then.'

Liam nodded and smiled at the teacher, who had obviously seen the funny side for once.

'Yes, Miss. Sorry, Miss.'

The class focused on the front of the room once more. Liam observed the book still on his lap and flipped it to the front page. The name on the cover was one Liam associated with someone he had grown fond of over the last few weeks.

Evidently, a friend in need.

'Here, Scott, pass that back across to Ferris.'

On receipt of her book, the owner glanced back at Liam with a genuine expression of care.

Not being accustomed to such treatment, Liam simply smiled back with a brief nod of the head and mouthed two words: thank you.

*****

Home time seemed to arrive rather quicker than normal. Liam put it down to the fact that his mind had been distracted from the mundane procession of the timetable by other more pressing matters.

A summer camping trip.

An unwanted secondment to his grandparents'.

Retaliation to an unknown perpetrator.

Yet his mind had also accommodated other thoughts. Pleasant feelings that he could not grasp the meaning of. Shafts of light that penetrated his bleak soul and surprisingly made him feel uplifted at regular intervals.

He could not place the source of this light.

But the light was definitely present within him.

And the elusive cause, although undisclosed, was far nearer than he could ever have imagined.

He approached the gates to the school where his friends waited. His stride suddenly halted to the sound of a familiar voice.

'Liam! Liam! Wait!'

Liam turned to see Mr. Smith trotting quickly toward him.

'I just want a quick word, Liam. It's about the Year Seven art class.'

Liam glanced to Elson and Jonka, who had already lit their first cigarettes of the afternoon.

'What about it, sir? I've got business outside. Can it wait?'

'Well, just listen. I'm giving you first refusal. The Head has granted us some time away from school to venture out and draw the local environment. Now we're into summer and the weather is better, I thought I'd take them out and draw some landscapes around town and such. They get a bit bored in the classroom and being young they appreciate a change of scenery.'

Liam did not understand the purpose of the conversation.

'What's this to do with me, sir?'

With a broad smile, Colin Smith elaborated.

'Well, my plan is to take them out a couple of times a week until the end of term.'

'Yeah...and?'

'Well, I'll need assistance with supervision. They're a bit of a handful on my own. Will you help me, Liam?'

Glancing to his friends waiting at the gate, Liam pondered the appropriate reply.

'Why me, sir? Why not anyone else? I ain't no teacher.'

Colin Smith's sincerity shone through.

'Because I don't *want* anyone else, Liam. I want *you*. Plus, with your talent you could pass on some tips for the budding artists. What do you say?'

The encouraging patter of the art teacher was undeniably persuasive. But Liam was taken aback by the prospect of being considered as some kind of role model for the youngsters.

'I'll...I'll think about it, sir. I'll think on it. I don't know. Head-case Harris won't agree with it, will he?'

'*Wrong*. He's given me permission to ask you. I've got every faith in you, Liam. The young ones would enjoy it and I think it would do you the world of good. Get your head out of the gutter and looking upward. Hey, what do you say?'

Liam smiled at the teacher's turn of phrase.

'Fine. I'll do it. When do we start?'

'Brilliant! I'll come and find you tomorrow and let you know the plan. You can shoot off and light a fag up with your mates, now.'

Finally merging with the small throng at the gate, Liam heard Mr. Smith calling out once again.

'For fuck's sake!' Liam muttered before turning around with an unlit cigarette dangling from his lips.

'What now, sir?'

Mr. Smith's pleasure was evident as he gave a thumbs-up across the playground.

'Just thanks, Liam. Thanks. That's all. You won't regret it.'

Having endured a comparatively positive day at school, the evening rewarded Liam rather less so. He scornfully scrutinised the plate of food that his mother had just placed on the dining table.

'What's this, Ma?'

Fully expectant of the critical response of her son, Stephanie was ready with her reply.

'You've had it before and liked it. It's lasagne. It's Italian.'

The voice of disdain mumbled from under a large hood.

'Fuck that foreign shit! I'll get a kebab later.'

Richard entered the kitchen having smelled the feast and the imminent argument. He sat opposite his son and joined the debate.

'Problem with the meal, Liam?'

'Yeah. It's foreign shit!'

'Your mother bought this especially for you. I suggest you adopt a more appreciative tone. Its only beef and pasta. It won't kill you. A kebab probably will!'

'But at least a kebab's English food!'

Mother and father smiled at one another. Sometimes there was a strain of humour in their son and his blissful ignorance. Sometimes it was best to avoid trying to explain things and leave him alone in his own little world.

Reluctantly, Liam reached for a fork and began to prod the content of his plate. Stephanie took her seat beside him and tried once more to encourage a sample onto Liam's cutlery.

'Don't play with it. Liam. God, listen to me. Talking to my fifteen-year-old like he's still in his bloody highchair!'

'Can't I leave the table unless I clear my plate then, Ma?'

'Well, you act like a child, so we may as well assume you are one.'

'I ain't no child!'

Richard watched his son become visibly agitated. Liam's fuse was so short these days. It was difficult to avoid rousing his temper with most casual issues. Time for change of subject.

'How was school?'

'Okay, I suppose.'

'You attended, then?'

Liam stared disparagingly at his father across the table.

'I always attend, Daddy dear. It's just that if I don't like some lessons, I bunk off for a while. Anyway, I was made an offer today.'

Richard and Stephanie looked at one another with practised concern.

'Not a job offer, then? Cruising on the Med? Bodyguard to a film star? Pro footballer? I'm sorry Liam but the law says you must stay at school until you're sixteen. That's another year by my reckoning. These aren't rules invented by horrible parents, you know.'

Liam placed a forkful of food into his cheek and leaned forward.

'Yeah. Laugh it up. But before you both jump of the cliff of conclusion…no…it's not a job offer.'

Richard smirked knowingly, waiting to be amused by the latest tall tale from his son.

'An offer from a female then? About time, too.'

Stephanie wanted to hear what her son was about to reveal.

'Richard. Let him speak for God's sake.'

'No. Not from a girl either. From a teacher. Mister Smith. From art.'

Liam had now captured his father's attention in an instant. Silence befell the table as parents listened to their wayward offspring and his pronouncement of partial conformity.

'Well, my lad? Go on! Tell us more.'

The son took a deep breath before continuing.

'Well…he wants me to help out with the first-year kids or something. To help supervise them. He's taking them into town to draw landscapes. He thinks it will be good.'

Richard stared at his wife.

This time, his smile was earnest as opposed to ironic or sarcastic.

'Honestly, Liam? You're not pulling my leg?'

'No, Pa. He's asked me to pass on some of my artistic flair.'

'But that's brilliant, Liam!' proclaimed his father. 'A wonderful opportunity in fact. When will this be happening?'

'Dunno. He says he'll speak to me tomorrow.'

Richard Warburton resumed with his dinner. For the first time since he could remember, a drop of paternal pride seeped into his heart.

'I told you he had time for you, didn't I? I'm really pleased. This is the best thing to happen to you at school for ages. What do you reckon, Steph?'

Liam glanced at his mother in mild embarrassment. Praise was not something Liam was accustomed to receiving. He barely understood its relevance. Although he felt a certain pang of pleasure in knowing that his parents supported his actions for once instead of conveying their usual policy of disapproval.

Stephanie's reaction to her son's news seemed to almost draw emotion.

'I'm really glad you're helping out, Liam. Giving something back. It'll do you good.'

Placing another morsel of lasagne into his mouth, Liam felt a tangible sense of achievement. His parents were genuinely pleased about something he was involved with. Even though he hadn't accomplished anything yet, the premise lifted his mood to nigh on sociable.

'You know, Ma. This foreign grub ain't bad.'

Stephanie simply shook her head and continued to eat. A minute or two's silence passed as the family dined in peace. However, the contentment was brief as Liam's brimming curiosity forced a query.

'Do you know when you're leaving for Greece?'

Richard looked toward his son who in turn did not lift his gaze from the plate in front of him. Immediately, he suspected an ulterior motive in asking the question.

'We don't know exactly. We must wait for Bill to get back to us. All being well, the end of July. About a month or so. There's been something of a delay in processing the necessaries.'

More seconds of silence as Liam's mind toiled.

'Why do you ask, son?'

It was time for a careful choice of word and tone for once.

'Well, the boys are keen for me to join them camping, like we discussed. They're on about the coast. Just two or three nights.'

His father set down his cutlery.

Now the picture was becoming clear.

'And you hoped to soft-soap your mother and me with this art class story? Hoping we'd change our minds?'

Liam felt affronted by the accusation.

'No way! It ain't no story! It's the truth!'

'Alright, son. Calm yourself down. At this moment in time, we don't know any confirmed details about the trip. So as things stand, I can't say yes or no to you jaunting off to the coast. Though it doesn't sound like a great idea to me.'

A disgruntled son slumped back into his chair and dropped his knife and fork onto the tabletop.

'What? Me, enjoying myself for once? No. I didn't think you'd approve, Pa. This fucking family. Its priorities stink, man! Thanks for the food. I'm outta here'

His mother and father watched as Liam scraped his chair backwards out of the way and exited the kitchen. The slam of the front door signalled the latest angered departure of the wayward young man.

The usual, daily mode of expression for Liam Warburton.

Richard and Stephanie did not even feel compelled to stop him. They no longer questioned him about his various evening destinations or the company he kept.

Sadly now, it was placation enough should they find him in his bed the next day.

*****

It was break time the next day when Colin Smith finally caught up with Liam in his usual spot, keeping his usual counsel under the veranda in the playground.

'Morning, Liam. Morning, lads. Where were you at registration, Liam?'

Sensing the attention from close by, Liam barked his reply.

'Late, sir.'

'Yes. I know. But I wanted to fill you in on what we spoke about yesterday.'

Elson and Jonka had not been informed as to their leader's invitation. As such, their interest was now firmly entrenched in discovering more. Liam felt uncomfortable with the line of conversation and the unwelcome audience.

'After dinner, okay? Room eight. I've cleared it with Miss Stock. I've excused you from double maths. You'll be able to catch up with the work though, won't you? I'm sure some kind soul will lend you their book. Don't forget. Room eight. One-thirty.'

Liam watched the art teacher as he walked back into the school building, sensing the eager eyes of his friends. Their expectation of some explanation was beginning to irritate him. Yet Liam had little option but to be honest. Elson could not contain his mirthful inquisition any longer.

'What's this shit, Warbs? You getting out of maths? For what? What's happening, man? Can we come too?'

Liam balanced his weight uneasily from foot to foot. The words did not come readily. His coy discomfort was now obvious for the others to see. Jonka compounded the issue.

'You're blushing, man. The leader of the Black Stars is shamed! What's to be shamed about, Warbs? What's up with Smithy? What you two planning together?'

Liam was trying desperately to appear relaxed. He was failing by the second, much to the growing amusement of his companions.

'He...erm...wants me to...help him.'

'To do what, man?' chipped Elson.

'Erm...supervise...'

'Supervise who?' smirked Jonka.

'Erm...the Year Seven art class. This afternoon.'

Elson and Jonka were now completely failing to hide their exasperation on hearing such news.

'What? You? Teaching? No shit! You're ribbing!'

'No, man. The truth. We're going out. Drawing the landscape.'

The explosion of laughter resonated around the wooden roof of the veranda, causing those nearby to glance across to the trio. Liam was now in the grip of all-out embarrassment. There was nowhere to hide as he watched his friends holding their sides.

'I don't believe you! My ears are playing with my mind! Liam Warburton. The man the future generations must admire! I've heard it all, now. Hey, I bet you have them smoking by home time!'

'Shut it, Jonks.'

'You gonna teach them how to pick Smithy's pockets?'

'Look. It's not *my* idea. Okay?'

'Sure, Warbs. You just want to hang around with little boys. We know all about you. You gonna wear the long coat with the hole in it?'

Elson didn't have time to smart at his own quip.

In a flash, his breathing had been restricted and he was involuntarily on his knees, gasping for air.

Liam's patience had snapped.

Jonka watched in horror as his two friends fought a one-way battle.

Liam was winning without a moment's resistance.

Veritably sucking the life from the lungs of his gang mate.

'Jesus, Liam! Stop! He can't breathe, man! We're only fucking kidding! You don't have to fucking kill him for it!'

Liam averted his gaze from the panicking figure at his feet as a crowd gathered to observe the action. He stared into Jonka's concerned eyes and released his grip. Elson collapsed to the floor, flapping like a grounded fish.

Squaring up to his friend, Liam whispered into Jonka's ear.

'You've seen what he got. One more word…will be your last. Clear?'

Jonka did not utter a sound as he watched Elson struggle to his feet. Both nodded their heads, leaving Liam to exit the arena, again triumphant in the contest.

The eerie, fearful silence that had descended during the fracas was graciously interrupted by the sound of the bell, calling the pupils back to class.

NINE

Liam did not speak to another soul for the remainder of the morning. Despite being in the same room as Elson and Jonka, they kept their distance.

In turn, they were not acknowledged.

They had crossed the line with Liam Warburton.

But they would eventually forgive him as he would certainly forgive them. After all, they were friends.

Liam passed the lunch hour pondering the prospect of spending the afternoon with Year Seven pupils. His instincts were telling him in no uncertain terms to go and find Colin Smith and tell him to shove the offer where the sun didn't shine.

But the alternative was double maths. And Miss Stock.

In truth, there was no decision to make.

*****

The time was one twenty-five. Liam waited outside the closed door of room eight. The uncertainty of the next two hours was almost unbearable.

Usually, he thrived on the unknown.

The thrill of the chase; the advance and the retreat; this was his customary staple diet.

But not now.

Not at this moment.

Somebody was expectant of him.

He suddenly realised he had to deliver.

As his mind toiled the door opened, and the smiling face of Colin Smith invited him in. Dual emotions swept through Liam's mind. The mild sense of superiority he would normally feel in such company evolved into a barely concealed meekness.

'Boys and girls. I'd like you to say hello to Liam. He's from Year Ten and has kindly volunteered to join us on this afternoon's session.'

A few awkward seconds passed as the youngsters observed the towering, intimidating figure at the head of the room.

Then, in unison, the class expressed their greeting.

'HELLO LIAM!'

More seconds of discomfort were endured by the teenager.

Liam quickly glanced toward the teacher. Then back to the smiling, innocent faces of the children sat before him. There was only one reply to give.

'Erm...hello, boys and girls.'

He felt like the intro turn at a Christmas pantomime.

Thankfully Mr. Smith took the reins once again.

'Now, I've asked Liam to join us because he is very good at art. In fact, he's not just very good... he's superb. During the course of this afternoon, I want you show him your work. Ask him what he thinks. And he'll give you advice on how to draw landscapes. Okay? Everybody got pencils and paper? Drawing boards? Let's get out there!'

It was a surreal situation.

Yet, suddenly, Liam felt at ease. Understandably, the youngsters looked at him warily at first, but did not ask questions. They did not judge the person they saw before them. It was a refreshing change. Despite his initial reluctance, Liam felt almost as if he belonged in that place at that moment.

Though, filing them out of the school grounds in full view of his maths class was not a prospect he was relishing.

Mr. Smith walked on ahead. Out of the main building, across the playground toward the entry gates. Liam followed up behind, automatically checking that the boys and girls were in pairs, in line and paying attention.

It was almost like an army drill.

Liam Warburton. Sergeant Major. Escorting his troops from the barracks.

Then came the shrill bang on the window from the second floor of the school building.

Liam glanced furtively upward, to Elson and Jonka, smiling their heads off at the spectacle below. Without further word, Liam reacted with his middle finger. A gesture of little consequence to him, but which caused much hilarity for some of the youngsters under his charge.

Realising his response had been spotted he was quick to excuse himself.

'Listen, kids. Never do that! It's rude and naughty. The teacher will tell you off for it!'

'Will the teacher tell *you* off for doing it, Liam?' came a tiny voice from the middle of the line.

'Probably! So, keep it shut. You never saw anything. *Okay*?'

The chuckling eleven-year-old pressed a forefinger to his pursed lips, causing Liam to smile.

'Good lad. You know it makes sense. Never snitch!'

Liam did not look back as the throng left the school grounds and ventured on toward the town centre. The boys and girls were remarkably well behaved. It seemed that Mr. Smith's analogy was correct. The change of scenery and sunshine was having a positive effect.

On Liam, especially.

He was actually enjoying himself.

It felt good to make some form of contribution.

It was also a relief to be relieved from the tiresome quandary of maths with Miss Stock.

After trudging behind their teacher for over twenty minutes, the group finally reached the chosen destination.

The elevated railway sidings on the edge of town provided wonderful views of the layout and buildings around Talworth, including the distant aqueduct. It was a peaceful location to sit and draw.

It was also a place of decidedly mixed memories for the assistant present.

With drawing boards placed on laps, the pupils sat in small groups discussing which areas to sketch. Liam watched Mr. Smith in action. He was confident and friendly. He knew how to get the best from his students. How to keep them interested. They responded in kind to his jovial manner. He treated the children like adults yet maintained an authoritative stance.

It was a strategy that produced immediate results. Within minutes, the discussions had ended and nearly thirty pupils sat contentedly drawing the views around them.

There was no need for arguments. No need for friction.

Only time for work. Work that was to be embraced.

Liam walked up and down the line without word. He wanted to see what the children were seeing. To gain their perspective on the world below. It was a fulfilling exercise.

As Liam observed the young artists, Mr. Smith covertly surveyed the whole scene with interest. There was an ulterior plan in inviting Liam. It was a chance to try and divert his attention from the negative aspects of his schooling. Indeed, from his life in general.

An experiment to invigorate lost ambition.

To make Liam realise once again where his strengths may lie.

That was the secret to anyone's chances of success in Colin Smith's book.

Making people aware of what they can do.

Not repeatedly remind them of what they are incapable of.

Every human being on earth knows what they *can't* do. Yet it seemed so few were given the opportunity to acknowledge and exhibit their inner ability.

Liam had slipped through the net at some point.

Colin Smith was desperate to ensure the lad was positively ensnared in his own convictions once again.

Liam Warburton avoided disturbing the line of boys and girls as they concentrated on their work. Maintaining his distance a few yards behind, he admired their seemingly natural aptitude for focussing on the task at hand and the accomplished manner with which they transferred the landscapes onto paper.

He felt strangely comforted being among fellow artists.

The inherent anger; the undying need to assert; the self-imposed will to prove himself. These binding, suffocating characteristics had disappeared within minutes of being in the company of the younger pupils.

As he studied the group, vague drawings gradually came to life on blank canvasses. In truth, he had fully expected the group to be chaotic, boisterous and disobedient.

Perhaps, as he had, they would eventually evolve into such creatures of disarray. The thought made him smile as a tiny female voice intervened in his daydream.

'What do you think, Liam?'

Liam glanced upward to the end of the line to see a pasty-faced little girl with pigtails holding up her drawing. Despite his acquired sensation of solace within the group, Liam felt suddenly unconvinced of the next appropriate move.

Once more, he was uncertain of direction in the face of the unknown.

Almost suspicious in fact, of the child holding aloft her work for his personal approval. Mr. Smith appeared next to him as though from thin air.

'Go and talk to her, Liam. She wants your opinion. Tell her what you think. Encourage her. Help her. And take that bloody hood off.'

Slowly Liam moved toward the caller on the grass verge, whose smile broadened at being acknowledged by the new class assistant. For that is what he was now perceived to be.

He nervously crouched down beside her and let his eyes meet hers.

'Hello. What's your name? I'm Liam.'

The little girl offered an expression of innocent bemusement.

'I know that already, *silly*! I'm Sarah. Sarah Buxton.'

Liam became quickly enchanted by the impish figure perched beside him and held out a hand for her to shake.

'Pleased to meet you, Sarah Buxton.'

'Thank you.' she replied with untypical juvenile bravado.

Offering Liam a purposed glare of inspection she then handed him the drawing board that dwarfed her tiny lap. He observed the precision of the lines on the paper. The comparison with the real scene spreading below was uncanny. Liam was impressed by the standard of work.

'Yes. I can see the church spire and the car park. And if I'm not mistaken, that's St. Forsters isn't it, Sarah?'

The little girl beamed with joy.

'Yes, Liam. That's right. Do you like our school, Liam? I think it's lovely!'

He thought hard about the relatively easy question and her wondrous perception. *Was* it such a lovely school? *Should* Liam feel glad to be there? *Should* he feel justified in projecting such despondency each and every single day?

The positive outlook of his junior companion was infectious. Liam could not respond with falsehoods to such an earnest enquiry.

'No, Sarah. I don't really like school all that much.'

The girl looked him squarely in the eye as she retrieved her drawing board.

'You should do. It's a happy place.'

As she resumed with the sketch, her words struck several chords in Liam's mind.

Was school a happy place?

If so, why could he not recognise such things?

Liam Warburton had been regularly intent on causing misery to so many in that supposedly happy place. A shadow of dread followed him through the school gates every morning. To those that knew of Liam Warburton, contentment was not an associated concept.

The puzzle revolved in his mind as he rose to his feet.

An elusive answer to a question that he had never even asked of himself: Why was he not happy? What would make him happy?

For little people such as Sarah Buxton, life was a daily source of enticing discovery. A chance to learn and interact. To make friends.

Not enemies.

How Liam secretly envied the young ones. How he craved their futures and rued his own history. How he inwardly wished he had the power to admit his failings and change himself.

But at that moment, he could not…and would not.

Not for school.

Not for friendship.

Not for parents.

Not for anyone.

Least of all, for himself.

Yet he was already unwittingly taking those first few vital steps to becoming somebody else.

'Liam, come and have a look at Simon's work, will you?'

Mr. Smith called from the other end of the group causing Liam to file away his self-analysis for the time being. Reaching his new destination, he sat down on the grass as the teacher offered them a casual introduction.

'Simon, meet Liam. Liam meet Simon. I think you'll be impressed by Simon's talent. A very observant eye. Reminds me of you, actually.'

Liam scanned the pencil drawing on Simon's board. He used the medium very well. He had successfully depicted light, shadow and shade. There was a real sense of perspective to the work. An ability to interpret yet with a feel for the reality of what was being viewed.

This time, Liam felt no awkwardness in his responses.

'This is good, Simon. *Really* good.'

He watched the young boy's eyes light up at receiving praise. It was inflating for Liam to behold. Just a few simple words of appreciation. That was all it took to convince the child that he was doing something right.

The irony was that Liam could not recall receiving such commendation in his life, yet he was suddenly able to offer it. Heaping praise on people was not a previous forte. Yet the pride in doing so swelled within him after seeing its effect on the boy.

With just a few mere words, Liam was making a difference.

As he stood to his full height to inspect other drawings in the group, every child wilfully called his name to demand his response. They wanted his input. They needed his contribution.

Colin Smith stood back and said nothing, quietly satisfied that the exercise had already been a resounding success.

*****

Eighty minutes passed far too quickly, and it was time to return to school.

'Okay. Everybody got everything they came with? Time to go, then. Liam will lead us back.'

Liam glanced furtively at the teacher. *His* teacher. He was little more than a boy himself yet felt so much more than that today. Almost a giant among the first formers. A man of responsibility. A person that others could have faith in. He had enjoyed the temporary feeling of belonging as opposed to standing aloof. Until two hours ago, such an experience had never touched the life of Liam Warburton.

Now the desire to be involved and connected was overwhelming. Now he was a name and a face. Not the name and face that had instilled fear into his peers. But someone who was ready to help. Willing to assist.

Not only the talker, but now the listener.

As the class filed behind him toward St. Forsters and back into the classroom, the joy of the children was in vibrant abundance. A united 'thank you' from the class registered somewhere in his heart.

A firm shake of the hand from Colin Smith was accompanied by hushed yet wise words.

'Think on, Liam. This is just a taste of things to come.'

*****

The bell resonated signalling the end of the school day. Liam collected his bag and sidled back into the sunshine to meet his friends who stood in idle readiness outside the school gates. Liam expected some banter for his newly adopted role.

He didn't have to wait very long as Elson opened the greeting across the playground.

'Hey, man! How's the new career going?'

Before he could respond Liam notice his two friends exchange smirks.

'Ah…you know. Better than double maths. Did Stocky miss me?'

'She didn't, no. But *somebody* did!' quipped Jonka.

Liam was momentarily intrigued but quickly gave up the chase. His friends had no intention of expanding on their riddle. Routing through his bag, he dropped it to floor between his feet in frustration.

'Crash us a fag, boys. I'm gagging!'

The trio stood on the pavement as the home time crush flowed around them through the school gates. A stream of pupils that seemed to go on forever, all engaged in chatter about the day's events and the prospective evening ahead.

Elson could not resist another jibe regarding Liam's temporary secondment to the Year Seven group.

'So…what's the next art class gonna be about? You gonna be a nude model for the sixth form to paint?'

Liam watched with partial amusement as his friends doubled up with a bout of hysteria.

'Shut your sick mouths before I shut them for you.'

Immediately ceasing their mirth, an awkward silence followed. Liam drew deeply on his cigarette as he eyed his shuffling cohorts. However, the entertainment was not long in rejuvenating itself.

A familiar tone altered the peace.

'Hey, Liam! You're too young to smoke! I still think you're cool, though!'

Sarah Buxton's voice carried across the street toward the trio, causing more than a little embarrassment for the subject of her commentary. Liam's normal reply would be instinctive, angered and crude. Yet he fumbled for an appropriate response to the youngster.

Eventually, he unearthed one.

'Sorry, Sarah. If you don't tell anyone about me smoking, I'll come to another art class!'

The pasty-faced little girl with pigtails smiled.

'Okay, Liam! My lips are sealed! See you next week!'

He could hear his friends giggling behind him.

It was understandable, he supposed. But no less tolerable for the fact. A warning stare from beneath his hood did little to detract Elson and

Jonka from their amused state. Jonka eventually felt obliged to speak on the matter again as he raised his palms in a gesture of peace.

'Sorry, man. Sorry, okay? But if you could see our point of view! The leader of the Black Stars becoming a hero to Year Seven. It ain't right, man. It just ain't right!'

Liam did not respond. He threw off his suffocating hood and stared upward to the brilliant azure sky above.

'You out tonight, Warbs? quizzed Elson.

'Where?'

'Dunno. The square? See what crops up?'

Liam continued to avoid eye contact with his friends as his irritable mood subsided.

'Yeah, maybe. If I am out, I suppose I'll see you there.'

'Okay. Listen, man. We're gonna shoot. Watching a film at Jonka's. Coming?'

Liam observed the remaining unburned section of his cigarette.

'Nah. Perhaps see you later, boys.'

Elson and Jonka sidled off in the opposite direction as the last few pupils filtered out of the playground. It had been a day of personal discovery for Liam Warburton. His enthusiasm for creativity was evidently still within his soul. He had enjoyed talking to the young pupils. There was no connotation of suspicion attached to the artistic exchanges on the railway verge.

Just honest expression and acceptance of opinion.

It was a refreshing experience.

Not having to fight to be heard.

Somebody genuinely wanting to listen to him.

Lifting his nearly empty rucksack from the floor, Liam flicked the cigarette butt into the gutter and crossed the road. His advance was short-lived.

'Oy! It's an offence to drop litter! Pick that up! Now!'

The words registered in Liam's ear. Who was trying to order him around now? After the good day he'd just had. Trying to spoil his moment? To ruin his temporary victory.

Stopping his stride, he turned in readiness to launch a tirade of abuse toward the source of the command.

Yet the figure standing outside the school gate in the short distance was far too pretty to shout at.

Carla Ferris chuckled as she skipped across to join him.

'Alright, Warbs?'

Liam chewed nervously on his lower lip as they strode together toward the main road.

'Not bad, Ferris. You?'

'All the better for seeing you!'

His eyes narrowed as Carla displayed another smile, accentuating her blue eyes and dimpled cheeks.

'And why would you be wanting to see me, may I ask?'

Carla began to nervously swing her bag forth and back as she spoke.

'I've been hearing why you weren't in maths this afternoon.'

Liam glanced at Carla, fully expectant of more derisory commentary regarding the issue. He replaced his hood as a gesture of retreat. Yet there was no sign of any forthcoming mockery. Carla's manner appeared genuinely impressed with Liam's newfound pursuit. His initial suspicions were soon proved incorrect.

'I admire you for what you did today. It took some guts.'

Liam smiled to himself and checked the position of traffic on the main road before they crossed together.

'Yeah. Well. You're in the minority. Most think it's a bit of a joke.'

'I don't see what's so funny about it.'

'Yeah? Well, it was better than double maths, any day.'

Carla smirked and checked her mobile phone for text messages.

'Well, it looks like Louise has stood me up. I'll have to walk home alone.'

The comment pricked Liam's curiosity. He tried desperately not to look at Carla as they walked. He was aware of a growing attraction. He had heard the rumours all week about her having a crush on him. She was evidently trying to encourage the situation to progress. Being the cool kind of guy he was, he would certainly not wish to show weakness and acknowledge her romantic interest.

Yet he failed badly and quickly succumbed to the temptation.

'Well...I...I...could walk you home...if you wanted.'

Liam's words were enough to induce the widest of smiles from his classmate.

'Oh, you're a sweetie! Not the bad boy of legend, after all! Do you want a fag?'

'Please. I'm out.'

Retrieving a packet of cigarettes from her duffel bag, Carla lit hers first before cradling the flame for Liam. As he inhaled, Liam sensed their closeness. His heart suddenly lurched. The excitation was overwhelming. A totally new sensation. A feeling that would last far beyond the few seconds of actual proximity that had been enjoyed.

They continued to walk through the town centre with arms linked. A mildly awkward silence was soon broken by Carla's assured tone.

'Anyway, you have to come back to my house.'

Liam was puzzled.

'Why?'

'To copy up the maths you missed this afternoon. It's been about tangents. Have you got a calculator?'

Liam shook his head. Carla knew full well that he never carried any required equipment in his bag. In fact, she was surprised to see that he had a bag with him at all.

It mattered little. Liam had other ideas on what to carry.

'I could get some booze to take back with us. Are your parents going to be home?'

Carla puffed out plumes of smoke into the sunshine.

'No. Not 'til gone six. I've got my own key. Where would you get drink from, anyway?'

'Elson's cousin. Works at Thistle's offy near the precinct. He sorts us out regular.'

This apparently accidental meeting was becoming more interesting by the minute.

*****

Liam stood in the hallway of Carla's home, scanning the décor and picture frames that adorned the walls. Pulling the ring on a can of lager, he pointed to a photograph of an infant.

'Is that you in a nappy?'

Carla's sheepish expression said it all.

'Cute!'

'Give us a drink, Warbs. Stop pissing about!'

Carla sipped the froth from the top of the can as Liam popped open his own beer and followed her into the kitchen.

'I'll tell you what, Ferris. Fuck the maths. Let's just get drunk.'

She giggled as bubbles shot up her nose.

'I'm up for that. Come on. On the patio. It'll be nicer out there.'

Liam felt unusually driven.

Waves of masculinity washed over and within his very being. Yet he was still in control - just. The trepidation of earlier had vanished. He liked Carla's company. He always had. The pair perched onto deck chairs facing down the garden.

'Did you like teaching the first formers, then?'

'I wasn't teaching them. Just supervising, really. Smithy thought he might need my expert advice!'

'That's a compliment to you then, isn't it?'

Liam gulped some beer and stared at Carla.

'Yes. I suppose so. Never really thought about it like that.'

'You're not used to compliments, are you, Liam?'

He simply shook his head and focused straight ahead. Her line of assessment was a little too personal for his liking. But he rode the personal insecurity whilst drinking more of his beer.

Just as he hoped that the awkwardness had passed, her next question threw him off his stride completely.

Out of the blue.

Unpredictable.

Direct.

'Liam. There's something I have always wanted to know.'

'What's that?'

'Why don't you have a girlfriend?'

Liam gulped more of his drink and sat up in the deck chair. He considered his response as the sunshine forced him to squint at her even from beneath his hood.

'Well...not really into girls to be honest.'

Carla was not to be dissuaded from talking about the issue.

'Yes, but...you must have found girls attractive before. They must certainly have been queuing up for *you*. Have you never had a crush on anyone?'

Liam was becoming slightly agitated by the scrutiny. Taking more deep swigs from his can, he struggled to maintain composure.

'You sound like my fucking grandmother. Why are you asking me these stupid questions, anyway?'

Carla could see she had both annoyed and embarrassed Liam but the intrigue was too much to ignore. She wanted to uncover the outer layers of this boy that had grown through school with her, yet she hardly knew anything about.

'Louise and me…we often watch you and wonder…'

Liam sat further forward, visibly concerned by Carla's statement.

'When? *When* do you watch me? Have you been fucking spying on me?'

She sipped from her can and shook her head.

'Warbs…you're paranoid. You know what that means, don't you?'

'Oh yeah? What does that mean, then?'

The pause was unwelcomed. Much like her answer.

'Guilty conscience!'

Her laughter echoed around the patio and garden as she watched Liam control his emerging anger.

'Liam…I'm joking! We've watched you at school. Break and dinner time. You don't mix all that much, do you?'

The line of questioning was now bemusing. Why couldn't she just leave the subject alone? Why the persistence?

Who cared, anyway?

Carla evidently did.

A fact that finally softened his initial objections.

'I have friends.'

'Yes…but it's the same two all the time, isn't it? Doesn't it get a little boring, just the three of you at the school gates, grabbing a crafty fag here and there? What do you talk about?'

Liam finished his drink and sat back in the chair. His eyes met Carla's, which now beamed with anticipation.

'Look, you don't want to know at the moment. In fact, the less you know…the better.'

Now it was Carla's turn to feel confused. She could not understand the need for secrecy. It made no sense.

'I still think about when I made you storm out of the classroom. I upset you, didn't I?'

Liam reached for a second can from under his chair before retrieving another cigarette from Carla's bag. He gazed at the girl sitting opposite as he lit the end.

'Want one?'

She declined, eager to continue with the conversation.

Liam fixed his gaze into the trees beyond the garden fence and inhaled the smoke. Drinking deeply again, he began to feel slightly numbed by the alcohol. It was a contenting sensation which he had become very familiar with of late.

'I was a bit upset, yes. But it's all in the past now. Well, nearly.'

'What do you mean...nearly?'

Liam watched the spiral fumes of his cigarette ascend in the sunshine as he attempted to avoid eye contact with his interviewer.

'When I've sorted who did Glendin. *Then* it will be done.'

Carla's features turned pallid as the meaning of Liam's words hit home.

She had sought to see the softer side of this mysterious individual, yet his true self suddenly eclipsed any positive element she may have detected in the previous half an hour.

Yet still she probed.

'When you say 'sorted'...what do you mean?'

Leaning forward once more, Liam let the cigarette hang from his mouth as he made his solemn pledge. His eyes appeared black and lifeless as he spoke.

'Retribution, Ferris. When he surfaces - and he will - I am going to finish him.'

Carla's skin crawled and sheathed itself in goosebumps. Despite the heat, a shiver went down her spine, accentuated by the expression of sincerity in her friend's face.

'You actually *mean* it, don't you?'

Liam nodded and smiled.

'An eye for an eye. The killer will die.'

Unsettled by the swift change of mood, Carla placed her drink on the floor and nervously lit another cigarette. A few silent seconds passed as the implication of what she had heard began to register.

The fact that she was sitting across from a potential murderer.

So young, yet so willing.

Not only capable, but positively fixated by the idea.

The realisation inwardly repulsed her. The scenario had blackened. She was no longer comfortable in the company of this maddened boy. She felt his inner rage, ready to erupt. Yet the exterior had seemed so calm.

Carla checked her watch. Her parents would not be home for nearly an hour.

The subject of Glendin Jones had made her wish that hour would quickly elapse, and her parents would arrive. She had inadvertently pushed buttons in Liam Warburton that should not have been touched.

Carla became fidgety as she smoked and drank. She was now torn between changing the subject or just asking Liam to leave. Yet there was a strange compulsion that stirred within her.

Something told her to press for more responses. To continue the quest to uncover the enigma of Liam Warburton.

'Why do you need revenge? What will it prove? It won't bring Glendin back, will it?'

Liam peered at her from the gloom of his hood.

'It's not about bringing him back. It's about me. *My* ambition. *My* need. *My* desire to inflict fear. I've decided that's what I'm best at. People fear me. Old and young. So they fucking should do.'

It was a sinister declaration for Carla to hear, yet still her curiosity demanded more answers.

'But you're better than that.'

'No...no...I'm not. That's the whole point.'

'But what about this afternoon...those kids in the art class...why not throw your energy into more of that...instead of this nasty shit?'

Liam squashed his second empty beer can with one hand and chuckled.

'Where is the victory in the classroom? Where is my superiority going to come from?'

Such a reckless and self-obsessed mission. Carla finally rose to her feet, having heard more than enough.

'You're pathetic. Immature and childish. You scare *me*, too, Liam! I want to like you as a person. But you make that impossible, don't you?'

He watched, smirking as she displayed her annoyance.

'You secretly *like* me this way though, don't you? That's why I'm sat here, isn't it?'

She pointed angrily toward the side gate.

'Just go. Please. Before my mum and dad get back.'

Liam's amusement was short-lived as he realised Carla no longer wanted his company.

'Oh...I get it. You're ashamed of me, now? Don't want to play anymore? Just like the fucking rest, aren't you Ferris? All stuck up. Think you're a notch above me? Typical.'

Carla's mixed emotions were rising to the fore as she opened the gate.

'No. Liam. I'm not typical. I'm *not* like all the rest. I *do* think differently about you. But you make it so hard. Just leave, please.'

Liam brushed past her onto the front driveway.

'Don't get upset, Ferris. I'm going. You can have the last beer. Just crash us another fag.'

She thrust the packet and lighter in his face.

'Here. Have them. Just fucking go, will you?'

Unbeknown to the pair of them at that moment, it was to be their final conversation before the summer break. Liam sauntered out without offering her a second glance.

Closing the side gate after him, Carla wondered if she had done the right thing. It was not easy asking Liam to leave. Not knowing of the path he would take. Yet it was a relief for her to be alone once more.

Alone with the crushing disappointment of failing to tame Liam Warburton.

In previous days and weeks, she had fought desperately to erase the dubious popular image of him from her thoughts.

The pointless fighting; the lack of any compassion; the apparent contempt for his fellow man.

Yet as she pondered his departure, it dawned on her that the pre-conceived impression of Liam was indeed born out of a harsh truth.

And to her immense frustration, there was evidently no other image of him that she could aptly present in its place.

TEN

The remaining three weeks of the school term passed without major confrontation for Liam. The altercation with Carla had secretly caused him temporary concern, yet he did nothing to repair the damage to what had been a potentially close friendship.

For her part, Carla maintained a safe, peaceful distance.

Liam's deliberation on the matter effectively overshadowed the days before the summer holiday.

Declining to attend further art sessions with the Year Seven pupils had left the youngsters in the class - not to mention Colin Smith – extremely disappointed to say the least.

It seemed that Liam was effortlessly letting people down. Yet he persevered with the notion that his way was the only way. Skipping lessons to amble round the local shopping precinct left his pockets crammed with stolen goods and his mind empty of creative impetus.

But he was still proving adept at using one particular talent. Liam was a practised hand at avoiding theft detection devices.

As with every aspect to his life, rules and boundaries were put there to be broken and crossed, after all.

Colin Smith felt very disheartened with Liam's sudden reversal in attitude, but as a teacher he had other priorities. The exam period was over, but there was a mountain of other academic issues to deal with. Liam Warburton did not wish to figure in those plans and as such he decided to leave Liam to his own devices until the new term started in September.

A few weeks away from the monotony of school routine would perhaps enable everyone concerned time for refreshment of approach.

Not that Liam was a stickler for school routine, anyhow.

Yet little did anyone know what surprises the summer break would comprise.

Or the motives for any possible changes in Liam's disposition that lay waiting to be discovered.

Richard and Stephanie had attained confirmation that their planned trip to Greece had been set for the beginning of August. They would not be back in the country until the end of September, but Liam had little complaint about foregoing the first three weeks of the autumn term.

If it were up to him, he would not be returning to St. Forsters at all.

Another plus was that he would be able to attend the proposed end of term camping trip along with Elson and Jonka.

Liam's parents were not completely enamoured with the prospect of letting their wayward son loose on the local seaside resort of Ilcombe, but the idea of him loitering around Talworth for a few days was infinitely less appealing.

Stephanie held a slight sense of private guilt regarding her son's imminent secondment to her parents. But there was no other conceivable option. The subject had been the source of much friction over the previous weeks.

Letting Liam free from his proverbial chains for a night or two at the coast would perhaps be an astute form of appeasement.

Appropriate preparation for his enforced retreat to the countryside.

At least, that's the strategy that Liam managed to convince his parents to digest as he left for the railway station to meet his friends.

As he waved his mother goodbye, little did Liam know just how ill-prepared he would be for what awaited him at Clearlake.

Still, that was still another week away.

The indeterminable shadow on the horizon could be ignored for the time being at least.

*****

'Crash us a fag, Elson.'

Liam squinted through the window of the train carriage as unfamiliar scenery flashed before his eyes.

'You're not allowed to, man. Non-smoking, see?'

Liam's scornful gazed rested on the red sticker emblazoned above the window. More rules. More prohibition. This was supposed to be a holiday.

'What fucking shit is that?'

Passengers in proximity winced at the audible profanity issuing from the back of the carriage. Liam smiled avidly at the disapproval he was incurring. It was a spur. Of course, there was no deterrent, now. Liberation was completely his, if only for the short term.

No mother and father to berate him.

No teachers to criticise him.

No law to restrain him.

'We gonna fuck us some seaside women, then Jonks?'

The group cackled loudly as more intolerant stares were aimed in their direction. Liam thumped the window and glared at the landscape beyond.

'How far is fucking Ilcombe, anyway? I'm ready for some action.'

Elson reached into his holdall.

'An hour away, man. Be cool. Have a drink. Compliments of my cousin.'

Liam laughed out loud as he took the beer can from his friend.

'You're a fucking hero, Elson!'

Boastful cries of male frivolity were interrupted by the sound of cracking beer tins, and frothing spillages. A moment of serenity reigned among the group once again as Liam raised his drink to propose a toast.

'To an absent friend.'

'And our mission to find the motherfucker responsible!'

'HERE, HERE!'

Indulging in their semi-tribal rant, the trio failed to notice a respectable looking gentleman in his forties who had left his seat at the other end of the car to walk toward the rowdy throng. Instinctively, Liam suspected the interruption was not to be of a social nature as he warily eyed the stranger's approach.

'Excuse me, lads. I don't want to spoil the fun, but alcohol is actually banned from public transport these days. Just thought I'd let you know before I go and find a guard to throw you off the train. And another thing, keep the swearing and shouting down, will you? There are children present and I'm trying to read.'

Other passengers sat in silent appreciation of their brave companion, whose misguided aura of victory accompanied him back to toward his seat.

But the apparent triumph was all too brief.

Liam stood to his feet, beer can still in hand.

'Hey! Hero!'

The man turned to see the tall, athletic-looking youth in the hooded top.

He said nothing, as did the other occupants of the car. Glares were exchanged for a few uncertain seconds. Elson and Jonka suddenly began to worry. They did not want Liam to be involved in trouble.

At least not until they reached their destination.

The audience watched in anticipation of a scornful reaction.

Liam maintained his focus on the gentleman in his forties. His inner rage bubbled, causing him to drink more beer.

Decision time was upon Liam.

Yet, strangely, he faltered.

Untypical thoughts diluted his normally impulsive demeanour. He remained standing; yet motionless. And still, he stood, without word. And he found himself able to do little else...but stand. The gentleman did not acknowledge Liam further. He simply resumed his chair and picked up his book.

Liam continued to hold his ground.

Until the time had passed. A comparative eternity.

Too late for responsive action, now.

Liam was pulled back down into his seat, greatly troubled by his own uncanny reaction.

'Later.' Elson whispered. 'Not here. Not now. Later. Just drink and keep it quiet.'

*****

The remainder of the journey passed in relative silence.

Having had their tickets checked, the Black Stars made their way through Ilcombe railway station, the self-appointed target now fully in view. He seemed to be alone as he departed the platform with his suitcase in one hand and book in the other. The crowd of travellers was dispersing. Even better, the respectable looking gentleman who had dared to publicly challenge them was seemingly headed for the toilet block.

With practised rhythm, the group assumed formation to commence their assault. Liam would exert the initial move whilst covertly guarded by Elson and Jonka.

As the scuffle ensued behind the locked door of the lavatory cubicle, there was little time for the victim to react.

The sequence lasted little more than thirty seconds. Pulling the cubicle door open and shutting his quarry in behind him, Liam ushered his friends from the toilet block and into the street. Humping their bags into the nearest taxi, they made a swift exit.

In the back of the cab, nothing was said. Liam hurriedly counted the bounty that had been acquired only seconds earlier.

Two hundred and fifty-two pounds in cash.

More than enough for the three of them to enjoy a good time.

'Where we headed for, boys?' asked the driver.

'Ilcombe Farm camp site.' came the anxious reply from the back seat.

Liam fondled the cash in his palm.

'And there's a good tip in it for you if you floor it.' he smiled.

The group gave little thought to the harrowing scene they had just left behind.

It had been a quick, decisive and profitable manoeuvre.

And as far as they were concerned, it was genuinely warranted.

Some way back, staggering from the toilets, a gentleman in his forties emerged, his face covered in blood. His nose had been smashed. One punch in the correct place had sent him reeling. He knew little else about the attack.

But he had a fair idea who the culprits might be.

Struggling to retain his vision, he reached the information desk and was assisted by two members of staff. Holding a handkerchief to his face, the nasal tones were surprisingly clear as his voice bubbled through a crimson calling card.

'Can you phone the police, please? I've just been robbed. I've got a good description.'

*****

'Do you know how to put this fucking thing up, or what?'

Liam reclined on the grass verge in mild amusement as he watched his friends berate one another.

'*You* should know! It's *your* fucking tent, after all!'

Liam continued to sit and absorb the welcome change of scenery, which was gradually becoming infested with campers. Similar quandaries regarding tents were seemingly being experienced within every new group of arrivals. Taking a deep draw on his cigarette, he opened a fresh can of beer and leant back onto his elbows.

Thoughts of what had been left at home only three hours earlier were placed firmly at the back of his mind. Talworth was a place of harsh reality – a concept he would endeavour to forget about for the following couple of days. Yet, attempting to focus on positives was not an easy task for Liam Warburton. As a tormented soul, he found it difficult to relax at the best of times.

Brooding seemed to be his second and first nature. But thankfully, two trusted friends were present to deflect the typical, self-induced bombardment of his mind and provide a modicum of comic relief.

'You twat! You nearly smacked my hand! Watch it or I'll plant that fucking hammer in your skull!' barked Jonka.

'It's not big enough to knock the fucking spikes in, man! How's it going to hurt *you*? Fucking useless, this is!'

Elson proceeded to launch the hammer toward Jonka as the tent collapsed into folds of canvas once more. Liam felt compelled to ease his friends' frustration.

'Why don't you two just have a drink and think about things for a minute? Come on. Chill out, will ya?'

Deciding it to be a welcome option, the two joined Liam on the grass bank behind their pitch. Each in turn sipped their beer and lit a cigarette as the mid-afternoon sunshine blazed down. One or two potential female admirers sauntered past the trio, inducing them to remove their tops and display supposedly manly upper physiques. The annoyance over tent erection was soon eclipsed by more pressing matters as the three boys observed the girls until they wandered out of view.

'Totty count aint up to much, Liam.'

Liam flicked cigarette ash onto the grass and sighed knowingly.

'Not that bothered, Jonks. I've had enough of bleedin' women for a while.'

Elson and Jonka smiled at each other as they allowed their mutual thoughts to become known.

'You mean you've had enough of Carla Ferris?' teased Elson.

Liam's attention diverted from the sedentary activity around the site and fixed itself on his friend.

'What you say, fool?'

Elson suddenly became nervous but would continue with the banter under Jonka's encouraging grin.

'Carla. We know you've been seeing her, Warbs.'

Liam became annoyed at the false assumption and sat upright.

'What are you talking about? I haven't talked to her for a month! Now shut it, fool!'

Jonka prepared to jump to Elson's defence, already sensing that the school rumour mill had got it totally wrong for once.

'So…you two…aren't…together…then?'

Liam simply shook his head in disapproval. There was little in the way of expression in his face, which served as neither a confirmation nor a denial of the charge. It was not conclusive enough for his friends, but enough persuasion for Elson to change the subject for the time being.

'What are we doing tonight, Liam? Going into the resort?'

Liam leant back on his elbows once again and surveyed the pile of material, poles and cord that they would be hopefully sleeping in later on.

'Yeah. Can do. See who fancies some action with the Black Stars in town, eh? Pass us another beer, Jonks. I'll see if I can get this tent up whilst you two idiots go to the camp shop and rustle up some supplies. I'm fucking starving!'

With considered reluctance, Elson and Jonka pushed themselves up and stretched their legs.

'What do you want, Liam?'

'Crisps. Sandwiches. Anything. Use your initiative, Jonks…if you know what that even means! See if there's a chippy on site as well.'

Both boys watched as Liam crouched among the tumbling mess of canvas and pegs. A good minute passed before realising he was still under vacant scrutiny from the counterparts he thought had been successfully despatched to the shop.

'What you two fucking waiting for?'

A short silence prevailed before Jonka sheepishly replied.

'You got the money, Liam.'

With mild exasperation, Liam searched into the pocket of his jeans and retrieved the cash acquired earlier.

'Here. Twenty quid. Now fuck off and let me get this bastard tent up in peace.'

Another discomforting hiatus ensued as Elson and Jonka continued to hover.

'Liam…'

With a disarming scowl, the leader of the Black Stars turned to his gangmates with hammer firmly in hand. It was a look that swiftly prompted the inevitable query from Elson.

'Do you know where the shop is?'

Liam instantly rose to his feet, causing Elson and Jonka to sprint in the opposite direction. As they ran, the tent hammer bounded around the floor between their legs and ricocheted amongst their feet, causing uproarious laughter from all three.

Liam's parting shot acted as a gentle warning for their return.

'And don't forget some more beer and fags!'

*****

Nearly an hour had passed before Liam finally resumed position once again on the grass verge, admiring the small two-man tent exhibited proudly before him. Taut and tight, it was cramped inside for the three of them but would suffice for the two-night duration of the stay.

As he sat under his re-applied hood, it was satisfying for him to know that he had achieved such a feat alone. But Elson and Jonka could be like old mother hens at times. Cackling and arguing about nothing. If Liam took control in such situations, it invariably brought peace and order.

Still, they were his friends. And he respected them for their frailties.

However, his period of reflective accomplishment was not to last long. Liam heard familiar voices in the distance before homing in on the distinctive vision of Elson and Jonka, scampering desperately toward him as though being pursued by a lion.

Then he saw what they were carrying.

Absolutely nothing.

No food. No fags. No booze.

Liam wondered why he ever entrusted them with any simple task. Yet his dismissive reaction was tempered by the expressions on their faces as they approached.

Something drastic had evidently happened.

He stood up to greet them and emptied the remains of the last can down his throat.

'Where's the grub and beer, fools? You've been gone for fucking ages!'

The only initial response from his friends was a mutual grimace of exhaustion. Panting for breath, they finally reached Liam and grabbed onto his top for support as they halted their stride.

'Watch the fucking hoody, boys! What's happening? You both look like you've seen a ghost!'

Elson looked into Liam's eyes, his own as wide and white as saucers. There seemed to be genuine fear in his tone as he spoke.

'Coppers, man. Now! At the front gate of the camp. We saw the squad car. They'll be looking for us, Liam! They'll be after us! We'll go down for what we did at the train station! I'm fucking telling you!'

The leader of the Black Stars was not perturbed by the warning of unexpected visitors. He looked across to Jonka, who also seemed unnaturally fearful. As usual, it was time for Liam Warburton to take command of matters.

'Relax, boys. All is fine. We just wait here until they go. No problem. They won't check every fucking tent, will they? I'll bet this is only one of a few sites along the coast. They won't be here long. They never are. Chill. It's all cool!'

Jonka was not overly convinced by Liam's optimistic appraisal of their predicament.

'That receptionist looked us up and down when we checked in. He knows who we are. He'll help the pigs!'

Liam was becoming a little angered by the expectancy of defeat that had suddenly instilled itself into his two gangmates.

'He knows shit! Absolutely nothing! Now sit and relax. Have a smoke. Be calm. We wait here. I'll scout until things are clear, okay?'

There was no reply from Elson or Jonka as they quickly placed lit cigarettes between their lips and drew heavily.

Liam turned to survey the landscape around him as an unrestrained smirk of arrogance emerged.

A few peaceful minutes passed before Plan A was rapidly employed by necessity.

'Shit! Get behind the tent!' cried Liam as he shoved his dozing friends into life.

All three crouched behind their pitch and peered studiously across the camp site. A police car was slowly weaving its way around the myriad of tents, stopping intermittently to allow the officers to speak to passing campers.

Elson's scepticism returned quickly to the fore as he observed the spectacle in the distance.

'If they see us, we've had it! The summer's over! I'm getting in the tent!'

The trio bundled over one another in their attempts to evade detection.

It was a crush, but a vital arrangement for the moment.

Liam zipped up the front curtain, leaving open the slightest gap at the top to allow him constant vigil over events outside.

Wary voices raised queries from under the increasingly hot canvas.

'Can you see them, Liam?'

'Ssh…I'm watching them now. Keep fucking quiet.'

Elson and Jonka glared nervously at one another as the temperature began to slowly rise inside the tent. The Black Stars were becoming steadily agitated as uncertainty grew among the group. The silence was agonising as their leader maintained his position on all fours as look-out.

Finally, a development was announced in firm, whispered tones.

'Okay. The filth are about one hundred yards away…'

'What are they doing?' asked Elson.

'Looking for us, you dopey twat! What do you *think*?' snapped Liam.

'What do we do? What do we do?' enquired Jonka.

Liam's voice was calming as his gaze remained focused out front.

'We sit like we're not here. Okay?'

Obeying the order, Elson and Jonka kept their quiet in the now searing nylon bubble. A minute or two later, Liam's hushed voice was just about audible but broke the deafening peace.

'They're near to us now. The tent across the path is empty. They're ignoring it. Shit! They're looking at ours right now!'

A deathly anticipation was countered by murmurings outside on the grass verge. Car doors could be heard to open. Liam could identify two policemen and the site receptionist – a bedraggled, overweight man in his late-fifties, who unwittingly pointed directly towards the tent containing Liam and his cohorts.

Liam could not decipher what was being said but listened and watched as though his very life depended on it.

Then, with perfectly inappropriate timing, Elson broke wind.

The attempts to stifle their erupting amusement combined with the ensuing scrutiny outside the tent were causing not a little discomfort among the trio.

Still the policemen asked questions. Still the receptionist pointed. Still Elson and Jonka fought to stem their writhing giggles.

Then, after what seemed like hours, the welcome sound of car doors closing was followed by the slight rev of an engine and they moved on toward the next batch of tents some yards away.

Liam began to relax amidst the sound of his friends' background tittering. Yet he remained on watch, mindful that the pursuers were not yet out of view.

'We clear, yet? It fucking stinks in here, man!' guffawed Jonka.

'No. Wait! Shut it!' came the reply from their leader.

Again, the police car revved and trundled further away to continue the search. More minutes passed as the heat in the tent peaked in tandem with the unpleasant stench.

Finally, Liam watched as the police car disappeared from view in the distance.

Jonka repeated his giggling request to evacuate.

'I'm fucking burning in here, man! We safe or what?'

Liam ripped open the front zipper of the tent allowing the three friends to pour out and take in welcome breaths of fresh air. This natural act was hindered by uncontrolled laughter. Luckily, the police had vanished, with little idea that the three suspects they had been searching for were rolling around on the grass holding their ribs in amused relief.

Liam, never one for taking his safety for granted, squinted into the distance once more to confirm their status with a sneering announcement.

'I think we're out of contention, boys. The pigs have flown! Smells like you were pretty worried, Elson.'

The friends shared the moment of hilarity before reconsidering the wisdom of their search for nourishment.

Liam rose to his feet to judge the lie of the land.

'Perhaps in an hour or two, boys. When the dust has settled.'

*****

The presence of the police had caused a change of plan. The duration of the first day was mainly spent patrolling the camp site and local village. Being under-age and possessing no formal faked I.D., the gang had successfully persuaded locals to obtain alcoholic supplies for them from the nearby grocery store. Yet the site seemed to be inhabited by an older peerage and any attempts by the Black Stars to cause distraction were in vain due to the daytime absence of many campers.

But fortune would favour the bold.

It was the second evening at Ilcombe which eventually brought with it the desired sense of excitement. Having kicked their heels for nearly forty-eight hours, the gang finally opted to visit the coastal resort to sample - and possibly spoil - the jovial atmosphere.

Alighting from the promenade shuttle bus, Liam, Elson and Jonka silently hoped for provocation.

They were not to be disappointed.

The mix of holidaymakers made for a far livelier spectacle than the farm site. Teenagers swarmed in and out of the souvenir shops, amusement arcades and burger joints.

Laughter and screams emitted from the rides at the nearby pleasure beach. The sights and sounds of the seaside were everywhere.

Liam turned to his colleagues and offered a knowing smile.

At last, the boys would be able to expend their pent-up energies in an experiment of exploitation.

The unwitting arena awaited them as they stalked and watched.

Having been drinking since mid-afternoon the gang was under considerable influence when Elson spotted a familiar face striding across the pier deck.

He pulled Liam closer whilst pointing to the subject of his curiosity.

'Hey…it's Barnesy…with his brothers by the looks of things.'

Despite the welcome change of scenery, Liam had quickly become bored. However, the opportunity to antagonize another member of St. Forsters was not to be passed up and he relayed his wishes.

Especially as the subject was Ryan Barnes, who had become something of a nemesis to the Black Stars over previous months.

'Come on. We'll hang out with them for a while. See what's up.'

Elson and Jonka followed Liam as they left the promenade bench and made for the pier in pursuit of their target. A small arrangement of children's rides toward the end of the pier seemed to be the destination and Liam's voice carried ominously over the pounding music.

'HEY! BARNESY! WAIT UP!'

Ryan Barnes turned to identify the caller and was not impressed to see the three eager faces that approached. He secretly had little time for Liam Warburton. He avoided him at school and certainly had no desire to spend any period of his holiday with the Black Stars.

In truth, the feeling was mutual.

Still, his greeting was barely convincing if well-acted.

'Hi, guys! What an unpleasant surprise! Out causing trouble, are we?'

96

Liam feigned a look of bemusement before addressing the quip.

'We never *cause* trouble, Barnesy. We just *finish* it.'

Pretending to chuckle, Ryan glanced to his two elder siblings and ushered them on with a stark statement.

'Well, there's none to finish round here so fuck off and bother somebody else, will you? I'm enjoying myself, see?'

Liam was initially confused before realising that young Barnes was not speaking in jest. He moved closer and lowered his tone so as not to attract unwanted attention.

'That's no way to talk to friends, Barnesy. You ought to be careful. We could take offence.'

'Take what you like and fuck off. You stink of booze. How many you had today? You're a bunch of amateurs. Amateur piss-heads!'

Liam's bubbling temper was quickly evolving into rage as he grabbed Ryan's t-shirt. Before the brothers could react, a punch landed squarely on Ryan's jaw, knocking him backwards.

All around eyes widened as the scene unfolded. Yet Liam remained totally impartial to events as he grinned at Elson and Jonka, rubbing his knuckles.

'Been wanting to do that for months. Tick it off the list, lads!'

Cradling his chin, Ryan was seemingly unperturbed by the attack.

'You don't scare me, Warburton. You're just a scumbag. You and your virgin mates. I bet they wouldn't be hanging around if they knew about Glendin. I bet they don't know it was all your fault!'

No sooner had the words registered with Liam then the fight broke out in earnest. A myriad of fists and feet moving in all directions. Elson and Jonka gave no second thought to helping their leader as he launched himself toward the source of his torment.

Ryan's brothers had little choice but to support the fracas as onlookers ran for cover. The scrum rolled its way through the smattering of rides and into the pier-end amusement arcade.

Punches landed with alarming regularity and precision as the scuffle's momentum increased. Ryan was not about to let this chance slip. He had beheld a silent hatred of Liam for many months, knowing full well about the legacy of the Black Stars.

Grabbing Liam's hooded top, he shoved him into a corner against a fruit machine. Then Ryan Barnes placed his nose squarely to Liam's and issued a distinctly unwelcome opinion.

'YOU GOT GLENDIN JONES KILLED, DIDN'T YOU! YOU AND YOUR POT-HEAD MATES! HE DIDN'T DESERVE TO DIE! YOU FUCKING DO, THOUGH!'

Liam, now totally consumed by fury, could only foresee one outcome of the argument, and reached down to retrieve his ever-reliable flick-knife from his sock.

Simultaneous to this action, a hand reached and grabbed Liam's shoulder, violently pulling him away from his intended target. Turning angrily, Liam threw a reactive fist in the direction of the interruption.

To his immediate horror, Liam realised he had just landed a perfect right hook onto the chin of a police officer – the very same officer that had patrolled the camp site the previous day.

As the officer stumbled back and prodded his cheekbone. Liam wasted no time in making his escape and pulled sharply on the wilting forms of Elson and Jonka.

'THE FILTH! MOVE IT! GO! GO! GO!'

Obeying their leader's command to retreat, the Black Stars bounded from the amusement arcade and past the fair rides. None of them looked back as they scampered along the pier, through its entrance and across the promenade.

'DOWN THERE! QUICKLY!'

Concerned children were moved aside by their parents to allow the escape. Making for the nearest side street, the pace was unrelenting as they forged a menacing group silhouette against a late summer sunset.

Once safely into the shadows, all three placed their backs against an alley wall and regained breath. Between desperate pants, Elson demanded some explanation.

'You fucking twat, Liam! I can't believe you still let Barnes get to you! You've pulled some shit, but that was crazy. What were you gonna do with that fucking knife, man? The pigs are really gonna be out for us now!'

Liam turned to his companion with a raised fist.

'Listen, fool! We're lucky the filth came when they did. I was about stick him for his disrespect!

Jonka could not believe his ears.

'Liam. You're mental! He was only having a dig, man. Just a joke! He didn't mean what he said about you and Glenners. It wasn't right, but he didn't mean it. You don't have to go overboard, do you?'

Liam regained his composure and checked up and down the darkened twitchel. Holidaymakers passed at either end, but it seemed that for the moment the three had slipped the net. Content that they were away from police scrutiny, Liam ordered a swift return to camp.

'Come on, pussies. We've got some beer back at the tent. I can see you're too chicken-shit to stay out and play tonight!'

Elson and Jonka looked at one another in bemused relief as Liam wandered up the side street laughing to himself. Jonka's tones were whispered so as not to interrupt their leader's obvious twisted sense of achievement.

'Elson…I think it's a good thing we're getting outta here tomorrow. That dude is gonna get us fucking locked away before long!'

*****

A peaceful final night resumed at the campsite. Liam became distinctly withdrawn as the other two sat and played cards. Drinking and mulling, he contemplated the events of the previous forty-eight hours, and the memories encouraged a smile.

He stared vacantly at the top of the crimson sun as it dropped below the distant ocean horizon. His friends were seemingly content to leave him alone with his thoughts. They knew where he was and could keep an eye on him.

At least he wasn't inflicting danger on anyone - or himself.

They watched him smoke his umpteenth cigarette of the day, wondering what it was that travelled around the beleaguered mind of Liam Warburton.

It was a deep, cavernous place.

Uncertain. Unpredictable. Unyielding.

Both watched respectfully as Liam immersed himself amid his conscience. Elson and Jonka were privately thankful that he would be elsewhere for the remainder of the summer.

A time for him to reflect.

Perhaps, even, time that would afford him to change.

ELEVEN

It was a sharp prod in the shoulder that first aroused Liam's senses as he stirred under the duvet. Not enough to wake him, but enough to interrupt a deep, cursed slumber. Yet a familiar voice soon began to invade his solace.

'What time did you get in last night? You know we wanted an early start today. Your father and I have lots to do as it is without you holding us up. Why is your phone turned off?'

His mother's mild tirade merely presented itself as an annoying background hum which varied in tone and pitch. Liam deciphered little of the monologue as he attempted to bury his head deeper into the pillow.

His efforts to eradicate any semblance of reality that may inflict itself on his state at that moment were instantly thwarted by the deflating knowledge of what the day was about to bring.

The thoughts began to build in his head as he fought valiantly to shut them out. How he wished he were back on the campsite with his friends. Or even back at school.

But today a different destiny beckoned him.

The secondment to his grandparents.

The grandparents he supposedly hated.

The grandparents that, he supposed, hated him.

A summer sentence to a distant, rural prison.

The dark shadow of Clearlake had been looming large over the previous weeks. Now Liam Warburton was fully enswathed in that shroud of dread.

The relentless sunshine that battled to penetrate his bedroom curtains did little to lighten his pessimistic appraisal of the uncertain encounter that lay ahead. Indeed, the scenario looked bleak for all.

The chance for fun had passed.

Playtime was well and truly over.

Though, instinctively he already suspected this swift change of emphasis. The thought of sleeping in a hard, cold, itchy bed had plagued him for days. He had tried to omit the inevitable from his mind, but now had little option but to embrace the plans laid down by his parents.

His stupid, selfish parents.

And their stupid, pointless business trip.

Attempting to keep eyes firmly shut only served to achieve the exact opposite.

100

Adjusting to the rays of invasive daylight streaming in through the glass, Liam then realised he also had to deal with the symptoms of an incessant hangover.

The result of last night's farewell party with Elson and Jonka. The music, the booze, the pills and the commiserations thumped around his skull like a bass drum. His eye sockets throbbed. His throat and mouth felt like sandpaper.

But how he and his friends had laughed together as they drank their way into wondrous oblivion by the canal side.

Untouched by the imminent schedule and its demonic guardians. The Black Stars had celebrated their ongoing survival…and the departure of a leader. Their union had been tested by recent history and its punctuated trail of misdemeanour.

Yet those boys saluted their future together.

An autumn reunion was a beacon of hope for all three.

Of course, there was also time to honour the absent member of the gang. His passing still acutely infringing on Liam's conscience. A conscience pricked regularly by guilt. And a secret desire to be anybody but Liam Warburton.

His soul rarely rested in peace.

Though such intermittent insecurities he would never willingly disclose to anybody.

The aroma of frying bacon and the sound of a slamming father were a potent combination when hindering recovery from over-indulgence. Falling from his mattress to the floor, Liam reached under his bed to retrieve the can of Red Bull that he felt sure had been rolling around the room for weeks on end.

Alas, all in vain. What he would give at that moment for such sweet liquid to quench the bitterness within. After grappling with and grabbing at shadow, dirty laundry and fresh air, he gave up the ghost.

Resigned to slowly becoming upright on both feet without chemical assistance.

The discomfort seared from the top of his head, through his jawbone and down toward a lurching stomach. Walking was barely achievable without discomfort. His eyes squinted automatically to reduce the intake of light.

Liam issued a desperate request toward his closed door.

'Dad. For fuck's sake, man. Stop banging, will ya?'

Richard Warburton peered from the bathroom and grimaced at the sight of his only child who stood in his bedroom doorway naked, and still slightly drunk.

'For Christ's sake, Liam! Get a robe on or something! And get a *move* on! Your mother and I want to be back here by tonight...not *tomorrow* night!'

Liam tried desperately not to listen to the continuous paternal rambling as he wavered on the landing, watching his father stomp an angered descent down the stairwell.

'Have you even packed? Have you eaten? No? Shift it then!'

Liam could not summon an adequate response to his father's demands. Only one whispered word emitted from his mouth as he entered the bathroom and donned a towelling dressing gown.

'Twat.'

Gulping cold water straight from the tap brought little in the way of relief from the remnants of alcoholic plunder, either internally or externally. Gazing into the shaving mirror, he barely recognised the face in the glass.

More headache. More water.

More slamming from the kitchen below.

'For fuck's sake! Ouch! Jesus!'

Liam shouted as he cradled his fragile head into his palms as his parents hurriedly prepared for the day ahead downstairs.

'Fucking pair of idiots!'

Finally at the breakfast table, Liam ventured to identify the items on his plate.

A smile emerged as he glanced up at his mother.

'Bit heavy this, mum! I might just throw it straight back up!'

Stephanie turned from the kitchen window, stirring her coffee.

'Better make the most of it. That's the last cooked breakfast you'll be seeing from me for weeks! Go and eat in the garden if you're going to be ill. I've just washed this floor! And hurry. We need to be on the road for nine.'

His vision barely accommodated the two hands on the kitchen clock. It could have said ten to nine. It could have said anything. He didn't really care for a timetable in his current state. Inserting a forkful of what tasted vaguely like tomatoes into his cheek, he glugged freely from the orange juice carton perched on the table.

102

Overspill covered his chin and trickled down his arm. But the temperature and effect of the drink gave refreshing respite from his green-gilled stupor.

The sleeve of his robe slipped as he held the juice carton aloft.

Stephanie observed the crimson lines of destruction etched upon her son's forearm. Her heart quivered with maternal anguish.

So many warnings; so many wishes for her son to stop.

Yet still, the terrifying evidence remained - and amassed.

Following a partially satisfying breakfast and an explosive ten-minute diversion via the toilet, Liam made a weary ascent back to his bedroom. His mother had laid clean pressed clothes on top of his miraculously remade bed. Without further thought, Liam dropped the lot into the suitcase that lay open for him on the floor and snapped the lid shut. Stephanie appeared without warning in the doorway.

'Are you taking your games console with you, love?'

His mother's unwelcome interruption of the packing process was given immediate vocal response.

'Fucking dead right! I'm counting on it to keep me alive among all the dead people! They have got electricity, haven't they?'

Stephanie shook her head as she observed her son slumped on the edge of the bed.

'Don't be so disrespectful, Liam. They're looking forward to having you.'

He did not answer. The premise repulsed him. He made little secret of the fact, either. Reluctantly pulling a holdall from the bottom of the wardrobe, he proceeded to gather vital items from around his bedroom.

'I take it the coffin dodgers have got a TV, too? Or do I have to pack that as well?'

Stephanie's voice carried across the landing from her own bedroom.

'Oh, that's a point. I think they've only got one television set. It's quite old. It mightn't be any use for your console.'

Liam slouched as disconsolation hit home. He considered his mother's words with simmering disbelief.

'You're having a fucking giraffe right, ma? This isn't fucking hell you're pushing me off to, is it? Is it true that Clearlake is devil-speak for torture?'

Liam detected his mother's chuckles from the other room.

It made him smile also, but his frustration was beginning to build as the scenario grew more damning by the second.

'Of course not, my dear child. But you'll have to watch the swearing. No f-words in front of your grandparents. Do you hear?'

Liam feigned a loud groan of trepidation.

'Why? What are they going to do? Wash my fucking mouth out with soap?'

Again, Liam listened as his mother's mirth rose to create an audible laugh. Liam's ready defiance was mildly entertaining at times, although she always endeavoured to hide her amusement from Richard if possible.

Liam waited for a reply to his last query regarding the probable punishment for profanity.

A reply that did not come.

*****

Liam threw his distressed form into the back of the car. This was the moment of realisation. The fateful and vain acknowledgement that he would give anything there and then to remain in Talworth for the summer.

Listening to his father slam the boot of the car down behind him, Liam plucked his mobile phone from his pocket and composed a simple text message which read: *Missing you already. Love L.*

The message was quickly despatched to three people.

Elson, Jonka…and Carla.

This final contact with the world he knew left him with a churning sense of anticipation. The thought that he should be forfeiting weeks of leisure time with his friends for an enforced break in the countryside did little to rouse enthusiasm.

On the contrary, Liam's mood was darkening by the minute.

The premise briefly entertained him that he might go on the run from Clearlake and hitchhike back. Yet realistically, it was a nogoer.

His parents had emerged victorious in this particular battle.

There was little alternative but to obey their orders.

The moment of private whimsy was suddenly interrupted by the sound of the car's central locking mechanism securing all in their positions. The clicking of seatbelts in front was a proverbial nail in Liam's coffin.

No way out now.

His father's jovial sarcasm as he started the engine only served to heighten Liam's overpowering disapproval of matters.

'Okay boys and girls! Next stop Clearlake! Sing a song if you want!'

Liam's silence encouraged his own unavoidable regret at being subject to such parental enforcement, and he merely pulled the brim of his hood further over his brow and sunk back into his seat.

The car glided out of Tennyson Gardens and onward past familiar buildings and landmarks of the local neighbourhood.

Into the main road; over the canal bridge; past the strutting architecture of St. Forsters Secondary School.

Onward past St Martin's church near to the park and cemetery. Through the market square, where many Black Star meetings had been held and numerous plans devised.

Then, out of Talworth town centre and beyond. To become part of a writhing mass of traffic, seamlessly joining and separating as it snaked toward territory unknown.

Liam stared vacantly through the car window as familiar ground gradually became eclipsed by strange frontiers. He was still close to home, yet far enough away to be lost.

Then a final glimpse of the last recognisable outpost. The welcome yet helplessly distant vision of the railway verge and aqueduct, where he had sat and talked to children about art.

Then, Talworth was no more.

The picture of reliability was gone.

Now there was only the expectancy of a feigned welcome from relative strangers in a faraway place. Yet, even as he currently dreaded the prospect, his preconception of Clearlake would be altered drastically over the coming weeks.

Everything he knew, and thought he knew, would be dramatically challenged from this point onward.

This troublesome and troubled boy, who believed he had all the answers, would soon be forced into a process of reassessment.

Although no longer under the safe regime of a school criteria, unavoidable lessons would soon be imposed at a rapid rate.

A new teacher awaited his arrival.

Not one to be the victim of misplaced criticism.

Nor a person to be ridiculed before an eager audience.

Unbeknown to him as the car joined the motorway, Liam would soon be confronted by an unprecedented opponent of worth.

Indeed, an adversary he would learn to fear.

II
INITIATION

TWELVE

Francis James Gould stood in the porch-way of his two-hundred-year-old stone cottage and embraced the arrival of another glorious summer dawn.

He was supremely passionate in his observation of developments at first light. The evolution of a rising sun that quickly ensures the cotton layer of mist on the horizon is gradually replaced by pure cobalt.

Shadowy limbs slowly exhibiting their sleeves of entwined greenery as the pallet of colour gains life.

He looked to the tips of the tall pines and poplars that touched the sky all around the village, framing the scene akin to a pleated, protective shawl of emerald.

This was the view that he had fallen in love with at first sight all those years ago.

This was Clearlake.

The disciplines of a long military career had instilled a strict regime into this mind of nearly sixty-years-old. Yet, the body belied such a passage of time. Fran Gould was as strong and able as a man half his age.

This attribution was helped not a little by his daily morning run.

A three-mile route that snaked in and around nearby homes in the area; up gentle hill and down gradual slope; each turn of the path was flanked by dense foliage.

It was a place untouched by the cynical stains of progress and trend. And he would readily absorb every familiar sight as he ran. Each day, becoming silently more appreciative of the jewelled hamlet he was proud to call home.

He appeared to glide through the landscape.

Light of foot; shallow of breath.

The movement of limb was fluid and efficient. He was blessed with a sense of natural co-ordination that had stood him in fine stead throughout three decades of service in the Canadian armed forces.

Honoured by his country for his bravery in adversity, Fran had purposely re-immersed himself in the sedentary haven of Clearlake on his stand down from office.

The setting for an idyllic romance which now stretched back some forty years. A place to marry his sweetheart. The chosen location to settle down and raise a family.

A man finally at peace; now the master of all he surveyed.

A man who had once earned the right to command…and punish.

His morning jog would take twenty-five minutes on average. Fran's wife, Barbara, would readily berate him for supposedly putting his heart at such risk. Yet that heart was mighty and strong, striking a persistent, steady beat that had never faltered.

On the homeward straight he would sprint the final one hundred yards or so. The marker to indicate his increase in speed was the gleaming red mailbox on the corner of the street.

Then, with muscles and mind attuned to the task, he would physically move through the gears until at his own front gate, before warming down with some stretching exercises.

'You're off your damned trolley, sergeant!'

Barbara's good humoured appraisal interrupted the splendid silence as she emerged from the side of the cottage to hang some damp laundry on the line that spanned the neat, square garden.

'One of these days, Francis Gould, you'll listen to me! One of these days!'

Fran smiled as he rested palms on knees, before blowing her a kiss in return. She meant well and was probably right. Perhaps he was placing his body under needless duress. But Fran was not a man to be deterred by probability or risk. The odds had never mattered in battle. His mindset was one of pure confidence.

He feared nothing…and no one.

The next part of the daily ritual was to shower and shave as his wife prepared breakfast.

Today was Wednesday.

Eggs and toast day.

Stepping from the shower into a steaming bathroom, the aroma from the kitchen alerted his senses to the imminent snack.

Drying his face with a towel, he cleared his throat. This in turn induced a raging coughing fit. A regular and more frequent occurrence in recent times. Fran had been told at the age of fifty-three that the cancer slowly eroding his throat lining was malignant and inoperable. The blame was laid at the door of his cigar habit.

A social sin that Fran had indulged in since the age of fifteen - an army custom that appealed from the outset.

But he would not relinquish his love of the luxury whether the doctor ordered him to, or not.

Yet the coughing was increasingly and excruciatingly painful, as though he was trying to regurgitate razor blades from the base of his gullet. Prescribed medicinal syrup was a temporarily soothing remedy, but not a long-term answer. Fran stubbornly believed that his cigars removed the discomfort just as efficiently and infinitely more pleasurably.

The smoking was a cause and a cure. This was his lame excuse to an understandably worried wife.

Sometimes the bouts of retching would last for up to half an hour. Thankfully, the symptoms dispersed quickly. Fran drank water as he dropped blood-stained tissue paper into the toilet. Watching it flush away, he pondered - momentarily - about the future, knowing full well that his battle with this most resilient of enemies was not going to end in glorious victory.

The subject was hardly referred to in open conversation with Barbara. She had given up on passing the correct advice. Fran would jokingly claim that man needed at least one of the four sins. Women, booze, and gambling were never on his agenda, so smoking was his last and preferred option.

Barbara understood her husband's prolonged condition would only worsen and in turn would eventually take him from her, but such negative thoughts dissipated immediately as she watched him stride into the kitchen in a crisp white cotton shirt and jeans.

The same, handsome specimen that she had fallen in love with all those years ago.

Time had not tarnished her love for Sergeant Francis James Gould. Similarly, his loyalty, trust and companionship had never waned. He had supported her as a struggling mother when baby Stephanie arrived and military duty dragged him away from home, but he would always return the same person.

The proud father; the doting husband.

His un-typically lean and muscular figure belonged to someone Barbara viewed as being the complete man in every way.

Her man.

Taking his customary seat at the large, oak kitchen table, Fran observed his wife as she prepared his food and placed it before him. He continued to watch as she carefully poured stewed tea into his favourite mug. Then finally, she sat opposite and spread butter onto a piece of toast.

Breakfast was a time to relax in the Gould household. Peace and quiet enabled thoughts on the day ahead to be assembled, although the radio would softly emit classical music on most mornings. Man and wife liked to catch glimpses of one another as they ate, usually resulting in earnest smiles of mutual affection.

Fran sampled his tea and began to eat his eggs.

'I heard you, sergeant…cursing in the bathroom. Did you take some syrup, yet?'

Fran nodded as he chewed, aware that his wife knew he was lying.

'You couldn't have done…because the bottle of medicine is still behind me above the sink!'

Fran glanced over his wife's shoulder to confirm her claim. With mouth full, he grinned broadly.

'How is your breakfast?' asked Barbara, knowing full well that the food would be met with his approval.

'Grade A, my sweet. As always.'

The morning sun was now filtering proudly through the kitchen window. Barbara squinted into the golden shafts as she crunched on her toast. The silence resumed for a short while as Vivaldi offered a gentle backdrop.

Another glorious day in Clearlake looked likely.

But a day with a difference, also.

Barbara was somewhat reluctant to engage Fran on the subject of their daughter's pending arrival, but she needed desperately to gauge his mood regarding the arrangements.

Arrangements that Fran had subtly objected to from the beginning.

Nevertheless, Barbara gently dropped the issue into conversation.

'Stephanie will be here around early afternoon, she said.'

Fran continued to eat without reply.

Undeterred, his wife continued with the prompts.

'I've prepared young Liam's room upstairs. Clean bedding. Cobwebbed and dusted throughout. I'll bet he's a strapping young man by now. Soon be sixteen. I can't believe it's nearly three years since we've seen him.'

Fran finished his eggs and set the cutlery on the plate, swallowing carefully as he did so.

Barbara knew that an opinion was forthcoming.

'Her choice, Barbara. It's Stephanie's decision to keep her family at arm's length. Not ours.'

Now Barbara could at least burrow a little further with the debate.

'I know, Fran, but they are busy people. With busy lives to lead. It's not like they're around the corner, is it?'

Fran drank his tea, wincing as the lukewarm liquid splashed over his etched throat. But the discomfort would not hinder the expression of his views.

'They could have been *closer*. *She* could've been closer! If she'd have taken that district nurse placement you arranged for her. Then she would have been a stone's throw away.'

Barbara watched her husband place his empty mug on the tabletop and dab his mouth with a napkin. Evidently, Fran's disenchantment with their daughter's will to leave the countryside still raged silently within him.

'But Francis, you're talking nearly twenty years ago. Stephanie's just not a country girl. She never was and never will be.'

Fran huffed as he rose to his feet and began to place the crockery into the sink.

'No. I know. The businesswoman. The executive. Always chasing the dream and the dollar. That's what she is. I know.'

Barbara stood up and began to help with the pots. Fran had strong feelings, but thankfully he was remaining calm in conveying them.

'Well Fran, judging by their need for us to have our grandchild come to stay, the dream seems to be working out for them.'

Fran rinsed the dish cloth and looked sternly at his wife. His words were almost prophetic, yet neither he nor Barbara could know just how much at that moment.

'My dear, when one is determined to pursue a life of money…the question arises: at what cost should the ambition be attained? There is *always* a consequence, Barbara. There's *always* a price to pay in the city. *Always.*'

Fran's words did not make complete sense to his wife as she continued to dry the plates and mugs with a towel. His anger with his daughter over the years had seemingly been eclipsed by a certain wariness. He loved his daughter. There was little to argue about that. But Barbara could sense an inner concern from her husband.

Yet at that moment, she could not identify where the concern could be centred and opted to change the subject.

'Are you going out this morning, sergeant?'

Fran had finished the washing up and was now opening the syrup bottle to ease his raw throat. Ingesting two tablespoonfuls of the brown coloured liquid, he pulled a face of acute objection.

'Goddamn stuff. Tastes like tar! Yes, my sweet. I thought I'd nip to the village and fetch a few things. I need to fix that fence as well. Plus, I'll be in the garage most of the afternoon, servicing the pick-up. If we're going to entertain our only grandson, I'd better make sure we've got some wheels, eh? I'll see you later, my love.'

Barbara smiled as her husband kissed her softly on the cheek. She understood that working on the car was a simple excuse for him to remain out of sight when the visitors arrived.

'Don't forget, Fran. Be back for dinner. I want you home for when Stephanie arrives!'

Francis James Gould blew his wife another kiss before shutting the front door behind him. Striding along the garden path, his thoughts centred on lighting the first cigar of the day. Turning the tip as he applied the flame, it took a full two minutes before he could begin drawing and inhaling deeply.

Then the secondary consideration arose as he dwelled briefly on the uncertain reunion with his family in only a few hours' time.

A prospect that, for some reason, he could not fully embrace.

*****

Whilst having travelled for the duration of the morning, it felt as though they had been on the road for days. Liam's vacant stare beyond the rear window of the car carried little in the way of conclusive expression. The battery of his I-pod was running low and so he had opted to save any remaining power until reaching the destination. An immediate charge-up would be necessary by then.

The journey had been blessed with intermittent rain showers, but on the distant horizon, pure blue crowned the tree-lined landscape. The motorway had given Liam little cause to be attentive. Text messages had been received from his friends. Friends that now seemed to be on another planet, somewhere. A particularly amusing reply from Carla Ferris offered to send out a rescue party. He was pleased they had settled the confused business of a few weeks earlier.

At that moment, Liam felt somewhat imprisoned.

114

The noise and bustle of the dual carriageway had been left behind some miles ago. The remnants of urbanism had all but disappeared. A different arena was being unveiled now. The roads had become narrower. The trees more numerous and gradually taller. More alarmingly to the uninitiated observer, the sightings of fellow man had also become sparser.

Unbeknown to Liam, the four-hour journey to Clearlake was nearing its end. Stephanie's trepidation as she checked the map was well concealed. The meeting with her parents was to be a supposedly positive event, yet gradually instilled dread as the miles clocked up.

Richard simply wanted to deposit his son and retreat. He had far more important matters in his head. A family meet-up was not a priority for him, especially considering the potential and probable friction that awaited them.

Grinding up and down the gears, the car slowly wound its way through deep cavernous drops and then emerged atop hillside views. It was a never-ending exploration, with every new scene appearing to be slightly different to the previous one. Liam realised that they were neither following other cars, nor were they being followed. The sense of isolation begun to grow as his already minimal enthusiasm for the venture only continued to diminish.

It was possibly the longest period that Liam had sustained without uttering a single word for some time. There was little to say that could detract from the feeling that he was meeting his destiny. Several weeks of enforced potential boredom, and of wishes being unfulfilled.

Liam fought with an undying desire to be back where he felt happiest…and safest.

Wherever that was, it was certainly not here among this rural splendour.

Giant trunks and canopies dwarfed the tiny road as the car climbed and coasted down gradients. The wall of greenery enhanced a remoteness that Liam could only imagine was increasing by the minute.

He watched his father in the rear-view mirror, whose eyes were firmly fixed on the scene ahead. He watched his mother, whose attention was firmly fixed on the map. The silence was overbearing; agonising; painful to endure.

Then, finally, a voice sounded.

A voice emitting words that caused Liam's heart to lurch.

'Half a mile, Rich. I'm beginning to remember it now.'

Liam perched himself between the two front seats as a village honed into view among the swathes of foliage. Ancient looking buildings forged from rock. Thatched roofs. Quaint pavements. Neat, untarnished gardens. The sanctity and undeniable beauty of the picture was almost depressing to Liam Warburton. Now there was no chance of escape from this cauldron of ancient civility.

He was trapped.

He would surely never survive the duration of the stay.

Such selfish thoughts were obliterated by another claim from the front of the car. His mother's startling affirmation providing the final jolt of inevitability.

'That's it! The next road on the left after the mailbox. That's it, Rich!'

Knocking the car down to second gear, Richard manoeuvred into the designated street and cruised up alongside the front gate of the cottage that had stood for two centuries. Outside on the wall, a hand-painted sign proclaimed the residence as *Summer Place.*

Liam slumped back into his seat, as though hoping to disappear through the back of it and not be discovered until back home in the protective haven of Talworth.

Yet again, his mother's tones only served to destroy the dream of escape as she turned to face him with a feigned expression of enthusiasm.

'Okay, Liam. This is all yours for the summer. Isn't it lovely?'

The son did not reply to his mother as he silently began to fume.

He would have given anything in the world to remain in the car and make the journey back home with his parents. But something instinctive told him to conceal his ill-feeling toward the situation.

His objections contained for the time being, he waited patiently for his father to open the car door.

Reluctantly, Liam alighted, into a new, uncertain world.

THIRTEEN

Stephanie waited at the gate and surveyed the vision beyond. Perfectly preened rose beds framed a manicured lawn, which in turn supported a line of billowing linen. This was an image that instantly took her back to her childhood.

Memories of summer days; of being young and carefree.

And of being bored beyond insanity.

Richard joined his wife as Liam stood silently behind carrying his hold-all and suitcase. His demeanour was now particularly sour; his facial expression resembling that of a convict in the dock. But Liam's obstructive disposition mattered little to his parents.

Within an hour, they would be gone again.

To journey onward.

To arrange business.

To make their money.

The importance of the next sixty minutes was to ensure a smooth passage of responsibility. Stephanie's parents would soon have to bear the brunt of any resilience from their grandson. By tomorrow she and Richard would be a thousand miles away and thankfully helpless to assist.

But for the immediate moment, courtesies had to be paid, and a suspected rift, overcome.

The light summer breeze delivered the aroma of a garden in full bloom across the plot of the cottage. Stephanie observed the serene domain of her mother and father. Whilst picturesque, it also seemed so dull and lifeless. So sedentary and lacking in vigour. Her glance diverted back along the road they had just driven.

Not a soul in sight.

Not a sound to be heard, aside incessant birdsong.

Yes, she thought to herself.

Liam might just find things a little difficult around here.

Then a familiar vision appeared in the cottage doorway. Barbara Gould dried her hands on a tea towel as she tentatively peered through the drying laundry toward the trio at the gate.

It had been over a year since she had laid eyes on her daughter, yet despite their petty quarrels the maternal pride had not diminished one iota.

The smile of parental recognition that followed was encouragement enough for Stephanie to acknowledge the elder greeter in the pinafore.

'Mother! Hello, mother! We're here!'

With a half-smirk of reassurance, Stephanie beckoned her husband and son to follow her lead through the gate and along the garden path.

Barbara's glee on seeing the new arrivals was evident and earnest as she held her arms open for her daughter to fall into. The embrace was meaningful and firm. Mother and daughter closed their eyes as they buried their heads in one another's love. That contact alone was sufficient to draw a single tear of emotion from Barbara Gould, which was dispersed immediately with a reflexive digit.

Drawing away from her little girl, Barbara looked admiringly into Stephanie's eyes. Though only months, it had seemed like a lifetime since they last saw one another. The moment was cherished for all it was worth. Then Barbara's attention diverted to the males in the group.

'Hello Richard, darling. How's things? Life being good to you?'

Stephanie watched as her husband followed suit and hugged her mother, somewhat less enthusiastically, but at least the attempt at affection was on public display.

'Things are good, Barbara. As you can see, I'm trying to take care of your baby for you.'

Barbara looked once more at her daughter's beaming smile and bright, brown eyes.

'Well, she sure looks good on it.'

Then a temporary silence prevailed between the adults. Attention was now becoming centred to the young man stood aloof of the group, just inside the gate.

With hood securely atop head, luggage by his feet and hands now thrust into the pockets of his jeans, Liam Warburton stepped forward for his grandmother to inspect.

Barbara scrutinised the boy that shifted his weight awkwardly from foot to foot and tried to avoid eye contact with her. The first time she had seen her only grandchild for an age. A hand went involuntarily to cover her mouth, in what was a reaction of genuine disbelief.

The initial shock rapidly turned to earnest pleasure as she admired the figure standing before her.

The vision of the fifteen-year-old evoked the widest of smiles as she calmly raised her arms to welcome her only grandson to the fold.

'My…Liam…my, how you've grown. My goodness. Such a handsome young man. Look at the size of you! Oh my…I can't believe what I'm seeing…come here, my boy, give your grandma a squeeze.'

Liam obliged the loving ritual with a detectable minimum of exertion.

The mild discomfort exhibited on the teenager's face caused more than a wry smirk to emerge on his mother's lips, but Stephanie retained her composure in honour of the exchange.

Finally, with the opening acknowledgements complete, Stephanie breathed a sigh of relief as her mother invited her family into the kitchen.

'Please, do come in. I've baked your favourites, Steph…cheese scones! I'm making fresh tea, too. I bet you all need a drink after the journey.'

Liam exchanged furtive glances with his father before looking upward to the pure azure sky. Summoning the least possible zest, he collected his belongings from the path and repositioned them by the front door. There was no going back now as the cutting realisation swiftly dawned on him.

This was his home for two months.

*****

Liam watched quietly as his parents and grandmother discussed the impending business trip. The tea was poured, and the cheese scones were sampled. It was the most civilized situation Liam had experienced for an age.

And the conversation bored him rigid.

He silently longed to be elsewhere.

Anywhere in the world but there at that moment.

Anywhere in the universe but Summer Place.

He watched with brimming annoyance as his father supplied feigned gratitude regarding the situation.

'This is really good of you and Francis. I'm so pleased that you've helped us out. This trip could make us ultra-successful as a business. We can't afford to miss this chance.'

Barbara briefly gazed at Liam before speaking. She noted his abject disinterest in the surroundings and the company. He looked to be a substantially unhappy young man at that moment. Certainly not the frisky twelve-year-old she had entertained during their previous encounter.

'Why couldn't you take Liam with you? I'd have thought a holiday in the sun would have done him the world of good.'

Richard was quick on the draw.

It was obvious he didn't wish for Liam to contribute a response.

'Erm...no...it wasn't really possible. We wouldn't be able to keep an eye on him for one thing. We need to fully focus on our work without unnecessary distractions.'

Barbara glared at her son-in-law and his unbridled sense of self-importance.

'Well, yes...he's only your son, after all. Don't want him getting in the way of a business deal...do we?'

Richard and Stephanie exchanged glances of simmering disdain across the table but opted to ride the moment of sarcasm.

'With all due respect, Barbara, you don't know what Liam's like. He can be a little bit...shall we say...boisterous?'

'Nonsense! That's what little boys are *supposed* to be, isn't it? What do you say, Liam?'

The slouching teenager simply smiled, grunted and nodded. Then an appropriately humorous reply popped into his head as he suddenly sat attentively forward. As usual, he didn't feel the need to hold it back.

'Actually Grandma, I can't wait to see the back of them. I've come here for a bit of peace!'

Barbara laughed out loud at her grandson's quip and rocked back in her chair.

'Splendid! Bless you, boy! Honesty is the best policy! Especially when it comes to your parents!'

Again, Liam's mother and father briefly engaged one another as laughter echoed around the kitchen, knowing full well that the apparently well-mannered, articulate youngster sat beside them could well turn out to be the Goulds' worst nightmare.

However, Stephanie decided to steer the conversation to the subject she had been trying to avoid.

'How's Dad? More to the point, *where's* Dad?'

Barbara glanced over her daughter's shoulder and through the kitchen window. She pointed with a bony forefinger toward the gravel-panelled garage.

'In there, somewhere. Trying to give the pick-up a clean, I think. He's always tinkering around with the damn thing.'

120

Then Barbara suddenly bolted upright in her chair as the subject himself unexpectedly appeared in the kitchen doorway in a set of oil-stained overalls. Wiping his hands on a dirty rag, the gruff voice, now cursed by fate, still carried a tone which commandeered the room's full attention.

'That "damn thing" as you call it needs some expertise under the hood, methinks!'

Four heads spun in the direction of the imposing speaker.

Francis James Gould stepped into the kitchen and eyed the occupants with a mild expression of pleasure. His Canadian drawl accentuated the introductory attempt at satire.

'Hello, strangers! Fancy seeing you way out here in the forest!'

Stephanie bounced to her feet and skipped into her father's arms.

Again, the embrace was warm and genuine on her part.

'Hi, Dad! I've missed you!'

'I've missed you too, sweetheart.'

Fran extended a soiled hand of greeting to Richard, who now also stood rigid as if to attention.

Fran's stare bore deep into him as the voice boomed once again.

'Have you missed me, too, Ricky?'

The responsive smile broke a momentary unease as he shook the iron grip of his father-in-law. Liam smirked at the use of the nickname, careful to conceal his mirth with a quick hand.

'Of course, Francis. Of course, sir. Great to see you again.'

Fran grinned wildly as his eyes sparkled with a dose of sour wit.

'You're still a bad liar, Ricky! Always have been!'

Liam, whilst amused by his grandfather's quips, was also instinctively observant of the tall, athletic looking elder man. Still adorning the hair cut of a crewman, he looked hardened to the bone.

Ravaged; world weary; unafraid.

All the things Liam truly aspired to be.

Then when his grandfather's attention was eventually focused his way, Liam sensed a sudden pang of that sensation that he had thrived on and veritably nurtured in recent times.

Yet this time, the coldest of all responses was not his to invoke.

The truest of unknowns was now Liam's to taste.

And Francis James Gould exuded authority from his very pores.

A large hand took Liam's and shook it firmly.

121

The dry Canadian dialect pierced the boy's conscience.

'It is customary to stand when your elders enter the room, soldier! Especially when those elders are your relatives. I'm Francis. We've met before. You've grown a lot. A fine-looking private in the making, I might say. Not too keen on the hood, though.'

Liam thought quickly, naively opting for humour.

'It's okay, Grandpa. I won't make you wear it if you don't want to.'

Reserved chuckles rippled from the observers, but something unspoken told Liam that his repartee was not received in the spirit he intended. Fran adopted a theatrical pose of surprise.

'Oh? A mouth? Stephanie, your son has a mouth! Barbara…our grandson has a *mouth*!'

Fran drew closer to Liam, still rubbing his hands with the stained cloth.

The delay in his grandfather's next line served to accentuate the point. The delivery was issued in a hushed tone.

'If you'll take my advice, and I strongly suggest that you do, you'll use that mouth a little more wisely, soldier. It might get you into trouble around here.'

Liam could not resist challenging the elderly aggressor as a furtive audience awaited the next exchange. The youngster's defiance came naturally. This sudden and unexpected offer of verbal combat was relished.

'I can see I've got some way to go before I can compete with your mouth, Francis. I think I'll be fucking deaf come September!'

Liam anticipated more laughter from the stalls.

Yet the audience stayed coldly silent.

A mother and father winced as their son let fly with his first, woefully misplaced profanity. Barbara looked helplessly at her husband, who in turn put his face ever closer to Liam's, now reducing his volume to a whisper.

Liam could now smell Fran's presence. His overalls exuded a potent mix of fuel and grime. He sensed the closeness of the lean, tanned flesh that stretched across seasoned features.

Yet Liam still dared to look his grandfather in the eye even from under the supposed protection of his hood.

The uncertainty of moments earlier was his sole encouragement in this inevitable battle of wits. Instinct was sending him contrary signals.

Fran was definitely a personality Liam would relish competing with.

But there would be only one winner.

A crocodile smile accompanied the stark, concise warning.

'You're unaware of my regime, youngster. So, it's only right that I induct you. First rule in this house…no disobedience. Second rule in this house…no cursing. Third rule…you obey the rules. You got that…soldier? I don't want to have to get the swear box out, do I?'

Liam looked to his grandmother and parents. He sensed their nervousness but didn't heed it, preferring instead to run the gauntlet of rebellion once again as he reclined in his chair.

'That swear box had better be big cos' it's going to be fucking overflowing by the time I've done here, then!'

Again, the response in the room was muted.

Within five minutes, Liam had already crossed the line of respect.

Fran straightened himself up and looked to the wall behind Liam's head.

Still wiping his hands, he turned to his wife.

The mood was now indeterminable.

The request was considered fit for purpose.

'Barbara…will you make me a black coffee, please? I'll be in the garage should you need me.'

Liam and his parents watched, as his grandfather made a slow, meaningful exit from the room.

*****

'Have you got all you need, Liam?'

Richard stood ready to close the boot of the car as he shouted to the front door of the cottage.

A nod from beneath the dark hood was the only reply, which duly prompted Stephanie to embrace her mother in a farewell that could not have come soon enough.

'Thank you, mother. Keep Dad calm, will you. Liam's just a little tetchy at the moment.'

Barbara looked her daughter in the eye. There was a definitive lack of conviction in her response.

'I'm sure they'll get on just fine. Enjoy your trip. Don't forget to ring when you can. Goodbye, Richard!'

With a slam of the boot lid, Richard offered an overdue wave of relief and eagerly slid behind the steering wheel.

Kissing her mother on the cheek, Stephanie then turned to her son and placed both hands on his shoulders. Glancing up into the shadow of his hood, she could feel his inner plight. But there was no other option.

'For Christ's sake behave, Liam. Your grandfather is not someone to suffer fools.'

Liam smirked as his reply came forth.

'Mum...'

'What is it?'

'You just swore, didn't you? You said 'Christ!' That's not allowed!'

Holding him tight, Stephanie contemplated saying goodbye to the crusty old man in the garage. She pondered the prospect of disturbing her father - for a disturbance it would certainly be deemed - as he played with his car. A single glance from her mother confirmed the initial feeling that it might be best just to leave whilst the going was good.

Barbara and Liam watched from the front gate as the car rolled slowly away from the cottage.

Away from the constant disapproval.

Away from dissatisfied parents.

Away from a scowling son.

Stephanie said nothing as she mulled over the potential powder-keg they were deserting. She could still detect her father's deep resentment. Yet it all seemed so petty and unnecessary. As the car turned the corner, Summer Place promptly disappeared from view.

Francis James Gould covertly observed the departure from his garage window. He then stared through the glass at the abrasive youngster in the hooded top before his attention reverted under the bonnet as his wife fussed over the new arrival.

'Bring your bags, Liam. I'll show you to your room.'

With minimal enthusiasm, Liam hauled his luggage from the kitchen floor and followed Barbara into the passageway. The shining wooden floorboards creaked with every step. Barbara gestured to a large oak door with a brass handle.

Delicately, she turned the knob and pushed the door open.

'Through here is the lounge. There's a radio and television. And a selection of books. Do you like to read, Liam?'

Staring at the perfectly arranged bric-a-brac and scented, polished furniture, his gaze finally rested on the large red leather armchair in the sun-drenched bay window.

'No…I don't read much. I like to draw, mostly. But I haven't done any drawing for a while.'

'Really? Why not? A God-given talent must be utilised, son.'

Liam shrugged his shoulders and peered from beneath his hood.

'I don't know. Friends and stuff get in the way.'

He noticed his grandmother trying to see into his shadowy features.

She found it bemusing that he should wish to obscure his face with the draping shroud hanging over his head.

'Tell me, Liam. Do you *always* wear that hood?'

Immediate suspicion guarded his response.

'In public…yeah…why?'

Barbara clasped her hands as she continued to stare into its maw.

'Such a waste…to hide those handsome looks of yours.'

'It's for protection.'

Barbara could not conceal her instant mirth at such a theory and giggled to herself as she continued ahead along the passage and up the stairwell.

'Protection? Protection from whom?'

The reply was forthright and issued with stark conviction.

'Enemies, Grandma.'

Now she stopped smiling, intrigued by his choice of word.

'But that's ridiculous! You surely don't have any enemies, Liam. Especially not here. Not now. Let the world see your head awhile. Show yourself off! Fran doesn't appreciate people that wear hats indoors. He says its twisted thinking. He claims it is distrustful and rude.'

Liam sought to bolster his explanation as they reached the landing.

'It's like in the Westerns, Grandma. The eyes give every emotion away. That's why they wore large brims. To hide the eyes. If your opponents can see the fear in you, you'll lose on the draw. You'll be dead before you know it.'

Again, Barbara chuckled heartily at Liam's logic as she swung open another large oak door with brass handles. Liam noticed the locking switch on the outside as he followed his grandmother into the bedroom.

'Here you are, Liam. This is your room. It's sparse, but clean. They'll be plenty of space for you and your things in here.'

Liam turned back to the door and gestured with a thumb.

'Why is there a lock on the outside of the door, Grandma?'

Barbara's uncertainty in the answer was evident. Her reply was equally unconvincing, to say the least.

'Oh…just security. That's all.'

Liam furrowed his brow and probed further.

'Security?'

'Yes, Liam.'

'Whose?'

Barbara turned away without replying and opened the window. It faced a portion of the garden, the nearest neighbouring cottage, and the street outside. Liam lowered his bags to the floor. There was evidently no explanation forthcoming on the issue of the lock. Despite his puzzlement, Liam let the subject drop.

'Are you hungry, Liam?'

The answer was typical yet supremely misplaced.

'Yeah…I could eat a fucking scabby horse!'

Barbara's disapproving glare needed no further expansion.

'Sorry, Grandma…I forgot!'

'That's alright. Your grandfather didn't hear you this time, I'm sure. There's stew and potatoes for dinner. I'll leave you to settle and unpack. Please make yourself at home, Liam. I'll be in the kitchen if you want anything.'

A question burned on his lips.

He could not resist the opportunity to ask.

'Grandma…'

Barbara's sweet smile would not serve to soften the justification of Liam's query. Or her expectation of it.

'Francis doesn't want me here…does he?'

She visibly struggled to maintain the positive expression upon her wizened features. Her obvious inner rankling told Liam all he needed to know. Her untruth in answering satisfied his curiosity.

'Don't be ridiculous, Liam. He's your grandfather. Of course he wants you here. He's been looking forward to having you stay.'

Barbara exited the bedroom and quietly shut the door behind her.

Liam looked at the dark oak chest of drawers and wardrobe.

He pulled open the doors to reveal a dozen or so coat-hangers. A coarse looking grey blanket lay folded in the bottom.

Glancing across to the bed, Liam sighed to see no sign of a duvet. Three more heavy blankets were neatly inserted into place around the mattress. As predicted, the bed looked small, cold and hard. Pulling the items from his suitcase, he arranged them in no particular order in the wardrobe.

If nothing else, such a foreign practice would pass some time. He opened the three drawers in turn, placing clean underwear and socks in the top two.

The contents of the bottom drawer held his attention for a few moments. Inside were several sheets of drawing paper and a packet of new pencils. They may have been put there for his benefit, but it bemused him as to how his grandmother could have known about his flair for art.

The discovery pleased Liam, though.

He closed the drawer, giving the issue no further thought.

He threw his wallet and mobile phone onto the dresser. Pressing the earplugs of his I-Pod into place, Liam reclined on the bed.

The music was a welcome reminder of home.

Of things preferred.

Of routines, places and of friends...currently foregone.

The mid-afternoon sunshine streamed through the window, bathing Liam Warburton in gold.

Gradually, slumber encroached and transported him into the enticing wilderness of his dreams.

FOURTEEN

The dawn chorus gradually roused Liam from a long, deep sleep. Though barely awake, he could sense the warmth of the rising sun desperately fighting a path through the drawn bedroom curtains.

Slowly but surely, his mind attuned itself to activating various parts of his body. It was at this point he realised he was under the sheets, adorned in only his boxer shorts.

As he strove half-heartedly to think back over the last twenty-four hours, he could not even recall getting into bed. In fact, little of the previous day was particularly clear in his head. Yet judging by the incessant birdsong that accompanied his reluctant reawakening, it most certainly was morning.

A hand emerged from beneath the sheets and grappled for the mobile phone on the chest of drawers. Pulling it close to his face, Liam still had to squint at the tiny display to ascertain the time.

Seven-thirty-two.

He must have been asleep for well over twelve hours. He did not remember saying goodnight to anyone. Nor did he take advantage of his grandmother's promised stew and potatoes. A rumbling stomach confirmed as much. Puzzlement abounded as he considered the length of time that had passed in his absence.

Thoughts invaded his solace. Why had no one called him for dinner? Why had they left him alone for so long?

Would he perhaps be fortunate enough to wake up in Talworth?

Perhaps his grandparents appreciated the fact he had endured a long journey and was tired. Even so, Liam had never slept continually for over twelve hours in his entire life.

The birds were now beginning to irritate him. He was not used to such persistent hindrance to his morning routine. It was as though they had gathered outside his window on purpose. Yet sing they continued to do, as though deliberately annoying Liam was now their aim having woken him. Hundreds of shrill calls per minute perforated his peace.

Succumbing to the inevitable, Liam swung his legs from the mattress and sat on the edge of the bed with head in hands. Moving the I-pod from beneath his backside, he detected that the battery had finally died. Picking up his phone once more, he checked for text messages from distant friends. The message box remained empty.

Floorboards creaked as he rose unsteadily to his feet and shuffled to the window. Separating the curtains almost blinded him, as searing sunlight flooded the room.

Still the birds provoked.

Liam reached up and pulled the top window firmly shut with a resounding slam. The feathered fracas outside reduced considerably as Liam stood and stared vacantly beyond the glass.

The tranquillity of the scene did little to inspire. Not a breath of wind. Not a murmur of life. He observed the deep blue sky, pricked by the tips of giant pines. Such a beauteous depiction of nature, yet it did little for the soul of Liam Warburton.

Then suddenly among the static backdrop, Liam spotted movement. A man in the mid-distance along the lane. A runner. An athletic-looking type. Graceful and swift.

Finally, his mind registered the identification of his grandfather on his morning jog. It came as something of a surprise to watch a sixty-year-old in such fine fettle. He continued to observe the figure until Francis James Gould merged with the landscape and disappeared.

Moving position back to the small, hard bed, Liam contemplated the day ahead and what it might bring. One thing he was certain of was a raging appetite. Two cheese scones consumed on arrival were hardly sufficient fuel.

Time to find some breakfast.

Tentatively moving to the door, he listened for possible movement in the outer passageway. Visual inspection confirmed that his grandmother must be in the kitchen.

Every footstep down the stairs seemed to be accompanied by creaking, as though the wood panelling had been specifically designed to do so. Perhaps to destroy the element of surprise and reveal the approach.

Peering into the kitchen, he saw the ever-busy form of Barbara Gould in her apron, stirring a pan at the stove. An orchestra floated from the small radio perched on the dining table - a potent reminder of breakfast time back home in Talworth.

'Morning, Grandma.'

Barbara' eyes darted in surprise across the kitchen, soon followed by a genuine smile.

'Well, well! Good morning to you, young sir! A little tired, were we? You're just in time. It's nearly ready.'

Liam scratched his head and positioned his near-naked form at the table.

'I suppose I must have been shagged out. I can't even remember un-dressing. I know I missed dinner though.'

Barbara looked at the wall above the stove with disdain as Liam's latest verbal slip-up descended on the room. However, she declined to mention it.

'Yes. You were out for the count when I peeked into your room. I bet you're famished, aren't you?'

Liam found himself struggling both to hear and be heard as the music echoed around the room.

His impatience surfaced once again.

First the birds; now the violins.

'Can I turn the radio off? Mum's always listening to this shit.'

Barbara was not willing to comply with her grandson's wishes. She did not look his way but instead continued to stir the pan as she issued her concise response.

'For your information, this is not...by any means...shit, young sir. This is Vivaldi. My favourite accompaniment to a summer morning.'

Liam leaned forward in his seat, hiding his face in his palms, as if to stifle the muffled retort.

'I say its shit.'

Now, he had mildly annoyed his grandmother.

She turned to Liam, with a hand on her hip.

'Young sir, your opinion of the piece is irrelevant, aside from being woefully incorrect. Your silent appreciation of my preferences would be beneficial for the both of us.'

Liam rolled his eyes. He couldn't be bothered with lectures. It brought out the worst side of his intolerant personality. Yet Barbara's tirade did not abate.

'It's going to be a long summer for you Liam if you aren't prepared to embrace a change of attitude. If not, there will only be one loser. And that loser will be you!'

Liam decided to sit back in his chair and showed both palms to his grandmother as a gesture of feigned peace.

'Okay...okay...chill out. I just asked if I could change the radio stations...that's all. No need to fucking go off on one! Jesus!'

Barbara moved away from the stove and towards Liam's disrespectful form.

Resting her hands on the dining table, she addressed him as his gaze instantly fell to the floor.

'And the answer…young sir…is *no*…you *cannot* turn the radio off! Please leave the radio alone!'

With his temper beginning to boil inside, Liam looked anywhere but at his grandmother. It was already like being back at school. Almost embarrassing to be chastised by an old woman. Yet the ultimate frustration came in knowing that he had little other option but to obey her decision.

Yet Barbara Gould held her position.

She had not finished putting Liam in his place.

'And another thing. It is customary in this house to wash and dress *before* breakfast. As your food is now ready, I'll pardon your ignorance in the matter. But bear this in mind for the future. We do not eat in our underwear around here!'

Liam was desperately struggling to contain his festering despair. Yet something unspoken told him to hide his angst for the time being.

He watched his grandmother walk back to the oven.

Yet still her list of disapproval continued.

'Oh…and another thing. *That* is your grandfather's chair. It would only be courteous if you were to park yourself in another seat.'

Now, Liam snapped.

'For fuck's sake! Shall I stop fucking breathing for you, as well? Would that comply with the fucking rulebook?'

Back at the stove, Barbara stirred and quietly giggled.

The boy was spirited, that was for sure.

'That…my dear young sir…is entirely up to you.'

Liam opted for silence as he brimmed with a maelstrom of emotion. He watched aghast at his grandmother as she retrieved a bowl from the cupboard and poured the contents of the saucepan into it.

If this was breakfast, it certainly didn't look like it.

His open displeasure only increased as he scrutinized the contents of the bowl laid before him. It was almost as though Barbara was waiting eagerly for his response as she stood at his shoulder.

'What..the fuck…is this…?'

Knowingly antagonising her grandson was not providing enjoyment for Barbara Gould. But she figured that Liam's argumentative and dismissive approach needed to be vanquished at the earliest possible opportunity.

'That…Liam…is porridge. Made with fresh oats and goat milk. It's good for you. Take my word for it. Eat it and be thankful for the privilege.'

Liam could not restrain an expression of pure horror at the prospect of consuming the sticky substance that lay steaming on his place mat.

'How the hell can you expect me to try and eat this?'

Barbara's answer was already primed and cocked in the barrel.

'Through that large, whining hole underneath your nose. The one where all the hot air comes from. You will find a spoon to be most helpful in the cause.'

Liam stood to his feet, almost knocking over the dining chair. He had endured enough.

'Is that it? Porridge? Nothing else?'

His grandmother gently pointed to the centre of the table.

'No. I've laid out some syrup to pour on it. Or there's jam if you prefer.'

Liam's stressful dissatisfaction was almost amusing to the elder lady.

'You can't do this to me! You can't make me eat this crap!'

Folding her arms in assumed victory, Barbara spoke calmly and clearly.

'I wouldn't dream of *making* you eat it. If you don't want it, then you'll stay hungry, won't you!'

Liam slammed his fist onto the table, upending the bowl, in turn sending hot porridge across the table surface and onto the floor.

'I fucking hate his place! It's worse than prison! I can't fucking stand it! I can't stand *you*, either!'

With those words of juvenile finality, Liam stormed from the kitchen and marched angrily back up to his bedroom. He cared little to offer his grandmother any consideration as he concluded his performance, the remnants of which she began to clean up with a damp cloth.

Slamming the bedroom door behind him, Liam bounded onto the bed and grabbed his phone. He had little credit left until he could find a shop to purchase some. Text messaging was his only bridge to the life and friends he had left behind in Talworth.

How he wished to be with them in that instance.

Yet further damning frustration ensued as the display indicated a complete absence of network signal.

So, in effect, his isolation was already complete. The concluding act of his tantrum was to launch the handset across the room, which clattered into the wardrobe, in turn dislodging the plastic casing. Liam hunched his knees up under his chin, silently rocking in his self-imposed exile.

Unbeknown to him, his grandfather had returned to the cottage some minutes earlier from his run. Remaining out of sight, he had witnessed the entire episode as it unfolded.

Allowing Liam time to vacate the scene, Francis James Gould entered the kitchen to find his wife mopping globules of porridge off the floor.

The feeling of inevitability was mutual as two grandparents exchanged glances of foreboding.

FIFTEEN

Fran assisted Barbara to her feet as she struggled against the wrench of an arthritic hip to stand upright. His stern grimace preceded a foregone conclusion regarding their grandson's behaviour, though his voice remained controlled and unthreatening.

'It's not going to work. The boy has no discipline. He's wild. Untamed. He's never been brought under control. I really didn't want the job…but it seems I have little choice.'

Wiping the remains of Liam's mess from the dining table, Barbara considered her husband's words with a due sense of dread.

'He seems so unhappy, Fran. He doesn't want to be here. That much is obvious. He feels unwanted by his family - including us. I really don't think that further punishment will help matters. Do you?'

Fran closed the door to the passageway so as not to be overheard.

'What I know is what I've just witnessed and listened to. And now I must watch you clearing the debris of his temper. It is not acceptable, Barbara. I won't allow it to continue under my roof. In less than twenty-four hours of being here he hasn't uttered a solitary word of respect. And you expect me to accommodate such an attitude? I don't think so.'

Barbara shuffled to the sink and proceeded to wring out the dish cloth and tea towel under the hot tap. She watched as diluted porridge gurgled down the plug hole. Yet still she resisted agreement.

'Try and put yourself in his shoes, Francis. Clearlake is hardly the hub of excitement for someone of Liam's age. He's bound to resent the situation. Stephanie and Richard are to blame if anyone. It was plain to see they couldn't wait to get out of here, yesterday.'

Fran sighed heavily as he reached above the sink for his bottle of throat syrup.

'He's too much like his mother if you ask me. Overly headstrong and naively wilful. But such disgraceful conduct to go with it. I heard the way he spoke to you. Don't tell me it didn't hurt, Barbara. The shouting. The cursing. The anger. He needs to see that it's wrong to act in this way.'

Barbara dropped her cloths into the basin and stared into the deeply concerned eyes of her husband.

'And I suppose that means some good old military-style measures, does it? Make him run ten miles with a sack on his back? Knock the fight out of him, eh?'

Fran was only partially in sympathy with his wife's reasoning.

'I'm just saying that I'm not convinced talking to him will solve the problem. No. He's already way off-track. He's far too arrogant to listen to wisdom and principle.'

Barbara dried her hands as Fran swallowed his medicine, wincing as it attempted to caress his throat. She suddenly felt immense sorrow as the man she loved tried to mask his pain.

Priorities returned to the fore.

'How are you feeling today, sergeant?'

Dropping the spoon into the soapy water, he replaced the bottle on the shelf behind her.

'Bearable. No better, for sure. But don't try and change the subject on me!'

Barbara smirked and kissed Fran on the cheek before whispering softly in his ear.

'Go take your shower and cool off, Francis. I'll cook your eggs and then I'll go talk to our grandson.'

Fran gazed at his wife's radiant features. She was still beautiful. Sixty-three years had not tarnished nature's gift. She could still melt his ever-hardening heart with one look. He slowly shook his head in reluctant agreement, but his customary disgruntlement was soon eclipsed by a joyous smile.

'Okay, my sweet. Whatever you say…for now.'

Playfully patting his behind, Barbara issued her final instruction.

'You know I'm right, sergeant. Now go clean yourself off. You're making my kitchen look untidy!'

*****

Liam lay on top of the bed, his mind filing through images of history and fantasy. He visualized his friends. He imagined holding court in the playground at St. Forsters and the market square in town.

Watching their admiring expressions as they held onto his every word.

Then thoughts transferred to Carla Ferris. He pondered their final exchange as she angrily ushered him from her back garden. He still struggled to ascertain her reasons for showing such disgust.

Although now some weeks ago, her distress and concern regarding his mindset continued to bemuse him.

Yet she referred to herself as being different to the rest. Of claiming to see a side to Liam Warburton that others did not see.

He silently probed these issues and others, whilst intermittently scanning the bare walls of the bedroom. Contemplation of the next two months in such foreign tedium cursed his being to the core.

Indeed, his inner turmoil was slowly becoming all-consuming.

No friends. No I-pod. No mobile phone.

Just himself. And his grandparents.

As he rankled with such pitiful conclusions, the creaking of floorboards could be heard from the other side of the bedroom door.

Somebody was outside in the passageway.

Strange, sinister thoughts encroached as three knocks were heard against the large oak-panel door. Then Liam shuddered inexplicably as he observed the brass handle turning.

It came as something of a relief for Liam to see his grandmother's gentle face peering through the narrow gap. She scrutinized the room, exchanging glances with the disgruntled teenager now spread-eagled on the bed with his hands behind his head.

Approaching with learned caution, Barbara searched for some credible line of dialogue with which to open the exchange. Yet to her surprise, Liam took the honour from her.

'Is Fran back, yet?'

It was an unexpected query for sure, but at least enabled a conversation to commence.

'Yes, Liam. Yes, he is.'

'What is he doing?'

Liam's sudden interest in the activity of his grandfather was a little puzzling to Barbara, but she obliged with her report.

'Well…he's had his morning run. Then he showered and shaved. And now he's having breakfast in the kitchen.'

Liam did not look at his grandmother as he followed with a question that he didn't really want the answer to.

'Did you tell him about what I did?'

Barbara would not lie to Liam. But nor would she reveal the exact truth that Fran was fully aware of what had transpired at the breakfast table.

'No…no, Liam. I didn't tell him.'

'I bet he doesn't get shitty porridge for breakfast, does he?'

Liam's mellowing of mood was evidently not going to last. Having glared at Barbara with his final verbal blast, he quickly averted his gaze to focus on the ceiling lamp. She could not understand his despondency over things so trivial and attempted to appease his unwarranted anger.

'I thought you'd like porridge, Liam. But I'll gladly cook you something else. All you need do…is ask me.'

Finally, after a few moments of thought, Liam turned his attention directly back toward his grandmother and sat up on the bed.

'Honestly, Grandma?'

'Of course, Liam. I'm always honest.' she smiled.

'Bacon and eggs?'

'I'll do my very best. All you had to do was show some manners.'

Liam began to feel suddenly uplifted by the simple development. He watched in satisfaction as Barbara straightened herself up and made for the door.

'I'll call you when it's ready. By the way, just one or two things.'

'What's that, Grandma?'

Barbara gestured to his unkempt form.

'You still have to get dressed and wash, first! And please…stop the swearing.'

With a false sense of victory, Liam lay back on the bed and smirked to himself.

Maybe the oldies weren't so bad after all. Maybe the change of scene would work to his advantage. Perhaps they would see that Liam's way was the only way things would work around here if they were to get along.

Pulling on his jeans and hooded top, the thought of a fried breakfast awakened his enthusiasm.

*****

Fran laid his plate and mug into the sink and observed his wife at the stove as she flipped rashers of bacon with a fork.

'So…you're accommodating the young one, are you? Pandering to his desires just because he throws a tantrum?'

Barbara turned to her husband, whose dismissive expression told her he could not agree with her solution to Liam's temperamental demeanour.

'I'm just trying to understand him, Fran. To work *with* him, instead of *against* him. It's only eggs and bacon, after all.'

Francis James Gould made his wife look into his eyes as he placed both hands on her shoulders. To put it mildly, he was aggrieved at her option to cater to Liam's whims.

'You're wrong, my sweet. He's laughing at you as we speak. He'll make a fool out of you. Mark my words. He's quite capable. But he won't make a fool out of *me*.'

'Nonsense, Fran. You're just looking for excuses to be angry at him. And you're frustrated because you have no real reason to be. Don't fall out with him just because of Stephanie.'

Fran walked toward the front door of the cottage and issued a stark command which Barbara took to be a solemn and earnest request. She would not disobey her husband when he adopted such a tone.

'Okay. You try it your way. And let me try mine. When he's had his fill, put him in work clothes and send him up to me on the verge. I'll be chopping wood for the village. I could do with a hand.'

Barbara watched her husband quietly shut the door behind him and continued to observe him through the window as cigar smoke trailed his route toward the garage.

SIXTEEN

With an inner smile that symbolically stretched from ear to ear, Liam watched as his grandmother removed the empty plate from the dining table. It felt good to be sated once again. His appetite had raged for hours. It felt even better knowing that he could still dictate when necessary.

'How was that breakfast for you, young sir?'

Finishing his mug of tea, Liam nodded and gave a thumbs-up.

'Okay, Grandma. Better than porridge…I'm sure of that!'

The classical music continued to penetrate Liam's peace. Subsequently, his fingers automatically reached for the dial to search for more fashionable listening. The radio waves whistled as the frequencies attuned to the next station.

Now overwhelmed by renewed vexation, Barbara turned from the kitchen sink to see her grandson intent on discovering something modern.

'What did I say about the radio, Liam?'

He did not look at her as he continued to fiddle with the set.

'Listen, Grandma. I can't sit and eat with this racket going on.'

Barbara walked to the table and plucked the radio away from Liam's fingers. Her grandson's smile was no longer concealed.

'I asked you previously to leave it alone. I meant what I said. Besides, you're finished eating now. There are other things lined up for your entertainment.'

Suddenly it was Liam's turn to be puzzled.

'Like what? You got Sky TV, then? Oh…by the way, I need to charge up my I-pod and phone. I take it you have got electricity in this place?'

Barbara was not to be outwitted by the runaway mouth of the youth slumped before her. Much as it annoyed her to admit it, Fran was already looking to be correct in his theory. That much was becoming more evident by the second. She needed to remain calm and respond with a level head. She could not let Liam adopt the upper hand.

'We do have electricity, young sir. Yes. However, we do not have central heating.'

Again, Liam did not fully appreciate his grandmother's apparently random musings.

'Central heating? What the fuck's that got to do with anything?'

Barbara moved toward the work surface behind Liam's chair and

139

retrieved a small pile of clean clothes, which she then placed on the table.

'These summer days are lovely, Liam. But cottages such as ours still require a little warmth at night. Just to keep the woodland chill away from the bones, you understand.'

Now Liam was very confused and showed little hesitancy in saying so. An exaggerated expression was accompanied by flailing hands.

'Are you finally off your rocker? Why are you telling me this?'

Barbara was becoming more than a little amused by the game of one-upmanship that she was winning capably against such a thoughtless, aggressive mind.

'Because we need wood...to put on the fires.'

'Yeah? So what?'

She leaned towards him and offered a knowing smile.

'So...these are the clothes you will wear when you go outside and help your grandfather to cut some. He chops wood for the local neighbourhood. It keeps him busy for one day a week. But its far quicker with some help. That's where you come in, young sir.'

Liam stood to his feet and observed the folded pair of tattered jeans and hideous brown woollen sweater that lay before him on the table. He tried to act with an air of invincibility, but the feeling of facing the unavoidable began to creep into his mind once more.

'I don't fucking think so. And definitely not in this garb. It looks like stuff bought from a jumble sale.'

Barbara's eyes widened to accompany her beaming reply.

'That's great guesswork! You're spot on! I got them very cheap. Specifically, just for *you* to work in! It'll save ruining the good clothes you've brought, won't it?'

Liam's tone became tinged with malice as he backed away toward the door to the passageway.

'No chance! I'm not your slave! I haven't come here to do your chores for you. Find another mug. This one isn't interested.'

Barbara sighed gently. Another pause was followed by another seemingly random query.

'What size shoe are you?'

Now Liam's exasperated form shrugged wildly, completely baffled by the seemingly crazed lines of questioning.

'Who fucking cares? Stop harassing me, will you?'

Barbara continued to gaze at the gesticulating form of her grandson and nodded to the floor by the front door.

'Just outside there you'll find a pair of Fran's old boots. They should fit adequately by the looks of it. Off you go! You'll find your grandfather on the forest verge behind the cottage. Go up behind the garage. There is a clear path. You might have to walk a good way to meet him.'

Liam stormed out of the kitchen and along the passage. Back upstairs in his bedroom his temper was now at boiling point. Yet even as he sat on the bed, the reality had already dawned that this particular summer was going to be like no other he had known previously.

His mind toiled with the quandary. Maybe the odds were against him after all. He was in foreign territory, with adversaries that were infinitely wiser and more determined than he was accustomed to in the pursuit of ruling the roost and laying down the law.

Despite his protests and misguided assumption of superiority, Liam already sensed he may be fighting a losing battle.

But he would not show any chink in his armour.

He was not quite ready to surrender just yet.

He would continue to play along with the charade for a little while longer.

*****

Liam looked and felt ridiculous.

The heavy, itching sweater was far too large and cumbersome for the time of year. The well-worn jeans hung just above his ankles. There was nothing remotely fashionable to ponder as he looked at his reflection in utter disgust.

Even worse, he could sense his grandmother's amusement follow his every step as he departed the kitchen doorway, thrust both feet into the pair of heavy leather boots, and staggered awkwardly across the lawn.

Barbara covered her mouth with her hand as she chuckled, eventually turning away from the window and the image of the dishevelled young figure outside.

Having been advised to check the garage for his grandfather, it was evident that Fran had already made his way to the wooded covert that stretched beyond the rear of the cottage.

Liam squinted through streaming sunrays into the tree-lined path.

He could hear little that seemed familiar and could visually identify even less, aside the mass of branches gently hissing in the morning summer breeze.

Embarking on the steep ascent, Liam suddenly felt nervous. His body began to perspire in the unsuitable clothing that had been purposely provided. His heart began to thump as the uncertainty descended.

With each and every step came the knowledge that he would soon be alone with his grandfather for the first time since his arrival in Clearlake.

And the thought was strangely discomforting.

As though he should feel cautious of what lay in wait.

Looking briefly over his shoulder he continued up the narrow, winding slope. Liam realised that he was now completely lost. He had walked for only ten minutes or so, but that short space of time had caused him to lose bearings with the cottage.

The situation was becoming more frustrating by the second.

He continued to scan the dense area ahead yet still there was no sign of his grandfather.

Everywhere he looked seemed to be the exact image of the glade opposite, as though he was exploring a hall of mirrors. Hanging limbs danced and teased above his head. It was almost claustrophobic. Surrounded completely by unyielding foliage, there was no sound detectable that even vaguely resembled the chopping of timber.

Onward Liam marched, now becoming distinctly angered by the apparent wild goose chase.

Liam did not like to play games if he couldn't commandeer the rules.

He was not attuned to such futile detective work, yet little did he know that it was all part of the plan.

Stopping for breath he contemplated a return to the cottage, he silently seethed as the sweat poured down his back.

But his anger was soon to be eclipsed by shock, as he advanced into a small clearing.

The final destination that would provide the arena for the contest.

'TOOK YOUR TIME DIDN'T YOU, SOLDIER?'

The rasping, authoritative tones of Francis James Gould made Liam jump out of his skin.

Turning behind him, Liam observed his grandfather, sitting cross-legged on the grass in a pocket of golden light. Cigar smoke partially concealed Fran's frowning features as it made a twisted ascent into the entwined canopy above. Liam said nothing as the elder man casually placed the cheroot to his lips, causing the sun to reflect off the shining copper bangle wrapped around his left wrist.

At Fran's booted feet were positioned a pair of small axes, as if ready and prepared for the impending duel.

The two protagonists faced one another in the silent seclusion of the copse.

Alone together for the first time.

Yet both knew who was now in ultimate control of events.

'I've been waiting for you, soldier. I didn't want to start the job without my shift partner.'

Liam shuffled his stance nervously, determined not to let a sudden surge of inner fear be displayed. But Fran detected fear easily. Especially the fear that resided within his grandson. Yet he remained typically calm and collected as he continued to draw on his cigar.

'Did you enjoy your breakfast?'

Liam swallowed a lump of trepidation as he considered his response.

He found it difficult to look Fran in the eye when he addressed him.

'Yes. Yes, I did. It was good. Thanks.'

Fran watched the edgy disposition of the boy standing before him. He was silently relishing the long overdue sense of supremacy over the teenager.

'Made quite a fuss in ordering it, though. At least, that's what I heard...'

Liam's mind flashed back to the scene in the kitchen with the porridge. Did his grandfather see the episode? Had his grandmother lied about keeping quiet? It mattered little at that moment. He had to think quickly.

'I...I...don't like porridge.'

Fran extinguished his smoke on the gleaming steel toe cap of his boot. He presented a half-smile to Liam, which was difficult to interpret.

'So why not just say so? Instead of spilling it around the room and upsetting your grandmother like you did?'

Liam was now afraid.

His grandfather was becoming more empowered by the second.

Liam's smart-mouth act would only land him into deeper trouble than he was already in. That much was obvious.

'I...I didn't realise I'd upset her. I'm...sorry.'

Fran rose ominously to his feet, retrieving the choppers from the grass as he did so.

'What you say, boy? Did you say you were...*sorry*? After all of that...cursing...hollering...throwing your weight around? You don't think that's going to upset a caring little lady like your grandma?'

Fran's physical stature became more imposing in such compact surroundings. He was not quite as tall as Liam, but evidently stronger in build. Liam could not face his grandfather's studious inspection and feebly looked to the floor around his feet.

Fran stepped forward and placed his face only inches from Liam's. The gruff voice now lowered to just above a whisper. The indeterminable half-smile had by now evolved into a black mask of dread.

'Let's be absolutely crystal clear on the road ahead, soldier. I know all about you and your pitiful little ways. I might not have been around you much, but I know full well what a complete pain in the ass you've become. And I know how to cure you of that little problem. But I'd rather you cure yourself. Save on the pain and inconvenience. You understand? If I ever witness another performance under my roof like the one I saw this morning, I'll kick your behind so hard you'll need to unbutton your collar to take a shit. Get me...soldier? It's all about discipline and respect. I hope the lessons are easy for you. And I hope for your sake you learn them real quick.'

Liam's heart banged wildly as if calling for the exchange to end.

Sweat ran from every juncture.

The stunted silence that followed was agonizing.

Finally, Fran's attention diverted over Liam's left shoulder to the weave of tree limbs behind them. A slow directional nod was followed by a welcome change of subject.

'Okay, soldier. You've obviously dressed for doing some work. We'll start on those branches over there.'

Liam's adrenaline raced ever faster as though ready to burst from his veins. He could see that his grandfather meant every single word of the warning.

Liam felt like a new private on parade.

Yet this was no military introduction.

This was supposed to be his family.

Liam stood by Fran's side and observed carefully as his grandfather showed him how to identify suitable branches for cutting.

'Thicker than the handle of your axe but not thicker than your wrist. We'll strip down lengths of five to ten feet to take back to the garage. Then I'll get you cutting them into twelve-inch sections. Then you can tie them up as required and deposit them around the village. Give you a chance to meet some of the neighbours.'

Liam did not respond.

The tedious prospect of the task ahead filled him with numbed frustration.

But his grandfather still wanted a response to the instructions and displayed his teeth at the sulking teenager.

'Any objections so far...soldier?'

Liam nodded with an expression of distaste.

'Good. This is your cutter. I'll chop one for an example. Then you can cut another. Do you think you have the strength for this, boy?'

Fran was amused by the suddenly dispirited features of his grandson. The arrogance of the youngster had swiftly dissipated, to be replaced by strained obedience.

Grabbing the branch with his left hand, Fran swung his blade onto the bark, cutting halfway into the flesh of the limb. Another rapid swing saw the axe re-enter the original cut, this time travelling clean through the wood.

The dual action was repeated some eight feet further down along the stem. Liam continued to observe without word. Within seconds his grandfather held aloft a detached branch and proceeded to trim off the smaller twigs along its length, in readiness to take back down to the cottage.

'Okay, soldier. Give me one exactly the same. You've seen how easy it is. Think you can do better than an old man like me?'

Determined to impress, Liam gripped the shaft of his axe with both hands and selected a suitable branch.

Fran stood back, barely concealing his enjoyment.

Aware of being under his grandfather's unsettling scrutiny, Liam held the branch of choice in his palm and drew back the chopper, before bringing it heavily back onto the bark.

To his astonishment, the blade hardly etched into the limb at all.

He looked across to Fran, whose pleasure at witnessing such a miserable effort was now clearly exhibited.

Liam repeated the action.

Again, the same, non-productive result.

'Not strong enough are you, soldier? And here's me, four times your age making it look like child's play! Well. Now I've seen it all!'

Liam's prickly temperament was now getting the better of him. He stared at his grandfather, who proceeded to light another cigar and effortlessly resumed his former cross-legged position on the grass.

'There's something wrong with this axe. It's blunt! It must be!' Liam shrieked.

Fran grinned behind a large plume of aromatic smoke.

'Maybe…maybe not. Perhaps you're just a weakling, soldier. Maybe you don't have it in you do perform like your granddaddy. What do you say?'

Liam's fury caused him to grab the branch once more. Incessant perspiration was making him feel very uncomfortable. Time and time again he swung down at the limb, each time the impact barely leaving so much as a scratch.

With each fruitless motion, Fran's laughter seemed to increase in volume. Liam's anger was now all-consuming. He was not used to being made to look foolish.

'It's fucking blunt! You *know* it is! You've done this on fucking purpose!

Liam finally snapped and threw his axe aside. He stormed toward his grandfather who casually offered his own tool to the fuming teenager.

'Give me yours! I'll fucking show you!'

Gripping the branch firmly once more, he didn't notice that Fran's amusement had suddenly ceased. The laughter had stopped, making way for a pre-emptive quiet.

Yet still the cigar smoke billowed upward into the clawing canopy.

Summoning all his might into one final attempt, Liam sent the blade of his grandfather's chopper completely through the limb…and straight into the top of his own leg. Retreating into the clearing as blood began to slowly seep through his tattered jeans, Liam shrieked in shock before desperately clenching his fingers around the wound.

He looked scornfully at the elder man perched on the floor, whose mocking air of indifference had now been firmly restored.

146

Liam restrained his tears but could not restrain the tirade as he hopped around the clearing.

'JESUS CHRIST! FUCK YOU! YOU PLANNED THIS! I WAS RIGHT WASN'T I? YOU FUCKING SET ME UP! FUCK YOU!'

Fran merely placed his cigar into his mouth and rose to his full height once again. Retrieving both tools from the base of the tree, he offered words of partial sympathy.

'It's only a skin wound, soldier. Your grandma will clean you up and hopefully repair the trousers. You'll survive…for now.'

Clutching his injured thigh, Liam watched in disbelief as his grandfather disappeared back through the trees toward the cottage. He offered no further word to his grandson, who hobbled unsteadily behind. An attempt to further provoke the situation seemed almost pathetic.

'What about our wood, you fucker? Are we finished? Is that it?'

Fran continued to stride away in front. This time he would honour his grandson with a response over his shoulder.

'You're not safe to handle a cutter. Can't keep yourself out of the way, can you? Dangerous things in the wrong hands. Better get you patched up.'

Puzzled and in pain, Liam had little option but to follow. His anger now tempered by the discomfort of the cut to his upper leg, he struggled to keep up with the nonchalant figure of Francis James Gould as they made their way back down the verge.

*****

'Just sit back on the chair. It's only broken the skin. You're very lucky. Those axes are sharp for a reason, you know!'

Barbara applied a damp antiseptic cloth to Liam's wound as he sat discomfortingly at the kitchen table in his boxer shorts. With teeth clenched and eyes fixed through the kitchen window, he watched with growing antagonism as his grandfather emerged from the garage and approached the cottage.

'He fucking did it on purpose, Grandma! He wanted me to look like a fucking idiot!'

Shaking her head slowly, Barbara continued to examine the pierced flesh at the top of Liam's thigh muscle.

'Please stop swearing, Liam. Okay…the bleeding seems to be slowing up.'

147

The teenager pursed his lips as the cleansing solution entered his broken skin.

'What are these strange scars down both your shins? You look to have been in the wars, boy!'

The stark remnants of his infrequent self-abuse mattered little at that moment as he persisted with his protest.

'I mean it, Grandma! He *wanted* me to fucking hurt myself!'

'You're being ridiculous, Liam. It was just an accident. That's all. You'll be okay. I'll wash your jeans for you. Be clean for tomorrow.'

Fran appeared in the doorway, immediately in receipt of Liam's malicious attention. The vexation continued in deliberate earshot of his grandfather.

'Don't bother washing them. I'm not doing any more of his stupid fucking jobs.'

Barbara's eyes widened as she too greeted the imposing figure of her husband. There was no time for her to interject on the exchange as Fran retaliated.

'While you're living under this roof, soldier, you'll do as we ask of you. Barbara...strap him up and get him out of my sight, please. He's of no more use to me today.'

Liam scowled across the room at Fran, who furiously scrubbed his hands under a hot tap, but this time the boy thought better of offering the reply that his instinct so compelled.

Liam was now officially the unwilling pupil.

His grandfather, very much the willing teacher.

And lesson number one had been successfully administered.

148

The rest of the day Liam spent largely alone in the lounge, flicking through the selection of old magazines and books that were neatly arranged in and around the dark oak bookcase.

A natural history publication generated fleeting interest but could not distract him from the utter tedium and unbearable discomfort of his circumstances.

Another blow was the discovery that the television set could only be operated manually. Barbara's revelation came after he had spent several fruitless and painful minutes on hands and knees searching for the non-existent remote control. The lack of visual stimulation only served to impress further frustration on Liam's tortured soul.

Following a welcome evening meal of boiled chicken, peppered rice and mixed salad, which Fran decided to eat separately and alone in his lounge armchair, Liam reluctantly offered his grandmother a semblance of gratitude and opted to while away the remainder of the evening in his room.

He was in little mood for the company of his elderly relatives. It had not been a productive day for their relationship. In fact, it had been totally regressive considering he was now hobbling around the cottage with a bandaged thigh. However, Barbara tried to reassure him that he would be right as rain within a couple of days.

In truth, Liam cared little for the opinions of his grandparents.

Especially the dubious motivations of Francis James Gould.

The mutual hostility was tangible and obvious. When alone with his grandfather, Liam felt both vulnerable and yet strangely drawn to the undefined challenge. Both opponents were seemingly in constant assessment of one another's strengths and weaknesses.

As for his grandmother's stance on the running duel, he could not yet ascertain. At the moment she was barely upholding the role as peacemaker. How she would have responded to the episode up in the copse, Liam would never know. But she was instantly dismissive of her grandson's claim that Fran was a willing tormentor. The briefly disturbing thought broached Liam's mind as to how events might transpire in her longer-term absence.

The warm summer day had evolved into a hazy dusk. Having wished his grandmother goodnight, Liam decided not to acknowledge his grandfather as he passed the open lounge door. The sound of the television suggested that he would only be disturbing Fran's concentration if he did offer as much as a word of courtesy.

Finally reaching the partial privacy of his room, Liam slipped inside and closed the door behind him, noticing once again the exterior lock. How he wished it were inside, to secure him some respite from his sufferance.

The air in the room was humid and made him perspire once again. Throwing off the woollen sweater was an almost heavenly sensation as he allowed the air to embrace his skin for the first time that day. It was pleasurable to experience such a simple feeling of release.

Briefly passing in front of the dress mirror, Liam observed the deep red scar lines on his forearms, which in turn were eclipsed by mental images of home.

Friends he longed to see once more.

And those he would never see again.

Thoughts of the past and future placated him temporarily, until his mind settled briefly on the ever-present issue of Glendin.

But there was little to be gained by dwelling on the subject. Nothing that had transpired in the recent past that could be altered. The future would not change things for the better, either.

Glendin was gone. Liam pledged to shoulder the guilt for the remainder of his life.

He removed his scowling reflection from the mirror and moved toward the window. The view beyond the glass was infinitely different by half-light. In the daytime, everything appeared orderly; neat; arranged.

Yet by early evening, nature came alive, enswathing the cottage and its surroundings with an enticing hue and intermittent programmes of unexpected activity.

Pushing open the window and securing the latch to the frame, Liam rested on the sill in quiet observation of the scene. The silence of his room suddenly became diluted by the call and cries of the unseen sources in the wood.

From all directions, a hundred birds bade their evening goodbyes to one another in differing tune. Yet the birdsong was no longer the irritant that accompanied his first awakening.

It was now a strangely pleasurable mystery to behold.

Such beautiful, vibrant noise from every direction. Everything audible…yet nothing visual. It was a timely and reliable beacon that confirmed his hopes that life still existed beyond the four walls in which he angrily resided.

Five feet above ground, dozens of groups of midges danced through the last golden shafts of a setting sun, which had long since been hidden behind the backdrop of the treeline. Black spines touched the crimson sky as though to close ranks on another glorious day, in turn making way for the uncertainties of another night.

Liam was totally transfixed by the unpredictability of this rural theatre. Every angle brought with it a new adventure. Curious mammals flitted in and out of the shadows. Ground dwelling scavengers scurried around the undergrowth, causing Liam to squint into the encroaching murk to identify them.

He thought he saw rabbits. Perhaps a humble hedgehog. The wily fox floated through the scene, never ceasing its seamless stride as it embarked on another nocturnal hunt.

Then, as Liam watched, the vivid realisation struck him.

All these things that played before him had always been there. Yet he had never appreciated the fact until this evening.

Whilst sitting alone in this foreign bedroom, nature's concerto had rapidly dispersed his previously overwhelming sense of isolation. He was now invigorated by the reality of what was happening outside.

He was involved in something honest.

Something exciting.

A myriad of living beings danced before him.

A personal parade…for his eyes and his only.

It was indeed an unprecedented privilege for Liam to watch night being created. The performers did not question the curiosity of their spellbound observer. Similarly, they neither requested nor required his presence.

This was nature in its perfect, modest form.

Untouched.

Untouchable.

Absolutely pure.

The time spent at the window was a glorious immersion into a previously unacknowledged reality. Almost an hour passed since Liam first opened his mind to the addictive spectacle, yet it had seemed little more than a few minutes.

Such was the extent of Liam's interest he now avidly awaited the next surprise to emerge from the darkness, as opposed to being confronted with it unexpectedly.

Then, just as he had accustomed himself to the exhibition of the idyllic playtime, it ended abruptly with the sound of the cottage front door opening and the instinctive retreat of a million creatures.

As though attempting to purposely interrupt the festival, the all too familiar figure of Francis James Gould appeared in silhouette against the greyness beyond as he checked and secured his property for the final time that day.

Liam watched from his secret vantage point the crude lumbering shadow of his grandfather by the garage. There was no grace about the man.

No beauty.

Just an obstructive, intrusive bulk that spoiled the canvas.

Then, trepidation shrouded Liam's disgruntlement as Fran began walking back toward the cottage, apparently satisfied that all was good outside. He stopped a few feet away from the front door and seemed to centre his curiosity on Liam's bedroom.

Liam felt his grandfather's eyes scanning the area around his window.

Both remained completely still, each anxious to avoid attracting the other's attention.

Then finally, after an unmeasured hiatus, Fran coughed heavily before continuing onward into the cottage and locking the front door behind him.

Retreating into the bedroom and closing the window, Liam's mind raced. The dissipating light had made it impossible to observe the external parade any further. Opting first to close the curtains, Liam sat on the bed and flicked on the bedside lamp.

Reaching down to the bottom drawer of the dresser, he retrieved a few sheets of drawing paper and selected a pencil from the tin.

Allowing wilful amusement to guide his hand, he proceeded to sketch out cartoons of his grandparents on the blank page.

He smiled as his grandmother came to life in caricature form. He exaggerated her pointed features, large bun of brown-grey hair and adorned her in her standard, ever-present pinafore.

Then, starting with a new sheet, Liam turned his attention to his grandfather.

152

The re-imagination of Fran's overly muscled physique, deeply embedded frown, and frothing grimace. Liam completed the image with an enormous cigar, a sergeant's peaked cap and crooked walking stick.

Observing the activity outside had seemingly re-ignited Liam's long-forgotten creative impetus. The lead tip moved freely on the page. His mind's visions were rapidly transferred into instantly recognisable representations of their subject.

More importantly, Liam found it a completely pleasurable exercise. Employing his talents, yet so subtle and simple to achieve.

Slowly but surely, Liam finished his sketches in competition with growing fatigue. He had completely forgotten about his bandaged leg. It was almost as though the accident with the axe had never happened.

Struggling to remain awake, Liam dropped the reams of drawing paper onto the floor beside his bed and turned off the lamp.

In tandem with the awakening wonders of the forest beyond, he succumbed to slumber as evening took its resilient hold.

EIGHTEEN

The first sight that greeted Liam the following morning was the folded pair of jeans, now laundered, pressed, and replaced on the chair beside the wardrobe.

The temporary sense of liberation he had experienced only hours earlier had rapidly dissolved, to be replaced by the stark, regretful recognition of his surroundings.

The sun blazed dutifully once again from behind the curtains. Liam stretched and reached over to peel them apart only slightly, shielding his face from the blinding glare that forced its way through and lit up the room.

On rubbing his eyes, another discovery was made.

The drawings had gone from the floor beside the bed.

Continually pressing his thumbs gently into his dazed eyeballs, he looked again. The cartoons of his grandparents had seemingly been removed from the room.

In turn, he instinctively glanced across to the bedside table.

No mobile phone. No I-pod.

Both were gone.

As were the battery chargers he intended to use that morning.

Remnants of sleep were rapidly shaken off as he sat on the edge of the bed and pulled open the drawers of the dresser.

His underwear and socks had been removed also.

As had his wallet.

In the bottom drawer, the blank sheets of drawing paper remained. He checked the tin of pencils. All were present, including the one he had used last night.

Whilst the evidence was puzzling, it suggested that someone had definitely been in his room during the night.

Clad in only his boxer shorts, Liam rose to his feet and instantly winced as the wound on his thigh became taut. He picked up the tattered pair of jeans. They were clean, but the blood stain was still present. He decided there was no way he would wear those again.

It was high time for a little fashion, even if it might look a little out of place in these rural surroundings.

But on pulling open the wardrobe doors Liam's anger was instantly fuelled by what he saw.

It too had been emptied.

No clothes. No shoes. Not even his holdall.

Nothing.

His mind raced with possibility. There could only be one perpetrator of these acts. Only one person could summon the inclination to devise such a futile and seemingly childish prank.

It was time to confront his grandfather once more.

With shameful reluctance, Liam pulled on the ragged pair of jeans and inspected them mournfully in the dress mirror before moving toward the door.

A due sense of caution encroached as he gripped the brass handle and gave it a sharp twist.

He was in no mood for playing games, now. Yet the joke was increasing its momentum by the second.

The door had been locked from the outside.

Puzzlement was now matched by severe indignation. Liam's mind was now in overdrive in consideration of the game that was afoot.

How dare Fran enter his room! How dare he take property that didn't belong to him!

Frustration slowly evolved into fury as he pondered two options.

Choice one…scream for his release. If there was no response, then he would break down the door.

Choice two…climb out of the bedroom window and mount a surprise entrance through the kitchen.

Swaying between the two alternatives, Liam eventually decided that the second choice presented a far more civilized approach to matters.

Padding barefoot to the window, he released the catch and tried to shove the frame.

It was with further immense disgruntlement that Liam discovered that the window had too been secured shut during the night. He scanned the outside of the window through the glass. There was no obvious obstruction, yet it had evidently been tampered with.

So, Fran must have seen him last night as he checked the cottage.

Another mindful attempt to constrict his grandson's freedom.

He could no longer contain his outrage.

Overcome with anger, Liam bounded back to the door and began to hammer it with his fists.

'YOU FUCKER! OI! WHAT ARE YOU TRYING TO DO TO ME?'

155

There was only a stony silence that followed, leaving Liam little choice but to continue his protest.

'YOU FUCKER! LET ME OUT! FUCKING LET ME OUT! YOU WON'T BEAT ME! I'VE SEEN OFF BETTER AND HARDER. YOU FUCKER!'

The click of the external latch confirmed the response to his barking. The door duly swung open, revealing his grandmother's understandably concerned features, yet her tone remained unsuitably tranquil.

'Liam! Whatever is the matter? Why the crude commotion?'

There was little time to contemplate any consequence of his misplaced anger.

'Where is that bastard? Where is he? I'll kick his fucking head in! The bastard!'

Untamed emotion dictated Liam's every word and thought at that moment. He stormed out into the passageway, almost knocking his grandmother to the floor in the process.

'Liam! Slow down! What are you talking about! Slow down I tell you!'

Liam was fully charged with fury as he bound downstairs and did not hear his grandmother's call. Reaching the lounge, he kicked open the large oak door, sending it crashing into the adjacent wall.

His grandfather was not there.

Onward into the kitchen, Barbara engaged in pursuit.

Again, there was no sign of Fran.

Out into the garden.

Then across to the garage.

Fran was nowhere to be seen. Liam turned to face his grandmother, who stood in the kitchen doorway with arms folded. The despair in her grandson's face almost made her want to smile.

'Satisfied, young man? He's not here! I could have told you, if only you'd stop and listen for once in your life! There's no need to behave like a rabid lunatic!'

But such behaviour was a natural reaction for Liam Warburton. He was not master of his own will when commandeered by an urge for violence. He made back toward his grandmother and spat his question across the front garden.

'Where is the fucker, then?'

Barbara raised her palms as a pleading gesture for the teenager to become calm.

'Stop swearing will you and come inside. Let's have a little serenity first thing in a morning. What exactly is the problem with your grandfather?'

Liam did not budge, aside from thrusting an accusing finger her way.

'He's been in my room! Last night! Took the fucking lot! Clothes! Money! Everything! What fucking right does he have to do that? You fucking tell me!'

Barbara closed her eyes in shame and beckoned him to enter the kitchen.

'Sit yourself down. You're bringing the neighbourhood into disrepute!'

Eventually accepting Fran's absence, Liam opted to talk sensibly to his grandmother at the kitchen table. His heart and mind raced with suspicion and anticipation, but in taking a seat he was also in position to listen as Barbara spoke softly.

'What makes you think your grandfather has taken your things?'

Liam bolted forward in his chair and offered the feeble evidence for his misplaced anger.

'Because he *can*! Because he *hates* me! All I had was this pair of fucking scruffy jeans! That's all I've got left!'

Barbara's emotionless response was bemusing for him to observe. But Liam's confusion was soon to be resolved as his grandmother pointed over his shoulder.

'Look out there, Liam…on the washing line. Recognise anything?'

Liam turned around in his chair and through the open door he could see his entire array of clothing flailing freely in the breeze.

'I like to wash and dry early in summer. The hot afternoon sun tends to make clothes go stiff and starchy. Everything you own has been cleaned. It will be back in your room by lunchtime.'

Liam was dumbstruck.

Completely lost for words.

He had jumped off the cliff with his shameful over- reaction. The misinterpretation of events began to cause him not a little embarrassment as he sunk silently back into the chair. But it was not long before his appetite for confrontation reared itself once again as the next issue came to the forefront.

157

'Okay. What about my I-pod and mobile? Don't tell me they're hanging on the fucking washing line as well!'

Barbara chose not to reply, but simply nodded toward the section of work surface behind her irate grandson's chair.

To Liam's unprecedented - and undisclosed - pleasure, he turned to see the items in question plugged into the wall sockets. Both batteries were nearly fully charged to capacity.

A strain of guilt tempered his will for further combat.

The final missing item on the agenda warranted mention.

'And my wallet? Where has that gone?'

Barbara observed her one and only grandson with distinct fondness. She could not help but be amused at his impetuous nature and lack of patience. Her voice softened to sweeten the pill.

'Well...Fran thought he might slip a little spending money in there...you know...as a little gift. But you can't wait long enough, can you? You've ruined the surprise, haven't you?'

Liam stared at the tabletop in vacant sorrow. He watched sheepishly as his grandmother rose and switched on the kettle. She turned to him, the permanent smile never fading.

'I suppose you're thirsty after all that screaming?'

Liam felt foolish but would not dare admit to such weakness. The negative issues surrounding his grandfather still burned deeply.

'So why lock my bedroom door, then? And why won't my window open? It gets too warm in my room at night. I struggle to sleep.'

As Barbara placed two mugs on the worktop, her customary sincerity shone through. Liam believed her answers to be truthful. He had little reason to suspect otherwise.

'I don't know, Liam. A habitual oversight on my part, perhaps? Don't take it too personally. And before you ask, I've cleaned both pairs of training shoes you brought with you. They were filthy! They're now in the outhouse, where we keep all footwear.'

Liam's flimsy affection for his grandmother was steadily growing by the day. She was evidently a woman of considerate nature. Judging by what had already transpired that morning, she cared a lot about Liam's contentment during his stay. Every puzzle that Liam uncovered, she had solved with a simple, logical solution.

All that is, except the one remaining quandary.

Francis James Gould.

As though through an act of clairvoyance or divine coincidence, the man himself appeared in the kitchen doorway as he always seemed to do. His acidic tone erased any temporary sense of contentment for the teenager.

'Quite the talented artist, aren't you, soldier?'

Liam froze in his chair as he became alerted to his grandfather's presence behind him. The inference to the previous night's drawings jolted him to attention. Barbara's conveyance of friendship evaporated as conflict again began to infect the atmosphere. From the corner of his eye Liam could identify the wavering figure, who had just returned from his morning run.

The icy silence was broken with further commentary from beyond the front door.

'A little cruel, though. In fact, I'd say nothing short of disrespectful. Although I'm sure your grandmother doesn't mind being mocked by you behind her back, especially when she's been up half the night doing your laundry.'

Slowly, Liam turned in his chair and faced the opponent. Standing in shorts and t-shirt, Fran lit a cigar and kicked off his running shoes. Liam remained composed as he offered an explanation.

'I've said I'm sorry. I didn't mean to mock either of you. But she didn't make it clear that she'd been in my room for a valid reason.'

Fran raised his left hand, allowing the copper bangle to glint in the morning sunshine. A forefinger extended to accentuate the response to his grandson's claims. Then with each stage of the statement, another finger flicked out to accompany the rest.

'Number one...I have not yet heard you apologise. Number two...*she* is your grandmother, *not* the cat's mother! Number three...the reasons for her entering your room were made perfectly clear, it's just that you have no patience to hear them. Number four...it is not...*your*...room.'

Liam's resentment at the provocation was beginning to surface once more. His grandfather seemed to have an uncanny ability to know everything that occurred around him, even without being able to witness it first-hand.

He tried to conceal his expanding disgruntlement with matters but could not resist the temptation to be sarcastic as he faced Barbara.

'Okay, Grandma...I'm sooooo...soooorrryy!'

His grandmother was rendered speechless by the insolent display. After all she had done for him that morning, Liam's ingratitude was unbearable. She turned away shaking her head and continued to prepare the pot of tea. At that precise moment, one of Fran's running shoes hit Liam firmly on the back of his head, causing the youngster to spin angrily in his seat and confront his grandfather once more.

'What the fuck do you think you're doing?'

Barbara listened intently to the altercation but did not dare to turn around. Fran entered the kitchen in his socks, trailed by the customary fragrance of his cigar. He walked toward Liam and moved his face close to the boy's, allowing him to convey his words with more pertinence.

'I'll tell you what the fuck I'm doing, shall I? I'm assessing what *you* will be doing today. Your grandmother is baking. *You* will help her. You'll enjoy that, won't you, soldier?'

Liam stood up, meeting Fran toe to toe and nose to nose.

'Sure...I'll help her. As soon as I get my stuff back.'

Fran removed the cigar from between his lips and blew on the tip, encouraging it to glow a deep red. He continued to observe the smouldering tobacco as he spoke.

'Son...in life, I find it's far better to *earn* one's possessions rather than just help yourself to what you want. That way you appreciate things far more. Don't you agree, soldier?'

Liam eyed the enemy with disdain.

'So...what are you saying? That I *can't* have my things back?'

Liam clenched his teeth as Fran's expression evolved into a veil of satisfaction, whilst simultaneously blowing smoke into his grandson's face.

'You'll get your things back...*when* I say so.'

Placing the cheroot back in his mouth, Fran turned his back on Liam and re-positioned himself just outside the front door.

Liam was now shaking with fury as he watched the elder man bask in the sunshine. In two minds, his attention flitted between both grandparents.

He could take no more of this incarceration.

His resolve and patience had reached breaking point.

He decided there and then that he would willingly run the gauntlet again with Francis James Gould.

'Hey...Fran...'

160

His grandfather did not look back as he spoke, keeping his admiring attention fixed on the garden beyond.

'Yes…soldier? What is it now?'

There was a momentary hiatus which allowed Liam time to consider the possible penalty for his next ploy. He figured there was nothing left to lose as he took a deep breath.

'Fuck you…'

The cold interruption to the conversation was almost painful.

There was no immediate reply to the proclamation of the youngster. Liam felt a sense of victory wave through his body. It felt good. He had confronted his fears and followed his instinct.

He was now attempting to tame the dragon in its own lair.

And he believed he had gained the advantage.

Or so it seemed.

If only he could have seen his grandmother physically cringe as he uttered those fateful, final words. Barbara closed her eyes and placed the tea pot on the kitchen table, awaiting the inevitable eruption.

Fran contemplatively continued to draw on his cigar before extinguishing it on the stone wall of the cottage. Quietly re-entering the kitchen, he faced his grandson, who had resumed his position in the chair with his back to events.

Fran's expression gave nothing away.

He glanced across to his wife who now knew that Liam had made a grave error in directing such profanity and disrespect toward his grandfather. Fran stood patiently with hands clasped behind his back.

'Barbara…I'll be ready for that tea in a couple of minutes. I have something to discuss with my grandson in the garage.'

Liam's attention flickered briefly across the room.

But it was far too late.

Without warning he felt two hands form a cast-iron grip around his throat. In the next instance, he had been wrenched from his chair and bereft of all breath as his windpipe was tightly squeezed.

Absolutely stunned by the surprise attack, Liam then felt one of the hands leave his throat and reach for his crotch.

Now in searing pain and choking wildly, Liam found himself being manhandled out of the kitchen like a rag doll, across the front lawn and toward the garage.

He could not summon sufficient air to scream.

His eyes bulged from their sockets as he fought desperately to open his throat to call for help.

But the steadfast hold of Francis James Gould was unwavering. Besides, there was nobody to help Liam, anyway. Nothing could have prevented what was to come. The vice that clamped on his body was completely debilitating.

He was now at his grandfather's mercy.

Like the quarry under the whim of a predatory animal, Liam was dragged into the garage before being roughly discarded on the concrete floor like a used toy.

He lay on his back in total disorientation. Still gasping for a single breath of oxygen, he felt down to his crotch, which felt as though it had been ripped completely away from his body.

His head span as stinging salt water flowed from his sore eyes.

Blurred light evolved into terrifying blackness as the garage doors were slammed shut, enclosing the two alone together.

Liam now had to face the ultimate disclosure.

Another lesson in recognition that his grandfather was the one that ruled the roost.

Powerless to resist or indeed defend himself to any degree, Liam felt Fran's full weight crash down onto his limp and ailing form. It hurt beyond belief as his grandfather sat astride Liam, pressing his knees into each shoulder, pinning him down against the hard, uneven surface.

Still struggling to inflate his lungs, further obstruction was administered.

Liam's nose was clamped tightly shut by Fran's thumb and forefinger, involuntarily causing the boy to thrust his mouth agape as he clamoured for precious air.

The teenager's suffocating brain became more oblivious to the punishment with each passing second. Then, just as Liam was ready to surrender and pass out, he felt a sour tasting liquid being poured down his throat.

The engine oil pumped steadily from the bottle, coating the inside of Liam's mouth, tongue and then quickly filling his throat.

Completely trapped by his grandfather, Liam began to drown as unconsciousness beckoned.

The relentless force clamping down on his chest combined with the silky, clinging oil were a potent, violating restraint.

Then his body began to convulse as a reflexive reaction to the danger, yet still Fran maintained his position and still poured until oil covered Liam's face and head.

Life began to ebb away. Vision slowly obliterated. His heart thumped madly, ready to concede. Liam's limbs thrashed wildly as his starving blood craved respite.

Liam lay trapped as the helpless, hopeless recipient of an age old yet horrifyingly effective penal code.

Under the complete jurisdiction of Francis James Gould, flashes of Liam's past appeared before him.

His parents. Mr. Smith. Carla Ferris. Elson. Jonka.

And finally, a smiling, waving...Glendin Jones.

Then, just as he prepared to succumb to the ultimate destination, the powerful curtailment lifted.

Liam was suddenly liberated from the manacle of his grandfather.

Instinctively hauling himself onto his front, he began to vomit with violent procession. The stinging oil, mixed with raging stomach acid, removed the skin from his throat as it passed upwards and back through his mouth and nostrils, coating the floor of the garage in a light brown tar.

Liam's body was now fighting for recovery.

And Sergeant Major Francis James Gould knew it, as he willingly stood by and watched the boy's struggle to survive.

The chemical reaction continued to lurch from his gut as Liam buckled unsteadily on all fours. Gradually, the extremity of the physical expulsion eased, and his vision slowly returned through shards of tears.

Liam lifted his head to gauge the whereabouts of the perpetrator.

In the vague murk of the garage, he thought he could identify a sinister silhouette.

His grandfather leaning against the brickwork, watching his own flesh and blood wrestle himself back to consciousness.

Liam could not speak as his stomach continued to twitch and cramp. Yet against the backdrop of his gurgling cries of terror, he heard a familiar, imposing tone carry across the room.

A calm, yet distinctly sinister voice.

Belonging to a man that Liam now detested with all his might.

'Cough it all up, soldier! Let's get that mouth washed out good and proper, now! You want to think yourself lucky. If I were your commanding officer, you'd have had to physically fight me off to stay alive! I was only playing with you just now!'

The darkness was eclipsed by welcome light as the garage doors swung open once more, allowing sunlight to bathe Liam as his palms and knees swished around the turgid residue of his ordeal.

Liam squinted to observe the outline of Fran standing on the lawn, contentedly re-lighting the remaining half of his cigar.

With his throat scorched and lungs bruised, Liam attempted to gather some thought. Panting in disbelief, he could never have predicted the brutal events of the previous minutes. Wading among his own mess, further tears of frustrated fear oozed forth.

Then another sensation encroached on his concentration.

Water.

A strong, piercing jet of cold water.

Assaulting his body relentlessly.

Drenching him hard and fast.

Forcing himself once more to glance upward beyond the garage door, he was treated to the sight of his grandfather armed with the hosepipe; a billowing cheroot clamped tightly between his teeth and an almost evil smile completing the vision.

'You made a hell of a mess of my garage, soldier! Still, I hope it was worth it. There's a hot bath waiting for you inside. Better get those jeans of yours washed again, hadn't you?'

*****

Like a lame dog crawling from its disgusted trainer, Liam inched out of the garage and away from the jet of water before pulling himself to his feet. With an unstable stride he made his way back to the kitchen doorway. A process that was both uncomfortable and humiliating.

Without a single word of consolation, Barbara escorted him to the bathroom, helped him undress and ordered him to bathe.

The bathroom door was locked as she departed, leaving Liam alone with his thoughts. Immersing himself into the steaming water felt like a journey into another, safer world.

With all but his head submerged, he silently contemplated what the future might bring should he display such disobedience again.

He was now officially the acknowledged understudy to his grandfather's perverted mastery.

164

Under a relentless shroud of dread, the boy considered his situation with great angst as he cowered and trembled like an infant in the bathtub.

Deeply fearful of the next uninvited lesson, Liam contemplated silently as the hot water cleansed and soothed.

NINETEEN

Liam Warburton was not accustomed to kneading dough. Yet as he stood beside his grandmother at the kitchen table, his mind was content to focus on this one simple task and eclipse the myriad of thoughts he had been experiencing over the previous hours.

His coarse, dry throat was being steadily re-hydrated with regular gulps of water. His voice was now a mere rasp compared to the angered bark of earlier. However, his speech was almost inaudible, and he winced with each frequent, instinctive swallow.

For the time being, the situation was more than satisfying for all concerned.

He did not really wish to speak.

In any case, there was little to say.

It had been made quite plain to him that his voice had been heard once too often for one day.

For Liam's part, he was more than happy to remain at peace and therefore supposedly out of harm's way.

Holding the bowl of cream-coloured mixture for Barbara, she then instructed her grandson in the art of rolling pastry.

'I've decided to make small fruit pies today, Liam. I want you to roll this pastry and cut the lids out for me. Can you do that without a problem?'

Liam dutifully smirked and nodded, thankful that the ship was seemingly on an even keel for the foreseeable time. Whilst abhorring the very premise of baking with his grandmother, complying with such a menial chore was comparatively pleasurable to facing the wrath of her husband again.

Taking the ball of dough, he followed Barbara's instructions to the letter. Sprinkling flour on the tabletop, he flattened the mixture by hand before adding more flour. Then, he spotted the large wooden rolling pin and picked it up.

It felt good in his hands.

Heavy.

Functional.

A potent weapon for use against potential enemies…and actual ones. Applying his weight to the pin, Liam rolled and squared up the dough.

166

This process continued for a few minutes until the ball had become a thin sheet ready for cutting.

Carefully, he placed each pie lid securely, sprinkled them with sugar and pricked them with a fork.

An amusing thought entered his head as he did so.

If only his friends could see him now.

Adorned in a pinafore, covered in flour, making fruit pies.

Yet he did not smile at such a predicament.

Liam was a boy very recently humbled by circumstance.

What would his friends have thought if they had witnessed such an act on their leader? Only the merciful facet of his grandfather's nature had kept him alive that morning.

The alternative sent shivers down his spine.

Having finished cutting the tray of pie lids, he swallowed more water from a large glass. Barbara covertly observed him as he battled to recover from her husband's diktat. She felt sad for Liam and his wayward inclinations, but his arrogance was crudely overbearing and intolerable for someone so young. Fran had been right to bring him down a peg or two. But she was by no means able to endorse such brutality.

Even if it was successful.

Secretly she hoped that her grandson had suffered the correct remedy and would quickly change for the better.

If not, she was aware that Francis James Gould was always willing to administer further educational tactics should the need arise.

The misguided youngster standing before her had no idea what he was taking on.

But then if truth be known...neither did Fran.

Barbara wished to broach the subject but had been forbidden to do so by her husband before he left for the village.

Analysis demeans action.

Those were the words of military prowess he instilled as she wiped away a solitary tear of sympathy at her grandson's sufferance. Although the innocent target of his vitriol, she felt no desire to inflict pain on the boy. As Liam shivered fitfully in the bathtub, Fran had left for the village with his warning to discuss nothing regarding the matter.

She would abide by her husband's wishes. Liam was now indoctrinated into the system of redress that his grandfather favoured.

Only time would tell if he would be deterred by Fran's short, sharp shock approach.

167

But Liam didn't seem to take on advice readily even though he had been offered chances to amend his undesirable habits.

He had been warned not to swear.

He had been asked not to swear.

He had been told not to swear.

Each stage to no avail.

Liam handed the full baking tray to Barbara, who placed it on the oven shelf.

'Twenty minutes, Liam. Maybe twenty-five. Then you can sample your own creations. How does that sound?'

Liam acknowledged Barbara before taking on more water. He had been permitted to wear his tracksuit bottoms and graffiti t-shirt due to the fact that his working jeans were once again being laundered.

He watched them dancing on the washing line outside before emitting a query that had been on his mind for a while. His impeded vocals could just about be heard above the sounds of the obligatory classical music.

'Grandma...where is he?'

In the mind of the recipient, the question was somewhat unexpected as she sat down at the dining table.

Barbara was surprised that Liam would want to know, or even care.

But she answered out of courtesy.

'Just gone to the village centre for some supplies. He'll be back soon.'

Liam seemed puzzled. Another question emerged.

'You mean...he's *shopping*? Fran's gone *shopping*?'

The image amused him. The mental vision of his grandfather steering a trolley up and down aisles; comparing prices; presenting savings coupons. Finding conflict.

'Well, it's not the conventional kind of shopping, Liam. In Clearlake, there are no supermarkets. We still have to go to specialist stores.'

Liam toiled with the conundrum.

'What? Like butchers and bakers, you mean?'

'Yes, sort of. There's no bakery. But there's a dry goods shop. A greengrocery. Your grandfather knows all the villagers. He takes over the place. He can spend all day there if it suits him.'

Barbara chuckled at her last comment, but Liam could believe it to be true.

168

He imagined Fran stalking through the main street whilst fearful shopkeepers slammed their front doors shut and dived for cover behind their counters.

'Does he threaten them, too?'

The question stopped Barbara in her tracks.

She turned the radio down and asked him to repeat himself.

'What on earth do you mean, Liam?'

'I mean...Fran...my so-called grandfather. Does he go around beating people within an inch of their lives when he's out in public...or is that treat reserved for grandchildren only?'

A lump of emotion formed in her throat as she observed Liam's unwavering eyes peering from under his hood. There was no flicker of flippancy in his expression. It appeared that he genuinely wanted to know the answer. Whilst still suffering the physical evidence from his last encounter, Liam was in no mood to surrender to his grandfather's assumed sense of authority. She could see that her grandson was a hardened soul for his tender years.

A tough nut to crack, indeed.

'No Liam. He doesn't like to make people afraid of him.'

Liam detected his grandmother's voice beginning to falter. This was an uncomfortable subject for her. She was obviously wary of her responses to such an issue.

'But *you're* scared of him...aren't you, Grandma?'

She looked beyond the kitchen window. The pause was pained. The answer already presented through her expression.

'I have to do my duty, Liam. I don't like some things about your grandfather, but there are many things about him I love. I can't change him.'

She folded her arms around her own midriff in a protective gesture, as though to prevent further intrusion into her thoughts. Liam moved behind her seat and placed a hand on her shoulder. The effort to converse was evidently difficult, but well worth it.

'Did he ever hurt you, Grandma?'

Now he was hitting a nerve. She had been forbidden to speak about such things for a lifetime. Yet this fifteen-year-old was drawing answers from her at will.

'No...never. Not at all. Don't ever ask me that again.'

Liam was temporarily stunted by her response, but his curiosity was not satisfied.

'What about Mum? Did he ever hurt Mum?'

Barbara was becoming visibly emotional. Liam was pleased that he had managed to generate a reaction in his grandmother, even if she was not actually disclosing very much detail regarding the past.

'Liam…you listen to me. He never touched a hair on mine or your mother's head. I promise. On my life. He never touched her. Now…please change the subject.'

Liam removed his apron and sat down at the table whilst Barbara instinctively moved from her chair and began to wipe down the work surfaces. His natural inclination was to press for further information. But it seemed there wasn't likely to be any forthcoming.

'He could have killed me out there in the garage, you know. I could have died.'

Barbara Gould continued with her wiping and her cleansing without being drawn to look at her grandson.

'It wouldn't have gotten that far, Liam. You're being silly.'

Liam shook his head angrily and gestured with his fist, slamming it onto the table.

'How do you know? You were hiding in here while I was being tortured out there. How do you know what he wanted to do to me? Even *I* didn't know, for fuck's sake!'

Barbara rinsed her dishcloth under the tap. Still she fought the will to face her grandson as she closed the issue.

'Your grandfather loves us all. Never forget that. His way is best. Now then…I'd better check the oven.'

A few minutes of silence was eventually accompanied by the re-ignition of the radio volume. Chopin broke the tension, culminating with a rousing symphony that accompanied the tray of pies being repositioned onto a cooling rack.

Finally, Barbara gazed at Liam and smiled.

'Try one for me. The fruit will be very hot inside, though. You'll need to blow on it, so you don't burn your tongue.'

Mildly intrigued by the prospect, Liam selected a pie from the rack. It was very warm to the touch as he passed it between his fingers. Placing it to his mouth, he blew and bit carefully into the pastry. It was a tender moment. A grandmother watching her grandson eat his own wares.

Every family in the world had experienced such a scenario. For the first time since his arrival, the cottage had become somewhere that briefly resembled a family environment as opposed to a barracks. The feeling was placating for both Barbara and Liam.

But that feeling was to last for only a few short seconds.

'HOPE YOU'VE WASHED YOUR HANDS, SOLDIER! I TEST THE COOKING AROUND HERE! PUT IT DOWN!'

Liam almost dropped the pie into his lap as the booming tone carried across the room, burning his lips in the process. He scowled toward the doorway, which had become occupied by the evidently irritated figure of his grandfather.

Fran dropped the bags of groceries onto the table and suspiciously eyed the rack of pies. Liam was inwardly angered by the crude interruption, but smartly opted to remain silent until asked to speak. He watched as Fran retrieved a pie from the tray.

He did not look at Liam as he spoke in a softer volume.

'You made these did you, soldier?'

Liam nodded without word.

'Surprised...thought you'd be more attuned to making *puff* pastry!'

Fran chuckled with a mouthful of warm fruit as he leaned over to kiss Barbara on the forehead.

'Is he behaving himself now, my sweet?'

'Yes, Francis. He's just fine.'

Turning back to his grandson, Fran presented a smug grin as he sampled more of the pie.

'That's very good, soldier. I knew you'd see things my way quickly.'

Liam stood up to oppose Fran's assumptive stance. He could see the fear in his grandmother's expression, yet she obviously dared not confront such an aggressive personality.

If the truth be known, she admired Liam for his spirit, whilst privately acknowledging that any challenge to Fran would be shot down in flames.

That was the historical pattern, anyhow.

Voice still rasping in recovery, Liam was quite prepared to open the debate once more.

'*Your* way? You mean...by nearly murdering me?'

Fran laughed out loud at the accusation.

'It's called discipline, soldier! Works for me! Works for everyone! And it's working for you! Keeps things in line! Don't you agree?'

171

Liam clenched his fists. He could still feel the bruised reminders of the earlier encounter all over his body.

Yet such mementoes only served to spur him on.

'Make you feel good, does it?'

Fran finished the last morsel of his pie and pulled a packet of cigars from his top pocket.

'What's that, soldier?'

'Ordering people about. Controlling them. Is that what turns you on… Grandpa?'

Apparently still amused, Fran nudged Barbara gently in her ribs and feigned a whisper.

'Seems that mouth I washed out earlier hasn't got used to staying closed just yet. Still a little dirt in there, methinks. Do you reckon the young one needs another scrub down, dear?'

Barbara did not answer. She continued to watch her grandson rise against her husband's omnipotence once more.

Liam was not perturbed in any way.

'Bring it on, Fran. You're either going to kill me…or cure me. I reckon that's fifty-fifty odds. I can handle that.'

Fran laughed out loud again as he lit his cigar tip.

'Soldier…you aint tough enough to handle your own tail! I suggest you beat it out of my sight. Your chores are done for the day. Leave your grandmother and me in peace.'

Liam's intense desire for a renewal of combat was now reaching the point of overspill. He contemplated jumping across the table and attacking his grandfather there and then. Fran moved to the kitchen doorway to allow his smoke to escape.

Barbara offered her grandson a respite as she left the room, asking for his help as she cradled a small stack of laundry.

Liam ignored her and stood rooted to the spot as Fran faced away and continued to produce a wreath of tobacco smoke. His voice raised in volume as it carried around the garden.

'You see, soldier. *I'm* in charge around here. Not *you*. It's that simple. Your customary ways are null and void out here. It's as if you don't exist anymore. Never forget who's the daddy…and you'll be alright.'

Liam spotted the rolling pin on the table. He eyed it considerately as his grandfather continued with the fanciful diatribe.

'My men were orderly, soldier. No objections. No breach of code. That's how life should be. Organised, with a firm chain of command. In this house, I'm in command. You understand? Is it going into that thick skull of yours yet?'

Liam gripped the rolling pin in his fingers. He wondered how much damage could be done with one, swift, unexpected blow to the head. He might not even knock his grandfather out. Then again…he might kill him. He placed his other hand around the wooden shaft.

It felt ideal for the job.

'I saw some friends in the village today - Thomas Henworth and Fred Jameson. I told them about you. They'd like to meet you. I've arranged a little surprise on your behalf.'

Liam was not listening. He continued to debate the options that whirled inside his head.

But the conspiracy was soon ended.

He had been discovered in mid-plot.

Fran spoke softly as he held the cigar between his fingers and thumb. He turned to face his young adversary with the widest of grins.

'I know what you'd like to do with that pastry pin, soldier. But it would not be a wise move. I assure you. Instead, I suggest that you go for a long walk and think about what I just said.'

Liam so wanted to use it.

To unleash his anger for one joyous moment of victory.

But he faltered.

His heart lurched as Fran moved calmly toward him before taking the rolling pin from his grasp. His grandfather's final words came as a thinly veiled warning.

'Get your shoes from the outhouse and get out. Don't ever think about doing anything like that again.'

Liam had finally reached the boundary of his own bravery.

He unwillingly hesitated, relinquished his conviction and finally deserted the room. Emotion welled within his soul as he tied up his laces and bounded out of the front gate. A maelstrom of feelings followed him as he strode quickly away from the vicinity of the cottage.

He knew not where the path would lead.

But he knew, for the moment at least, that being as far away as possible from Francis James Gould was the wisest choice.

*****

173

Liam walked alone for over an hour. The sun shone high against an azure screen. Despite the negative aspects of his stay so far, he was slowly beginning to appreciate the authentic beauty that Clearlake possessed.

He had made a point of staying on the road. Travelling through woodland was fine for the adventurous and knowledgeable, but Liam was in no mood for the unknown at that moment.

This was a period for honest reflection and for earnest thought.

A chance to debate what had occurred and how he should proceed in the immediate future.

There had a distinct absence of fellow man on his ramble through the winding lanes of the local area. Yet he did not feel threatened by the isolation.

It was placating; welcoming; yielding to his presence. A light breeze cooled his forehead. If nothing else, it was pleasurable to adorn the familiarity of his own clothes once again. It gave him some of his identity back.

Liam felt like his old self yet placed in such foreign surroundings it was increasingly difficult as time went on to decipher who he was supposed to be anymore.

Talworth and its constituent ingredients seemed to be on another planet.

The road began to slope slightly away, causing him to adjust his stride. The never-ending curtain of trees had gradually been replaced by waist high stone walls which segregated the fields around and beyond. He gazed across the scene of rural solace, hoping to see something of vague interest. There was no livestock to catch his attention and because there were no trees in proximity, the familiar backdrop of birdsong was notable by its absence.

There was just Liam.

And his enveloping, soothing solitude.

He continued his trek, scanning the area stretching out before him yet paying little concern to time or direction.

Considering re-tracing his steps, his attention was drawn to a mystical image in the distance. An unusual vision that seemingly appeared from out of nowhere, about half a mile walk across the landscape toward the horizon.

In the middle of the sparse vista was situated a formation of tall pines. They appeared to be positioned in a circular pattern.

But from his location at the roadside, he could not identify what it was they concealed.

But they were certainly definitive by their outward arrangement. Highly visible for miles around. Almost symbolic and contrary in context of the surroundings.

An untouched place by the initial looks of things.

And it captured his imagination instantly.

Armed with compulsive curiosity and typical lack of hesitation, he navigated the stone wall and began to walk through the meadows towards the strange oasis.

Getting closer to his destination he continued to observe the fields behind and beyond. Liam was literally alone in the wilderness. It felt so invigorating, as though he was a king inspecting his realm. Nothing and no one were present to question his approach. Everything seemed to draw him toward the trees, as though this place possessed some magnetic force.

Now only yards from the pines, it was still awkward to ascertain what lay beyond the veil of foliage. The trunks stretched upward into to the blue yonder, almost making him dizzy as he followed their ascending might with eager eyes.

On reaching the outer wall of greenery, Liam looked around once more to check that he had not been detected by a chance passer-by. The last thing he needed at that moment was for some farmer to accuse him of trespass and escort him back to his grandparents with a shotgun.

Fran would not have appreciated such an episode, for sure.

Liam attempted to obliterate any downbeat thoughts that may have entered his head. There were gaps in the curtain of greenery that would just allow him access to the clearing beyond.

No further deliberation was required.

In a split second, Liam had breached the boundary and was on the other side of the tree line.

What he saw took his breath away.

The lake was an almost perfect circle, completely secluded by its natural, protective shield of pines.

The surface of the water shimmered like silver as it reflected a golden sun.

Liam stood in awe of this unexpected haven, before seating himself on the grass bank in overwhelming admiration of his newly discovered beacon of tranquillity.

The birdsong that had been absent from his journey had now returned in full chorus. He sat and closed his eyes…and listened.

It was a strange, singularly sensual experience…to utilise only one of his senses and simply listen.

He had done so little of it in his short life. Yet suddenly he realised the benefits of opening himself to other voices. There was nothing intrusive about the sound anymore.

It bathed him in spiritual contentment.

It allayed his fatigued and unsettled mind.

Cross-legged on the plush verge, Liam was taken away to another place in his own head. There was no aggression; no opposition; no quest.

Just a need to be. To breathe; to engage with nature.

To allow his physical body to respond to the moment rather than his mental instinct taking control and causing its typical chaos.

It was a high that eclipsed any effect of any drug he had ever tried.

The minutes passed as Liam allowed the ambiance to fill his every pore. It was as though he was under some magical spell. It was completely alien to his previous existence, but instantly addictive.

He had re-discovered the place he had only briefly sampled outside the bedroom window the previous evening.

He was back there.

The Liam Warburton that had arrived in Clearlake had already altered in the space of a few short days. He wanted to encourage the evolution in his character. The change was invigorating.

Eventually, he opened his eyes to embrace the scene once more. Now completely calmed, he immersed himself in his own visual study.

Then, without warning, the picture became complete.

From the other side of the water, a family of swans had commenced its hourly ritual and began to glide toward him across the glimmering surface of the lake.

Liam was spellbound by the endearing display of unity.

The mother led her seven cygnets in single file in a boastful parade of majestic splendour. The father kept close vigil at the end of the line, scanning the lake for any potential threat. They moved with a skilful, silent grace, so unlike any other creature.

Naturally proud of her brood, the mother held her head high, as a captain would steer a brand-new cruise liner from dock.

Liam maintained his position as the family closed in on the bank where he sat.

They did not even seem to notice him. He felt need to do no other than succumb to total reverence. His senses were more than adequately responding to the spectacle.

One by one the swans left the water and positioned themselves in a small group a few yards from Liam's position. The cygnets were only days old by the looks of their unkempt grey down and comical uncertainty when out of water.

Eventually, the seven babies followed their mother's lead and began to preen themselves vigorously, as if to specifically entertain the singular audience. The father did not engage in the task, preferring to stand tall at the water's edge as an all-seeing guard to his offspring.

As Liam watched, he realised he was smiling at the sight evolving before him.

A genuine, unprompted, wilful expression.

Wide, appreciative, and handsome.

For the first time he could recall, he felt happy inside. Not an exuberant sensation of silliness, but an inner tranquillity that had previously eluded him.

The interaction of the swans was addictive viewing, even for someone of Liam's limited appreciation of the wildlife community. He studied the order of the formation. How the youngsters imitated their mother and snapped beaks at one another as the father stood aloof, yet still avidly watchful over his brood with every passing second.

Then Liam's thoughts turned toward his own situation.

The relationships with the people in his life.

Parents; peers; grandparents; friends.

The faces of every one of his family and acquaintances flashed before him.

As he continued to fight the visions away, they grew larger and more imposing. Keeping close vigil on the family of swans could not detract from the frailties that were still present in his soul.

His habitual unsociability. His frequent instinctive rebelliousness. His regularly violent temperament.

All so unnecessary.

The will to inflict harm on others...and himself.

The lack of concern for the existence of others.

Especially those for whom life had already ended so cruelly short.

The vision of the swans recalled Glendin Jones' family to mind.

A mother and father, now without their baby.

Then he thought of the adult swans on the bank without their little ones beside them.

So unthinkable.

It would be such a crude, wasteful travesty of nature.

The investment of so much time, love, and attention, given such a tragic and pointless resume.

Liam was taken back to the cemetery. To that night where the fate of one bright, young boy was prematurely decided.

One swift movement of a blade. Friends helplessly ignorant.

Possibly uncaring.

A life lost; a spirit gone forever.

Back on the banks of the lake, Liam was no longer smiling.

As he wiped away the onset of tears, they fell in abundance.

Liam could not stem his tide of personal remorse.

Yet if he were forced to succumb to such emotion, he would not let the swans see him upset. He did not want them to suspect the darkness that lurked within their admiring observer.

Rising to his feet, he bade his feathered friends a promise to return as they continued to preen, oblivious to the continuing plight of the young man that stood before them.

Liam turned away from the water and climbed back through the tree line, thankful that no one was in proximity to witness his sufferance.

TWENTY

Accompanied by a perpetual release of emotion for most of the way, the route back through the outskirts of Clearlake was retraced with little effort. The sun had begun to drop below the tree line by the time Liam approached the front gate of the cottage.

His grandmother was in the garden sprinkling flowers and plants from a tin watering can. He dared not announce his presence before wiping his eyes and adopting a typical if feigned air of confidence.

Barbara turned to refill the can from the tap in the wall.

'I'll do that for you, Grandma.'

Spinning in shocked surprise, the smile was instant as Barbara greeted her grandson.

'Liam! You've been gone an age! Where have you been all afternoon?'

Liam walked across the garden toward the open arms of his grandmother. They embraced tightly. It felt healing.

'Oh, just for a walk. Have a look around. Here…give me that can. It'll be heavy.'

'Why…if you insist. I've put all your clothes back in your room. They smelled wonderful. I've aired the room as well. And fixed that darned window. You should sleep fine tonight. I bet you're hungry as a hunter, aren't you?'

It was nice to feel welcomed. Liam revelled in the attention.

'Yes, Grandma. Starved.'

'You finish off out here while I prepare your supper. I'm so glad you're okay. I had no idea where you could have gotten to!'

Liam upended the can and made his way around the remaining plants and borders. It was a vibrant display of colour, even more so now that light was slowly fading.

Standing in the garden he watched as the early evening visitors gradually made their entrance. The birdsong gradually reduced its intensity, paving the way for insects and mammals to perform their various dusk routines.

For a short while he forgot about his own private turmoil and was back in that special place.

But only for a short while.

The distant sound of a car engine drew gradually nearer.

As Liam refilled the can with water once more, he was startled by the interruptive rattle of his grandfather's pick-up pulling onto the drive and coming to a sharp halt in front of the garage.

He really did not want to acknowledge the shadowy driver at that moment. It would only serve to spoil the mood. Liam's reaction was instinctive and deep. The thought of conversing with Francis James Gould made his heart want to leap from the cradle of calmness that he had nurtured for most of the afternoon.

But Fran was nothing if not unpredictable.

He alighted from the car and made straight for his grandson. His stride was swift. His expression indeterminable. The permanent cigar in place as ever, readily emitting its trailing plumes.

Liam began to get nervous.

'Hey there, soldier! You're back! Had a good jaunt, didn't you? You make the lake?'

Liam was again confounded by Fran's ability to *know* things. He could have been anywhere during the afternoon, but his grandfather presumed correctly without hesitation.

'Yes…it's beautiful. Amazing.'

'You bet! The babies should have hatched by now. You see them?'

Liam set down the watering can as Barbara emerged from the doorway.

'Yes, the swans were on the water. They're just…incredible.'

Fran's attitude seemed to have altered in Liam's absence. He conveyed an untypical sense of companionship and an eagerness to be in his grandson's company. It was a refreshing change of approach, but Liam could not help but question its authenticity.

Barbara's smile had not waned either as she enquired as to the success of Fran's little excursion.

'Did you sort things for tomorrow?'

Fran kicked off his boots into the outhouse and took the cigar from between his lips.

'Yes, my sweet. We are to meet Fred and Thomas in the square at five am. Should be on the river and catching by six; back home and frying by nightfall!'

Liam watched confused as his grandfather turned to him.

'You ever fished a river before, soldier?'

Liam suddenly realised he was to be an integral part of the following day's plan.

180

'No, sir. Never. I've never fished, anywhere.'

A firm yet possibly friendly hand slapped him on the shoulder.

'Well…tomorrow's the day you learn! I've just been for bait and to confirm arrangements. I'm going to introduce you to a couple of old friends. You'll like them. Be good for you to escape the monotony of this place for a while. Don't you agree?'

The last thing on earth Liam felt like doing was spending an entire day with his grandfather. However, it was obvious he would have little choice in the matter.

He met Barbara's understanding gaze as he answered.

'Yes…whatever you say, sir.'

'That's right, soldier. Whatever I say. I knew that walk would do you good! Barbara, I'll be in the garage sorting out the tackle for the morning. Give Liam a little supper, will you? He's got an early start.'

'It's already on the stove, Fran. Already done.'

*****

Liam sat eating in quiet contemplation of what the next day would bring. The meal of braised beef and vegetables was gulped heartily. Barbara could sense her grandson's trepidation regarding Fran's fishing itinerary, but typically opted not to open discussion on the subject.

Retiring to his bedroom after kissing his grandmother on the cheek and thanking her for supper, Liam quickly scanned the contents of the wardrobe and dresser. Everything was back as it was. The mobile phone and I-pod were fully charged once again. The phone was useless without credit or a signal, but the music was most welcome.

Pressing his earplugs in place, the pounding beat reminded him of home.

The adrenaline-fuelled excitement; the discussions; the planning; the troublesome adventures of the Black Stars.

Then, without prompt, another image came to the forefront of his mind.

A vision of swans in single file, gliding across a silver lake.

Reaching down to the bottom drawer of the dresser, Liam retrieved a couple of sheets of drawing paper and a pencil. As his mind conjured the memory, his hand freely relayed the imprint to the page.

He was careful to accentuate their physical prowess. The upright posture of the adults. The long, slender, curved necks. The wary, astute eyes sitting atop firm, capable beaks.

Then of course, the youngsters.

Little, innocent bundles of grey plumage.

So naïve.

So in need of parental protection.

So vulnerable.

Finishing the drawing, Liam quickly began another.

The family on the bank. The young tending to their dishevelled feathers whilst under supervision of the cautious adults.

It pleased Liam to recreate the pivotal events of the day. Putting things on paper seemed to be a sure-fire way of preserving any positive recollections.

The mind's capacity to remember was undeniably brilliant yet faltered at critical times. Simple marks on a piece of paper would last for a lifetime.

This would be the policy he needed to uphold from this point on.

The pleasurable aspects of life should be retained always.

This was Liam's final thought before fatigue carried his body and soul into a far-off land.

TWENTY-ONE

Liam was still half asleep when the pick-up rolled into the main square of the village. The warmth promised by the day ahead was already in evidence, even though the hour was only just approaching five a.m.

Bundled from his bed, he could remember little of his grandfather's excited ramblings at the kitchen table. Barbara had laid out toast and cereal for speed and convenience and provided a hearty picnic for the fishermen to enjoy during the day. She had also placed the tattered old jeans and jumper for Liam to wear. He dejectedly observed the blood stain and holes in his trousers as the pick-up pulled into the village centre and came to a stop.

Fran yanked on the handbrake and reached into his top pocket for a cigar.

'I can sense a good day ahead for us today, soldier. A clear sky means good fishing. Plenty of food and a case of strong beer in the back for the boys. This is living, isn't it?' he grinned whilst sucking on the end of his smoke as it ignited.

Liam nodded without reply and gazed through the dusty windscreen at the square beyond. It looked clean and orderly. Hand-painted signs hung above shop windows to indicate the category of goods for sale. It was like something from another century. A quaint time capsule that had obviously not heard of modern trend or brand.

'Does it get very busy here, Fran?'

His grandfather fiddled with the radio reception as he spoke.

'Yeah...sometimes. Most days. I come here most days for supplies. I know most of the citizens of Clearlake. They know me. We get along. Pass the time of day. You know.'

Liam rubbed his eyes and yawned as music filled the cab.

'Do you like rock n roll, soldier?'

Liam smiled at the noise emitting from the crackling speakers.

Trying to stem his mirth, he searched for a respectful answer.

'Yes. But modern sounds. I don't know this one. It sounds old.'

Fran chuckled and wound down his window.

'Here's a thing to bear in mind. Your modern sound originated from this old stuff! Buddy Holly. Elvis Presley. That's where it all began. You ought to thank them and embrace their music. They are the only reason you have what you have today, soldier.'

Liam could not think of an appropriate response to continue the debate, so instead opted to say nothing and just listen.

The silence between the two was a pleasant contrast to the bickering that had ensued over the previous week. Fran was evidently looking forward to the next few hours. Liam was secretly pleased to be away from the confines of the cottage but was withholding judgement on the potential company he was about to share.

Just as the thought entered his head, another beige pick-up very similar to his grandfather's appeared from across the other side of the square. Fran jumped out of his seat and beckoned Liam to join him.

'Come on, soldier. Don't be shy. I want you to meet my friends.'

The pick-up pulled next to the pair and the two occupants alighted, accompanied by a rapid exchange of greetings and banter.

'You got the booze, Fran?'

'Ready to lose your money again, Tom?'

'Thought you'd gone into hibernation for the summer, Fred!'

After much hand-shaking and back slapping, attention turned to the teenager stood quietly beside the group. Fran opened the introductions.

'This, gentlemen, is Liam. My fifteen-year-old handsome grandson. He'll be joining us for the day. We'll show him how to enjoy himself, hey boys?'

The first of the men stepped forward. A tall, thin dark-haired man with a wispy beard offered his hand.

'Pleased to make your acquaintance, son. I'm Tom. Glad you're here.'

Liam nodded confidently.

'Thank you, sir. I'm…looking forward to it.'

The second, a stocky, red-faced balding man laid a hand on Liam's shoulder and squeezed, causing not a little discomfort due to the bruising caused by Fran the day before.

'Hi, junior. I'm Fred. You're a strong looking lad for fifteen. A good looker, too! How long you here for?'

'The whole summer.'

'Well, wait until the local girls get a glimpse at you! You'll be fighting them off with a cattle prod, I reckon!' proclaimed Fred.

As Liam blushed the three adults burst into laughter at the youngster's evident discomfort with the subject. His grandfather did little to help stem the embarrassment.

'Don't mention females around him…I think he's still to get it wet…if you know what I mean, boys!'

More chuckles ensued at Liam's expense. The thought crossed his mind that he wished he had Barbara's rolling pin to hand. He felt sure he could take all three of them out with one blow each. Fred feigned an expression of sympathy which only served to fuel Liam's mild annoyance.

'Aw look…I think he *is* still a virgin. He's not arguing on the case, anyhow!'

Liam offered a stern glare as he clenched his fists. Thankfully, the arena closed on the issue as Tom proposed movement.

'Well, let's get on that riverbank. I can feel my line twitchin' already! Hey, Fran, your good lady done the deed again for us?'

In reference to the picnic, Fran gave a thumbs-up.

'Yeah…and the beer's been in the cool house all night.'

Fred in particular seemed filled with joy at the thought of food.

'Beautiful! Okay. Let's go. We'll lead, Fran. You follow on with the virgin!'

Liam watched Fred's portly frame climb back into Tom's pick-up. Containing his disapproval of the mockery, he could not help but whisper his feelings under his breath as he got in beside Fran.

'Fat fucker.'

The vehicles pounded their way out of the square and through the winding forest of pines before hitting relatively smooth country lanes. There was little indication as to the destination, but it mattered little to Liam. Within minutes of the journey, he was embracing the prospect of a day by the river.

Fran tuned the radio up, encouraging the growing sense of liberty that Liam was beginning to adopt. He was even developing a liking for fifties' rock n roll.

It was a good half hour before both pick-ups pulled to a stop beside a stone walled lay-by. Everybody jumped out of their seats and into the golden rays of another hot, humid day. Still only just before six am, Liam had now engaged his mind and body to the task ahead.

'Grab some gear, soldier. I'll bring the tackle. You get the beer and food.'

Liam reached into the back of the truck and pulled out two large green canvas bags. It quickly became obvious that hauling both bags at once would require considerable energy. Liam guessed they must have weighed at least ten to twenty kilos each. A fact that played on his mind as he followed the three men across the stile in the wall and on towards what he hoped was a nearby location.

The minutes ticked on and still the group of three men walked ahead, eventually reaching a spot indicated by half a dozen leaning trees. Liam's arms were aching for respite, but he could not show weakness in front of his grandfather. The teasing would be merciless.

On finally ceasing their march, Fran gestured for Liam to set down the bags. Looking up beyond the bank, the snaking river demonstrated a steady flow. The fishing platforms were spacious and conveniently spread apart.

Liam was suddenly enticed by the idea of catching his tea for the evening. Maybe it was time to show the old folks a thing or two, even if he had little idea of how to indulge in such a pastime.

He stood patiently aside as his grandfather and both his friends assembled their equipment on their chosen platforms. There was a definitive air of competition as they threaded lines, attached hooks and baited the waters in front with crumb and worms.

Fran seemed suddenly anxious about the prospective day now that he had arrived at the riverbank. He was unusually quiet and far less aggressive and imposing in the company of the others.

Evidently, Tom and Fred were adept at the art of angling. They were ready and waiting for Fran within ten minutes, as he still persevered in tying his hook.

'You feeding or floating, Tom?'

Fran's query was met with a concerned gaze up along the bank.

'Why feeding, of course. The flow's a little strong for sticks, today.'

Tom's reply was accompanied by a haughty chuckle from Fred who sat between the pair.

'Looks like the sergeant's gonna try his luck with a float! Might just hook a tiddler with that! Looks like the money's ours, Thomas, my man!'

Liam coyly observed his grandfather, who now seemed so different to the ominous figure of authority that Liam had become accustomed to back at the cottage. When with his peers, he was just a man like them. There were no grandiose statements, arrogant responses, or prophetic

186

advice. Even a friend calling Fran 'sergeant' was a form of belittlement in Liam's eyes.

He watched his grandfather struggle to set his rod and trace as he dangled it in the water. Still his friends continued to mock as they sat impatiently.

'I say Fred. What time are we due home tonight? If the sergeant takes much longer, we won't even get chance to wet our lines!'

'It's okay, Tom. The fish don't go to bed until after dark, anyhow. I just hope I can stay awake!'

Liam was not used to witnessing Fran being ridiculed. He appeared much less significant in the company of his friends, but it pleased him to observe it develop. It was entertaining to see his grandfather taste his own medicine. Liam was gratified to watch Fran swallow his pride and keep his mouth closed for once.

Finally, his grandfather announced his readiness for battle.

'Okay you lubbers! I'm ready! What's the stakes?'

Fred quickly glanced toward both men in turn before proclaiming the rules for the day.

'Usual entry of ten each. Then depending on the fishing, an extra ten per hour to stay in. It's now six-thirty. We fish until six-thirty tonight. Twelve hours equals a final pot of three hundred and sixty. Everyone agreed? What do you say, boys?'

Tom hollered from his position.

'Fran…you can get the virgin there to hold the pot. He can collect every hour.'

All three nodded eagerly toward Liam and reached into their pockets.

Liam watched without word as Tom and Fred each placed their stake money inside an envelope which Liam collected before returning to his grandfather's side.

Then it was Fran's turn to produce his contribution to the kitty.

Liam could not believe his eyes as Fran nonchalantly stood up on the fishing peg and retrieved a familiar looking wallet from his trouser pocket.

Liam's wallet.

The one taken from his room. He had completely forgotten about it. Then the realisation quickly dawned that Fran was using Liam's money to gamble with.

Confusion was eclipsed by severe irritation as Liam watched his grandfather take a note from the wallet and place it in the envelope with the others. He did not acknowledge his angered grandson and obviously did not feel it warranted discussion.

Liam, however, was not so reticent regarding the issue.

'What the fuck do you think you're doing?'

Fran finally engaged his attention with the fuming teenager who forcefully re-stated his position.

'That's *my* money! You can't fucking do that!'

Continuing with his act of ignorance, Fran sat back down in his deck chair and pulled a packet of cigars from his pocket.

He proceeded to light one in his customary nonchalant style.

'Fran…that's all the money I've got! That's all I brought with me!'

Still his grandfather said nothing in reply and puffed heavily on the smoke. Fran was in no mood to quibble and feigned inspection of his rod and line.

But the silent treatment did not rest easily with Liam, who felt justified in knocking the cigar from his grandfather's mouth with a swift motion of his hand. It hissed as it hit the surface of the water lapping at the base of the platform.

It was a prompt that proved sufficient in finally forcing a reaction.

Fran turned to his grandson with a glint of menace in his eye. Out of his companions' earshot and line of vision, he grabbed Liam's arm and pulled him towards his scowling face.

'You…ever…do that again, soldier…I'll pull your arm from its socket. You understand?'

Liam's heart banged like a drum as Fran's fingers dug deep into his skin. But he would not back down this time. He had sensed weakness in his grandfather. He had worked it out. Fran was actually afraid of losing the fishing match to his friends. Particularly as his grandson would be there to see events unfold.

His mood was tense; he looked nervous. He was certainly not at ease in such a competitive environment, even if it was only fishing with his friends for a day.

'But that's *my* money, Fran! You can't just take it! It's mine! It's not fair!'

'Listen soldier. Cut your moaning, will you? I'll wipe the floor with these two hippies. Then we'll split the winnings between us tonight. One-eighty each! What do you say?'

Liam could find no argument. He was powerless to intervene in such a plan. The grip around his arm relinquished.

All he could do was sit, and watch, and wait.

*****

Two hours passed before a single fish had been caught between the trio.

Fred eventually found success first, landing a beautiful bream which weighed in at over four pounds. It seemed to kick start a procession of bites for Fred and Tom, who were seemingly netting a fish between them every few minutes.

But Fran was way behind in the race. Not a single hint of interest from the occupants below the surface. Not even a nibble on his bait.

Liam had dutifully collected the stake money every hour and handed out the sandwiches and beer on request. The comments directed at Fran by his friends were essentially good natured and harmless, but Liam could detect a gradual blackening in his grandfather's mood.

Francis James Gould was not accustomed to coming last at anything in life.

With the combination of the hot sunshine, lack of reward and intake of beer, Fran was silently fuming as morning evolved into afternoon. His body language was twitchy, impatient, and aggressive, giving Liam concise indication to steer clear and keep quiet.

Yet still Liam's money was thrown into the pot by the hour. There was surely little chance for his grandfather to better his friends' achievements with the clock counting down. He was effectively out of the running already. Yet still he continued to empty the contents of Liam's wallet without thought or hesitation.

As the time approached five-thirty pm, Liam collected the final round of stakes. The men were becoming tired. The weigh-in would inevitably be between Fred and Tom as opposed to the three-way tussle predicted earlier in the day.

But with all prize money in the pot, Liam contemplated spending the remainder of the summer without a penny in his pocket.

Fran's selfishness had reached new, unbelievable heights.

By this time, both grandson and grandfather were ready to erupt with frustration. The minutes passed as Fred, then in turn Tom, added another fish each to their keep-nets. They weren't landing monsters by

189

any stretch of the imagination, but their total weights would need to be eclipsed by one mighty catch if Fran were to upset the applecart.

With only half an hour remaining before the end of the competition, Fred conveyed an observation which touched a nerve in Liam's fuming grandfather and sent howls of derision echoing around the riverbank.

'Hey, sergeant! I think you'd better let the young one take over for a while! You can hand out the beers instead whilst you count how much money you've lost!'

Further laughter resonated between Tom and Fred. Liam would have felt like laughing too had he not supplied a third of the winnings.

The strain of the competition was finally getting to his grandfather, who promptly slammed the rod down and retreated up the bank. Slumping onto his backside, he opened another tin of beer and lay back on the grass. He mumbled frustration beyond earshot of his companions.

'Fucking stupid sport!'

Fred observed the display of submission, not resisting the temptation to invite the young substitute into the fray.

'Come on down, young one! The sergeant looks to have had enough punishment. Chance your arm! Pick the rod up.'

Liam looked across to his grandfather who vacantly returned the gaze before shrugging his shoulders and swigging his beer. Liam decided to accept Fred's invitation.

Clambering down to the platform Liam retrieved the rod from the floor and reeled in the hook.

It was quickly discovered that Fran's bait had long since wriggled free. Fred again supplied the appropriate commentary.

'Christ, Francis! Even your worm has had enough of you!'

Liam attached another morsel from the bait bucket as he had observed his grandfather doing all day. Then a thought struck him as he glanced across the water.

'Fred...how deep is this river?'

'Oh...I'd say, ten feet. Perhaps twelve. No more.'

Without instruction, Liam rearranged the weights and float to match the estimated depth. He added another little weight near the hook to sink the bait, before casting out.

Fran had suddenly become alerted to the actions of his grandson and spoke with a fresh cigar billowing smoke from between his lips.

'What do you think you're doing, soldier? Thought you said you couldn't fish?'

190

Liam dipped the tip of the rod under the surface and drew out the slack in the line with the reel. He did not reply to Fran's comments. It was time to try a new approach.

Sitting back in the chair, Liam waited and watched the bright orange paint at the top of his float.

The minutes ticked on.

Nobody in the group of four uttered a single word.

Liam determinedly squinted at the surface of the water, hoping that the dream finale might materialise.

There were approximately ten minutes left in the competition. Tom and Fred had converged onto one peg and were discussing the potential weights in their nets. Fran remained at the top of the bank, not wishing to speak to his competitors or observe the climax to the day's events.

Little did they know that the true conclusion was yet to be established.

Liam twitched forward in his seat as the top of his float suddenly disappeared under the surface and remained out of sight for a good second or two. He carefully picked the rod up from the rest and gripped it firmly as the head of the float reappeared.

Re-checking his hand and finger position, Liam's adrenaline began to run fast and hard. His mind also raced, contemplating what may lie in the depths below.

The tip of the float danced above the surface once again.

None of the adults had noticed his change of luck or altered posture.

The silence was deafening as the float was firmly dragged under once more.

Having observed Fred and Tom all day, Liam whipped the rod quickly to one side to secure the hook in the mouth of whatever had taken a fancy to the bait.

Only then did the battle commence.

'Jesus Christ! Fred! Look at the young one! He's damn well got something on! Fran! FRAN! LOOK! Your grandson's showing you how to fish! Who'd have thought it?'

The three men made their unsteady path down towards Liam's platform, who continued to wrestle with the unidentified monster from the depths. Varying instructions were bellowed to assist him.

'Keep the rod up, boy!'

'Make sure the line stays tight!'

191

'Let him run, now!'

'Reel some in!'

Fred and Tom teetered with excitement as Liam began to overpower his squirming quarry.

'Jesus! A bream! But way bigger than mine! Big as a dustbin lid! Look at the *size* of that thing, Tom!'

Francis James Gould said nothing as he watched with a stony expression of embarrassed disapproval at what was unfolding before him.

Tom applauded as Fred scooped the fish safely into the landing net and rested it down on the platform.

'Must be ten pounds at least! I'll get my scales!'

Scrambling back up the bank, Fred did not see the hatred in Fran's eyes as he quietly observed his grandson's success. No one could know of the fury that cursed through the veins of Francis James Gould at that very moment. Little did Fred or Tom understand that their unrestrained enthusiasm for Liam's achievement was only serving to increase the resentment Fran felt inside his soul.

A sense of distaste that emanated from Fran's very core as Fred returned with the scales and weighed the large, circular fish in the net.

'I declare we have ourselves a winner, gentlemen! With the net, the weight is thirteen pounds four ounces. I know for an undeniable fact that the net alone is ten ounces. That makes for a fish of twelve pounds ten! Neither Tom nor I can match that! No chance! You are today's winner, son! Congratulations!'

Liam's euphoria was shared with Fred and Tom, who shook his hand and slapped his back in appreciation of his wildly unexpected contribution to the event's closing moments. Fred pulled a camera from his pocket and captured Liam and his prize-winning catch through the lens for posterity.

Fran was once again the automatic butt of the joke from his friends.

'Bet your grandaddy will want to retire from fishing in shame now, boy! Wait until the rest of the gang see this photograph!' teased Fred.

Tom joined in with the merciless taunting of their counterpart.

'I think you ought to teach the sergeant how to go on in future! Lucky you brought him along today, Francis! Hope you watched carefully and learned something.'

The atmosphere among the group was descending into friction.

Again, Fran declined to contribute to the celebration and proceeded instead to pack away the tackle. Liam stood aside and counted the money in the envelope as Tom released the winning fish back to the water.

Liam studied the obvious strain in Fran's movements as he crudely packed various items into his fishing box.

He could feel his grandfather's vexation as his rod was stripped and separated.

Liam had effectively defeated the elder man at his own game.

In front of his own friends.

He would not miss the opportunity to volunteer some opinion of his own as Fred and Tom began to prepare for departure along the bank.

'Well, Fran...I take it all back. I'm *glad* you used my money for the stake. That means I get to keep the winnings. I reckon I've three times as much as I started with this morning. Thank you.'

Fran continued to collect his things together.

Still the wall of silence held firm.

Still the bubbling temper raged inside.

Still Liam pressed his grandfather's patience.

'I'll do you deal, Fran. If we come fishing again, I'll use *your* money for the stake and let *you* keep the winnings. Of course...I'll have to come along to catch you a fish as well and...'

Liam's monologue was suddenly ceased by a severe jolt to the chest as Fran grabbed him by the jumper with one hand and pulled him close. Liam could smell the tobacco and the distaste on his grandfather's breath as he spoke. It almost made him feel sick.

Fran glanced furtively along the riverbank to check that Fred and Tom were out of earshot before he emitted a disarming whisper.

'Shut your fucking smart mouth, soldier! The money's all mine! And so are you when we get back home! Now get your sorry fucking ass into the truck. I don't want to hear another fucking peep!'

Liam's legs began to shake as Fran released his hold and hauled some fishing gear under each arm. Picking up the canvas hold-alls, Liam tentatively followed the group back to the two pick-ups.

Fred and Tom did not have a chance to say goodbye as Fran wrenched the car into reverse. With a screeching halt, he then slammed the gear box into drive before placing his foot to the floor.

Liam watched without word as scenery flashed passed.

Potholes in the road felt like ramps as Fran's foot never left the throttle.

193

His grandfather's white-knuckled hands never left the wheel.

Liam could only guess at the nature of the inevitable punishment awaiting him back at the cottage.

But this time, he was more than ready to defend himself.

TWENTY-TWO

Barbara stood at the garden fence to meet her husband and grandson as the pick-up pulled up in front of the garage.

Liam edged from his seat to greet her as his grandfather remained in the cab. Her expression conveyed sincere elation at their return.

'Hello, Liam, darling! How was fishing?'

Waiting until he was standing next to his grandmother before replying afforded him the luxury of whispering.

'Well, Grandma…I ended up taking the winnings, can you believe? Though I don't think a certain someone is so happy with the outcome.'

Liam and Barbara watched as Fran slowly emerged from the far side of the truck and offered a half-hearted wave. Making his way over to the pair, a forced smile broke out as he placed a firm hand on Liam's shoulder.

'Liam did me proud today, Barbara! Showed them hippie friends of mine how to go on didn't you, soldier! Biggest fish I ever saw. Too nice to bring home. Cruel not to let it go again. Besides, we couldn't eat it. Wonderful catch, though.'

Fran's choice of words resonated in Liam's conscience. It was the first time he had been addressed by his Christian name since his arrival. Yet his grandfather had not yet finished with the appraisal.

'Funny thing was, Barbara…we got to the river this morning and I realised I'd forgotten my money. And do you know? Liam offered to foot the stake from his own wallet! He's turning out to be a fine young man.'

The lies were almost unbearable to listen to. Yet Barbara was evidently fooled as her response carried pure pleasure.

'I'm so relieved it went well. I'm so glad you're both bonding at last. Come inside and get washed up. Dinner's almost ready.'

Fran's grip on Liam's shoulder tightened, causing him true discomfort before he managed to escape and trooped into the kitchen behind his grandmother. He could sense Fran's eyes burning into him from the garden. But he would not give credence to the septic atmosphere by returning the glare.

He was more than content to let his grandfather continue to fume.

It was no more than the elder man deserved.

A welcome meal of shepherd's pie with vegetables was followed by fruit crumble pudding. Fran sat at the head of the table, eating in stony silence as Liam and his grandmother sat opposite one another and discussed the day in finer detail.

Fran clanked and clattered his cutlery as an indication of his disgruntlement, but neither Barbara nor Liam paid attention as they mused.

The exchange was only interrupted when Fran rose to his feet, causing the chair to scrape across the tiled floor behind him. The noise pierced the banter in the room, paving way for an announcement.

Fran glanced through the kitchen window. Dusk seemed imminent as light was fading by the minute.

'I'm going to put the car away. It's getting late. Liam, you can give me a hand sorting out the tackle if you would. Thanks for dinner, Barbara. I'm stuffed.'

Liam watched as his grandmother clasped her dainty hands and rested her elbows on the table.

'That's fine. I'll wash up and then make a fresh pot of tea. Don't be too long, boys!'

Fran prodded a forefinger into Liam's back as he moved away from the dining table.

'Come on, soldier. Everything will need a wipe down before it can be stored away.'

The teenager sensed threat in his grandfather's true intentions. He was not willing to get drawn into battle so easily again.

'Do you mind if I stay here and help you, Grandma? There's a lot to clear up. I could dry the pots for you.'

Fran did not wait for his wife to reply to Liam's futile diversion tactic.

'She can cope…I need you outside…*now.*'

Barbara watched helplessly as her grandson mulled over his elder's command.

With considerable reluctance, Liam rose from his seat and followed Fran across the garden toward the pick-up. He did not speak as his grandfather swung open the garage doors and gestured for Liam to come closer.

'At the back there somewhere, I put my leather rod case. Can you switch on the lights and get it for me?'

Liam peered further into the murk. He did not even know where the light socket was situated.

Before he had time to enquire, an almighty shove from behind sent him flailing across the floor of the garage and into the back wall. Clattering into a toolbox and step ladder, Liam next heard the slam of the two doors as Fran shut himself inside with his grandson.

With Fran now evolved into a fearsome dark silhouette, it was difficult for Liam to ascertain exactly what the next move would be.

He did not have to wait long to find out.

The punch came from nowhere.

Hard, low, and just above the groin, it completely winded Liam, who collapsed in a whining heap on the floor, gasping for breath as dust filled his nostrils. The wooden step ladders tumbled down on top of him, colliding with the back of his head.

Fran stood above the crumpled figure of his grandson; so close that his steel toe caps touched the boy's forehead as he lay holding his stomach.

The gravelled voice that carried from the elder man's throat was predictably menacing in tone and adequately disguised any sign of ailment.

'Think you did really well today, don't you, soldier? In fact, all you did was make life harder for yourself. You see…you made me look a fool in front of trusted friends. Now…I don't appreciate being made a fool of…especially by a young virgin like yourself. This is just a reminder for you never to do it again…okay…soldier?'

Fran reached down and grabbed Liam by the scruff of his t-shirt, before yanking him back to his feet. Liam was breathing a little easier, but still wary of a secondary attack. He maintained his distance as Fran continued with the instruction and pushed open each of the garage doors.

'Now…get back to your grandma and tell her that I didn't need you after all. There's a good boy.'

Liam did not move. Instead, he responded to the goading from his grandfather standing ominously by the doorway.

'You're pathetic, Fran. You know that? Fucking pathetic! You're a coward and a bully! You should be fucking locked away. You're not right in the head!'

Francis James Gould simply laughed at the accusations from his grandson.

'You're the pathetic one, soldier! You're the virgin! I've seen the scars on your arms. Supposed to be a sign of strength?'

The teenager did not offer any response as his grandfather persisted.

'A symbol of rebellion, are they? You trying to pretend to be a real man by cutting yourself up? Does your mother know you do that to your arms? Don't talk to me about being pathetic! Get out of here!'

Yet Liam remained, unmoved by the words of his older relative.

He had something to counter the accusations.

Far more than Fran Gould was ready to hear.

'You don't frighten me! You might frighten Mum. You might frighten Grandma. But not me! You're fucking *scared* of me…aren't you, Fran? I'm a *threat* to you, aren't I, Fran? I'm stronger than you…aren't I, Fran?'

Another punch emerged rapidly from the murk, landing in Liam's side, right below his kidneys. The pain was intense as he went to ground once again. Fran gave a quick glance toward the cottage before dragging Liam back to his feet, spitting into his face as he issued his warning.

'Now listen up, soldier. If you want more pain, then I've got more pain to give. Don't make me hurt you. Or I swear to God you won't get up at all!'

Liam feigned injury as he observed his grandfather from the corner of his eye. Fran was up for a fight. That was for sure. It was difficult to resist such a challenge. Liam felt as though he was back within the realm of the Black Stars, such was the anticipation of the unexpected and the customary rush of adrenaline.

He flexed his muscles in the encroaching darkness.

Waiting for the right moment.

Then when the time felt upon him, he swung a punch in his grandfather's direction.

Liam completely missed the target, serving only to knock himself off balance. And what followed from Fran was an unstoppable barrage of retaliation.

Blow after blow landed on Liam's body.

Front, back and sides took the brunt of the pounding before Fran stood off. Liam eventually made his way out of the garage in agony.

The assailant had been very careful not to damage his grandson's face. The evidence would be damning should Barbara be able to see it.

Liam fled the scene and hurried past his oblivious grandmother who was busy at the kitchen sink.

Onward into the passageway, up the stairs and beyond the large oak door with the outside lock.

Liam would retire to the supposed sanctity of his bedroom for the evening as bruises bled inside and swellings grew around his torso.

As his head nestled gingerly into the pillow, a myriad of positive thoughts flashed through his whirring mind, each in turn being overshadowed by the menacing spectre of Francis James Gould.

Liam prayed for slumber and the end of his terrifying ordeal at the hands of the oppressor.

Harsh reality slowly ebbed away as a youthful mind eventually drifted from the hurt.

III
INFATUATION

Liam's contemplation of the unbelievable events since his arrival at Clearlake did little to dissuade him from his negative demeanour.

Almost a month had passed since he set foot in his grandparents' cottage. It was no exaggeration to claim that for the duration of his stay so far, his constant sole wish was to return to Talworth.

Unsure what the future held in terms of his unstable relationship with his grandfather, Liam had decided that toeing the line was the policy most conducive to easing tensions. He secretly hoped that the remainder of the summer could pass without further hostility and antagonism.

Yet irony ran in tandem with these prevailing thoughts. Liam had evolved greatly as a person in such a short space of time. He had learned lessons. Especially in the art of employing thought before action.

His rural surroundings had also been a subject of increasing appreciation. He now embraced the inherent sense of solace that Clearlake offered. It was a place that had served to encourage an inner contentment on regular occasion, so his contrary desire to return to his hometown and all its dubious influences was causing him severe consternation.

Despite the bouts of confrontation with Fran, he had become physically and mentally healthier for his days away from home. But open acknowledgement of the fact would prove an elusive admission at that moment.

Liam Warburton was still uncertain of many things.

In fact, his mind was being bombarded with a labyrinth of unfamiliar emotions that accompanied the passage of time. Barbara and Fran were a stark contrast to the adults he had been accustomed to in his short fifteen years. They upheld stern principles and had strict rules. It was uncomfortable for Liam to adhere to even a mild request, let alone be persuaded to obey orders. But he was gradually realising that a policy of coexistence in the short term would entail obedience and respect for his grandparents' wishes.

Since the last altercation with his grandfather, Liam had indulged himself in all manner of household chores. From dusting and hoovering, to tending the garden. Painting the boundary fence of the property was a sedentary occupation but the accomplished result was most satisfying to behold. He had also finally heeded the dangers of cutting firewood under Fran's renewed tutorage.

Nothing had been said regarding the events that unfolded during and after the fishing match. Liam had certainly felt no obligation to discuss the topic. The winnings remained in the envelope, which surprisingly was still in the top drawer of his bedside cabinet where he had defiantly placed it. His wallet had also been covertly returned to his possession in the drawer.

Interaction with Barbara was as amiable as ever. He still sensed her inner trepidation towards her husband's authoritarian approach to domestic life. But Liam figured that, as she was his wife, Fran was *her* problem. After all, she did choose to marry him.

Liam had turned an efficient hand to baking bread and meat-filled pies. His cheese scones were as good as his grandmother's ever tasted, but such an outcome was relatively predictable as he was following her recipe.

But inevitably, Fran's long shadow readily cast itself across most of the daily timetable. His attitude to his grandson seemed to have softened, but this was probably due in no small part to Liam's cooperative reappraisal of his holiday.

However, despite his adherence to the regime, he was still a teenager in need of fun. The tedium of life in the cottage was slowly beginning to wear him down. He feigned enthusiasm to appease his hosts, whilst knowing that it was all an act for their benefit. His façade of civility would only hold for so long. If not soon presented with some diversion or stimulation, the peace that currently reigned within Summer Place would be a short-lived experience.

Little did Liam know that the excitement he so craved would originate inadvertently from his grandmother's suggestion one morning at the breakfast table.

The presently stagnant existence of Liam Warburton was about to become disturbed in the most positive way imaginable.

*****

Finishing his bacon and eggs, Liam placed his plate in the sink with the earnest intention of washing the pots. His grandfather followed suit and placed his plate on top of Liam's as Barbara squirted bubbles into the hot water.

She picked up a dishcloth and gingerly began to wipe the crockery.

204

'Francis…if you're going to the village today, I should like to come to. I bet Liam would like a change of scenery as well.'

Whilst in earshot of the conversation, Liam cared little for returning to the village centre and did not hesitate to offer an alternative suggestion.

'I'll stay here and listen to some music if that's okay. I'll be fine.'

His grandmother frowned at the idea.

'Oh, I think you ought to come and see some new people, Liam. This cottage will send you batty if you don't get out occasionally.'

It was surprising, bearing in mind recent history, that Fran too seemed keen for Liam to accompany them.

'Come on, soldier. Get your best rags on! I want to show my grandson off to the neighbourhood.'

Typically, Liam felt he had little choice but to accept the invitation, which was effectively another thinly veiled instruction. Indeed, it struck Liam that Fran had been quite reticent thus far in displaying even a modicum of pride in his teenage relative. Indeed, when considering his draconian approach to discipline, the very notion was preposterous.

Up until this point, Fran had presented himself to be little more than a pompous bully. Liam hoped to change his personal perception of the man, but only time would tell if that would be possible.

In his bedroom, Liam pulled on a pair of his own baggy jeans and a white hooded top. Keeping the hood off his head would be a necessary measure of compliance with his grandfather's wishes.

He then debated the idea of pulling up his sleeves as the weather was very warm. The instant reflection of his own self-abuse startled him away from the idea. He studied the deep red lines on his forearms. Scars that would fade with the memory but never disappear completely.

Despite his overwhelming sense of dejection since arriving in Clearlake, Liam had not once felt the need or urge to cut himself. He had successfully concealed the markings from his grandmother, although Fran had briefly glimpsed them and dispensed little sympathy.

His grandfather saw such action as sign of weakness and was not reserved in conveying his views. But Liam himself now struggled to justify the marks of self-mutilation on his body. It made no sense now yet seemed such an appropriate form of remedy in the past.

His puzzlement was interrupted by a gentle knock at the bedroom door, which prompted him to roll down his sleeves to hide the shocking evidence once again.

He turned to greet the visitor, who peered around the door and offered her customary smile.

'Why don't you bring a little of that spending money with you, Liam? You never know what bargains you might uncover!'

Liam paused for a moment. It was difficult to think of any shop in the village that might accommodate his taste in clothes or music. The next issue to cross his mind was ridiculous yet understandable.

'What about Fran?'

Barbara appeared to be confused.

'What about him?'

Liam gestured to the top drawer of the chest containing the money.

'Maybe he won't want me to spend it, bearing how I won it. Perhaps it isn't such a good idea I come with you after all.'

Continuing to display her customary positivity, his grandmother shook her head.

'I promise you he'll be fine about it. Your grandfather was the one who suggested it in the first place. Now...hurry. Time's a ticking!'

Liam felt suddenly charged with a pang of pleasure and hurriedly prepared himself.

Standing at the front gate with his grandmother, they watched as Fran reversed the pick-up out of the drive and pulled up beside them. Liam climbed into the cab, sandwiching himself between his grandparents. With the driver engaging a shift of the gear lever and a puff of cigar smoke, the pick-up chugged its way toward the village.

*****

Liam's expectations of the day ahead were given a surprising need for revision as the trio left the pick-up and walked toward the village centre.

The square was vibrant with sights, sounds and smells. So different to the tranquil deserted arena that Liam remembered from the day of the fishing match when waiting for Tom and Fred. Still, that was at the crack of dawn. The centre presented a very different picture at the peak of market day.

There were people everywhere. Perhaps five hundred; maybe even a thousand. Ambling arm in arm in twos. Chatting in groups. Bartering with stallholders. The air was alive with voices from all directions.

Fran had parked the pick-up down a side street, leaving his wife and grandson to venture alone for a while. The three had arranged to meet at one o' clock for a bite to eat. Until then, Fran declared he would keep himself occupied and leave the other two to shop at leisure.

The plethora of activity fuelled Liam's senses as he observed shoppers of all ages inter-mingling. The smell of fresh meat and bread wafted above the multi-coloured selection of canopies that kept goods under cooling shade. Liam meandered not far behind his grandmother, scanning the various traders barking for custom. He had seen nothing quite like it in his life. The whole place appeared to thrive on interaction.

He felt rather dubious about being in such a scenario at first, but within minutes was comforted by what he saw and heard. So many different faces to behold emitted a multitude of strange dialects to identify and a hundred differing conversations ensuing at one time. Men, women, boys, and girls battled to speculate at each stall.

This was the essence of community spirit.

This was Clearlake at its most traditional.

The centrepiece of the market was a staged area to the side of the main square which provided local musicians with a platform to impress the locals. Barbara manoeuvred her way through the dense throng with Liam in tow until they gained a suitable view of the day's visiting band.

Resonating over the entire square, rhythmical violins carried the sound of Irish folk songs. It was strange for Liam to think that strings could induce a response that sufficiently stirred his soul, but Barbara's lifelong appreciation of such music assured them a front row view.

The fast-flowing tempo of the music had encouraged dancing among the crowd and within seconds Liam was addicted to the beat. With feet tapping and head nodding, he was beginning to actively immerse himself into the unexpected excursion. Happiness again threatened to breach the mindset of Liam Warburton.

He was in that rare, special place once more.

Untouchable.

Lost in a bubble of contentment.

And his handsome smile returned without prompt for the first time in what seemed an age.

Barbara could see her grandson's pleasured expression and hollered during a break in the music to get his attention.

'You stay here and watch if you want. I'll go and find your grandfather and do some browsing. Take your time. Enjoy it! We'll see you this afternoon at the clock tower to decide where to eat.'

Liam nodded in acknowledgement, barely glimpsing his grandmother's carefully navigated departure from the scene. The crowd bustled and jostled as another tune commenced and immediately roused the senses of all in earshot.

Liam suddenly felt liberated. And he felt trusted to be alone. Away from all that was familiar and constrictive. He had not experienced such inner freedom since the coastal camping trip with his friends.

But this was different, somehow. Here he had no image to emulate or emboss. He could be his natural-born self, easy-going and free from scandal.

There was now no need for him to act up to the audience.

Unbeknown to Liam, others had paid him silent appreciation of the tall, handsome stranger in their midst. With his physical stature, dashing young looks and urban attire, Liam stood out from the crowd without effort. Yet he was not aware of such a natural ability to attract admiring onlookers.

Historically, his usual tendency had been to attract negative attention wherever he went.

For once, the picture he painted of himself was honest - and infinitely endearing to the distant eyes of most in the vicinity.

And for one particular female in close yet unseen proximity, the vision of the good-looking boy among the large gathering of marketgoers was completely intoxicating.

Applause rang out as the current tune ended and another quickly began. Liam began to let his attention drift from the musicians, and he started to scan the varying faces of those around him.

It was such a joy to behold the villagers taking so much pleasure from something so simple.

He watched as a mother laughed with her two youngsters. An elderly couple - far older than Fran and Barbara - stood arm in arm and swayed to the memories of their youth. Groups of adolescents of similar years to Liam mocked, pointed and sniggered. Men and women jigged merrily to the sound of the band, as was the custom for such open-air plays.

Then he saw her.

No more than twenty feet from his own position, through the heaving throng of bellowing traders. His eyes rested easily on the girl, and she in turn never once averted her own alluring gaze once they connected.

A smile so enchanting. She was a beautiful creature, adorned in a cream summer dress. Auburn hair hung loosely in ringlets around her shoulders. Blue eyes accentuated the odd freckle against her lightly tanned skin.

It was a vision from heaven.

And Liam was immediately transfixed by its powerful hold.

The band played harder and faster as if to accompany the pounding in his chest. The reaction of mind and body was like nothing he'd ever experienced.

And still she stared. And still she smiled.

Until embarrassment finally rained down over his masculine aura, forcing him to divert his attention for only a few seconds. He sensed her eyes still boring into him. But he could not look. He felt his cheeks flush, and his body become hot.

Yet he felt like a giant among dwarves. The sense of superiority that he had purported for so long was now authentic in conveyance. He was truly a king for that moment in time.

A moment of addiction for him that seemed to last forever.

Casting his attention back to the source of the music, he attempted refrain from returning her fond attentions.

For just a little while longer, at least.

Just to digest his response and summon some courage.

Having steadied the ship of surging emotion for a full minute, he was finally ready to engage with her image once again.

Summoning the bravado, he tried to reacquaint himself with her location in the heaving crowd.

Yet she was gone.

Vanished into thin air. With dozens of strangers, unfamiliar faces and unidentifiable voices that combined and heaved into one forceful, confusing mass. Frantically searching among the myriad of bobbing heads, frustration quickly developed as he realised the beautiful vision may have been lost forever.

It was as though she had woven some magical spell then deliberately disappeared to leave him floundering.

Beyond range of sight. Beyond reach of touch.

Gone.

Dejection slowly crept back into his soul as the band stopped playing again and the dense audience began to disperse.

Ultimately now disappointed by the all too brief exchange with the gorgeous stranger, Liam glanced around once more before checking his mobile phone for the correct time. He scanned the display as he walked slowly away from the stage area.

There was still no signal. But he still had no credit to spend, anyway.

Floating on a lost premise, he placed the phone back into his pocket and opted to find his grandmother, who would no doubt be shopping at one of the stalls.

'Hello, handsome!'

It was a voice he had never heard before. Yet strangely, he recognised the possible owner in an instant. Turning to his right, the angelic vision had reappeared. Still separated by a procession of passing shoppers, he returned the greeting.

'H-Hello. How are you?'

Her beautiful smile never faded; only seeming to widen by the second. Liam's pulse raced beyond control once more and his left leg began to quiver uncontrollably. Yet there was no fear, no discomfort or disapproval about the moment.

Everything was suddenly pure and earnest.

Especially her accent. Rural, quaint and soft, with the hint of a West Country dialect. He wallowed in the tones as she spoke once more.

'Did you enjoy the band? I saw you, earlier. They were very good, weren't they? I really like your clothes. I'll wager you didn't buy them from the market!'

Stuttering for only a moment, Liam eased himself into the conversation as the pair were constantly jostled on either side by shoppers.

'Yeah…the band was excellent. By the way…I'm Liam.'

The girl held out a gentle hand of greeting through the moving conveyor belt of people.

'How do you do, Liam? I think they're here next week as well. Do you like to dance? I do.'

Honesty may not have been the best policy regarding such a subject. Confusion resulted in a multi-layered mess of a reply.
'Yes, well…maybe…well, no…I've never really…'

There was little time to finish the speech. The girl checked her watch before glancing across the square.

'Look, handsome. I'd better be getting back to my stall. I've got someone covering for me. Will you come by again next week? I'll make more time.'

Liam's head was spinning. Even before he could conjure another sentence, she was retreating into the crowd. But not before turning to face him once again as she did so.

'Well? Are you coming back to see me next week...or what?'

Liam nodded with mouth agape. Fighting desperately for some last offer of communication, it finally emerged.

'Yes...maybe...hey! You didn't tell me your name!'

The flame haired girl began to disappear among the multitudes once more. She smiled, waved, and shouted to be heard above the incessant din before merging completely with the crowd.

'MY NAME IS TISSY!'

Liam studied the empty void where she had stood only seconds earlier, which was soon filled by the ever-shifting horde of Clearlake locals.

*****

The rendezvous with his grandparents came all too soon. Liam could not get her out of his head. He could not fathom why his mind should have reacted as it did. He felt warily confused, yet incredibly enticed. He had subsequently wandered around the dozens of stalls, but little else had captivated his interest.

Nothing could fuel his curiosity as the girl called Tissy had done.

She had deserted him when he wanted to talk. He was uncertain of her motives, yet he wanted to know far more than just her name.

The contrary and distracting thought process persisted for the remainder of the day. Having lunch with Barbara and Fran in a cosy tearoom just off the main square did not divert his concentration from the events of the morning.

'You spend much, soldier?'

Liam gazed vacantly through the window of the café and to the activity beyond. He did not even hear his grandfather's voice, let alone digest the words spoken. Fran set his teacup back onto its saucer and repeated the question.

'Sorry? Er...no, sir... I...I didn't really get chance to look round.'

211

Fran pulled the packet of cigars from his shirt pocket and lit one whilst keeping vigil on his daydreaming grandson. Barbara too felt compelled to enquire about Liam's apparent air of bewilderment.

'You alright? You seem a million miles away from here.'

Again, Liam failed to respond.

His attention was indeed centred on somewhere far away. An amazing place. Yet where it was, he knew not. Fran looked to his wife in feigned exasperation.

'Well sweetheart, I'm ready if you two are. I've had enough of folks for one day. I'll load the shopping into the truck. You follow on with him. If you can get him to prise his nose from the windowpane, that is.'

Barbara smirked as Fran left his seat and paid the bill. Only when he had left the café did she remark as to Liam's apparent disinterest in his present company.

'You sure you're okay, Liam? You've been awfully quiet since you met us for dinner. Did you not enjoy your burger?'

Finally, Liam faced his grandmother, though instead of an answer to her query, he posed a question of his own.

'Grandma…'

'Yes, my dear…what is it?'

He swallowed a lump of hesitation before reaffirming the words in his mind.

'How do you know when a girl you've never met before likes you? I mean…*really* likes you?'

Barbara looked at her grandson in amazement. She was very curious as to the reasons for such a question.

'Explain, Liam. What's happened? I knew something was on your mind. You haven't been with us at all, have you?'

Liam's cheeks began to flush with mild embarrassment, but his desire to understand had eclipsed any discomfort regarding the subject. Yet, he suddenly withdrew from continuing the debate.

'It's okay. It doesn't matter.'

'Are you sure, Liam? You can talk to me if you want, you know. I might be old, but I know a few things. I might be able to help you.'

Liam stood to his feet as a look of bemusement befell his features.

'No. It's okay. I'll deal with it. We'd better go. Fran will be waiting. Don't want to annoy my grandpa now, do I?'

*****

212

Getting ready for bed that evening, Liam could barely keep his mind focused on anything for longer than a few seconds. He tried reading a magazine. Listening to music. He picked up pencil and paper. But all to no avail.

Leaning across to the window, he opened it wide and rested his elbows on the sill. Nature had long since been at play. The moon was high and from the dark wilderness of the woodland, varying animals cried out to each other. It was a humid evening. Not a breath of wind.

Between the shriek of the fox and call of the owl, there was silence.

A silence that Liam occupied with a single image of loveliness and a solitary thought in his head.

Whilst he barely knew the girl, the future was destined to torment him unless he made her acquaintance once more.

The only obstruction to such a plan was an unbearable passage of time.

Although a full week away, the next market day would see him return to the square with a definitive mission in mind.

TWENTY-FOUR

Time was not usually an issue that incurred any relevant bearing on the life of Liam Warburton, but the past seven days had crawled past as though it were an entire year.

The wait had agonised him like no other experience in his life.

It was the most anticipated of all Tuesday mornings when he opened his eyes.

Market day at Clearlake.

He did not succumb to the usual struggle of waking and rising.

With a heart already beating to a rhythm of expectancy, Liam quickly threw on his clothes – the ones that Tissy said she liked. He has made sure that they had been laundered in the meantime. Parting the curtains, he observed that the sky held a strange hue. A slate greyness that hinted at rain. He had become accustomed to pure unbroken sunshine since his arrival, but whatever the weather, it would not dampen his enthusiasm for the task ahead.

'Morning, Grandma! What's for breakfast? I'm starved!'

Barbara filled the tea pot and set it down to stew a while as Liam entered the kitchen. Even the obligatory backdrop of classical music was reasonably bearable.

'Whatever you want, Liam. But you'd best be quick. Your grandfather needs your help today. He's ready to go when you are. You'd better change your clothes into scruffs as well. Might be a little rough going.'

Reality quickly dawned on Liam's island of dreams as he sat to the table.

'What's up with Fran? Where are we going?'

His grandmother pointed through the kitchen window toward the blackening sky.

'You see that lot up there? That paid us a brief visit in the night. And it's on its way back soon. Fran has a farmer friend out at Mawsby who has one hundred livestock to gather. The only problem is Fran's friend has injured himself and is struggling alone. You and your grandfather are going to help him herd them today. The storm is going to batter Mawsby, apparently.'

Liam pondered the words Barbara had spoken.

'I didn't hear any rain. I had my window open all night.'

Barbara noticed the immediate disgruntlement in her grandson's expression as she placed toast on the table.

'I'm not debating the issue with you. You've had your instructions. The herd will need at least three people. Now…what will it be for breakfast?'

Alarmed by the intrusive and disastrous alteration to his itinerary, Liam thought quickly as the likelihood of missing the market began to register.

'But I don't know anything about gathering cows.'

'Neither does your grandfather. But he's pledged to help his friend - and he's volunteered your services as well. There's nothing spoiling here. You may as well go, hadn't you?'

Herding cattle all day meant no visit to the village.

That meant no meeting with the girl.

Disbelief evolved rapidly into desperation.

'Are we not going to market today, then?'

Bacon began to sizzle in the frying pan causing Barbara to speak a little louder.

'I wouldn't have thought so, Liam. Being as Mawsby is twenty miles away from here. Why would you want to go back there, anyway? You looked bored out of your mind last week! I've cleaned your work clothes. They're in the outhouse with your boots.'

Liam fumed silently as he waited for his breakfast. Though he could not show his emerging temper in front of his grandmother. She would suspect he were up to something. A sense of trust had built up over the past fortnight. There had been less friction. Liam was being seen to pull his weight on most issues.

But he had endured so patiently for a whole week, so anxious was he for this day to arrive. He was not willing to allow any unwanted influence to deter him from the mission.

Seven entire days that had seemed like a lifetime in that cocoon of a cottage.

Tissy would be waiting for him at the market.

So that's where he would have to be.

Breakfast was wolfed down and pots were washed, dried, and put away in record time. Repeated instructions for Liam to attire differently fell on deaf ears.

'Hurry, Liam. There's a day's work ahead of you. He's waiting.'

'Okay, Grandma.'

Barbara left the kitchen for a moment.

Liam's mind raced to formulate a plan.

He had a vague idea how to get to the village centre but if he was going to make a dash for it, then now was the time. Rising from his chair, he checked that his grandmother was out of visual range. Checking his wallet was in his pocket, he picked up his mobile phone from the worktop behind him and scanned the display.

A futile exercise.

No credit. No signal. No text messages. Fully charged battery.

Still, it might just prove useful to take it with him.

Carefully listening for the footsteps of his grandmother on the creaking floorboards of the passageway, he satisfied himself that she would not detect his departure.

Thankfully. out into the garden, there was no sign of his grandfather, either.

He crept up to the garage window to see Fran placing his overcoat into the back of the pick-up. Liam left the garden via the front gate and made a hasty route along the lane.

He jogged in the direction they took last week. He knew it would lead him to the main road, where any passing traffic would no doubt be headed to the village. There was no other place it could go unless it was intending passing through Clearlake on towards the villages beyond.

The grey skies looked threatening, but Liam's enthusiasm for the day remained positive. Looking behind him, there was no sign of life. Reaching the T-junction, he paused to remember the route to the village centre. It was right to the river, so he opted for left.

At a guess, Liam reckoned the market was at least an hour on foot.

Consumed by will, he began the adventure.

The Gods were on his side for once. Within a couple of minutes of walking, a goods wagon followed behind him. Liam opted to flag the driver down, who courteously pulled the lorry over. A window lowered, which unveiled a thin-faced man with a lop-sided grin. However, his manner was obliging, which only helped to fuel Liam's vigour.

'Where you headed, young one?'

Liam pointed into the distance.

'The market…if you're going that way.'

The driver nodded and kicked open the passenger door.

'Hop in, son. You'll only wear your shoes out treading it there.'

Liam hauled himself up into the passenger seat, content that the first section of his quest had been achieved.

He just hoped that the journey would prove to be worthwhile and that the sole object of the exercise would be there for him at the other end.

*****

Fran entered the kitchen and turned the radio off.

'Barbara? Barbara? Where are you?'

From behind a closed door, a feint voice traced down the stairwell.

'I'm in the bathroom, Francis. What's the problem? I thought you'd be long gone by now.'

Suspicion shrouded the scene as Fran looked back to the garden with a furrowed brow before marching down the passageway. He checked the empty lounge before stomping upstairs and pushing the door open to Liam's vacant room. Knocking on the bathroom door, Fran waited politely before his wife eventually revealed herself with a towel wrapped securely around her head.

'What is it, Fran? You sound a little annoyed.'

The responsive tone was indeed laced with aggression.

Fran's customary grimace was firmly back in place, encouraged by the discussion about a wayward grandson.

'Liam? Where is he?'

Barbara's eyes widened as her forehead creased with confusion.

'Why…I sent him outside to you. A good while ago. Did you not see him?'

Fran did not reply. Now inwardly fuming due to the disappearance of the teenager, he stormed out of the cottage and jumped in the pick-up.

Black clouds formed above as Francis James Gould steered towards Mawsby…alone.

217

'Are you new in town, young one? I don't recall seeing you around these parts before now.'

As he studied the passing scenery, Liam began to recognise certain landmarks from the previous week. It was exciting to know that he was on the right path to his destination.

'No...I'm not from Clearlake. I'm staying with my grandparents on the outskirts.'

The driver continued to concentrate on the road ahead as he spoke.

'Oh? Might I know them?'

'Maybe. The Goulds...Fran and Barbara.'

A silence followed as the lorry slowed and navigated a sharp bend.

'The ex-army officer, isn't it? Is it Sergeant Francis?'

This was a small village. It wasn't a complete shock to realise that everybody probably knew of each other.

'Yeah...that's him.' Liam sighed.

The driver seemed friendly enough. Liam was happy to talk about his temporary circumstances and the motive for his solo visit to the market. He figured that disclosing his plans would make little difference to his mission. Once Fran caught up with him there would be hell to pay, anyway.

But Liam cared little for the consequences of his unannounced departure. He had one ambition in mind. Nothing could be allowed to obstruct him today.

It was a powerful compulsion, the likes of which he had never experienced before in his life. The inner desire to behold the girl once again had consumed him completely.

Liam glanced at the driver who checked his rear-view mirror. Spots of rain started to fleck the windscreen.

'Always seemed a tough nut to me...your grandfather. Never really spoke to him to be honest. I've only seen and heard about him if you know what I mean. Is he as strict as he looks?'

Liam smiled to himself which gave the driver a fair indication of the answer.

'Only if you pay attention to him.'

The driver's laughter echoed around the cab, and he made a rapid conclusion.

'I guess you don't pay attention to him all that much, then?'

'No, sir. I'm on the run as we speak! Best part of it is he's sat back at home thinking I'm still eating my breakfast!'

Liam and the driver chuckled at the prospect. Familiar buildings honed into view as the lorry hit a slower stream of traffic heading into the village centre.

'Well…from what little I know of him, junior…sooner *you* than *me*. If you jump out from here you'll get there quicker on foot. There's always a tail back for a mile or so. You'll get there a lot sooner than me, anyhow.'

Liam thanked the man for the lift and alighted from the wagon. The implications regarding his grandfather's reaction played on his mind for a few seconds, before renewed concentration on a beautiful stranger eclipsed the perils of discovery.

Just as the previous week, the market was throbbing with life. The sudden unpredictability of the weather had not deterred the scores of patrons and traders. In fact, at first glance, the square appeared even busier than on his first visit.

Snaking his way slowly among and around the crowds, Liam's sense of anticipation was overwhelming. He had never felt such motivation; such passion for wanting to confront the unknown.

He had always thrived on the thrill of the chase back in Talworth, but this was infinitely different.

Whilst on this daring quest to enter an unheralded situation, it did not instil the usual trepidation and rush of adrenaline that fuelled his typically arrogant determination.

Instead, the internal feeling was warm. Of wishing to enter some haven and never leave. To ensure peace instead of conflict. There would be no jeopardy attached to this liaison. Making the girl's acquaintance last week was nowhere near satisfactory enough and it had set the seed of curiosity burning within his soul.

For the first time in his life, he wanted to give of himself, rather than take from another. He wanted to present a positive portrayal of Liam Warburton as someone who cared as opposed to a lone figure of coldness.

But most of all, he needed to feel that he was wanted; that being in his company was a pleasure instead of a hindrance. The knowledge that his presence was welcomed and not resented was something he craved dearly, yet his constant mask of disdain readily hid this true whim in everyday routine.

But in just a brief exchange of glances and a few words across a crowded square, the girl called Tissy had reinforced the self-belief that Liam Warburton longed for.

He had tasted the potential benefits of harmony and attraction.

It was an alien concept, but more inviting for the fact.

However, weaving his way through the market dwellers was proving to be initially unrewarding. He recognised many stallholders and their wares. But Tissy was nowhere in sight. The splashing of rain had thankfully abated, now allowing streams of golden sunlight to bathe the shoppers.

Still, he searched and scrutinised.

Yet increasingly, his exploration seemed destined to bear little fruit.

After almost an hour of laborious observation, Liam must have circled the market at least three times. Every pass revealed something not seen before, but not the elusive beauty he sought.

The inspiration that accompanied his awakening that morning was now all but vanished to be replaced by exhaustion and despair.

Then, at the very point of conceding to fate, he thought he saw her through the myriad of moving heads.

A tiny stall in the far corner of the square.

A red-headed girl with the ringlets he fondly remembered now tied back with a white ribbon. Dressed in expectancy of cooler weather, she still sparkled in black jeans and knitted red pullover. He remained fixed to the spot, covertly enjoying the spectacle of watching her at work. Customers stood admiringly as they browsed her selection of handmade jewellery whilst enjoying her playful chants and business banter.

The stock made an impressive display. Gold chains and bracelets, silver trinkets and coloured stones set in rings were arranged on black velvet trays, each tray adorned with a price tag.

Whilst entertaining a small group of prospective buyers, her attempts to drum up any profitable custom seemed to be failing. Whilst being amused by her witty repartee, no one in the gallery was parting with money.

Whilst her voice remained loud and buoyant as she encouraged passers-by to peruse her wares, Liam saw the evident strain in her eyes. She appeared to be tired of the routine and might well need some inspiration.

It was time for Liam to make his entrance.

Jostling through the shoppers, he was only a few yards from her stall when a customer picked up a broach to scrutinise. Liam held back once more.

Reaching down behind the counter for a box to place the purchase in, Tissy did not detect Liam's approach.

He waited expectantly to the side of the stall as she stood up once more and exchanged money for the broach, graciously accepting the customer's offer to keep the change.

Then the façade dropped. With the customers gone, Tissy looked distinctly bored, until her head finally tilted in Liam's direction

Her weary eyes immediately lit up when they finally acknowledged his presence.

Liam's heart began to beat quickly, and his legs buckled under his weight. She looked even more pleasurable to behold than he had remembered from seven days earlier. The auburn hair was actually a vibrant copper-red mix, and her oval face appeared all the prettier due to the revealing ponytail.

But one thing was missing.

The incredible smile.

Her first words to him were brisk and to the point.

'You're too early yet, handsome! I can't break off for you just now. You'll have to go and mingle for a while. I'll shut up shop at midday. Then you can buy me lunch.'

Liam could not help but be amused by her blunt demands. His response was automatic and effortless.

'You might at least pretend to be pleased to see me by flashing me a grin. I kept my promise, after all. Anyway, what if I haven't any money on me to buy dinner?'

Her piercing blue eyes engaged fully with Liam's as more shoppers perused her bangles and beads. Finally, the smile he recalled so vividly emerged in tandem with the increasingly warm sunshine.

'Well first of all, you wouldn't be much of a date turning up skint, would you? Second of all, I can't pay cos I've made jack-all here this morning. Barely enough to cover my frigging pitch!'

Liam laughed out loud.

A gorgeous girl that also liked to curse. He was in heaven.

'What's so funny, handsome? I'm not here to amuse you. Piss off and watch the juggler if you want entertainment.'

Yet again, Liam made no effort to conceal his mirth as more customers shoved their way to the front of the stall.

'Look, you're good to look at but you're getting in the way of my trade. You're wonderful eye candy for me, but a bit of an obstacle for them. If you must hang around, come my side of the counter, will you?'

Without further prompt, Liam re-positioned himself to the opposite side of the table next to Tissy, who proceeded to pat him gently on the behind.

'There's a good boy. Now behave yourself!'

After failing to impress an elderly lady with a mock-pearl necklace, Tissy finally turned to Liam who had perched himself on a wooden casket at the back of the stall.

'Do you want a drink? There's a flask under your feet somewhere.'

Liam declined the offer, preferring to talk.

'Why were you staring at me like that last week?'

Tissy pretended to act dumb, but there was little reticence with her answer.

'Because you're handsome...and I like handsome men. That's why I call you handsome. Simple, isn't it? Right...my turn for a question. Why did you come back to see me today?'

Liam felt himself blush slightly but managed to keep his true coyness well hidden behind a facade of playful sarcasm.

'Because you asked me to. I had a gap in my diary, anyway...'

Tissy placed her hands on her hips and feigned offence with her abrupt retort.

'Oh...*really*? Well...it's *soooo* good of you to fit me in to your hectic schedule! Anyway, how come I've never seen you in my life before last week?'

Liam's attention was temporarily diverted to a tall, pale looking youth who seemed overly interested in the conversation he was having with Tissy. The figure stood against a wall behind a group of shoppers as though minding his own business, but Liam had become very adept at sensing when attention was focused his way.

With one cautious eye on the stranger, he continued.

'I'm here for the summer. Staying with my grandparents in the sticks.'

Tissy could not fail to disclose her sympathy.

'Wow...sounds absolutely riveting for you! You poor creature!'

'Yes…so I've escaped for the day. Just to see you. But I'll probably be in the deepest of deep shit for it.'

'Don't you worry about that, handsome! I'm well worth the risk, aren't I!'

Liam stared intently at the girl, and she duly stared back before crossing her eyes, sticking out her tongue and giggling. For Liam it was idyllic to become lost in her gaze. Her company was so easy and free from constraint. Bravely, he spoke again.

'Oh yes…you're well worth it, alright…'

The tall pale youth had moved from his position near the wall and had disappeared for the time being. More enquiring customers interrupted the flow of conversation for a minute or two. For saying she wasn't taking much in the till there was plenty of interest in her merchandise. Liam had one question that he just had to ask.

'Tissy? What is your real name?'

Now it was her turn to become thoughtful in response. She rolled her eyes and smirked mischievously. Liam's curiosity was well and truly provoked. She stalled on her answer.

'Come on…it can't be all that bad.'

There was evident discomfort in her manner as she pondered the issue of revealing the truth. Eventually, she succumbed to Liam's insistent and inviting glare.

'Oh, fuck it then…my real name is…'

'Yes? What?'

Tissy pursed her lips as the word reluctantly emerged.

'…Patricia…'

Liam sat back. He could not summon a response that fell into either humour or sorrow, sensing that honesty was infinitely the best option.

'So…what's wrong with that? Patricia's a nice name.'

She eyed him with practised suspicion, until she realised that Liam's reaction was earnest.

'WHAT? You mean…you actually *like* the name…Patricia?'

'Yes. A fine name for a woman!'

'Well, I fucking *hate* it! If you ever call me Patricia, I'll cut out your tongue off. Do you hear me?'

Neither could maintain a straight face and exploded into fits of laughter. Liam was now completely taken with this incredulous young woman.

Out of the scores of people of his age in the area, the first and only one he had spoken to was on his wavelength straight away. The chemistry was uncanny, and he relished every second of it.

Having decided Liam to be trustworthy, Tissy quickly became confident in revealing more about herself.

'It was my great grandmother's name. Wasn't I the lucky one?'

'But you prefer Tissy?'

Her temporary look of sternness was soon betrayed by a cheeky smirk of warning.

'Yes!'

Liam was now totally relaxed within himself and leaned back against the back wall of the stall.

'But Patricia is far more respectable. Far more…I don't know…it's just…more impressive.'

Tissy wagged a forefinger in Liam's direction.

'Listen, handsome…it's far too late for me to try and adopt an air of respect. Listen to my untrained mouth! That tells you all you need to know!'

More chuckles ensued, which were halted abruptly by the sudden reappearance of the tall, pale youth at the front of the stall. Liam studied his wild eyes and growth of stubble. He appeared agitated and was dressed like a tramp in ragged dark jeans that hung low off his hips.

Wary, wily, and obviously after something aside jewellery, he edged closer to Tissy to convey his words in a whisper.

It came as something of a surprise to Liam to realise that Tissy and the scruffy-looking figure knew each other.

'Hello, Tiss.'

Tissy turned to Liam and rolled her eyes before emitting an exaggerated sigh of frustration. Liam watched the youth as he spoke, but opted not to intervene, figuring that Tissy could handle her obvious displeasure at seeing the unkempt individual standing before her.

'Hello, Ray. What can I do for you, today?'

Despite the warm weather, the suspicious looking visitor seemed to shiver in his own skin, even though attired in a big black overcoat. He looked ill, certainly under-nourished at best.

'I wonder if we can meet up, today?' he mumbled.

Tissy again glanced toward Liam before declining the invitation.

'No…I'm sorry. I've made very little money this morning. Besides, I've already arranged to meet with someone.'

The youth's attention immediately fixed on Liam, who casually returned the stranger's steely glare without word from under his hood.

'Who might this someone be, then?' asked the man called Ray, still maintaining focus on Tissy's new friend behind the counter.

Tissy looked to Liam again as if struggling to summon an appropriate answer. The hiatus in conversation was unwelcome. Finally, she interrupted the uncomfortable silence.

'Liam's just a local trader. He's new to the area. Listen...come by the house later in the week, Ray. I'll have something for you by then.'

In an instance, the man bid his farewell, but not before unloading a departing warning toward her.

'You've had my cash! I want my smack!'

And then the man called Ray was gone, merged back into the crowds.

Liam did not feel particularly uneasy about the visitor, but he could sense the discomfort that had been awoken in his newfound friend. Tissy shuffled nervously before changing the subject and making an announcement.

'Well, Liam. It's been a shite morning for trade I have to say. I'm ready to wrap up for the day. What do you say to something to eat? I'm hungry as hell.'

*****

It took little time for them both to clear the stall and pack the stock into two battered suitcases. Liam trailed Tissy with a case in each hand as she carried the table. She guided him among the shoppers to a rusting tin outhouse behind the square, the wooden doors of which were secured by a large brass padlock.

Fumbling in her pocket for a key, Tissy muttered an instruction under her breath as she released the doors.

'Just chuck them in here. They'll be safe enough.'

Liam lowered the cases into the murk of the small lock-up. It was hardly the ideal place to safely store her entire stock.

'Will they be safe in here? Whose garage is it?'

Tissy simply smiled at the naivety of the query.

'Mine of course...you dummy!'

Liam observed Tissy's infectious independence as she secured the premises once more.

225

Finding a table at the local diner, Liam gazed through the window at the bustling market, whilst Tissy ordered cheeseburger and chips for two. There were inevitable questions which burned at the forefront of his mind as she returned to sit opposite him with two milkshakes.

'I hope you like vanilla…cos that's what you're getting!'

Liam sampled the cold, sugary liquid through a straw. He was physically struggling to take his eyes off his companion for even a second such was the masculine elation she had unknowingly instilled in him.

'I thought you said you were skint! I could have bought these.'

Her gorgeous features veered closer to him across the table.

'Listen Liam, my lovely. I tell people what I want when it suits…okay? So, stop quibbling and enjoy it. You can buy next time, okay?'

The implication of another date pleased him so, unlike the image of the loitering tall youth at the market. Liam waited until the food arrived before broaching the query. Sprinkling salt and vinegar onto his chips, he could sense Tissy's awareness of the next conversation.

'Who was that guy earlier? At the market? What did he want from you?'

Tissy chewed into her burger vigorously. It was a delay tactic which did not throw Liam off the scent. Finally, she revealed the answer after swallowing the food.

'Look. I'll be straight with you. He's Ray Trencham - an ex-boyfriend. Not a great friend anymore though, I hasten to add. We had a habit together for a while. But he fell out with our dealer. I didn't. I'm clean now, though. However, he's not. So…he gives me money and I go and get his stuff. Okay? Simple, isn't it?'

Liam was mildly disappointed. Tissy seemed far too attractive a creature to even be associated with trying drugs, let alone indulge in supplying.

'Bit risky, isn't it?'

She looked sternly into his eyes as she chewed.

'What…around here? We haven't seen the police for months! It's only dodgy if people open their big mouths. You can get away with anything in this world if you don't boast about it. Get my drift? Anyway…forget about him. What are we doing this afternoon?'

Liam thought it wise to change the subject once more as he watched Tissy place two chips between her lips and offer that smile of all smiles.

*****

The next few hours left Liam feeling as though he had entered a dream.

A world of joyous fantasy.

The storms that his grandmother spoke of at breakfast did not materialise. The skies had threatened intermittently but did not intend washing away Liam's growing contentment. Sunshine won the battle for most of the day.

All obstructive thoughts regarding his own situation were eliminated by his incredibly engaging counterpart. They laughed as they toured the market and mocked the locals. They danced together - Liam somewhat awkwardly - to the visiting band. He observed her natural rhythm and eye for performance. In turn, she admired Liam's guts to have ago despite an acute lack of musical coordination.

Obtaining half a crate of ale from the local pub's unsecured back yard, they covertly drank and became merry down a side alley behind the Council House. Liam won Tissy a stuffed bear on the coconut shies which she cradled for the remainder of the afternoon as if protecting her own child.

Neither secretly wanted the union to end.

Yet only too soon the hours crept by into evening and a dropping sun signified the time to part. Liam held Tissy's hand as they ambled back through the now empty market square. The area was shrouded in silence in stark contrast to the bustling activity of earlier in the day.

Tissy stopped her stride and drew her face close to Liam's. Standing in the shadows, they felt that no one would disturb their intimate final moments together.

'Wow – your heart's doing ten to the dozen, handsome! I can feel it!'

With any awkwardness between the pair long since dissolved, Liam said nothing of his intentions. The temptation had plagued him all day. It was time to succumb to the point of no return. Lowering his face to hers, he kissed Tissy softly on the lips, closing his eyes as he did so. She welcomed the gesture fully. It lasted for a few halcyon seconds which could have been a passing lifetime as the pair entwined.

Then, quite naturally, the moment passed. Reality bored crudely into Liam's conscience, despite the fight to keep it at bay.

'I'd better go, Tissy. They'll be sending the sniffer dogs out if I'm not back soon.'

Tissy looked to the ground as if hearing such words plunged her into deep sorrow. Her gaze rose again as she buried herself into his embrace once more and placed her head on his chest.

'When will I see you again, Liam?'

His emotional frustration preceded an indefinite response.

'In all honesty, Tissy...I haven't a clue. Do you have a mobile phone? Give me your number. I'll call you.'

Dejection befell her features as her focus dropped to the floor once again.

'Shit! It's at home. I don't want to disturb my father. I don't even know my own number anyway!'

'Okay. It doesn't matter. Would you like me to see you to your door?'

She shook her head, causing the copper ringlets in her ponytail to catch the remnants of fading sunlight.

'No...thanks...I'm fine. I'll tell you what, Liam. *I'll* come and find *you* next time. I'll surprise *you*...like you surprised me, today.'

Liam seemed puzzled by her statement.

'But I told you I'd come and see you. Did you not believe me?'

She grinned broadly. Yet appeared far from happy.

'I've not had too many promises made to me in my life that have been kept. It makes a change for me to pledge my time to someone I think I can rely on. Especially when it's someone as impressive as you.'

Liam was flattered for sure, although still a little concerned as to her obvious underlying issues.

'But you don't know where my grandparents live.'

Tissy engaged his attention with a final declaration.

'Don't worry, handsome. I'll find you.'

With a parting kiss on the lips, she let go of his hand and ventured into the growing murk of a side street. Liam stood and watched her disappear down an alleyway before reluctantly commencing his own way along the vaguely memorable route back to the cottage.

Where somebody undoubtedly lay in wait for his return.

TWENTY-SIX

The rains that had threatened all day finally decided to fall as Liam closed in on his destination. Like the evening sky, Summer Place was in darkness as he approached and quietly pushed open the front gate.

He had little idea of the time. He could only hope that his grandparents were sound asleep.

Only then did Tissy's enduring image finally leave his mind to make way for the likely probability of reproach for his desertion tactics that morning. However, there was little time to ponder what might be.

Two hard facts now had to be confronted.

Firstly, that he was probably locked out.

Secondly, he had to somehow gain entry without detection.

Scanning the front windows of the cottage there was little sign of life from inside. In his heart, Liam hoped to see the smiling face of his grandmother who would allow him inside and discreetly to bed.

No such luck.

Yet, suddenly, his emerging despondency lifted.

Tiptoeing around to the side of the house, Liam breathed a mental sigh of relief to see that his bedroom window was open and latched to the sill. It was a sight almost too good to be true. Hauling himself onto the kitchen window ledge, he pulled his weight upward and smoothly fixed a foothold on the bedroom sill before stealthily lowering himself through the open window.

Turning to check the area outside to confirm that his entry had not been observed, Liam then closed the window and familiarised himself with the shadows in the bedroom. The floorboards seemed particularly creaky as though purposely attempting to betray Liam's return.

Feeling carefully for the bed as tired eyes adjusted to the murk, he slowly rested his backside on the mattress and proceeded to remove his sodden clothes.

A sense of inner relief encroached as Liam removed the rain-soaked trainers and socks. Thoughts of the penalty that inevitably lay ahead were temporarily erased as he concentrated on resting his aching, soaking limbs.

He fought the negative potentials to think instead of the wonderful day he had just experienced.

But something was not right.

Something seemed out of place.

Liam's instincts had always been sharp yet were now on red alert.

Then the citric aroma hit his senses.

The distinctive, foreboding scent of cigar smoke.

It lingered silently as a warning ghost, piercing his nostrils as though preparing him for imminent confrontation.

Liam stopped breathing momentarily as his attention slowly focused on the unlit room. His eyes strove to identify various items as he sat on the bed. He recognised the wardrobe and the chest of drawers.

The small table against the wall seemed untouched.

Nothing seemed to be obviously unusual.

All appeared normal.

All except…the chair…in the corner…by the door.

A chair that remained unused most of the time, aside embracing a large cushion sleeved in a white woollen case.

But that was not the situation tonight.

Liam immediately traced the fragrance of burning tobacco to the area in question.

In the next instance, he rapidly assimilated the silhouette of his grandfather, sitting patiently in the chair. The crimson glow of his cigar tip was now highly visible against the menacingly hued backcloth.

Then it came…the voice of doom, in a considered tone lined with nurtured malice.

'You had your grandma worried sick, soldier.'

Liam's blood froze in his veins as the opening statement of Francis James Gould lingered around the darkened chamber. Paralysed by a mix of shock and surprise, Liam's mind failed to summon a suitable response before his grandfather continued.

'Hell…you had me wandering all over creation trying to tail you, boy. But I figured I may as well go help herd them cows alone. Then I'd come right back here and wait for you. I knew you'd turn up sooner or later. Mind you, you missed a hell of a storm at Mawsby. I hear it was dry as a desert where you were, though. I passed on your apologies to my friend. We could have done with that extra pair of hands I promised him.'

Still Liam could not muster any form of reply.

This was a typical build-up to a typically explosive reaction from Fran. Yet his grandfather stayed seated and smoking, encouraging some form of customary retort from his grandson.

Liam remained on the edge of the bed and fiddled for the switch on his bedside lamp. No light was emitted as he clicked open the circuit.

Fran remained on his adoptive throne by the door.

His face hidden in shadow. His voice stark and clear.

'Seems your bulb has blown, junior. I don't have a spare. Shame.'

Liam was puzzled by the seemingly random observation. It didn't have any relevance to the situation.

Or so he thought.

The red-hot tip of the cigar glowed brighter once more, as more pungent fumes filled the blackened room.

The elder man continued with his sermon.

'You have no respect for us do you, soldier? You continue to abuse our good nature and ignore our fair-minded rules. You disappear for a day and don't even bother to inform us of a place or time. And that makes me angry, soldier. That makes me very angry because I thought I taught you pretty well how things work around here. You were doing good, too. Real good. But the message hasn't quite gotten home yet, has it?'

Liam's heart pounded as anticipation now combined with raw fear.

Then he began to sense the move from his grandfather. He grappled with himself for some feeble explanation. Still those elusive words of defence would not rise to the fore. Liam silently cursed the sudden absence of his usually reliable bravado.

However, it mattered little.

Fate was ready to deal with the issue efficiently enough.

In a lightening quick movement, Fran duly asserted his position. Liam was punched squarely on the side of the head and knocked backward onto the bed. He had little time to react.

The murky surrounding of the bedroom evolved to a whirring, pained tunnel in an instant. Under the iron grip of his grandfather, he was then effortlessly tossed over onto his front and had both arms forced high up his back. Facing down into the mattress, he screamed as his shoulders were almost wrenched from their sockets. Yet those cries were quickly muffled as his head was pushed deep into the pillow.

Then…the struggle to breathe commenced.

His grandfather's full weight pressing down on him, Liam was pinned to the bed. He felt a steely palm pressing down onto the back of his head. Liam wriggled for respite from the vice-like trap, but Francis James Gould was once again the immovable object of superior power.

Yet again, Fran had the upper hand.

And as before, Liam's battle to escape seemed futile as his oxygen levels receded and his mind began to recoil. Then his body began to panic in a series of reflexive motions.

As he battled furiously, one arm freed itself, only to be quickly restrained and returned to position.

The agony continued as he felt his shoulder ligaments strain under pressure. He felt as though both arms would break. Liam's lungs pulsed for life, yet their called went unheeded for second after desperate second.

Then as before, upon the point of mortal surrender, the torture ceased.

Joyous air fuelled his grateful body once again, replenishing drowning lungs and fuelling a frantic heart as it regained a steady rhythm.

His upper body burned beyond belief as he slowly flexed his torso and limbs back to something resembling a normal position before rolling onto his back.

Stinging eyes blinked away the onset of acidic tears. Liam drew himself up as he tried to stem his weeping. He stared through the gloom toward the door where his grandfather's menacing form had been sitting only a minute earlier.

Yet the chair was empty.

There was no sign of Francis James Gould.

Or any evidence to suggest he had been in the room at all. Even the pungent aroma of tobacco had dissipated. The large white cushion was back in its rightful place.

Pondering this unearthly conundrum, Liam Warburton gradually dispersed the whipping tide of his emotion and laid his weary head down.

Retreating slowly away from the brief chapter of terror, his mind created a soothing vision of a beautiful girl which accompanied his determination to fend off the demons of the night.

Another lesson administered.

Another cause for hatred effectively implanted.

TWENTY-SEVEN

'Liam, darling. Guess who's on the telephone? Quickly, get up. They want to speak to you! Hurry!'

The previous day's storm clouds had passed over, allowing golden sunshine to bathe the bedroom once more. Liam squinted as his delicate eyes responded to Barbara's sudden entrance.

Sitting up in bed he was given sharp reminder of the most recent encounter with his grandfather. The tendons in his shoulders screamed on being used to elevate his body upright. Then Liam's attention immediately fixed itself on the chair by the door.

Had last night's confrontation with Fran been a figment of imagination? It was difficult to determine. His mind was confused. Yet his body paraded all the evidence in regularly searing twinges around his back and arms.

Aside swollen muscles and some mild bruising, there was little else to suggest that any altercation had taken place. But Liam knew he had been beaten again.

Anger over the issue surfaced as he gingerly prodded the painful areas.

Throwing back the blankets, he sat on the edge of the bed in his underwear. The warm rays of daylight were only mildly comforting.

Then an enduringly brighter image entered his conscience.

The profile of a red-haired girl with the sharpest wit and softest lips. Her face was never far from his thoughts now. Her voice was rarely out of his head. He wallowed in the moment of incredulous placation. The longing to see her again had embedded overnight and had taken a firm hold, ready to embrace his arousal from sleep.

Then a familiar voice again interrupted his temporary distraction.

'Liam! Telephone!'

His grandmother's excited tones echoed along the passageway from the lounge and up the stairwell, jolting Liam from his romantic whimsy.

'Okay. I'm coming!' he mumbled, begrudgingly.

Observing the pile of damp clothes on the bedroom floor, Liam padded from the bedroom in just his boxer shorts and downstairs into the lounge. Waiting by the telephone was the fidgeting form of Barbara, a smile on her face as wide as the bay window of the cottage.

'It's your Mum, Liam! She's calling all the way from Greece!'

Such a strange sensation; the thought of speaking to his own mother. It had seemed an age since his parents waved themselves away and departed for foreign lands, unknowingly leaving him at the mercy of the unknown.

Fran perched silently in the leather armchair by the window. He simply stared through his seething grandson as he entered the room. Greeting Liam with a narrow line of a smile, he revealed no inkling of the thoughts that lay behind the unreadable expression.

With only a cursory glance toward his grandfather, Liam took the receiver and placed it to his ear. The intensity of Fran's presence made him nervous.

Liam's fury gurgled within him. Retribution was uppermost in his head as he prepared to talk to his mother. He wanted to hurt Francis James Gould so badly. But now was not the time.

Though Liam secretly pledged to himself that the time would surely come.

Nevertheless, he remained calm and maintained his position of indifference under the unwarranted scrutiny of the elder man.

Yet that briefest exchange of looks revealed so much to Liam.

Fran had a definitive fear in his eyes. Suddenly his actions and attitude were in danger of being revealed to an unsuspecting world. The pendulum seemed to have swung temporarily in Liam's favour.

He enjoyed his special moment of perceived superiority as the conversation with his mother evolved.

Francis James Gould listened carefully to his grandson's responses, never taking his eyes off the teenager for a second as he digested Liam's instant and unadventurous replies.

'Hi, Mum.'

'Yeah fine…we're getting along…fine.'

'It's okay. A bit quiet I suppose. How's the trip going?'

'Oh…good. Worth going out there, then?'

'No…nobody's phoned me. There's no signal out here.'

'I haven't spoken to anybody, really.'

'Yeah…baking, gardening. Chopping wood every week.'

'Yes. I'm always a good boy.'

'Okay, it rained last night but it's hot again now.'

'Quite a bad storm yes.'

Liam's voice began to tremble as emotion threatened to unveil his true predicament. But he took several deep breaths and maintained composure under the incessant analysis of his grandfather.

His next question masked so many feelings.

'How long do you think it will be before you're back?'

'Oh. Okay. No…that's cool.'

'How's Dad?'

'Good.'

'Okay, then. Speak to you in a couple of weeks perhaps.'

'Love you both. Bye.'

Exchanging a final look with his grandfather, Liam handed back the mouthpiece to Barbara who continued the chatter.

Back in the sanctity of his bedroom, he searched through his wardrobe for clean clothes. Opting for a dark tracksuit top with yellow trim and white bottoms, he examined himself in the mirror.

Fran's approach at the open doorway went unheard and subsequently unacknowledged.

The gravelled voice had softened recently due to the undisclosed and worsening condition in his throat, but still did not serve to ease the trepidation that Liam always seemed to experience in his grandfather's presence.

Fran cleared his airway before commencing the statement.

'You did well, soldier. You didn't squeal. That's good. Perhaps you're learning after all. I'll see you later.'

Liam said nothing, opting to maintain his gaze at his own reflection in the dress mirror. Then Fran was gone again.

Liam's heart pulsed as he observed the elder man from his bedroom window. A welcome sense of peace descended as his grandfather reversed the pick-up from the garage, before cruising away into the rural backdrop.

Relief was the overriding sensation as he underscored his fresh attire with a dry pair of training shoes.

The phone call from his parents was an unexpected yet strangely welcome surprise.

Little did Liam know that the day would soon bring another.

TWENTY-EIGHT

After breakfast, Liam encamped in the lounge, plugging himself into his I-pod. The beat of the music again revived pleasant memories of home.

Speaking to his mother had inadvertently heightened the urgent need to get out of Clearlake. It had become a constant, daily struggle. The unpredictable episodes of violence and unnecessary feuding with his grandfather had begun to weigh unbearably on Liam's mind, not to mention his body.

But Fran was correct in one belief. Liam was no grass. He would deal with the situation in his own time in his own way.

Just as he always did.

The tranquillity of the sunlit scene beyond the lounge window was a pleasant accompaniment to the sound of the music, so much so that an hour passed seemingly within seconds.

Barbara entered the lounge and smiled as Liam's legs dangled lazily over the arm of Fran's favourite chair. He bobbed his head silently to the pumping rhythm. Appearing in his eyeline, she signalled to Liam that she needed to speak, which duly prompted him to remove his earphones. Unusually, he offered a word of concern for her puzzled expression.

'Are you okay, Grandma? What's happened?'

Barbara paused to summon the words.

When it came, the proclamation was initially baffling.

But as the implication of her announcement registered, his eternal shroud of despondency was immediately eclipsed by sudden euphoria.

'Liam. There is a young lady at the door. She wishes to see you.'

Liam's heart skipped as he pondered the hopeful prospect of seeing Tissy.

Dashing through the passageway and upstairs, he rapidly checked his appearance in the bedroom mirror once more. He looked okay. Not perfect by any means, but okay. He noticed his hair was slowly growing and thickening. It had been a few weeks since his last cut.

The hood would remain off today, though.

Convincing himself he looked at least presentable, he ventured back down into the kitchen. Grinning at his grandmother and offering her a mischievous wink, he moved to the open doorway, which framed the beautiful red-haired girl from the market.

Her smile was radiant. Her copper ringlets now loose and free around the shoulders, danced in the sunlight. Her short pale blue summer dress was a most striking change from the denims and woollen jumper she had adorned yesterday at the village centre.

Liam studied her appearance approvingly.

The butterflies in his stomach felt like birds.

Barbara intermittently gazed curiously at the pair whilst pretending to attend to some dishes at the sink.

Liam's mouth hung open at the vision of beauty standing before him. A hesitancy that urged the visitor to commence the conversation.

'Well...are you gonna gawp all day or can I come in?'

Liam heard his grandmother's laughter in the background as he brought himself back to earth.

'Erm...yeah...sorry...Jesus...how did you find me?'

Entering the kitchen, Tissy smirked once more as she fully engaged with Barbara's affectionate stare.

'Listen handsome, when you've a mouth as big as mine you tend to use it for two things: shouting at folks and asking questions. You weren't hard to find. I asked around. A friend from the market dropped me off. He's collecting me tonight at six.'

Grinning from ear to ear at Liam's unimpressive lack of social skill, Barbara felt compelled to offer an introduction, which Tissy duly reciprocated.

'My real name's Patricia, but I prefer Tissy. How are you, Mrs. Gould?'

Liam eyed his grandmother as she responded. He noticed a light in her eyes which he had not seen previously. It was as if Tissy's presence pleased her beyond a will to convey mere civility.

Barbara appeared almost thankful of another person in the house, especially another female. It was good for her to see that Liam had spent his brief time away from the cottage to some positive use.

'I'm very well, thank you dear. So nice that Liam has met a friend at last. I think he's been pretty lonely over these past few weeks.'

Tissy chuckled and patted Liam on the shoulder.

'We met at the market a couple of weeks back. He won't get lonely with me around. I tend to stick like glue to people I like!'

Tissy's hand moved to her mouth to feign a humorous whisper.

'And...Mrs. Gould, don't tell Liam...but I quite like him, you know!'

A knowing glance accompanied Barbara's next comment.

'And I suppose that's where you were yesterday was it, young man? The market? When you should have been herding cattle in the rain with your grandfather?'

He nodded without word. It was evident that his grandmother knew nothing regarding the altercation with Fran on his eventual arrival home. Now was certainly not the time to raise the issue. The discomforting thought was evaporated by Tissy's demanding tone.

'Where shall we go then, handsome? It's a nice day.'

He needed little time to decide.

'Do you mind if we just go for a walk? I know just the place. Let me get one or two things, first.'

Liam left the two ladies in the kitchen whilst retreating up to the bedroom. It was as though instinct compelled him to gather a few vital accessories for the excursion. It required no thought or deliberation.

Delving into the bottom drawer he retrieved some sheets of paper and a couple of pencils. He also made a point of taking the sketches of the swans from a couple of weeks earlier. Grabbing his mobile phone and I-pod, he swiftly re-joined Tissy and his grandmother downstairs.

'Have you got a bag, Grandma? Just want to throw these in it.'

Barbara reached into a cupboard and pulled out a small blue backpack.

'Perfect!' Liam beamed.

'Would you like to take a drink with you? You'll need it if you're walking in this heat. I've a bottle of lemonade in the fridge. Just enough to wet your whistle! Here...take some of these crisps and cakes as well.'

Liam smiled at Tissy as his grandmother packed the bag and heaved it onto his shoulders.

'There you go. All ready for the journey! What time can I expect you both back? There's a joint going in the oven for supper. If you both want to eat with us that is?'

Liam and Tissy smiled simultaneously at the thought of some authentic home cooking.

'I've got my phone, Grandma, so I can check the time. Before six, because of Tissy's lift! Definitely!'

'Well. Enjoy yourselves. And behave yourselves! See you later, then!'

Barbara Gould stood in the kitchen doorway with arms folded.

238

She felt a certain pride in watching the pair as they ambled out through the front gate and along the winding avenue.

The enchanting image recalled memories of Stephanie when boyfriends used to come and call for her.

She observed Liam's cocksure stride as Tissy bounced along beside him until they disappeared among the greenery of the lanes.

The young lady was quite taken with her grandson.

That much was obvious.

*****

'So then, handsome. Where are you taking me?'

Liam looked into the eyes of the gorgeous girl walking beside him. It all still seemed like some vague dream. But she was there for sure.

It was all real.

She was all real.

And it felt incredible.

'Somewhere I fell in love with a short while back. Somewhere secret.'

'Okay, I'm easy. Your grandma's a lovely lady. You're so lucky. I never knew my grandparents.'

Liam glanced across the featureless landscape in search of the first landmark of his personal oasis. He felt unusually content to discuss personal matters with Tissy. There was an unspoken, instant loyalty between them. It had been there from the first time they met. As such, Liam had little hesitancy in declaring how he felt about the subject of his older relatives.

'Yeah…well, *she's* okay I suppose. I don't get on so well with my grandfather, though.'

Tissy squinted ahead as she pondered his statement.

'How do you mean?'

Liam's emotions began to well within his gut. It was the first time he had openly spoken about his tempestuous relationship with Francis James Gould.

He may have been willing to debate the situation openly, but it was nonetheless a difficult prospect to encounter. But he trusted Tissy, even though their friendship had barely begun. He felt instinctively safe in the idea of telling her anything.

When they finally came, his words were concise and clear.

'He doesn't like me. I don't think, anyway. And he's…strict…'

Liam's voice tailed off as his attention was taken to the distant arrangement of trees across the meadows.

He hoped that the conversation would change course, but Tissy watched him as they walked and pressed for some more detail on her companion's relationship with his grandfather.

She could also detect the upset that verged within him.

She reached for his hand as a gesture of reassurance as they strolled.

'In what way…*strict*? How is he strict? Does he shout at you?'

It was an emotive moment. Liam was untried in such legitimacy of exchange. He halted his stride and purposely engaged Tissy's cobalt blue eyes. They smouldered with sincerity and drew him in. He made a point of not physically touching her and pulled his hand free from hers. This particular union comprised only the joining of minds.

'No…no…he never shouts. That's one thing my grandfather never does.'

But Liam stalled in completing his confession. Maybe it was cowardice. He just didn't feel it quite the correct time to indulge her. They began to walk again amid a few seconds of mutual silence, continuing toward the fence that flanked the field.

Liam helped Tissy over the stile before clambering beside her. Tissy's curiosity had been alerted even more by Liam's sudden reluctance to continue with the revelation.

'I don't understand what you mean. Does he have harsh rules? A curfew and the like?'

Liam scrutinized the distant scene ahead. He could not wait to reach the sanctity of the lake.

'No…not really. Not rules as such.'

Now Tissy stopped her own buoyant gait and stood face to face with Liam in the field. He didn't want to encourage her, but the subject was now unavoidable. He could see that Tissy's desire for learning about him had been awoken.

Despite his apparent unwillingness to hold hands, she made a point of loosely holding a couple of his fingers in her own gentle grasp. Her interest was genuine.

'I don't get what you're saying. Liam. What is it, then?'

The hiatus in response seemed to last for an eternity.

Finally, Liam suppressed his inner frustrations and summoned the words that he had fought to hold back for so many days.

'He…he…*beats* me, Tissy. He *attacks* me. He's violent. It's like he wants to punish me for something I haven't done…then stops for some reason and no more is said. He seems to resent me being in his home. I…I don't know what to do about it, aside run away. He's really scared me a couple of times since I arrived here.'

She did not appear particularly shocked by the disclosure. In fact, her slow shake of the head and stern expression indicated a rather contrary response.

'When was the last time?'

'Last night. He was waiting in my bedroom when I got back from seeing you at the village. He tried to suffocate me. On my own bed! It's like a form of torture. He did it before. Nearly dry drowned me. It's like he's keeping me in check every so often. As if to teach me some kind of lesson. I haven't told my grandmother. I can't. I don't think she would believe me anyway.'

Tissy firmly clasped Liam's now shaking hand and beckoned them on through the sun-baked meadow, ever nearer to the enticing arrangement of trees.

'You don't need to tell her anything, Liam. She knows it all. Believe me…she *knows*.'

Liam's confusion at becoming a target of his grandfather's bullying temperament had now only been compounded by the discussion of such behaviour. It must have sounded horrific to a practical stranger such as Tissy, but she somehow understood.

In a way, Liam was greatly relieved to have shared his burden with somebody else. But he could not fathom why he should have so much faith in this girl whom he hardly knew. It was also disturbing to openly acknowledge the evident lack of trust he held in his grandmother.

But he was aware that she would never willingly take her husband to task over his attitude and actions regarding anybody or anything.

Indeed, Francis James Gould was the affirmed king of his particular castle.

Yet Tissy's interest had unwittingly injected Liam with an alternative perspective on the issue. He had a renewed overview. Suddenly, his secondment to Clearlake had adopted a whole new meaning. For the first time in his life, he had made a connection with somebody. It was a placating sensation. The concept of such a spiritual friendship had never touched the existence of Liam Warburton before.

Yet here he was, walking hand in hand in a foreign place with somebody he hardly knew.

And it felt like he had been mysteriously ordained to do so.

The wall of pines beckoned the pair ever closer as they navigated the final field.

Tissy had given serious contemplation to Liam's circumstances. Whilst feeling some sympathy for him, she was also bemused by the fact that such a tall, athletic young man would allow himself to be victimised in such a way, especially by somebody who should supposedly love him.

Liam was brash and brutish on the exterior, anyhow. Certainly, he was someone who gave the impression he could ably handle any would-be assailant.

He was a quandary for sure.

But Tissy's own private plight also rankled in competition with his situation. She had her own secrets to tell. And as they approached the perimeter of trunks and limbs, it seemed as good a time as any to disclose them.

'Do you remember the guy from the market?'

Liam heard what she said but didn't feel totally at ease in discussing her other male accomplices. Yet he was also obliged to display some interest.

'The drug-head? What about him?'

Tissy altered her step to avoid a clump of thistles. She also tried to avoid Liam's incessant stare.

'Well...I told you, didn't I? That I sometimes get gear for him...'

Liam did not interrupt her flow as the anticipation increased.

'...well...he sometimes gets angry. You know, if he's given me money...and I can't get hold of anything...even though it's not my fault. Well, he's hit me before now.'

Somehow, Liam already knew that Tissy might be in trouble with the scenario back at the village centre. He stopped dead in his tracks and faced her once more, placing both hands on her shoulders. His inner fury made him dig his fingers slightly into her skin, but she did not flinch.

'You mean that fucking dirty bastard has laid a finger on you? Just because of his own drug habit?'

His inflamed response to her disclosure caused the emotion to well within her.

Her moistened gaze was evidence of a failing struggle to maintain an outer composure. She looked beyond Liam, to the scene of mystery that lay beyond. It helped distract her from the inevitable.

Finally succumbing to the need for security, she let herself be drawn into his embrace, which gradually tightened around her, enabling calm to prevail over the pair once more.

Silent, aching seconds passed as two hearts shared their mutual battles.

Then the seconds elapsed into minutes.

The haven they had finally encountered within each other was immensely pleasurable. There was no reason to leave the moment until both were ready.

Liam observed the top of her head as she buried herself within his salvation. She may have wept a little. He could not tell. Nor should he wish to know.

Then, hand in hand once more, they completed the final leg of their journey toward the lake. Their honour toward one another had been established. No further words needed to be exchanged.

United by their past, their present - and possibly by their future.

Having reached the treeline, Liam carefully guided Tissy through the dense foliage until they both emerged on the banks of the shimmering lake.

Brushing herself down, she stood in awe at the scene before her. Liam did not wait for her to speak.

His personal promotion of the location was not withheld.

'Amazing, isn't it? This place? It's like part of a dream. Where you can come and fantasize. You can feel anything you want to feel here.'

Tissy admired the picturesque view. She analysed the silver surface of the water as protective brown and green limbs hung all around, preventing the real world from intruding upon the private splendour.

'It's truly beautiful, Liam. I've never been here before. How did you know it existed?'

He drew her close once more, his confidence in their companionship growing with each passing minute. Liam looked into her eyes and spoke with effortless sincerity.

'Something brought me here. I don't know what it was. Or why. Something guided me. Unseen, yet it was definitely there with me. I didn't know this place existed either until I stood here for the first time.'

Tissy's eyes darted all around. Her cutting sense of humour had been absent for most of the journey but made a thankful return to break the protracted solemnity of the moment.

'Jesus! It's damned warm today. Any chance of cracking that lemonade open? My throat is like a legionnaire's flip-flop!'

Liam chuckled as he lowered the rucksack to the ground and retrieved the drink. Tissy sat beside him and guzzled deeply from the bottle, in turn handing it over to him and admiring his chiselled features as he studied the tranquil waters that stretched out before them.

Walking had obviously given Tissy an appetite.

'Are you saving those muffins for somebody else? Or do I get one?'

Liam laughed heartily and handed her the box of cakes.

'Did you come to the cottage to see me or just to get a free picnic?'

Smiling at him, she chose from the box and ate ravenously whilst keeping one eye on her companion. Even though he looked contented, there was still an unidentifiable intensity bubbling away underneath his serene exterior.

'You're an unusual mix of a boy, Liam.'

Still his gaze remained on the far side of the lake, scanning every distant movement on the opposite shore.

'Why? What do you mean?'

She finished the cake and licked her lips.

'That was deee-lish! Give us another drink, please.'

Tissy took another swig from the lemonade bottle and screwed the top back on.

'Well...as I look at you now. So appreciative of what is around you. So considerate. So gentle. Yet, I still sense a darker side underneath. It's as if there is somebody else in there that I haven't seen yet.'

Now, finally, Liam turned his attention to Tissy.

The smile remained in place, but his reply was rather unexpected.

'Would it surprise you to know that you're right?'

Her eyes widened as curiosity fuelled her.

'No, Liam. It wouldn't. I've thought about it since the first time we met. You're a walking irony. You're only showing me your soft underbelly. You're concealing the harder edge, aren't you? And there is a harder edge...isn't there?'

He chuckled again and in distraction attempted to take a swig from the lemonade bottle.

'Christ, you've done this up tight! Yes. You're quite privileged. Normally, I only display my temper and my teeth to strangers. Not my nice side.'

A playful slap on the arm further roused him from the scene around them.

'Hey! I hope I'm still not classed as a stranger!'

Now he laughed out loud. Then he pointed.

'No. Definitely not. Not anymore. Oh wow! There they are. LOOK!'

Both cast their attention across the water to embrace the advancing parade.

The swans honed into view from the shadows across the far bank of the lake. The mother led her family of growing cygnets, with father trailing reliably as family look-out.

'They're just amazing, Tissy! Incredible creatures! They are the *real* reason we came here today. To see *them*!'

Admiring silence followed, allowing both friends time to absorb the scene as they watched the feathered guardians guide their offspring silently across the surface. Liam simply stared in total reverence. But Tissy was not one to stay quiet for long. She smiled inwardly at his childish enthusiasm for something so simple.

'I can see why you like it here, handsome. Keeps you sane, doesn't it? Stops the demons tormenting you, doesn't it?'

The girl spoke to him as though she had known him for a lifetime. Their mental connection was uncanny. It was as though she had always been around him.

And he always around her.

Liam had never previously harboured the need to acknowledge such a close companion. He was always the leader back home. Always the loner. Yet this brand of friendship made him feel spiritually anchored. He allowed his mind to mull over the representation of beauty sitting beside him on the grass bank.

'You're very perceptive, Tissy. As well as very special. And do you know...I haven't even asked how old you are!'

Her angelic features engaged him so. Her fiery ringlets glinted around her shoulders against the light blue of the dress.

'Well, it's very impolite to ask a girl her age. But as you're so interested...I'm seventeen. And a half!'

The swans continued toward them in single file as she mulled over her revelation.

'So that makes you...*nearly* the same age as me?'

Liam could not help but chuckle.

'Two years less.' he mumbled.

'Jesus! I could be labelled a friggin' cradle snatcher! But you haven't really answered my question yet! What is it that encourages your hidden demons to appear then, Liam? Tell me...I'd like to know.'

Tissy glared directly at Liam. She was serious in her request.

He shuffled on his backside and adopted an air of apparent discomfort. She had perhaps probed a little too far for the time being.

'I'll tell you one day, maybe, if I ever find out myself! Anyway. I'd like to draw you this afternoon...if that's okay?'

Tissy offered an expression of earnest bemusement.

'Pardon me? You want to *what* me?'

'*Draw* you. Draw your portrait. Here. Now.'

She seemed almost embarrassed by the idea and put her hand to her mouth in coy retreat. But Liam's expression did not waver. His eyes bored into hers, willing her compliance with his wish.

'But...nobody's ever drawn my portrait before! What do I have to do?'

Liam stood to his feet, shifted position on the bank and squatted behind her. His voice nestled softly around her ears as he placed his chin onto her shoulder and pointed out to the water.

'Look at the swans, Tissy. Admire their grace. It complements your own. Just watch them. Ten minutes. That's all you have to do. That's all I ask of you. Just watch the swans.'

And so, she did as Liam asked.

Liam studied her as his pencil danced across the paper, bringing her image to life. Her expression altered slightly as she observed the cygnets flapping after their mother atop the glass surface of the water. Her face visibly lightened as the family of birds edged ever closer to their usual spot on the bank. She could not help but snigger and turned to observe the artist at work.

'No...don't look at me, Tissy. Look across the lake. I need your profile.'

Sitting with her legs crossed and hands on her lap, she looked every inch the regal lady.

A young woman of distinction.

So different from the brash stall holder Liam had first encountered in the market square.

She may have found Liam to be a curious mixture of mood and emotion, but in truth, he found her to be infinitely more fascinating. Never had another human being intrigued him so. He had learned to peel away the layers of his practised façade. In turn, she had allowed him to do so unto her. The girl captured his imagination to the full, as he captured her on the page.

The swans finally waddled their way from the water, shook their tails in turn and took up their customary position on the grass at Tissy's feet.

Her expression was now one of complete endearment toward the vista. She pointed to the babies and looked to Liam for an explanation, as child would to its parents.

'They've come to say hello. It's what they did last time I came here. They're pleased to see us Tissy. They're seeing if we're both okay. And letting us know that they're okay, too.'

She giggled as the cygnets began to preen their soft, unkempt grey down, fully aware that their father remained ever watchful of the surroundings in the background.

'I can't believe how tame they are, Liam! They have no fear! It's as if they trust us. They are happy to be here in our company?'

'Of course! Their parents keep them safe from harm.'

He smiled and eventually presented her with the fruit of his labours. Tissy sat aghast as she studied the piece of paper. Dumbfounded at the incredible talent that Liam evidently possessed. Her beaming expression could have said any one of a thousand words.

But no words were needed.

Tissy was touched by Liam's romantic tendency. Such consideration was sadly lacking in her life. Liam did not know it as he hunched behind her looking at the drawing, but he had reached the girl in so many ways through such simple yet significant actions.

Again, the young swans captured centre stage as they battled for space next to their mother on the bank.

'Yes…they trust your company implicitly, Tissy. And so do I.'

His words temporarily diverted her attention from both the birds and the drawing.

'It's amazing, Liam. The likeness. Am I truly this beauty on the paper? Others should see your fantastic ability.'

Liam continued to study his work over her shoulder, the scent of her perfume gradually intoxicating his natural reticence.

'My art teacher says I'm good. But I'm not so sure.'

'You should place more reliance on the opinion of others. Not shun their views as unimportant.'

Liam again glanced toward the feathered family on the bank as his mind delved for sincerity in response.

'Self-belief isn't really my thing. I'm not that confident.'

Tissy swivelled to face him and focused with intent.

'Listen to me, Liam. The words of others can give people wings. They can help you climb mountains. Look at what you've done for me in a few minutes! Imagine what you could achieve in a day…never mind a lifetime! You have been given a gift. Don't ignore it.'

The proximity of their bodies had initiated a common train of thought that only encouraged the mutual compulsion. Their minds had connected instantly in the marketplace. Now their hearts were following suit.

Neither needed further reason to wish…or resist.

Tissy raised her hand to cradle Liam's face as he drew her closer.

The kiss was lingering and gentle, yet wildly thunderous in effect.

And conclusive for both parties.

The swans consoled themselves as they buried beaks deep into their plumage. Their knowledge now appeasing their purpose.

Tissy drew away and averted her gaze, only slightly discomforted by her boldness.

'I'm sorry, Liam. I really wanted to. But perhaps it was wrong.'

His heart beating hard, Liam gently turned her concerned features back to face his.

'No. It wasn't wrong. It was nice. It was right. And do you know what?'

Tissy frowned, intrigued by Liam's impending statement.

'No…I don't, unless you tell me…'

He gulped as the nervous electricity shot throughout his body.

Yes, he would tell her. There was no reason not to, now.

'I'd like to do it again…'

Tissy's heart melted at the earnest innocence of the handsome young man beside her.

Yet he was no youth at that moment. Losing herself in him, she held his face once more and leaned toward his ear with a solemn, inviting whisper.

'How much would you like to kiss this woman again?

The union by the lake was complete.

As they lay in the sunshine, riding the wondrous wave of unexpected gain in their lives, certain joy enshrouded the pair.

The swans eventually concluded with their preening, and under the reliable scrutiny of their loyal observers, made back for the water.

The feathered family departed the grass bank for the opposite side of the lake, as two friends exchanged their respectful, loving caution, for intimate, mutual desire.

TWENTY-NINE

The bond that had been augmented at the lakeside needed no further authentication. Liam and Tissy had revelled in one another's company in that place of solitude for the entire afternoon. But inevitably, as the sun passed high above and slowly began its descent, passage of time dictated their withdrawal from the centre of their personal paradise.

Yet even though they walked slowly back to the cottage, now arm in arm, they took the spell of the lake with them.

Both were encapsulated by an aura of enlightenment. Something positive had been ordained upon the pair during the previous hours. The potent image of the swans remained at the forefront of their minds, combined with an inner knowledge that witnessing such simple grace could convey utter delight.

And for both teenagers, the belief abounded that they could return to the life they had temporarily forgotten, armed with a revitalising inner strength to fight the negative aspects they may have to engage again in the future.

Francis James Gould heard the youngsters' voices echoing down the lane as he tinkered under the bonnet of the pick-up. From the open garage window, he suspiciously observed his grandson and the attractive female companion that waltzed after him across the garden and through the kitchen doorway.

Liam lowered his rucksack to the floor and offered the single most cheery greeting that he had emitted since arriving at Clearlake.

'Hi Grandma! We're back. Hey, we did well! It's not even five o' clock yet! Told you we'd be back on time for tea!'

Barbara unsheathed her yellow rubber gloves and dried her hands on a tea towel as she watched the lively duo take their seats at the table. Her expression was one of wary pleasure. Whilst enjoying the affectionate display of friendship between the young adults in the kitchen, one eye was kept firmly on the garage outside as she welcomed Liam and Tissy back to the cottage.

'So…where did you two get to? The lake, no doubt?'

Tissy nodded eagerly.

'It's truly glorious out there! Like another world. You're very lucky to be living so close to such natural beauty, Mrs. Gould. I can't believe I didn't know about it before now!''

'Please, Tissy. It's Barbara. No more Mrs. Gould. You make me sound like a schoolteacher! Okay? Now, do you have time for something to eat? The joint will be out of the oven in twenty minutes.'

She looked across to Liam whose beaming smile and rapid nod made her decision without delay.

'Please, Barbara. Only if there's plenty to go around, though! I'm famished! I only ate three of your muffins! Thank you!'

Barbara turned to retrieve her oven gloves from the hook above the stove and proceeded to check on the state of her culinary efforts.

Liam nudged Tissy playfully under the table with his knee, causing her to giggle. It was unusual for Barbara Gould to hear genuine laughter in her presence. The typical greyness and discipline of the daily routine was suddenly splashed with infinite colour and personality. She was quietly overjoyed that Liam had at last found something positive to centre his days around.

For Barbara also, it was a most pleasant change to welcome another guest into the fold, if only for a short while.

But as was the custom for Barbara Gould and her grandson, the diversity they quietly craved and indeed nurtured at that moment was interrupted by the ever-present sound of authority.

Suddenly the resplendent air was gone.

The greyness had descended once more.

The ominous black shadow standing in the kitchen doorway dispersed the joviality instantly.

Liam observed his grandfather. Fran swayed as he grasped a large spanner in one hand. The elder man found little reason to hold his tongue as he stared at Tissy.

'So...*you're* the reason my grandson hasn't been attending to his domestic duties! A mighty fine distraction, though, I must admit. Pleased to make your acquaintance, Miss.'

Extending a free if oily hand of supposed welcome, he watched as Tissy warily mirrored the gesture.

'I'm Francis. You must be the Tissy of legend that Barbara has told me about.'

Despite having learned about Liam's relationship with his grandfather, Tissy upheld the act of pleasantry as Fran hovered menacingly above her in his soiled overalls.

'Good to meet you, Francis. I've heard a lot about you.'

Tissy glanced across to Liam who had now become visibly uncomfortable. He would not even look at his grandfather as the veiled courtesies continued.

'Really? Not all bad...I hope?'

'No...' smiled Tissy. '...not *all* bad.'

It was evident that the genuine welcome extended by Barbara was not in tandem with that of her husband. He was a bad actor and brought waves of negativity into the room. Having been alerted to his repute, Tissy was instantly on her guard.

'You staying to eat with us, young lady?' charmed Fran.

Barbara interrupted the exchange in an attempt to distract her husband from his obvious irritation.

'Yes, she is, Francis. Now go and wash up, please. It's almost ready.'

Francis James Gould simply nodded and stood back outside to remove his boots and overalls.

Liam detected more trouble ahead.

*****

It was an uncomfortable dinner. With Fran, silent and slightly influenced by intrinsic anger at the head of the table, nobody dared to speak without invitation.

Tissy quickly finished her meal and kept stern vigil on the kitchen clock. She willed the minutes to pass until finally she could offer her excuses to leave.

'Thank you for dinner, Barbara. I'd better be going. My lift will be waiting at the junction.'

Ever the gentleman, Fran opted to break his unpredictable mood and offered his services.

'I can give you a ride back to town if you need.'

Tissy observed Fran's steely expression. Even when trying to be truly sociable, his eyes belied his intentions. He seemed to be a hateful, resentful person. Perhaps lonely. Probably bitter. The chemistry between grandfather and grandson was explosive, even in relative silence.

'No, really, Francis. Thank you. But I'm fine. It's all been arranged.'

Liam also took his opportunity to escape the scene.

'I'll walk you to the junction. Leave the pots, Grandma. I'll wash them when I return.'

Barbara rose to her feet and embraced Tissy with a farewell peck on the cheek.

'Please, call again, my dear. You're welcome here anytime.'

Fran offered Tissy another shake of the hand and a kind word to depart with.

'Barbara's right. Come back soon. You seem to keep my grandson in better check than I could ever manage.'

The young couple exited the cottage and made their way along the lane to the main traffic junction. Liam was the first to express his relief as he glanced behind them to see they weren't being followed.

'Fuck me! I'm glad to be out of there!'

Tissy smirked with a certain reservation.

'Your grandfather seems okay. Perhaps a little intimidating. Was it me or had he been drinking?'

Liam nodded wryly and placed an arm around her shoulder as they reached the pick-up point.

'I've never seen him with a drink in his hand, ever. Well, except when we went fishing. I'll tell you about that episode, someday. Hopefully you won't have to get to know him much better. It's not worth the trouble most of the time. Tissy, I know the phone signal is not good around here, but I'd really like your mobile number. If you don't mind giving it to me, that is.'

Without hesitancy, she delved into her handbag and read out the digits from the display. Liam inputted the number into his contact list.

'Jesus! How weird. This is the first time I've picked up a signal since I've been here! Must be a coincidence!'

Liam rang Tissy's phone to confirm her number.

She laughed as a bail wagon pulled into view in the short distance.

'Probably not! But we've been blessed by the swans now you know! Okay, I've got your number too. I'll have to go. My lift is here. Thanks for an amazing afternoon. I'll send you a text, later.'

A lump of emotion emerged within Liam's throat as they embraced in the low sunshine.

The truck pulled up to the sound of squeaking brakes. Liam tried to whisper as the wagon's engine rumbled heavily in earshot.

He felt like crying with happiness.

'This is going to sound crazy, Tissy. But I feel as though I don't want you to go. Just in case I never see you again. I don't want to forget what you look like. Does that sound silly?'

Tissy placed her forefinger on his lips and offered her assurances.

'Don't worry handsome. I'll be back soon! Keep my portrait handy. That will remind you until next time.'

With that, she climbed into the truck and with a wave, a chuckle, and the blow of a kiss, was away into the distance.

Back to her real life.

Leaving Liam with the real life he decided he no longer wanted.

*****

On his return to the cottage, a menacing atmosphere had gathered momentum. Liam's head was already in turmoil due to the experiences he had been privy to that day. It was all so new and strange, yet so invigorating.

However, the dubious familiarity of the cottage served to rapidly dilute his memory. As did the recognisable snap of his grandfather's voice as he entered the kitchen doorway.

Yet, the kitchen was vacant. The pots had been washed. There was no sign of his grandmother.

Fran was back in the garage, shouting through the open window towards his grandson. He beckoned Liam over with a gruff observation.

'Your grandma says you've been out most of the day with the girl. What did you do together?'

Liam entered the garage to find Fran buried under the pick-up bonnet yet again. The suspicion of inebriation was confirmed as Liam eyed an empty bottle of scotch on the garage floor. So Tissy was correct. He *was* under the influence. A nervous tension filled the air of the arena.

A familiar, clinging pressure that warned of things to come.

'We...we went to the lake. We saw the swans. They're...growing just fine.'

Liam tried to divert Fran's attention from the issue.

'Is there a problem with the car, again?'

Fran lifted his head from the engine and proceeded to wipe his hands on a rag. Shifting position from the front of the vehicle, he slowly advanced toward his grandson.

'Nothing I can't handle. Did your young lady like the swans, soldier?'

Liam watched with trepidation as his grandfather edged ever nearer in the half light.

'Yes...very much. I like it too...its relaxing.'

Now the tone of the conversation took on a sinister slant, as Fran frowned disturbingly at the teenager whilst still rubbing his hands on the dirty cloth.

'Okay. So...we've established what *you* like. Do you know what *I'd* like, soldier?'

Liam's voice would not react to his mind's commands. He could not summon a response quickly enough, aside an instinctive dislike of the elder man standing before him.

There was little time for him to provide an answer to his grandfather's query, anyhow.

'What I'd really like is for you to attend to your duties here before you go waltzing off around the countryside with your girlfriend. Your grandmother needed some help today.'

Liam interrupted Fran's flow.

A mistake.

But he was becoming distinctly bored by the unnecessary brow-beating approach of Francis James Gould.

'She's not my girlfriend. And anyway, Grandma said it was fine to go out. She didn't need me for anything.'

Dropping the oiled rag to the floor, Fran inspected his nails for remnants of grime. He remained still as his visual inspection revealed no blemishes. Yet as he spoke, he did not look his grandson in the eye, maintaining his focus on the palms and backs of his hands.

The tone was low and brimmed with foreboding.

'Do you know what I think, soldier? I think you are a cheeky little bastard. Always taking. Always demanding. Never giving in return.'

Liam was now becoming angry at the unjustified assessment.

This was an argument for the sake of it.

The same old empty, futile argument.

There was no true motive or reason for his grandfather's latest tiresome offensive.

The teenager had run out of patience.

Liam stood his ground and returned the verbal volley.

'Like I said. Grandma had no problem with me going out. So…it shouldn't be a problem for you either…should it?'

Fran stared through his grandson.

Liam trembled with anticipation at what might come next. He could now smell the booze on his grandfather's breath. Yet he felt strangely compelled to draw Fran into the ring. As if he now felt ready for the attack that was undoubtedly springing forth.

Indeed, enticing his grandfather into battle as opposed to fearing him seemed to inject Liam with untold confidence. He decided to increase the provocation to actively encourage the inevitable onslaught.

'So, Fran? What life-changing, Earth-shatteringly vital duty do you want me to attend to? What's so fucking important? What absolutely necessary planet-saving chore have I neglected so fucking carelessly today?'

Fran's mouth visibly trembled as he compiled a response. The anger crashed violently within his soul, but without just cause.

Finally, after a few seconds thought, he calmly conveyed his wishes to the youngster in a barbed whisper as he turned back to the car.

'Just…get the fuck out of my sight, soldier. That's what I want you to do.'

Now Liam's vexation was on the verge of erupting.

He could not abide his grandfather's vindictive attitude.

So unwarranted; so nasty.

So unyielding and unloving to his own flesh and blood.

Yet, a truth had unveiled itself. The dynamic had altered.

Liam now *wanted* the fight.

He had been beaten before and lost all battles. It was time to try and even the score as contrary emotion cursed his train of thought. But it was unusually obvious that his grandfather was not up for such an extreme exchange at that particular moment, despite his acid-tongued appraisal of Liam's newfound friend.

Even more reason for Liam to initiate proceedings, perhaps.

Yet instead, bound by a potent mix of learned fear and deep-rooted frustration regarding their relationship, Liam opted to turn away from the sorry figure of Francis James Gould.

Supressing the inner will to oppose the elder man was a contest in its own right.

Then Liam conceded once again to his rebellious instinct.

He would not walk away and decided to turn once more, lighting the blue touch paper with one more contribution to the debate.

A contribution that Fran was secretly counting on.

'I fucking hate you! You're no grandfather of mine.' Liam muttered, his heart twitching with anxiety.

His half-hearted attempt to return to the cottage was halted by a muffled response from the rear of the garage. Staring back toward the pick-up, Liam observed Fran walking slowly toward him once again.

His voice sounded coarse and gruff because of alcohol.

'What did you say to me, boy?'

Liam did not look directly at the taunting enemy.

But his words carried quite adequately.

'You fucking heard me. I don't need to repeat it. Can I go now?'

Silence resumed as both parties contemplated their next move.

Finally, Fran offered to conclude the exchange.

'Yes. You can go. By the way, soldier...there's just one more thing...'

Liam was in no mood for further lectures. He had listened far too much to this bitter, old man. He had heard more than enough.

Pumping with adrenaline, Liam tilted his head, just as a swinging fist connected with his temple, instantly knocking him off balance and causing him to stumble into the garage wall.

Slightly dazed yet inwardly appreciative of the invitation for conflict, Liam quickly regained his balance, rubbed his forehead and bided his time.

Fran stood defiantly with hands on hips, baiting his grandson with further mockery. The alcohol now fuelled the vitriol as his grandfather laced every syllable with abject distaste.

'Is that your first girlfriend, is it, soldier? Your first taste of womanhood, is she? You sampled that little pussy of hers yet, soldier? Do you think she wants you to? I bet she does...'

Liam regained his composure as unbridled fury galloped through his veins. He clenched his fists, but still did not respond to Fran's jibes, which continued unabated.

'I guess not, then. Do you really think she'd want a numb nut like you messing about down there? You wouldn't have the first clue, boy. The virgin from the city. Never touched a girl. How sweet.'

Liam wanted to shut his grandfather up once and for all.

But an unfathomable respect for the grotesque monster standing before him prevented the boy acting on any desperate whim for immediate retaliation.

'What's the matter, soldier? Need your Grandaddy to show you the ropes where girls are concerned? By the time I was your age I was giving lessons! Well...I tell you something...I sure wouldn't mind delving down on that little redhead myself...'

Liam executed his first assault through the murk of the garage and the brawl ensued.

A wild dogfight.

Propelled by an unprecedented mix of poisoned, flowing emotion.

Fran was strong, but Liam seemed stronger still.

And more willing in the race to victory.

The pushing and shoving and despicable commentary continued for no more than thirty seconds. Limbs grappled as knuckles connected with vulnerable flesh covered bone.

Until a victorious strike ended the vicious argument once and for all.

The trial by combat ended abruptly. A victor had been declared.

Tipping weightlessly through the air in a haze of whisky and mild shock, Francis James Gould suddenly felt the back of his skull connect heavily with the concrete floor of the garage. Head spinning, his eyes rolled to the top of his skull as he struggled to focus on surrounding splinters of light that rained down from above.

Prostrate and reeling from the fall, he vainly flexed his legs to ascertain his position.

One eye socket hurt badly and was already swelling rapidly to the point of closure.

He felt like he had been hit by a hammer.

Yet after twenty seconds of bewildered contemplation, he suddenly began to laugh.

A loud, raucous belly laugh that indicated to Liam that Francis James Gould was not yet fully vanquished.

Yet he could not summon the physical strength or the mental wherewithal to pull himself upward. Instead, he carefully cradled the bleeding wound at the back of his head and gently prodded his throbbing eye.

A feint shadow dispersed remaining fragments of sunlight in the near distance.

The shadow of a grandson whose resolve had been broken.

And then pieced valiantly back together.

A boy who had suddenly proved himself to be an opponent of worth, with one, swift, decisive, telling punch to the elder man's face.

An elder man he should be able and willing to love - not resent.

As Fran fought his increasing dizziness on the garage floor, his throat suddenly lurched and stomach began to wretch in a reflexive, coughing fit which brought the inane laughter to an end.

Doubled up in agony, Fran heaved violently as his body reacted to a premise of incoming fate. As his limbs relaxed once more, he tasted the blood as it dripped from his mouth onto concrete.

And he briefly pondered the fact that nobody was there to help him.

Francis James Gould was alone.

The cause of his trauma calmly entered the kitchen, picked up his rucksack from the floor and went upstairs to his bedroom.

Once inside, he shut the door and placed the solitary chair firmly underneath the handle.

As the grandfather writhed in pained reflection, the grandson sat upright on the bed, listening to the echoing signal of his own personal triumph beyond the window, and contemplating the immediate future.

From another, secluded vantage point, Barbara Gould watched her husband eventually clamber to his feet and stagger back to the cottage doorway.

She had witnessed the latest contest in its entirety.

And whilst not holding to religious faith in any form, she silently prayed to God that it would be the last.

THIRTY

Liam slept soundly. Content in the knowledge that he had delivered a clear message to the enemy. Hopeful that the message had been understood.

Then reality roused him rapidly from his dormancy.

Rubbing tired eyes to focus on the room, he noticed the chair was still in position under the door handle. Evidently, Fran had opted to go to bed rather than protract the debate.

Liam was placated by the fact and swung his legs from the sheets.

He studied his features in the dress mirror. Incredibly, there was not a blemish to be seen. No swelling. No bruising. No tell-tale sign that anything untoward had occurred the previous evening. How he had avoided displaying any injury was something of a mystery. He felt as though he had taken his fair share of punches, but the fact remained that he had not been visibly tarnished by the encounter.

Gathering his thoughts, he pulled on his track suit trousers and carefully debated the next move. As he did so, he listened. There was not a sound to be heard from elsewhere in the cottage. Perhaps boldly showing his face would be the most appropriate action, as opposed to hiding away from any potential consequences that may be in store.

Nervous energy encouraged his heart to pulse once more as he donned a t-shirt and pulled the chair from the door. Barefoot, he padded along the creaking floorboards of the passage which, inconveniently, seemed to be creakier than ever. As did the stairway, despite his gingerly placed steps.

Poking an inquisitive head into the lounge as he passed revealed a vacant room. It was then that Liam heard the floating strings of a nearby concerto accompanied by the aroma of frying bacon.

On reaching the kitchen, Liam was cautious not to announce his presence. Peering through the gap between door and frame, he observed his grandmother, flitting between the dining table and the stove. Brahms provided the music. Liam opened the gap a little wider to try and obtain sight of his grandfather.

Only when he had opened the door and fully scrutinized the room, did it become clear that his grandmother was alone.

Now Liam became agitated at the prospective reaction to what had transpired the previous evening. Deliberating on the best possible approach, the honour of a morning greeting was taken from him as Barbara turned to place cutlery on the table.

'Ahh…good morning sleepy head! You had a good snooze! Would you like fried breakfast or cereal, today?'

Liam fought to respond normally. He grasped between utter disbelief and a slight pang of pleasure. His grandmother's mood seemed particularly upbeat. There was no apparent trace of the expected disapproval in her tone.

In fact, quite the contrary.

'Yes…fried please, Grandma.'

'Sit yourself down, my love. Do you want the whole works?'

She was now smiling at him. She seemed genuinely pleased to see her grandson. Her demeanour was altered somehow. Not that this should have been classed as unwelcome. But it was not the reaction in her Liam had predicted.

'Yes, please.'

'Fried bread as well as toast, my love?'

'Yes, please…if that's okay.'

Barbara began to hum along to the radio as she filled the teapot with boiling water and placed it in the centre of the dining table. Liam quietly perched on a chair and waited to be spoken to. The sudden sense of security he was experiencing may have been premature. He'd been in this position once before. He was prepared to hedge his bets for the time being. But of course, the inevitable question burned away in his mind, and eventually thrust itself to the fore as he observed Barbara tending to the grill.

'Where's Grandpa?'

She heard him, despite the spitting of fat in the frying pan and the incessant radio. Yet the uncomfortable hiatus in her response suggested that all was probably not well.

Liam began to fret once more as the exchange was hit by a perturbing silence. But he was becoming strangely impatient and needed to know the answer to his query.

'Grandma…where's Fran?'

Again, Barbara stalled her reply as she set cooked rashers of bacon onto a plate. Why would she not answer? What was the problem?

Liam glanced through the open front door toward the garden. The garage doors were shut, so Fran could not have been in there.

Placing the small mountain of fried food before him, Barbara's smile widened even further as she gestured over Liam's shoulder.

'Don't panic, my love. He's just showered. He's right behind you.'

The fragrance of Fran's shaving balm hung heavily under Liam's nose. Yet he dared not turn to face his grandfather.

With attention firmly fixed on his breakfast, Liam involuntarily tensed every muscle as Fran's presence temporarily dissolved the upbeat atmosphere of seconds ago. The premise of further friction was unbearable. Thankfully, Barbara smashed the ice that was rapidly forming.

'You were coughing something terrible last night, Francis. Make sure you take some medicine before your eggs. They're nearly done.'

Fran cleared his throat as he edged around the room. Liam was tempted to steal a glimpse of his grandfather's face, but resisted the will, instead choosing to stare through the surface of the table.

The eventual sound of Fran's voice startled him, but Liam remained calm.

'Where is my cough syrup, Barbara? You're always moving things around.'

Still Fran stood with his back to his grandson as he scanned the cupboards.

'It's above the sink on the shelf…where it always is. It's *you* that doesn't put things back in their place.'

Liam listened as his grandfather swallowed some of the liquid straight from the bottle and slowly turned to take his seat at the head of the table.

Then finally, the eyes of the protagonists met.

They stared at one another. Studied one another.

Yet thankfully, there was no hint of intimidation from either party.

There was an unprecedented air of calm between them. Both men could detect a distinctly different balance in the relationship, even though neither had even uttered a word.

It was at that point that Liam caught a full view of Fran's left eye.

Swollen and bruised, it looked very tender.

The signature of a young man's resistance, no less.

Perhaps a lesson taught…and maybe even a lesson learned.

Fran stirred the teapot and proceeded to fill three cups. With each passing second, Liam's trepidation regarding their latest encounter was

262

dispersing. Yet still he could not conjure the appropriate words, choosing instead to pick up his cutlery and concentrate on eating.

Inserting a first mouthful offered Liam a chance to divert his attention from his inner turmoil.

Surprisingly, the feeble diversion tactic was short lived.

'Good morning, soldier.'

It was a courteous gesture.

Softly spoken and seemingly earnest in motive.

For the first time during his stay at Clearlake, Liam felt at ease in exchanging pleasantries with his grandfather.

'Good morning, Grandpa.'

Fran held a puzzled expression as he observed his obviously wary grandson from across the table. Liam in turn continued to chew, whilst covertly inspecting the damage he had inflicted on the elder man. Sheer disbelief enveloped him. The fact that he could cause such a disfigurement to his own flesh and blood unnerved the teenager.

But it appeared not to concern Fran one iota as he nonchalantly continued the conversation.

'How's your bacon, son?'

His grandfather's tone was much more amiable and inviting to a response. But before Liam could answer, Fran launched into another coughing fit. A sound of agony that welled deep from his gullet, ripping the delicate, worn flesh as it rose upward to mask the strings of the radio symphony.

In an incredulous yet instinctive turn of dynamic, Liam thought it appropriate to offer a sympathetic enquiry.

'Does it hurt, Grandpa? It sounds terrible.'

Fran gazed vacantly at the boy's concerned features whilst gulping back a taste of blood. He had learned to conceal his pain from a watching world. Even from the wife he loved so dearly.

But Liam was not so easily fooled.

'It's nothing to worry about, son. It always plays up after my morning run. It'll pass.'

Fran knew that such a comment would not convince either Barbara or Liam, but discussion on the issue was strictly forbidden. On a positive front, it was a pleasant change for Liam to be in such proximity to his grandfather and not feel intimidated.

The switch in mindset was mutually tangible.

It was as though last night's altercation had changed everything between them. Liam couldn't nail it precisely, other than a vague perception of a drastic evolution in attitudes. It was as if each of them had woken up as a different person.

The sociable interaction - albeit limited - was refreshing for all concerned.

A few minutes later the setting down of cutlery onto empty plates signified the end of breakfast. Within seconds, Barbara was on her feet and filling the sink with hot water.

'I'll clear up, Grandma.'

Liam stood and took the washing up liquid from her grasp before proceeding to clear the table. As he did so, he heard the coarse echo of Fran's throat, once more succumbing to relentless symptom. The sound shook the walls, forcing his grandfather to hastily retreat from the room to gain fresh air in the garden.

'That damned syrup does nothing, Barbara! Tastes vile, anyhow! A cigar will sort it out.'

Liam quickly washed the pots as his grandmother dried and put them away. Still perplexed by the events of the morning so far, he considered the lone vision of Fran through the kitchen window. It was like last night never happened. The current aftermath of acceptance was completely baffling.

Yet apparently, somehow relieving to the inhabitants of the cottage.

There was no anger in the air. No sarcasm. And no criticism. His grandfather had said some pretty horrible things in his state of inebriation. But now it was as if nothing had been said at all. Liam even felt guilty as the intermittent glimpses of his handiwork shone like a ripe plum on the side of Fran's head.

But now, he was just plain old Francis.

Not the daunting figure of the recent past.

No longer the authoritative, unquestioned master of the house.

He was simply the husband and grandfather that duty required him to be. Yet the elder man appeared to have acquired a new mystique in the eyes of his grandson. He projected a completely different personality when not trying to impart his misguided wrath.

Standing quietly in the garden blowing his cheroot smoke up into the morning sunshine, Francis James Gould looked a much stronger man for his silence.

But unbeknown to an admiring grandson, this strong man's days were now numbered.

Having finished washing the crockery, Liam tentatively opted to join Fran on the lawn. He approached his grandfather from behind and observed his clean taught physique, which crumbled every few minutes due to a convulsing diaphragm. The copper bangle glimmered as Fran lifted his hand to cover a quaking mouth. The aroma of burning tobacco was pleasant, not unlike the moment.

Yet still the struggle for words continued between them.

Liam felt he should be offering some kind of apology to Fran yet could not quite justify doing so. Irony soon played its part in proceedings however, as the elder man turned slowly to face his one and only grandson.

The eyes of Francis James Gould observed the handsome features of the teenager stood before him. Fran's customary glare had adopted a softer hue. He no longer conveyed aggression. He seemed willing to embrace the vision of the youngster. A gentle voice conveyed the cleansing, appeasing reference.

'Well…you sure shut my mouth for me last night, soldier.'

Liam looked to the perfectly manicured grass at his feet. Guilt was now eclipsed by embarrassment over the state of his grandfather's bulging eye.

Yet Fran apportioned no blame and spoke with no malice as he inhaled again from the cigar.

'Before you go getting all edgy about things…I need to tell you something.'

Liam waited for the toll of the bell. What he heard truly astounded him.

'I deserved it, son. And…I'm…I'm very, *very* sorry.'

The coughing returned to the forefront of proceedings, creasing Fran at his midriff. Liam laid a helpless hand on his grandfather's shoulder. The sixty-year-old suddenly appeared weak and in need of assistance. Not a sight Liam had become accustomed to over the past six weeks.

Within a few seconds, the retching fit had passed once more. Throwing his cigar butt to the floor, Fran straightened up and immediately lit another. Liam still felt it right to stay silent for the moment as his grandfather composed himself.

More words of kindness were then conveyed as he closed his silver lighter.

'Are you…planning to go and see your ladyfriend today?'

Frowning with suppressed emotion, Liam's heavy heart suddenly filled with light at the thought of seeing Tissy.

He felt it timely to offer some honesty.

'I'd really like to. I don't know how many more times we'll get the chance to meet up before I leave. It's market day. She's not expecting to see me, but I'd appreciate the chance to try and see *her*.'

Fran drew deeply on his fresh cigar as he scanned the surrounding scenery.

'I could give you a lift into the square…if you wanted me to, that is.'

The offer was most welcome, but Liam secretly appreciated his time alone. Away from the scrutiny. A chance to study his own thoughts.

'No. Thank you, Grandpa. I'd like the walk. It's a nice day.'

A knowing wince of approval gradually befell Fran's features as he delved into the pocket of his jeans. Retrieving his wallet, he removed a few notes and handed them to his curious grandson.

'Here. Take this. Treat yourselves. You deserve it. Enjoy your time together. Like you say…it might be short lived.'

Liam tentatively took the money as Fran choked once again.

Mixed emotions cursed the teenager's conscience.

Gratitude. Sorrow. Sympathy. Relief.

Each fought for prominence as Liam watched Fran's agonized struggle. He had not really noticed his grandfather's ailment before. Other aspects of their relationship had clouded a close-up view.

'Go on soldier. Get out of here. Away from us old folk! Have yourself a good day.'

With reluctance pawing at him, Liam left the garden. He entered the cottage and confirmed what had transpired with Barbara. Again, she had witnessed the entire exchange.

And she too was now experiencing her own inner conflict.

Indescribable pleasure at what had just occurred outside between the husband she loved so dearly and the grandson she felt she hardly knew. And simultaneously, a creeping fear for her husband's obviously worsening condition.

*****

The bedroom was now bathed in sunlight and warming rapidly. Liam showered and choosing his favourite attire from the wardrobe, he checked his form in the dress mirror.

His heart veritably bounced with excitement.

Euphoria that was about to be shattered.

Confirming he had pocketed the money from his grandfather, Liam then picked up his mobile phone, which as per the habit of late, had been turned off. As he bid farewell to his grandparents, Liam switched his handset on and set off on the trek to the village centre.

Having become resigned to the poor phone signal over previous weeks, the sudden blurt of his message tone startled him. Evidently there was a mobile network in Clearlake somewhere, even if it was very temperamental.

He pulled the phone from his pocket, hoping that Jonka or Elson had decided to send him some crude joke or other. The names and faces of his friends back home flashed briefly through his mind. It had seemed like an eternity since they had played any relevant part in his life.

Then he observed the display on the tiny screen.

He saw that he had missed a call during the night at three-ten a.m.

He stopped his stride and read the adjoining message.

He was quickly transfixed as he saw it was from Tissy.

His heart warmed to the mere fact she had communicated with him.

Yet the text she had sent rapidly made his blood run cold.

Sent at three-twenty-five that morning.

Whilst he had lay dreaming about her, she was evidently indulged in a far less pleasurable scenario.

HELP ME LIAM. I NEED U.

THIRTY-ONE

The sweat soaked Liam's back as he ran along the road. He pondered turning back to ask Fran for a lift but didn't want to involve his grandparents in any potentially dramatic situation now that life at the cottage finally appeared to be mellowing.

He had tried ringing Tissy straight away whilst the signal persisted, but predictably, her phone was off. His mind was now set on getting to the village as quickly as possible. Typically, in such an hour of need, not a single car or lorry passed him by en route.

So, Liam had no other option. He continued to gently pound the full distance, until nearly an hour later, he was finally among the vibrant throng of shoppers and stall holders in the market square.

Drenched in perspiration, he forced his way through the crowd and duly located the area in the far corner of the square where Tissy's stall had previously been pitched.

The space stood empty and lifeless.

Now his concern quickly evolved into genuine anxiety. He turned to face the bustling myriad of villagers, hoping that somebody would be able to help him in his quest.

A couple of traders claimed that they did not recall a girl called Tissy ever holding a pitch at the market, let alone knowing who she was or where she may live. He moved quickly from stall to stall, repeating the question and description of his beautiful friend with the auburn hair.

He felt desperately lost in his quest. After many fruitless minutes spent searching for clues, Liam simply stood amid the crowd and let his gaze wander. Despite being amongst so many, he felt so alone in the mission.

He was required to be by his girl's side yet had no clue where to continue with his search. The frustration was slowly getting the better of him.

The customary fury within him was beginning to resurface.

The Liam Warburton of old was still there in his heart.

Clearlake had taught him so much and made him so different in such a short space of time.

Yet there were still active remnants of the previously bullish teenager that had unwittingly descended on the area several weeks ago.

He was glad to have re-discovered something of the Liam that time had tried to vanquish.

He needed his anger at that moment.

Yet there was a subtle difference in his motive for feeling so incensed.

Whereas before he would become annoyed for the sake of it, he now had earnest foundation for his distress.

And deep down, he believed that reason may possibly be love.

Even though such an emotion was completely alien to him.

Or so he thought.

'You're after the jewellery girl…aren't you, young one?'

The frail voice that disturbed his concentration was meek in tone, yet muttered words of overwhelming solace. Liam spun around to find an elderly lady with white hair, wrapped in a large black shawl. It was a hot summer's day, yet she appeared to shiver uncontrollably in the sunlight. Liam observed her time-worn features as she spoke through a toothless mouth.

'I am right, aren't I? You want the jewellery girl? She has red hair…yes?'

Relief washed over Liam as he realised somebody remembered Tissy. And even more surprisingly, the old lady also recalled seeing him from his first visit.

'Oh yes. Caused quite a stir you did. We don't get many good-looking young men out here. We all remember you, my lad.'

The old woman cackled to herself, but Liam was rapidly becoming bored with the futile exchange of pleasantries. His voice now carried a mark of urgency as he gestured toward the corner of the market.

'Her stall…it isn't there! She's not here today. She must be at home! But I don't know…'

The old lady interrupted his panic-stricken flow with a raised forefinger.

'Behind the church. Dawson Street. Number twenty-one. That would be her address if memory serves. But be wary. She's lived alone with her father since her mother passed on. He's very protective. Doesn't like strangers.'

Tissy never mentioned the loss of her mother. She never even talked about her parents. It added a whole new drama to the impending encounter. Liam simply nodded and rushed back into the crowd. Roughly shoving his way through and incurring several looks of disapproval as he did so, Liam's focus centred totally on locating the house.

269

On finally reaching the church, he quickly ran around its grounds and discovered the street in question. The rusting name plaque protruding from a hedgerow confirmed his correct passage.

With adrenaline pumping through his veins and nervous hope emitting from every pore, Liam jogged along Dawson Street scanning the numbers on front doors.

On finding twenty-one he stopped dead in his tracks and scrutinised the exterior of the house. Although in need of a fresh lick of paint, the red door stood out against the others in the street.

He wasted no time and begun to knock vigorously. The sound resonated between the houses, causing one or two residents to poke inquisitive heads from their own abodes in wonder at who the strange visitor might be.

The seconds passed without response.

Liam knocked again. He would not give up. He thought of the message on his phone. If only he had left it on last night. He could have been there for her. Hours had elapsed since. The lack of knowledge only served to compound his throbbing desperation.

Still his fists hammered relentlessly on the red door.

Yet still no one answered.

Taking a few steps back, Liam scanned the upstairs bedroom. As he glanced up, the curtains twitched.

Somebody was at home after all.

'TISSY! TISSY! IT'S LIAM! I'M HERE! TISSY!'

Nearing the point of concession, Liam was alerted to the sound of a latch being turned. Then slowly, the front door was peeled open to reveal an unfamiliar face.

A middle-aged man, tired looking with a few days' growth of stubble peered through the gap and looked Liam up and down. He carried an expression of instinctive wariness. Liam did not hold back on announcing the reason for his intrusion.

'Hello…I'm Liam…Tissy's friend. I was told she lived here.'

The gap in the doorway remained at a minimum.

The man continued to stare at his visitor as Liam explained further.

'She tried to call me last night. My phone was off. Is she alright?'

Still the man remained unresponsive.

He continued to observe the vision of the worried teenager, whose impatience began to overwhelm the exchange.

'Damn it, man! Does she fucking live here or not? I need to know if she's okay! She said she needed help. *Speak* for Christ's sake!'

The evidence of Liam's undeniable concern finally compelled a response from the suspicious occupant, but in a whispered line of enquiry.

'Patricia lives here, yes. I'm her father. How do you know of her? What is your connection?'

Yet again, relief overcame trepidation as Liam pleaded his identity.

'She came to my house yesterday. We're friends. What's happened? Is she okay?'

The man glanced to the floor and shook his head slowly. Then a noise back inside the house alerted him to be cautious.

'No. No, son. She's not up to visitors. She's taken a real beating last night. She's resting up.'

Liam's heart sank as her father's words registered. His fury now bubbling within, he was not prepared to stand helplessly by for much longer.

'I *have* to see her, sir. Who did it? Who hurt her?'

As Liam's emotions began to get the better of him, Tissy appeared at the door behind her father. Wrapped in a pink dressing gown, her perfect features were now spoiled by a hideously swollen mouth and blackened eyes.

Yet she seemed so pleased to greet Liam and begged her father to let him inside.

'Please, Daddy. It will be okay. Let him pass.'

With great reluctance, Tissy's father finally stood aside and allowed the young caller to enter the hallway before shutting them all in.

Without further thought and with only a brief glance at her injured face, Liam's arms fell open and embraced the suddenly vulnerable young woman that had brought so much light into his previously shadowed existence.

As her father watched the couple comfort one another in sorrowful silence, she began to weep without restraint as Liam's protective hold tightened ever more.

Any remorse or lame excuse for not coming sooner was rendered futile.

He simply pulled her safe and close until she felt ready to draw away and talk.

Liam gently cradled her cheeks in his palms and properly studied the horrifying evidence of a truly savage attack. Exchanging a gaze of sorrow with her watching father, he turned back to Tissy.

The Liam Warburton of old could no longer retain his composure.

'Who the fuck did this to you? I want to know. Now.'

Yet the emotion of the moment continued to constrain her admission.

Liam understood her upset and opted not to press the point. He held her close once more and looked to her father for answers.

'Well? Who? You must know who could do this to your daughter!'

Her father looked to the floor once again and sighed in resignation.

'She was set upon in the square last night. After Eric Hilton dropped her off as arranged. About seven. You can't do anything about it, young one. I told her months ago she was mixing with the wrong crowd. They dabble in bad things. But you just can't tell her. The business is best left alone, son. I appreciate your concern.'

Once more Liam studied the bloodied and bruised visage of the beautiful girl in his arms. The sight of her confounded belief.

Only twenty-four hours ago she arrived at the cottage as a picture of summertime perfection. Laughing; smiling; radiant.

Now that same young woman sobbing before him was merely a vulnerable, battered victim.

Gathering her emotions, she too expressed a wish for Liam to let the matter drop.

But this was a side of Liam Warburton she had yet to experience.

He was not familiar with the practice of ignoring the plight of true friends.

Loyalty was an issue he abided by in the extreme. Yet Tissy would still try and dissuade him from his instant thirst for vengeance.

'It's *my* risk, Liam. I took his money last week. I got let down by my supplier, so he got angry. It's all been my own fault. My father's right. I should have listened to sense a long time ago.'

The culprit whose identity they were attempting to conceal suddenly became blindingly obvious to a streetwise mover of Liam's experience.

'It was him! That Trencham guy! It was fucking Trencham wasn't it? The bloke from the market. When we first met. You told me only yesterday that he gets nasty. *He* did this to you…didn't he?'

Her renewal of tears only served to confirm his suspicions.

Liam pushed Tissy away to engage her attention. He glanced to the remorseful expression on her father's face, evidently crucified by the treatment his daughter had received. Even more so, for the fact that it had obviously been long predicted.

'You can't let him get away with this, Tissy! I'm going to find the bastard. Now!'

Tissy tugged all her weight on Liam's shoulder as he turned for the door.

'No Liam! He's dangerous! You don't have to be involved in my mess! You might get hurt, too!'

'Then why did you try and contact me last night? What do you expect me to do? Sit here and look at you in that state? You don't know the real me, Tissy. I've been a good actor for a few weeks. Nobody does this to someone I care about and gets away with it! Nobody!'

Tissy was now resigned to the inevitable.

Inconsolable, she rushed upstairs.

A stony silence descended in the hallway.

Rage consumed Liam completely as he roughly grabbed the lapels on her father's shirt.

'So...where can I find this fucking animal? If you don't tell me, I'll find somebody that will!'

In the event, there was very little reluctance preceding her father's revelation.

Secretly, he had willingly hoped for Liam to seek retribution for his daughter's injuries. The knowledge that he alone was not capable of fighting his daughter's battles was almost shameful. But he dearly wished that Liam would act on his behalf.

'The Malt House. The inn on the main square. He'll be with his mates, no doubt. Even at this hour of the day. He's a soulless sort.'

A further warning from Tissy's father was accompanied by a pointed forefinger as Liam pulled open the front door.

'Be careful, son. He has no conscience when it comes to hurting folk.'

The teenager stepped onto the pavement before briefly glancing back at the forlorn looking figure in the doorway.

His departing words left Tissy's father inflated by silent gratitude.

'Yeah? Me neither!'

The large double doors of the Malt House Inn had been propped fully ajar to allow air to circulate around the room. The occupants had been drinking since the premises opened for business almost an hour earlier.

Liam sauntered to the bar and pulled his hood further over his brow.

He then turned to study the activity around the pub lounge.

In a corner snug, an elderly couple sipped halves and played cards.

A man in a cloth cap with a scruffy looking mongrel at his feet perched on a stool at the other end of the wooden counter.

In another corner, a gang of young men bantered, colluded, and conspired, with intermittent revelations about their recent dubious exploits. It was this part of the room that drew Liam's attention.

The conversation was loud, lewd, and littered with profanity that echoed around the lounge and into the street beyond.

The men were indeed a daunting spectacle to the casual observer.

Already mildly inebriated despite the early hour, Ray Trencham held court with his misguided gaggle of disciples.

Anyone overhearing their discussion would have been repulsed, as the finer details of his latest triumphs were relayed to the group. Awful phrasings representative of terrible deeds. Including one such tale about a pretty young girl who had failed to deliver on time and paid a heavy price for that failure.

The group listened to the toxic diatribe for a good five minutes, silently appreciative of the master in their midst. This feeble excuse for a man conveyed his supposed boldness by professing to issue a repeat of the treatment if the pretty young girl in question did not produce the goods by the end of today.

It was an unpleasant lecture in brutality.

Not for the ears of the feint hearted.

And a chronicle of violence that served to remind Liam Warburton of his own frailties, as he moved position and stood silently in the open doorway, listening intently to every last word.

The bartender observed the imposing silhouette of the stranger as the backdrop of shoppers heaved en mass behind him.

Confrontation was imminent.

It was only a matter of time.

Liam had found his man.

Now all he needed to do was choose the moment to strike.

The hideous laughter continued from the corner, with none of the group aware that they were now under scrutiny.

Liam's adrenaline flow was at its most empowering, so much so that the thought briefly crossed his mind that he hadn't felt such a sensation since leaving Talworth a few weeks earlier.

The desire to inflict pain ruled him totally.

Without moving from his covert position, Liam eyed a glass ashtray on the nearest table. It looked sturdy enough for the intended purpose, but also old enough to be carrying a few useful rough edges.

He watched as Trencham emptied his beer bottle down his throat and encouraged the gang to join in a tasteless chant before buying the next round of drinks.

Liam could barely stand to hear any more as he watched the merry party ensue. He tried to decipher the continuing conversation within the throng but could not ascertain it clearly.

Unbeknown to the participants, it seemed to be misguided celebration, for sure.

But now it mattered little.

An image of Tissy's bruised and battered face brought the stakeout to an end.

It was time to launch the assault.

Liam grabbed the ashtray and moved swiftly toward the group without further thought or word.

None of the merry throng saw him coming.

Subsequently, not one of Trencham's companions could react in time to stop their leader's head from being wrenched violently back by the hair, in turn almost dislocating it from the upper vertebrae in his neck.

In fearful, stupefied astonishment, Trencham's four accomplices sat vacantly by as their adopted messiah was rendered totally powerless by one swift finger punch to the throat. Already gasping for air, he was then winded completely with a second, excruciatingly timed kick to the ribcage.

In only three moves the enemy was down and convincingly beaten.

He was also clamouring desperately for oxygen as Liam casually kneeled over him and placed the jagged ashtray to his eyeball.

Now completely disorientated and defenceless, Ray Trencham quivered like a child under the assailant's guard.

No more laughter. No more chanting. No more idolisation by his companions. The opponent was rendered completely vulnerable and at the mercy of a mystery attacker. Resistance was futile.

Liam Warburton had ruthlessly imposed himself on the scene and had controlled it within seconds.

The glass was pressed further onto Trencham's eye socket, just waiting to gouge into the flesh should it be deemed necessary.

And after the actions, must come the words.

Now it was time to speak calmly to his unwitting victim.

The dominance Liam exuded felt so good to his soul.

It had been such a long time since he had worn such a mantle of strength.

Playing to a captive audience was an art he thought he had forgone.

But they all listened wide-eyed and open-mouthed to every word of the warning that followed.

'You don't know me. But I know who you are and your pond-life mates. We have a mutual acquaintance. The girl you attacked last night.'

Trencham's terror-stricken face showed a brief flicker of recognition, but incredibly, his voice remained aloof and arrogant as he panted.

'She fucking deserved it, man! She took my money.'

Wrong response.

The connection of knuckles with cheekbone resonated with a cracking sound that lingered around the room. Still Trencham's friends stood back and did nothing, as blood began to ooze from their illustrious leader's mouth.

'And you deserve *this*…my friend.'

Another punch landed squarely on Trencham's nose as he stared upward, in turn splitting the bone across his face. Now blood poured everywhere, beginning to choke the sprawling, quivering prey that Liam held firm within his grasp.

Yet this sense of supremacy that he had so dearly missed, he also slowly began to abhor as he towered above his disabled, whimpering quarry.

Despite having won the contest without a hint of hesitation, Liam suddenly felt a strange pang of inner remorse over his actions. A wave of guilt flashed through his mind as disturbing images of the past flickered through his conscience.

The fear he had imparted in this moment encouraged another upsetting vision of Tissy.

Then Liam's mind turned over his own sufferance at the hands of his grandfather. How Fran had held him down just long enough to scare the life from his cowering form.

Then another face honed into view.

The familiar features of a friend he had not thought about for so long. Glendin's customary smile was suddenly eclipsed by his tears.

Then in turn by anguished pain.

Then, by eventual loss of his life as darkness enshrouded the image.

Liam's attention reverted to the pathetic, wounded figure that lay at his feet, writhing and moaning in his own mess. His glance then lifted, to observe four terrified young men who could not believe the unremitting punishment they had just witnessed.

Yet this was a dish of revenge, served ice cold.

The thunderous flashes of regret did not cloud Liam's judgement as he tossed the ashtray aside which shattered against the wall and then he looked down to the heaving, buckled form that was once the mighty Ray Trencham.

'If you ever so much as *look* at Tissy again, I'll be back to find you. And when I find you, you'd better see me coming. Or I'll take your last breath away. You...*fucking...lousy...cunt...*'

Three more kicks to the gut accompanied each of Liam's final three words, which induced screams of agony that perished the walls of the pub and penetrated to the square beyond.

Yet hardly anybody heard those screams.

Certainly, nobody saw the perpetrator of the punishment.

He was away from the scene, running as fast as his legs would carry him. Along the silent country lanes once more.

Back to being alone with a toiling mind.

A mind that had enjoyed its last foray with the nonsense of such brutal action.

No more did the adrenaline spur Liam on.

Now it shrouded him in dread to his very core.

The parting thought entered his mind as he scampered frantically from the village centre, that he was also running away from the ghosts of his former life.

And away from the person he once was.

A boy who in his young life had perpetrated a personal inventory of violence.

A legacy of sufferance unto others.

A boy who now so wished it had could have been otherwise.

THIRTY-THREE

His grandparents seemingly suspected nothing of the fracas in the village. Liam maintained a low profile in the days that followed. The possibility that the police may have become involved gradually diminished with time. The cottage was secluded in location. In truth, only Tissy knew that he was staying there, anyway. The luxury of such remoteness was now taking on an all-new dimension.

But Liam now felt lost inside. He had exerted a terrible retribution on behalf of somebody that in truth, he hardly knew. Yet he cared so deeply about the girl. The contradiction was sheer torture.

The quandary of wanting to return to Tissy's home was fraught with danger. Yet staying away was proving just as difficult to reconcile.

In trying to assist someone, he also felt that he had lost them forever. He felt repulsed by his actions, yet also confident that he had committed a virtuous act.

But he was not alone in his torment.

Liam's inner struggle had been identified long ago by a man who himself had undergone many conflicting thought processes throughout his life.

A strong man, who had been honoured for a life's work in believing he was acting properly through duty and within accepted rules.

Francis James Gould knew more about loss than most men would ever know.

Loss of friends.

Loss of identity.

Loss of conscience.

He saw very familiar symptoms in the grandson that had come to stay with him over the past few weeks. He had maintained a distant eye on the growth of the youngster in readiness for their eventual, inevitable reunion.

Liam's secondment to Clearlake had been a vital learning curve for the grandfather and the grandson.

Both were deeply passionate.

Consequently, both were vulnerable.

Both were in fear of the characters they had presumed to become.

Fran approached Liam one afternoon as the teenager sat on the outer wall of the garden, vacantly scanning the vacant road for a sign of life. He had noticed a distinct unease in his grandson's temperament over the previous few days.

It concerned him that such a feisty young man should be troubled so.

It also worried him that he might just understand the reasons for Liam's despondency.

Fran perched next to his grandson and followed his gaze up and down the junction for a few seconds. Finally, Liam accidentally caught his attention. They stared at one another as Fran lit up a cigar.

'You've been quiet of late, soldier. Something bothering you?'

Liam's expression betrayed a certain reluctance to answer his grandfather's query. He bowed his head and stared at his feet.

'If you're worried about that ass hole you popped off his throne last week…don't be.'

Now Liam looked astonished, as well as mildly amused by Fran's laid-back analysis of the beating of Ray Trencham.

'Yes, soldier…I heard all about it. I have contacts, you know. It's the latest buzz about town. The big man brought to his knees at last…by a fearless young stranger, apparently. Of course, I didn't let on I knew it was you. The Godfather of Clearlake got himself taught quite a lesson by all accounts.'

Liam could not summon any sense of achievement regarding the situation. He had hoped to forget the entire episode completely. Yet his grandfather's next comment swiftly changed his entire outlook.

'They're pretty proud of you, youngster. In the town, I mean. That vile motherfucker has had it coming for a long time. Guess he picked the wrong girl to mash up, eh?'

Still Liam offered no response.

He continued to stare vacantly into the uncertain future. The scent of burning tobacco was soothing. It was the reliable, aromatic signature of Fran's presence.

'I'm proud of you too, soldier. Not only for what you did…but *why* you did it. True friendship is a rare thing. It's admirable that you show your compassion for the friends you've made.'

Liam could not look Fran in the face. The emotion began to stir memories of so much that had happened in his recent life. Particularly regarding the death of Glendin. The awful things he had done. And the praiseworthy things he had not done. The teenager became full of pained regret at that moment.

Yet the words of his grandfather went some way to easing that remorse.

And there was more comforting appraisal to follow as Fran studied the empty road and continued to enjoy his smoke.

'It's hard, aint it, son? Being of a destructive nature, I mean. I should know. That's all I've ever done is hurt people. Physically, mentally, emotionally. I've crushed many a soul in my time with the decisions I've made. The words I've spoken. The action I've taken. Lost many good friends through my principles and my personality. Take this bangle I wear. Belonged to a fellow officer who died in my arms on the battlefield. I've never taken it off. It reminds me of who I no longer wish to be. I've had to fight with my true self since I was your age. Always resentful. Always spiting others. The only one who stuck by me is that little lady I married. And God knows why she's hung around. All I ever seem to do is disappoint.'

Liam sensed his grandfather's tone becoming gradually uneven.

Whilst still beholding a low, gravelled consistency, it could not hide the fact that Fran's façade of assumed superiority was beginning to falter.

He became transfixed by the veiled confessions of the elder man sitting next to him on the wall. It was the most constructive conversation that the pair had ever had.

Drawing again on his cigar and examining the glowing tip, Fran then observed a departing magpie that shot from the tree line as he pondered his next statement.

'It's damned hard, soldier. Living with yourself. When every time you look in the mirror you despise the reflection. Don't be like me, boy. Choose a different path. While you're young. Don't leave it too late. Don't inflict your own failings on an unsuspecting world. It doesn't work. The problem won't cure itself like that. You must solve yourself from the inside. In your own heart; in your own mind. Sort it out in there. Not on the streets, by spilling someone else's blood. Because one day, that pool of blood will be your own. There's always a stronger fighter around the corner. I guarantee it. And I wouldn't like to think of my only grandson walking headlong into such a thing.'

Liam wiped his moistened eyes and fell into the waiting embrace of his grandfather.

They held one another tightly on the garden wall.

Liam nuzzled into Fran's protective shroud, as two minds finally met as one.

Barbara kept a silent vigil from the cottage doorway.

The sight playing out before her eyes brought immeasurable comfort to her breaking heart. Her husband, finally displaying his love for a grandson he had hardly seen and hardly knew.

Yet now, strangely, apparently seemed to understand so well.

But she also acknowledged the true significance of the embrace on the garden wall.

It was a profound moment that the two men would never be able to indulge in again.

The sound of a distant car engine disturbed the pair from their tender solace. The noise came and went past the main junction.

Liam slowly lifted his head and looked into Fran's eyes.

'Grandpa…you're crying…why?'

Fran rubbed his eyes to clear his vision before a forced smile eventually emerged.

Taking a final puff of his cigar, he placed a hand on Liam's cheek.

'All soldiers cry at some point, son. All soldiers cry. Now. I think I know what you'd like to do…and where you need to be.'

His grandfather's perception was precise and timely.

'I have to see Tissy again, Grandpa. I want you to take me to her. Please.'

Fran delved with affection into the sufferance of his grandson.

'Go wait by the pick-up. I'll let your grandma know what's happening.'

*****

It was with immense reservation that Liam knocked tentatively on the front door of number twenty-one, Dawson Street. His grandfather had parked discreetly around the corner.

As expected, there was no immediate answer.

Liam rapped more assertively a second time, in turn glancing up and down in anticipation of an unwelcome interruption. Finally, the door opened, revealing the weather worn features of Tissy's father. Understandably, he looked extremely wary of the unexpected visitor.

Liam's instinct suggested that all was not well.

'Hello, again, sir. I've come to see your daughter. Is she getting better?'

The man shook his head slowly, as though dismissing a complete stranger.

'I'm sorry, son. She's not here. I believe she's staying with her aunt on the coast. She thought it best to be out of the area, what with the Trencham business and all. Besides, if you're capable of putting a grown man in intensive care, I dread to think what you'd do to *her* in anger. I've had enough of the hatred and the violence. I'm washing my hands of it all. Goodbye, son.'

The door began to close, slowly inducing Liam's latent temper.

Obstructing the door with his foot, he demanded further explanation.

'Did Tissy honestly say that? Did she say she feared me because of what I did? Is that why she hasn't tried to phone me?'

Tissy's father glanced up and down the street beyond Liam's shoulder, as if cautious that the youngster's presence might drum up further trouble.

'It doesn't matter what she said, son. You won't be seeing her again in a hurry. And that suits me just fine. Like I said…goodbye!'

Her father tried to close the door again, forcing Liam to use his arm in an attempt to keep it open.

'This isn't fair! I *must* see her again! You can't just hide her away from me! When will she be back?'

Now her father's tone became laced with an impatience of his own.

'Listen here, boy! It wasn't my decision for her to go without as much as a word to you! It was her choice and hers alone! She doesn't want any more problems. She's had her fill of mindless bullies!'

Liam slammed on the door with the bottom of a clenched fist.

'Is that what you think I am? Is that how she looks on me? A bully?'

Tissy's father wearily observed the seemingly lost cause standing before him.

'Young man…what I think of anything don't mean jack to anybody. She's gone and that's that! And she's left her phone here so no one can reach her. I'm sorry. I can see that you're upset about it. But I can assure you that you're not as upset as I am. So long and good luck!'

With that, Liam surrendered his increasingly desperate position as the door affirmatively closed in his face.

Now completely lost for direction, Liam ambled back to his waiting grandfather around the corner.

He felt empty once more.

How he so desperately needed to see her again.

If only to confirm that their friendship had survived the recent trauma. Or, unthinkably, if it had perished.

Her face would not leave his conscience.

He shut his eyes and there she remained, fully occupying his mind and tormenting his spirit.

He could think of little else.

He hoped that she in turn, wherever she was hiding, might possibly be thinking about him also.

Such simple knowledge would placate him for the rest of his days.

Yet sadly, as he wearily pulled himself into his seat beside Fran, a breaking heart was the only remaining evidence that he had ever encountered the beautiful girl from the market at all.

IV
REDEMPTION

The skies above Clearlake had adopted an unusual, yet appropriately darker tone on the morning that Barbara Gould delivered the news.

Liam had spent a couple of hours cleaning the pick-up with his grandfather and the pair of them had their heads under the bonnet examining various mechanical aspects. The younger man listened intently to Fran's explanation of the finer workings of the modern combustion engine, whilst asking his own questions in response.

Liam had managed to concentrate on being positive during the past week. Fran was more than determined to assist his grandson in trying to overcome his recent difficulties. In truth, the relationship between them had blossomed beyond anybody's expectations in the space of a short few days.

They were enjoying each other's company in the remaining time they had. The benefits were mutually satisfying.

Unfortunately, that time together was to become suddenly finite.

Barbara scampered quickly across the lawn and stopped at the open garage doors.

'Francis! Liam! I've something to tell you both. Can you come outside for a moment?'

After much mumbling and fumbling, both men emerged from the murk rubbing their hands on oily rags. Fran smirked as he nodded to his grandson.

'What's so urgent, Barbara? We were just about to clean the air filter!'

Liam watched as his grandmother clasped her hands together in excitement. Taking a deep breath, she almost burst before relaying her news.

'Guess who just called on the telephone?'

Both men looked vacantly at one another before urging Barbara to continue.

'Stephanie!' she shrieked.

There was no reply from either Liam or Fran.

'Stephanie! Your daughter, Francis! Remember? Your mother, Liam? Don't tell me you've forgotten her already!'

Fran's features furrowed as he briefly glanced at his grandson and reverted his bemused gaze to his wife.

'Well?'

Barbara was temporarily puzzled by her husband's reply.

'Well *what*, Francis?'

'Well…what did our daughter telephone for?'

In his heart, Liam already knew.

But the last thing he wanted to hear at that moment was the cutting truth.

'They're home! Back from Greece! Back in Talworth! And they wanted to know if their son is ready to go home yet?'

With a scowl of disapproval, Fran diverted his focus and inspected his hands and nails for stubborn dirt.

'Well…ring her back and tell her no, he's *not* damned well ready to go home, yet! And I apologise for the curse, but it was no accident!'

Barbara chuckled at her husband's bluntness.

'Francis! That's the first time in an age that I've heard you swear!'

'Well? I'm allowed one little one now and again, aren't I?'

Liam's astonishment spread broadly across his face, but the amusement was short lived as Barbara conveyed arrangements.

'Well, he'd better be ready the day after tomorrow, because that's when they're going to be here for him!'

She engaged with her grandson's disgruntled features in expectancy of some celebratory reaction.

But it was not forthcoming from either Fran or Liam.

Both continued to wipe their hands, evidently disappointed by the fact that the summer for them was soon to be over when it had truthfully only just begun. Both men retreated across the lawn, both a little sadder for hearing what Barbara had told them.

'Well don't' shoot the messenger, boys! I thought you'd be pleased!'

Fran threw his rag to the ground in mild temper as he threw a reply over his shoulder.

'What the hell is there to be pleased about? I'm going to lose my grandson again. Why the fuck would I be happy about that?'

Rendered speechless by her husband's outburst, Barbara felt little alternative but to return to the kitchen.

Liam leaned on the hood of the pick-up.

He could not summon words to summarise his immense disappointment.

The symptoms of recent previous heartache now returned and crushed the optimism Liam had nurtured for the past few days as his grandfather re-joined him back into the garage.

It was a premise that would have encouraged exaltation eight weeks ago.

Now the notion of leaving Summer Place supplied him with nothing but relentless upset.

THIRTY-FIVE

It was a sight that almost made Liam feel sick to his stomach as he peered undetected through the curtains of his bedroom window.

He watched as the car approach, slow down and park in the road beyond the cottage.

He resentfully observed the two occupants in the front as they slowly emerged onto the pavement.

Tanned, smiling and evidently successful in their business dealings abroad. He saw them wave as the elderly lady rushed through the open gate to embrace her daughter, then in turn, her son-in-law.

Everybody seemed to be happy.

Everybody but Liam Warburton, whose world was about to collapse around him. The foundations that had taken a summer to construct were now about to crumble like sand.

Despite finding the situation completely untenable at the outset, he had grown to love the rural haven that had been his home for two months.

He did not wish to leave Clearlake.

At least, not just yet.

He had loose ends to tie up, not least with his grandfather, who had opted to seclude himself in the lounge with a newspaper for the morning.

Sitting on the edge of the bed, Liam studied the suitcase and large holdall by the door. His grandmother had cleaned, ironed and packed his clothes for him in readiness for departure.

But Liam was anything but ready to depart.

Reluctantly he pulled the bag from the floor and swung it over his shoulder before dragging his disillusioned form along the creaking outer passage with the suitcase. As he passed the open lounge door at the bottom of the stairs, he poked his head through the gap to announce to Fran that his parents had arrived.

The elder man did not shift his attention from the page.

He simply nodded and uttered a reply under his breath.

'Fuck.'

Being reunited with his mother and father was mildly tolerable, but Liam could not lift the pain from his heart.

The pain that would have to travel back with him to Talworth.

A pain that he may never have chance to extinguish.

Summoning his manners, Fran rose from the lounge chair and stood in the doorway of the cottage.

He watched the apparently joyous scenario play out between his family, but for him there was little personal satisfaction to be derived from the spectacle.

Stephanie's beaming smile carried across toward her father, who welcomed her eventual embrace with an indescribable emptiness.

'You okay, Daddy?'

Fran forced a smile to placate the eager audience.

'I'm fine, honey. I'm just fine.'

'How has he been?'

Fran gazed at the despondent figure of his grandson standing by the gate and nodded slowly, fighting to constrict the welling emotion in his throat.

'Stephanie...your son...is a fine, upstanding young man. It's been...a total pleasure.'

She looked into her father's eyes. It was as though he wanted to convey far more in those few seconds of intimacy, but the moment had gone.

Fran again looked away from his daughter and briefly observed Liam's forlorn expression. He became inwardly annoyed. His tone boomed across the garden, interrupting the upbeat mood and interaction.

'So, how was Greece? Prosperous, no doubt?'

Stephanie hesitated before responding. She detected the usual disapproval in her father's tone. But she couldn't ever identify a reason for it, aside from his long-standing distrust of her lifestyle.

'Yes, Dad. It went very well. We're doing...really...well. Thanks.'

Barbara offered to feed the throng before they embarked on the return leg of their journey.

'No thanks, Mum. Just a quick drink, please. Richard and I need to be back in Talworth by tonight. We've got to catch up on our paperwork. You know. Stuff like that.'

An uneasy silence descended upon the kitchen dining table as Barbara prepared a pot of tea for the travellers. Nobody saw any good reason for protracting the farewell. No sooner had the tea been consumed, it was time for the Warburtons to bid their goodbyes.

Fran moved slowly behind the group as they shuffled back out toward the car.

He offered a hand of congratulations to Liam's father, whose responsive smile was rather misguided.

'I'd like to wish you all the very best for your life of impending wealth, Ricky! You smell great already!'

Liam smirked once more at Fran's barely concealed sarcasm, although Barbara offered a rather disapproving stare in response to her husband's feigned ignorance.

Parents embraced their offspring as the car became occupied once more. The raw of the ignition supplied a disarming backdrop to the inevitable upset.

Liam bent down slightly to kiss his grandmother delicately on the cheek.

'Thanks for everything, Grandma.'

'Be good, Liam. I'll miss you. I hope you'll come back soon.'

Liam nodded, his emotions verging on eruption as he reluctantly turned to his newfound mentor.

He could offer no words of summary to his waiting grandfather.

As such, the moment proved to be too much to contain within his heart.

And he let his tears fall without semblance of embarrassment.

There was only true sorrow for the fact that he felt the need to cry at all.

Fran pulled a distraught grandson into his tight embrace as Stephanie watched completely dumbfounded from the car passenger seat.

The union between generations was long, warm and close.

Close enough, warm enough and long enough to calm the young man's internal storm.

Close enough, warm enough and long enough for Fran to retain the precious memory for his remaining days.

The final whisper between them was earnest.

'Take care, my strong, strong soldier. And don't be afraid to change. Don't make my mistakes. You promise me that much.'

The departing message into his grandson's ear was of vital significance for two very important reasons.

Sixty years of experience; a lifetime of lessons learned, now imparted into the mind of a once misguided youth.

And unbeknown to the stricken teenager at that moment, as he clambered into the car behind his parents.

He had heard the last words he would ever hear from Francis James Gould.

Loving grandparents waved their family goodbye from the front gate of the cottage as the car began to roll slowly away along the tree-lined lanes, and finally out of sight.

Liam strained his neck from the back seat, engaging with the scene of the cottage before his last glimpse of that old stone house disappeared completely from view.

Summer Place was no more in his sights.

Once the car had vanished, Barbara turned her attention to Fran, who carried a demeanour of sorrow that she had never seen in him before.

For the very first time since meeting her husband all those years ago, he looked truly sad.

She watched without word as he ambled back to the cottage; back into the lounge; back into his armchair; back into his thoughts.

As destiny waited to descend.

*****

'Damn it! I've taken a wrong turn. I think I'm lost, Stephanie! I knew I should have taken a left at that last junction. All these lanes look the bloody same!'

Stephanie did not reply to her husband's frustrations.

She simply stared through her own window, contemplating the incredulous evidence of family love that she had witnessed earlier.

Compelled to see her son in the back seat, she swivelled her shoulders to cast her eyes over him.

Liam's concentration was also elsewhere.

His mind filled with images and memories of the recent weeks' events.

Thankful for the fact that he had repaired one long-term relationship, whilst another enthralling yet woefully brief liaison had seemingly disintegrated forever before his very eyes.

Alone with his reflections, he simply gazed at the passing scenery through the glass.

Yet gradually as the minutes elapsed, the surrounding vista carried a vague familiarity. He couldn't quite place it, but he was certain that he had been in the area before.

Liam instinctively bolted upright in his seat as his puzzled father briefly noticed his son's excited image in the rear-view mirror. Richard

293

looked across to his wife, who appeared similarly perplexed by Liam's sudden interest in the countryside beyond.

Liam's father maintained an uncertain course through the narrow lanes until the forestry all around became gradually sparser, eventually to be totally replaced by meadowland.

In the distance across the fields, Liam spotted the landmark he had expected to discover.

His initial suspicions were proved quite correct.

The hidden fortress looked majestic from this side - the opposite side to which Liam had viewed it previously. As the car glided downhill, Liam hoped the spectacle was seemingly becoming closer. But to no avail. A teasing glimpse of water through the tree line was all that fortune provided.

It was the lake, for sure. But Liam resigned himself to the fact that he would not get his chance to take one last look at the beauty concealed within that circular wall of greenery.

He accepted denial of the final visual treat as the car began to veer away. With despair cursing his conscience, Liam disappointedly moved his nose from against the rear window and said nothing more on the matter.

THIRTY-SIX

Liam hardly discussed the details of his summer vacation. Not on the journey home. Certainly not once back in Talworth. He didn't think it worth wasting his breath. The minds of his parents were already distracted by future business plans.

The apartment construction project in Greece had been given the green light. Richard and Stephanie would be making regular visits to the location over the coming months. This was not to Liam's detriment. In fact, he was now trusted by his family. There was even an inference towards him taking a break with them in the sunshine, but it was not a priority as far as Liam was concerned.

Other pressing issues occupied his mind.

The new term at school had begun in his absence.

Liam's eventual return took place in the third week of September.

Walking back through the double iron gates of St. Forsters was a strangely unsettling experience.

Before the summer break, Liam had been the uncrowned king of the playground, but he no longer wanted such an unpleasant accreditation. He moved meekly among the throng before registration period. Not in a definitive attempt to avoid being spotted. It was more a case of wanting to blend in, like most of his peers had always been happy to do.

Finally finding a place of temporary solace under the science block veranda, Liam lowered his school bag to the floor and checked his mobile phone.

He lifted his head and scanned the bustling throng of pupils. Some of them eyed him with caution, wary of the reputation that he had nurtured. His hair had not been cut since the previous June and was acquiring a deceptive length to the onlooker.

Liam nodded and smiled to some pupils that passed by, but their response was either confused or they simply ignored him. Many didn't recognise the handsome face of the teenager due to the fact that his features had historically been shrouded by a large hood.

Such a disguise had been abolished for his return to school.

The subtle change of identity was taking some getting used to.

He felt like an alien in these academic surroundings. It was discomforting to feel such isolation. To see that others were still wary of him.

Whereas before, he positively clamoured the notoriety.

The fact that people would actively avoid him spurred him on and he gained strength through the fear of others.

But quietly sitting under the veranda was not the Liam Warburton that everybody thought they knew. This was a remodelled version.

The arrogance of old had been eclipsed by an earnest sense of inferiority among others.

The desire to be revered no longer stirred within his soul.

Yet many of the other pupils still opted to give the scowling teenager in the corner of the playground a wide berth.

All, that is, except one.

'Yo! Liam! My man! Where the fuck you been? Not the barbers, I see!'

Elson came storming through the crowd to greet his estranged friend. The smile was genuine, as was the ritual hand greeting of the Black Stars.

Yet Liam felt distinctly uncomfortable at being seen with Elson.

Yes, he was a friend. But not the friend of old. Not the associate that Liam wanted to remember.

It was through a false, almost embarrassing sense of duty that Liam acted pleased to see his one-time accomplice.

'How's things, Elson?'

'Real good, man! We thought you'd emigrated or left the fucking planet or something! Hey! You lose your phone out in the sticks?'

Liam chuckled.

'No. There was hardly any signal. Too many trees!'

'What about ladies? Too many ladies too, yeah?'

The comment brought one particular female back to the forefront of Liam's mind, but he would never wish to cheapen the brief encounter with the beautiful red head from the market by boasting of it.

'No, man. No ladies at all! Just my grandmother!'

Elson's features expressed sincere sympathy for his friend's apparent plight.

'What? You kidding? Jesus! I thought you went out there for a holiday, man! You sure you aint been to prison instead?'

Liam laughed. A genuine, heartfelt, belly laugh. It had seemed a lifetime since he had felt such sincere amusement.

Elson continued with an update of Talworth's latest news.

'Hey, listen up! The filth has nabbed someone for Glendin's murder! Some dude from the other side of town. We don't know him, though!'

Liam's heart lurched at hearing such news regarding the departed. He hadn't really discussed the situation in depth with anyone. It was something of a surprise to hear that the police had been successful in tracing the killer so quickly.

'When's the trial?'

Elson checked for anyone being in unwelcome earshot.

'Not set yet. The fucker admitted it, though! Well, couldn't really deny it. The fucker's stuck two others since! He's going down, boy! Hopefully we won't have to go to court. Anyways, I aint got no fucking suit to wear!'

Yet again Liam found himself at the mercy of Elson's quick-fire humour. He had secretly missed his friend's company but had little inclination to relight old fires.

But Elson had not quite finished with his bulletin.

'Hey, man!' he sniggered. 'You'll never guess who's having a kid!'

Liam was now intrigued as to the truth behind such a common story.

'How the fuck should I know? I haven't been here, have I?'

Yet again Elson mischievously checked that their conversation wasn't being overheard, increasing Liam's impatience on the issue.

'Well? Who's up the duff, then?'

Elson partly covered his mouth as his eyes widened.

'Ferris!'

Liam was genuinely shocked.

'Jesus Christ! Carla? You're having a laugh! She's had a busy summer then! Who's the guilty party?'

Elson chuckled whilst being wary of the next line he wanted to deliver.

'Hey, man! Rumour had it that it was *you*! That's why they say you did your jaunt to the sticks! Tell me that it aint true, man!'

Liam was now truly overcome with mirth at the very thought of such a frightening predicament.

'Listen, Elson! Call me old fashioned, but I still thought that you had to have sex with someone before you could get them pregnant!'

His friend now looked rather bemused as he eyed Liam with blatant suspicion.

297

'You mean…you never did? Not with her? So…it aint your kid?'

Liam duly dismissed his friend as the registration bell sounded.

'Fuck off outta here, man! I'll catch you later! Give my hello to Jonka when he shows up.'

'Will do, man!'

Still giggling, Liam switched off his phone, picked up his schoolbag and with an unusual spring in his step, strode confidently into the main building.

*****

Liam's schooling for the next few weeks elapsed without problem. After several weeks of self-scrutiny, he had secretly made the determined decision to concentrate on his studies on returning from Clearlake. The renewed attitude had been noticed swiftly by pupils and teachers alike.

For the first time since he could recall, Liam was enjoying the experience of St. Forsters.

It was just as well.

Important exams beckoned the following spring.

Colin Smith was particularly gratified that Liam had opted to channel his natural energies into something positive. He had always had faith in the boy's ability.

Equally, it became quickly clear that Liam had not lost his talent over the past two years.

Only the will to utilise that talent, had diminished.

Now back on track academically, he also gradually began to distance himself from out of school involvement with Elson and Jonka. The three were still good friends, but the unruly evening activity that they had customarily been involved in was now a relic of the recent past.

Thankfully for Liam, Jonka and Elson did not need the message enforcing to any degree. They registered with Liam's change of heart.

To a lesser extent, they sympathised and understood.

As far as the gang members were concerned, their reign as an active force was at an end.

The Black Stars were no more.

*****

298

Christmas came and went, with the new year soon evolving into the middle of January.

Night threatened Clearlake as winter's frosted shroud beckoned ever colder. Trees all around stood bare and lean, whose strong limbs once proudly wore flourishing sleeves of green.

And would soon begin to do so again.

The sixty-year-old man sat in his armchair.

In his lounge, alone.

Listening to the television but not watching it. A tedious political debate, the subject of which he had become disinterested in a good half hour back.

His stomach suddenly twitched in a demand for food.

A short-term staple diet of scrambled eggs and soup was no longer palatable due to a swift deterioration in the condition of his throat.

Yet he was so hungry. Especially when he thought of all the wonderful food that was once devoured with such relish.

How he longed to indulge the healthy appetite of his younger days.

All he ever did now was spend his time thinking about the past.

For him, the future was a concept of minimal consideration.

He felt increasingly tired. His strict exercise regime now reluctantly abandoned. Yet his physique remained impressive, even if it were insufficiently sustained, relatively unused and slowly but surely eroding away.

Despite his still impressive muscular build, the regular morning runs would now simply induce a coughing fit that was relentlessly painful. The consequences of even attempting to achieve what he could ably do only a few months before, would only lead to unnecessary sufferance.

In his eyes, there was now little benefit in trying to stay healthy.

Such a policy would not stave off the inevitable.

His loyal wife entered the room with a pint glass containing a thick, brown fluid that supposedly provided all the necessary nutrients that solid food could provide.

But it didn't taste like his favoured rump steak, well done with mushroom and onion sauce. Or fresh haddock pie in homemade pastry with parsley sauce. Or lamb and vegetable stew with sweet dumplings.

Despite only being tepid in temperature, the sickly substance still scolded without remorse as it passed down into his gullet.

The sixty-year-old man winced in fragile anger as his wife grimaced in wrenching pity.

Through a hoarse whisper, he thanked her as she smiled at the ever-present glint in his eye, before taking the empty glass back to the kitchen.

So that was dinner; over and done with for another evening.

How he craved one of his favourite cigars. But alas, such a soothing treat was now also out of the question. The nicotine now scorched his tender throat to unbearable levels of agony.

Indeed, any avenue of pleasure that Francis James Gould had become accustomed to had now been forcibly closed off in the space of a few short months as his unseen enemy had suddenly become aggressive beyond all restraint.

Yet he had lived with that enemy for an age.

It had resided silently within his body for the longest time.

But this man would not succumb to predicted fate, instead opting for a long-term policy of ignorance.

Only now, there was no option to take, aside a rapid physical demise which was increasingly clouded by inner regret.

As he sat in deep, solitary contemplation, he felt sure he detected a gentle knocking at the front door of the cottage. Surely no one should be calling at this time in these frigid temperatures. Before he could decide in his own mind whether or not it was worth getting up to answer, Barbara had already taken the honour from her husband.

Fran listened carefully to the distant conversation.

He could detect excited chatter that resonated through the kitchen and along the passageway. The muffled exchange continued for a good few minutes, but still Fran could not decipher what was being said.

He attempted to shout to his wife in enquiry as to the visitor's identity, but his voice would not allow the necessary pitch and volume.

This strong, proud man, who had bellowed orders at armed battalions and whose bark had echoed menacingly along silent barrack rooms was now confronted by a peace enforced by fate.

In acute discomfort once again, he feebly decided to sit back and relax in his favourite chair.

Within a few seconds, he had drifted into a temporary yet contented light slumber, just as Barbara entered the lounge carrying a pen and notepad.

Quickly scanning the bookcase behind Fran's chair, she removed her address book and proceeded to flick through the pages until locating the required details.

Scribbling them down onto the notepad, she replaced the address book on the shelf and kissed her dear husband on the forehead as he snoozed.

By the time he was reawakened by the closing of the front door less than a minute later, the visitor was gone.

Fran never knew who had come to the cottage that night, but he made a mental note to enquire the next time Barbara entered the room.

But the thought to do so deserted his enquiring, tired mind as rapidly as it had entered.

THIRTY-SEVEN

February the twenty-second would register itself as a bleak day in the history of Liam Warburton.

The telephone call came in the middle of the night. Liam was roused from his dreams by a muffled wailing sound emanating from the next room.

His parents' bedroom.

After a few minutes of attempting to identify the source of the disconcerting noise, he heard his parents emerge onto the landing. Richard opened Liam's bedroom door and tentatively asked him to join them downstairs.

Nervous expectation filled the air as he sat across from his distraught looking mother and straight-faced father at the kitchen table. The wall clock depicted the time to be nearly three am.

He scanned their concerned features, and quickly concluded that the news they had for him was certainly not good.

In truth, it was mind-numbingly painful to hear his father's words, which were interrupted by the unrestrained weeping of his desolate mother.

'Liam. Your grandmother contacted us about an hour ago. I...don't think there's an easy way to tell you this...'

Liam could not distract his gaze from his mother as she succumbed further to the unforgiving grip of emotion.

'What is it, Dad? What's the matter? Why is Mum crying?'

Richard leaned across the table and took his son's hand in his own, whilst simultaneously placing an arm around Stephanie's shoulder.

'It's...its Francis...he's...he's gone, Liam. Your grandfather... has...gone.'

The son looked to his parents in sincere confusion. He hoped that the implication of his father's words had been misinterpreted.

'What do you mean...gone?'

It did not take long for the mental translation to take effect.

'Not...no...not Grandad...no...'

A numbed silence was the only initial reaction that Liam could muster. His mother reached over and grabbed his hands, squeezing tightly as she looked upon her only son through tear strewn eyes.

But Liam could not weep at that moment.

He simply stared at his parents' fearful expressions, as though they were in expectation of some violent reactive display of temper.

But the mind of Liam Warburton remained calm and clear.

There were issues to address.

Evidently, he had not been fully informed.

He had questions that needed answering.

'How did he die? What happened to him?'

In a disjointed and purposely brief account, Stephanie relayed the terms of her father's illness. The teenager's eyes widened as curious pieces of the previous summer's jigsaw fitted neatly into place.

'Cancer? So that was the cause of his cough? And all along...I never suspected! Jesus! Why didn't anyone *tell* me? Why did Grandpa keep it a secret? He must have known what was coming... Jesus...'

No sooner had the urge to uncover truths descended on the scene than Liam rose to his feet with the certainty in his mind that he would perhaps rather not know any further details.

The uneasy response from the grandson was confirmed with a resounding slam of his bedroom door.

*****

The news of Fran's death had an unprecedented effect on Liam from the moment he heard.

He had enjoyed an altered disposition since arriving back in Talworth. The all too shallow relationship with his grandfather had nevertheless plumbed depths within his soul that no one had ever come close to touching before. The fruition of this inner discovery was, he had hoped, going to continue when they next saw one another.

But now, such positive aspirations were never to be realised.

The lessons he had learned in Clearlake were at times unflinchingly brutal in nature, and in hindsight, completely necessary if Liam Warburton were to place his life back on a track of supposed normality.

Of course, restraining his penchant for operating outside acceptable guidelines had not been an easy policy to employ.

He was, after all, a streetwise fifteen-year-old. Soon to be sixteen. A craving for excitement still burned within him, though instead of being a persistent source of torment as before, it now seemed to ebb and flow with the mood of the moment.

In tandem with this need for adrenaline, his desire to be reunited with Tissy remained a lingering if now futile dream. It was even more frustrating that she had vanished from his life as quickly as she appeared. With no cooperative point of reference and no clues to work with, Liam had resigned himself to the fact that he had lost the two people that he had felt truly closest to in his entire life.

The actuality that he would never see his grandfather again began to hit hard in the days that followed.

Despite Francis James Gould being a relatively unknown quantity in the immediate lives of the Warburtons, his grandfather's spirit had inspired a long-standing reformation in character.

A secretly harboured ambition to return to Clearlake was about to be achieved, but certainly not for the reasons that Liam had intended. Indeed, the unexpected posthumous farewell and funeral were definitely not part of his plan.

In the cold light of day, Liam had to accept that there had been two recent sources of divine inspiration to change his perspective on life.

Both dalliances had been tragically brief. Both had now ended against his will and beyond his control.

Not being made aware of his grandfather's illness rankled with the boy as reality began to settle into his conscience. By keeping him in blissful ignorance, Liam's parents had made an error. They had believed that their son could not be trusted to handle such knowledge. They could not rely on a composed response.

Whilst admittedly justified on their part, Liam believed the decision to be wrong.

Circumstances had conspired to keep him in the dark. Yet harbouring frustration about the fact was pointless. His renewed mindset would have to afford him a degree of maturity regarding the whole issue. But the past was gone. Nothing could be altered. But still his mind toiled at being forcibly and unwittingly detached from the truth.

He had watched his mother cry over the loss of her father, yet Liam could not help but feel that he had gotten to know Fran better than anybody in those few short weeks. No one seemed to truly understand Francis James Gould the man, or what made him tick as an individual.

Fran was neither a conventional grandfather, nor role model to Liam. But his principles and beliefs had instilled a legacy in Liam's mind that was worth a lifetime of mandatory hugs and pointless presents. The need to pretend had been eradicated from Liam's psyche. He had been taught to be his own person and not fear the opinions of others.

He had descended on Clearlake the reluctant pupil.

He had departed Clearlake the accomplished learner.

As such, his rate of progression in the academic scenario had evolved dramatically in the schooling periods before and after Christmas. With the sinister ghosts of his wavering history seemingly defeated, Liam found purpose and a will to embrace the future regarding his education.

Although the day of the funeral was imminent, his newfound role at St. Forsters continued to gather positive momentum. The daily routine of school was now something to creatively embrace, as opposed to a chore he would actively shun.

The final two terms of his education had become an equal priority to the emotional conflict he had to contend with.

*****

It was at break time one morning that his focus turned to Carla Ferris. Liam hadn't seen her for months. The news of her pregnancy had jolted the entire school. Although his vague friendship with her had effectively petered out, her new circumstances displayed to Liam just how reality can come crashing in on a once carefree existence if one's guard is left down.

In truth, Liam felt a certain sadness for Carla's predicament.

The gulf that had grown between them in recent times had seemed unbridgeable. Suddenly, Liam realised that he felt differently about their relationship. He thought about her for most of the day, trying to empathise with her situation.

The lack of guidance in her life had led her to make an irretrievable mistake. Where was the personal source of comfort for her?

Was she now fearful for her own future? Or could it be presumed perhaps that Carla was contented with her life plan?

He analysed the innocent faces around him in the classroom and playground. How many of his peers trod the fine line as he had done? How many of them would succumb to an unexpected bolt of fate that hits between the eyes without warning?

He compared his parents' influence with the likely roles of other mothers and fathers.

305

He spent time considering how he had so recklessly run the gauntlet for so long and yet still emerged unscathed.

Was he simply lucky; smart…or indeed blessed?

He had never turned to either parent for support yet support him they undoubtedly did. But perhaps providing food and shelter was not enough to steer the young from danger. Mothers and father needed to tap into the minds of their offspring if they truly wish to have influence over events. Rules and regulations needed a human face.

More worryingly for Liam, no one was either able or willing to stop him in his consuming quest for notoriety. The wheels had fallen off long before his stay in Clearlake. He was ultimately on a shrouded suicide mission. He had pledged himself to adopt a dark, vicious persona that rendered him effectively invulnerable.

Indeed, the self-induced scars he hid from the world were evidence that he was capable of far more harm to himself than any other being could inflict upon his person.

Consequently, he was in danger of severing all links of security in his life. He truly believed that the fortuitous vacation with his grandparents had been pre-ordained.

The last safety net for Liam Warburton.

Former fifteen-year-old tyrant.

Unluckily for some such as Carla Ferris and Glendin Jones, one single instance of reckless action had incurred permanent consequence.

Deeds that could not be undone.

Paths trodden that could never be retraced.

This was the scenario for Carla.

One simple irresponsible choice - the ramifications of which would last forever.

She had been on Liam's thoughts intermittently for several weeks, but only when he learned of his grandfather's passing could he feel justified in attempting to initiate a line of communication with her, whatever the outcome might be.

He had spent the best part of a school day tracking her whereabouts, with everyone coming to the same conclusion that she had retired away from school life due to impending motherhood.

Opting to try her at her home address, Liam sensed the irony.

The scene of the breaking point in their ambiguous relationship would hopefully provide a fitting setting for their reunion.

Liam made the diversion straight after the final school bell, recalling the location without effort. He could remember the street, but not the house number. Thankfully, he recognised the plastic tubs of flowering plants either side of the large, wooden front door and wasted little time in making his presence known.

Within a second or two, a blurred and wary image emerged through the circular section of frosted glass in the door. Even in such a distorted format, Liam instantly saw that it was Carla.

As he observed her hand reach for the latch, Liam remained unsure as to whether a grimace of concern or a cheeky smirk of greeting would be appropriate. He need not have worried. Carla's expression as she pulled back the door was one of instant pleasure. Her attractive smile beamed at Liam. Although in truth, Liam Warburton was the last person she expected to see on her doorstep at that moment.

Yet strangely, she was so thankful.

Of all those she knew at school, Liam was probably the one face she wanted to see most of all.

'Hi Carla. It's been a while. How you doing?'

Wryly patting her stomach, Carla's smirk was accompanied by a tone of sarcasm.

'Well, you know. Been better. As you can see.'

Liam followed her gaze to the small bump protruding under her jumper.

'Yeah. I heard. How far gone are you?'

'Five months…just over.'

'Jesus.' he muttered. 'I suppose school's been giving you a hard time?'

Carla looked over Liam's shoulder to glare at a passer-by before answering.

'Well. I hardly go now. It's far easier not to bother. I can't really sit my exams anyway. School don't care anyway, do they? No…it's my parents that have gone up the wall about stuff. Mum reckons she's too young to be a grandma just yet!'

Liam chuckled. If nothing else, his perception that Carla might be buckling under the strain seemed to be unfounded at that moment.

'Really? You do surprise me! Where is your mom and pops? At work?'

'Yeah. Come in for a coffee. They'll be ages yet. I'm glad to see a friendly face for once. They're in short supply at the moment!'

307

Liam followed Carla into the kitchen and perched at the dining table as she filled the kettle. It was pleasing to know that his uninvited arrival had been welcomed.

'I didn't know whether we were on speaking terms these days. I haven't had much to do with you since…well, you know.'

Carla turned to face him, the smile never fading.

'People change, Warbs. Life changes you. We're both different from this time last year. You've definitely changed! You've become Mister Sensible whilst I've become Mrs. Stupid!'

Liam observed her striking features as she stared sullenly at the table- top.

'Why do you say you're stupid? Because of getting pregnant?'

Her voice lowered to an almost embarrassed whisper, as though she didn't want anyone else to hear what she had to say on the subject.

'Well…wouldn't you consider it a pretty stupid thing to do at my age?'

He shook his head slowly and reached for her hand.

His first instinct was evidently correct.

Carla Ferris was not dealing with the issue too well after all.

'You've always been someone I could relate to, Carla. You're no fool. Not in my eyes, anyway. And believe me…I know what real fools are capable of.'

Carla did believe Liam. She knew his words were sincere and that the touching of the hand was maybe a knowing gesture to what may have been in the past. She had frequently harboured thoughts of how different life may be if her relationship with him had evolved into something other than estrangement.

'You've spent most of the past few months staying out of my way, Warbs. And I don't blame you. I suppose I overreacted by kicking you out.'

He squeezed her hand tighter as to offer further reassurance.

'Like you just said, Carla. I have changed. That idiot from last year…and the year before…well…I aint him no more. He's gone for good.'

Carla seemed rather bemused as she stood up to finish making the drinks.

'So…what changed you? You're the opposite of the person you used to be. It's like you'd rather not be seen in the crowd these days than

308

stand out in it. I'm interested to know what made you alter. Where's the rebel gone?'

Liam was genuinely placated by Carla's curiosity.

He had hoped that she would ask such questions. The opportunity to present the honest answers would not arise very often. He felt no fear of being judged by her. He fully understood that the brute he used to portray had made her justifiably cautious of him. But even in mutual mockery, Liam and Carla had maintained an honesty between them. There was never a hint of deceit or malice in their school relationship.

The vague romantic attraction was still tangible, but such a consideration seemed wholly inappropriate in the current situation. Yet Liam still felt at ease in relaying some of his experiences to her.

'Last summer…whilst you were enjoying yourself making babies…'

Carla rolled her eyes and smirked as she stirred two mugs.

'…I was sent to my grandparents out in the country for a few weeks.'

The coffee was placed on the table as she resumed her position across from Liam.

'Sounds nice…' she grinned. 'Nice and boring!'

'Yeah…well that's exactly what I thought. Until I got there! My grandfather was in the Canadian Army. High-ranking. A hard-liner. Shall we say…he taught me a few things…showed me where I was going wrong in life.'

Carla chuckled and rocked gently on the back legs of her chair.

'Are you trying to surprise me, Warbs? I bet you were a pain in the arse to him from the word go! I bet you menaced the whole town!'

She continued to laugh, but Liam did not see the funny side.

'No. That's the weird thing. Somehow, he already knew what a little prick I'd become. How he knew…I don't know to this day. But I never got chance to step out of line. He hit me like a fucking steam train. More than once. Knocked the aggression right out of me. The way he saw things, I wasn't being punished. I was being…re-educated. Shown a new view of life.'

Liam pondered whether to indulge Carla as to Fran's death. But she seemed despondent enough without having to heap sympathy onto his own situation. Indeed, any semblance of humour had now vanished from the conversation.

Her laughter had been through nerves. In truth, Carla was envious of the reformed teenager sat before her.

'I tell you what, Warbs. I wish someone would have held my hand before I got into this fucking mess. Too late now though, I suppose.'

Now it was Liam's turn to smile, which in turn reignited Carla's deeply buried light-heartedness regarding the matter.

'Elson says that the bookies had me down as the father. Not much chance of that is there!'

There was a moment of whimsy before she disengaged her glance from his and towards her drink.

'Sadly not.'

'So…who is the lucky boy?'

Liam had obviously asked the one question that Carla was truly afraid of. Her mood became slightly melancholy once more as she stared fearfully into her mug.

'I…I don't know. It was a fairly wild time, you know. I was, like I say…stupid…two or three times.'

It took a lot to shock Liam Warburton, but his surprise at Carla's behaviour was difficult to conceal.

'Jesus Christ, Carla! How many times?'

The temporary silence betrayed her lie.

'Five…perhaps six…'

'Fuck me! You *were* a busy girl! And you've no idea who the dad could be? Fucking hell!'

'Yes! Fucking hell, *indeed*! Tell me about it! My parents wanted to drown me! But now I've got to face the responsibility. They're still pretty pissed off at me, but I'm going to be a mum. And they are going to be grandparents. That's that!'

Liam watched her expression flicker between optimism and outright dread. He felt so sorry for her but was anxious to sooth her trepidation regarding the future.

'Not the words of Mrs. Stupid. More like Mrs. Clued-up, I'd say! So…what about school?'

Carla let out a huge sigh as though she was now bored with discussing the subject of impending motherhood.

'I don't know. The baby's due in June. I can't revise and give birth at the same time, can I? I might have to re-schedule my exams for a later date. I really don't know.'

Liam moved around the table and took both Carla's hands into his. Looking into her eyes, he realised that perhaps things should have been different for them both. But it was too late to change facts.

'Is it a boy or girl?'

'I don't want to know until the birth. If it's a boy, he'll be called Thomas, maybe. A girl…Emily, perhaps.'

A tangible sadness descended on the exchange once more. It was becoming hard for Carla to uphold the act of enthusiasm.

'Listen, Carla. I'm your friend. I'm here for you. You know that don't you?'

She tried to raise a smile as a ploy to stem the onset of tears.

'Thanks, Warbs. It means a lot. I might well need you if my mum and dad don't begin to chill out about things.'

'They'll be fine. They love you. And they'll love their grandchild. You'll see. Come here.'

Friends reunited in an embrace that had been long overdue for both parties. It was a bittersweet moment. The pair had only ever known playground antagonism. Yet in a few short minutes, they had discovered that their bond went far deeper than swapping classroom insults. They laughed whilst hugging, enjoying the unity that unexpected loyalty had provided.

Liam broke the tender exchange with a final query.

'If you do decide to come back to school in a hurry, I'll help you if you want to sit your exams. Just say the word. I mean it.'

Carla wiped her moistened gaze with her sleeve as she showed Liam to the front door.

'Thanks for being there, Warbs.'

With a smile and a jovial wave, he was away along the street and finally gone.

But not gone forever.

Carla Ferris instinctively knew that Liam Warburton was the true friend he professed to be.

Possibly the only one she had left.

THIRTY-EIGHT

The funeral took place in Clearlake fifteen days after his passing. The service was to be held at midday in the grounds of the church by the market square. A quaint setting, the church was surrounded on three sides by the cemetery. This would be the fitting final resting place for Francis James Gould.

Liam did not want breakfast that morning. The watery sunrise had just begun to peek over Talworth's roof tops as the Warburtons commenced their trek. It would be a long, silent four-hour journey. Barbara had offered to accommodate the family for the night, but as per usual, business demands would call for an early start the following morning. Staying away from the office was out of the question for Stephanie and Richard.

Liam would have gladly stayed with his grandmother for a month but was not consulted on the issue. Mixed emotions cursed his mind the moment he awoke from a poor night's sleep.

It was so ironic that his initial visit to Clearlake was under extreme protestation. Yet he anticipated the return with such relish.

As he sat vacantly watching the passing scenery from the back of the car, he longed to reach the destination as quickly as possible. Such a long haul would test his patience. The only way to pass the time satisfactorily was to employ his I-pod. He checked his phone for text messages. He had hardly received any for weeks. The latest was from Carla two days ago thanking him for his concerns and his friendship.

In disconsolate silence, Liam stared between the heads of his parents at the flow of traffic beyond the windscreen. His mind ventured briefly to the subject of Tissy. He wondered if she might be awaiting his arrival. He secretly fantasized that word might have got back to her that Liam Warburton was due in Clearlake once again.

Whilst wholly pleasant, such thoughts were the stuff of whimsy. The unflinching truth was that Tissy had fled for her own peace of mind and safety. It was no accident that she failed to reveal her intentions to anyone. It was her right to remain concealed from any apparent danger she may have perceived.

It was her prerogative to start afresh someplace else. If she wanted to stay hidden, then Liam was powerless to find her.

Yet, such truth cut like a knife.

He had not forgotten her. Nor would he ever do so.

He could not erase that beautiful face that had brightened his existence for a woefully short span of time. The vision of which had burned at the back of his mind for months since. Their liaison may have been all too brief, but the memories were clear and fresh.

Time had not tainted his feelings for her in any way.

'Do you want a sandwich, Liam?'

His mother's query did not penetrate the pleasant concentration of her son. His father offered a prompt.

'He's got his bloody music on, Steph. He won't hear you.'

But Liam's music had in fact been switched off. His mind now distracted by the imminent events of the day. The uncertainty of how he would respond was almost like torture. He simply did not feel like grieving. It wasn't like Fran had died at all. Far from it. If anything, the spirit of his grandfather was now stronger than ever.

'Liam, love. Do you want a sandwich? Cheese...or...ham?'

Stephanie watched as her son grimaced at the very suggestion of food. Nourishment would not appease his swirling gut. He needed sustenance of the mind, not the body. His parents' seemingly indifferent approach to the day ahead began to gnaw away at him as the journey rolled on.

Whilst she may have lost her father, Liam felt his mother could never have loved Fran properly. Certainly not in the intimate manner in which she should have been able to. She had never unearthed the true man behind the stone façade. To her, Fran had never stopped being the soldier.

It was sorrowful that within this seemingly untamed, powerhouse of a figure was actually an unseen and unstoppable enemy that gradually eroded him to the core.

Another issue of reverence for Liam was how Fran had dealt with his pain so capably. It must have been physically unbearable to swallow and be racked with agony every few seconds of every single day for several years. But there was not a syllable of complaint.

It was his own private battle; one which Fran had opted to confront alone.

It was mainly for this reason that Liam felt deep sympathy for his grandfather's solitary plight. And strangely, he felt little for those that Fran was leaving behind.

They were too ignorant and selfish to even begin comprehending their loss.

Having spent years running away from the supposed ogre instead of befriending him, they now had to live with their lack of courage. Fran was a good man inside. Even more telling is that the hidden positive aspects to his persona were only brought out by the challenge from his own grandson.

A mere teenager, once so rabid and unruly.

But it was exactly that rebellious streak that had quietly impressed Fran.

Most probably because he could see a lot of himself in Liam. His often cutting and brutal responses to the arrogance of youth mirrored his own experiences whilst growing up. Perhaps Fran had administered the treatment he endured as a teenager. The will to eliminate the aggression and channel that energy in a positive way.

But in the army, the anger of young men is their lifeblood. Without it, their duty as soldiers is only rendered all the tougher.

Demons are not cured in the military; only encouraged.

Yet now, in death, Fran had been salvaged to some degree.

Liberated from himself in his final, glorious conflict.

This was the reason Liam felt a need to celebrate Fran's passing as opposed to mourning a loss. Fran was now undoubtedly content. No longer was he burdened by a lifetime of self-discipline, inherent regime, and inward torment.

He had won the war against his own instinct, in turn helping Liam overcome his own ongoing problems.

No. Liam would not cry for Francis James Gould.

Today, of all days, he would stand proud for his grandfather.

*****

Barbara Gould moved unsteadily with the aid of a walking stick. Her mild arthritis always seemed more potent during winter months. Viewing their arrival from the kitchen window, she moved onto the garden path to greet her family as Richard pulled the car to a halt outside the front gate of the cottage.

An exchange of warm embraces left Liam feeling distinctly cold inside.

314

His mood matched the striking appearance of the surrounding scenery. Clearlake in the grip of winter was a sparse and grotesque version of its flourishing summertime vista.

The nameplate depicting the cottage as 'Summer Place' was never more inappropriate.

Black, dangling limbs clamoured among one another as far as the eye could see, as though reaching for something untouchable. Naked without their customary foliage, the trees conveyed a seasonal frontage that only served to intimidate and deflate the observer.

Liam glanced to the white skies above as his grandmother kissed him firmly on the cheek. His gaze reverted to her eyes as he searched for a modicum of authentic emotion.

Perhaps a sense of loss.

Any visual clue that she was feeling the deprivation that occurs when a hero is no more.

Instead, Liam thought he saw lifelessness in his grandmother's eyes. Dark, empty windows displaying a hollow soul. A conveyance that the departure of her husband was perhaps a burden lifted. Relief that he had finally succumbed to the inevitable.

His pain was now at an end.

Perversely, so too it seemed, was his widow's.

Perhaps Liam was jumping to infinitely wild conclusions.

But he did not wish to encourage conversation with anybody.

Whereas his previous aloofness could have been attributed to wilful arrogance, now it was a policy adopted out of earnest respect. So far as Liam could see, any dialogue exchanged during the day would fail to distract from the reason for being there.

Fran was gone. Sociability in his absence seemed so inadequate.

Just at a time when Liam was ready to learn more from his newfound idol. Destiny had deemed that those few precious lessons of the previous summer would be the only ones. This was the quandary for Liam and was immensely difficult for him to accept.

He wanted so much more of what was now impossible to attain.

The thought of indulging in pleasantries with the locals would not serve to divert a grandson from his turmoil.

*****

The silver funeral car containing Barbara and the Warburtons crawled behind the sleek hearse containing Fran's coffin. The journey to the church seemed to take forever.

Liam looked beyond the window to the bleak, country lanes, only slightly consoled by thoughts of times past.

On reaching the practically deserted market square it became quickly obvious that most of the villagers had convened in and around the churchyard to pay their last respects on this dank, dismal day.

Tom and Fred made a point of briefly reacquainting themselves with Liam. They mentioned last summer's fishing episode and the fact that Fran was the talk of the village for days afterwards.

But they would never know how Fran suffered within himself over such an embarrassment, nor would they know of the affliction Liam faced as a result. But the belated appraisals for his grandfather repeatedly hit a raw nerve.

Eventually, Liam's anger was conveyed in a concise and clear reply to the throng of supposed well-wishers.

'If you thought he was so great, why didn't you tell him when he was alive? Because he never understood how great he really was, you know. And he did need to be told. But it's too late now, isn't it?'

A shocked silence followed Liam across the burial grounds as he joined his parents for the final farewell.

A subdued service was led by the village priest, Father Carrick. A tiny bespectacled man who spoke in soft, velvet tones. His words induced tears in a few, but the grandson held firm as he watched his mother and grandmother openly display their belated emotions.

Don't cry for him, now.

It's too fucking late.

Another dead hero.

Liam felt a sense of honour as he observed the coffin being carefully lowered into its grave. Once at rest, the tributes ended, paving way for Liam to drop a single white rose onto the coffin lid. He tried vainly to ascertain the expression Fran's face through the thick layer of varnished teak. He imagined a wry, uncomfortable smirk, clamped around one of his favourite cigars.

The end of the funeral brought welcome and overdue relief to Liam. He walked among the mourners, scanning the myriad of faces for a flicker of familiarity or even humility.

There was some vague recognition of stall holders from the market, but nothing definite. There was certainly no sign nor mention of the one person he wanted to see most of all at that moment.

The congregation gathered back at the cottage for a low-key wake.

Photographs of Fran adorned the tables and mantelpiece. Liam studied one or two of the black and white stills of his grandfather as a teenager, briefly believing that he was truly studying his own reflection.

The similarity was uncanny. Fran looked every inch the soldier, ready and willing to take on the world. And he was probably capable of doing just that. At a time when his mental and physical prowess were second to none.

When Francis James Gould would have felt immense, invulnerable, and invincible.

A very familiar mindset to the admiring grandson that studied the bygone memories in their age-old frames.

*****

Departure for Talworth at the end of the day could not have come soon enough. Having arrived only hours earlier with the intention of embracing the visit, Liam had quickly tired of its pointless rigmarole. He had hoped for the event to have brought something different. Something positive. Something of inspiration.

But alas, it had evolved into a tedious chore.

Yet something tugged gently at the back of his conscience as the time to leave beckoned.

A calling from an undisclosed source.

A nagging sensation that his business in Clearlake was not quite over and done with.

Barbara left her friends and acquaintances in the cottage to oversee the farewell. She obligingly thanked the Warburtons for their attendance as they gathered at the front gate.

A mother held her daughter long and tight, as though it would be the last time they might ever see one another. Stephanie carried mixed feelings as she eventually approached the car. Richard started the engine with his thoughts centred on the business of the following day, checking his mobile for missed calls.

As ever, the scant signal in Clearlake had prevented such a possibility.

Daylight was drawing in and he became quietly impatient with the thought of having to drive the majority of the way home to Talworth in the dark.

Barbara knew exactly what her daughter was feeling as she motioned for Liam to get in the car. The lack of a relationship with her father had been a disabling feature of her entire life. Fran had played little part in guiding his daughter through the last two decades. He was practically a stranger to Stephanie. Certain bridges had been burned long ago that could now never be rebuilt.

The mutual regret and sense of guilt would never diminish.

Liam allowed his grandmother to kiss him goodbye. Instantly after doing so, she pulled away and walked quickly back to the cottage.

'I nearly forgot, young man. I have something for you. Wait right there.'

A little confused, Liam glanced over to his mother and father who sat waiting in the humming car. Richard tutted at the extension to the delay. Mildly intrigued, Liam shrugged his shoulders in response to his mother's expression of confusion.

The wait was short-lived as Barbara reappeared carrying a package wrapped in brown paper and tied with string. There were no markings of disclosure on the outside of the parcel, which was the size and weight of a pillow.

Now engaged by the offering, Liam listened carefully to the words of his grandmother. He detected a hint of emotion in her voice as she handed it over.

'You turn sixteen in a couple of weeks, Liam. This is your birthday present. From your grandfather and myself. But you must promise to wait until the big day! Don't peek before then! Do you hear me loud and clear, soldier?'

It was the very first time his grandmother had addressed him in such a way. The memories flashed through Liam's mind once more as he gently held the package from his grandmother.

Barbara's smile was bright and earnest, allowing Liam to finally see the recognition of loss in her eyes. The dark, empty holes he had perceived earlier were now full of life and light.

He had been far too judgemental. Perhaps she did understand after all and appreciated the true person that her husband was.

And the incredible influence he had cast over a once wayward grandson.

As final confirmation, she pulled Liam toward her frail form once more, and began to weep like a child.

Openly bidding farewell to one chapter in her life, whilst giving her sincere blessing to the beginning of another. Squashing the parcel between them, Barbara heaved and swayed with her tormented release.

When she drew back, her frosted whisper carried across the cold, still air of the garden.

Barbara Gould acknowledged her husband's true spirit in words that Liam would always remember.

'You know something, Liam? Despite your initial differences with him, you were the one person who eventually managed to inject a little happiness into Francis' life. He loved you dearly...and so do I. Never forget us.'

The eventual goodbye was tinged with incredible sorrow.

'Don't worry. I won't ever forget you or Fran, Grandma. I promise.'

Liam's act of bravado was stripped as he studied his grandmother's face. He finally took his position in the back of the car and wondered if he would indeed ever see her again.

As the Warburtons car slowly pulled away, the white shroud that had being hanging above them all day suddenly cracked, belatedly allowing the sun to penetrate and briefly wash Clearlake in gold.

Barbara proudly stood her ground and waved her family into the distance until they vanished from view into the tree-lined avenues beyond.

*****

The car had only travelled for a mile or two when it hit Liam like a thunderbolt. The nagging thought that had plagued him all afternoon. Departure had suddenly provided the solution to his puzzling irritation.

It was as if the sudden sunlight had revealed the answer to him.

He needed to visit the lake one last time. The compulsion was powerful and all consuming. The calling had come from within his soul. Liam was under order by his own instinct. He lurched forward in his seat.

'Dad...take a diversion...I'll tell you where...this won't take long...please...its important!'

*****

319

Richard pulled on the handbrake, understandably bemused by the choice of location. He and Stephanie waited in the car as they watched Liam alight. He walked to the boundary fence of the field and clambered over the stile. In the distance, a circular formation of spiny, black silhouettes guarded unseen territory beyond.

This was the target that their son seemed to be heading for.

His parents observed through the windscreen and simply wondered, knowing that Liam had made his appreciation of the vital detour quite clear. Richard voiced his irritation to Stephanie yet again about the lack of daylight and the need to get on the motorway. But they were now far from Liam's thoughts as he moved purposely across the meadow toward the hidden oasis.

Liam noticed the surrounding wall of limbs and trunks in the near distance. Now so bare and bleak - so different in appearance from the image in his memory. As he bounded purposely along, he re-imagined holding Tissy's hand as they walked across the exact same spot some six months or so earlier.

He could visualise her blue dress and copper twirls of hair. Skipping along by his side as she struggled to keep up with his long-legged stride.

The lake beckoned him ever closer.

With heart now racing, his little corner of heaven came ever nearer. He did not look back to his parents. He was focused totally on the site of beauty expanding before him.

Destiny had demanded his final attendance at this wondrous, mystical place.

On through the second meadow, the shrill air blew open the jacket of his black suit and made his tie flail wildly, but he felt no coldness; only an increasing warmth in his heart and soul which spurred him onward.

Finally at the tree line, he briefly hesitated to detect a suitable point of entry, of which there were now many due to the absence of foliage. Within seconds, he had penetrated the protective boundary of the lake and stood at the water's edge.

Slivers of precious diminishing sunlight bounced off the surface, which was as still and smooth as glass. He avidly scanned the scene for any signs of life, but at that moment the area stretching before him yielded nothing.

He walked a few paces along the bank, as further thoughts of Tissy entered his mind.

He pictured them lying together on that idyllic summer's day. The ground was now heavy and laden with dew. His eyes moistened at thoughts of what had passed and what could never be again.

The moment of reminiscence swiftly evolved into a consuming regret that he had not made more of the friendship with the angel from the market.

A once in a lifetime opportunity, gone.

How he wished he could turn the clock back to the previous summer.

He studied the water and the trees across the other side of the lake.

Nature's piece of paradise seemed so uninviting now.

He seemed to have made a wasted visit.

As his malaise took a firm grip, there was a sudden distraction from overhead.

A flash of movement in the corner of his eye.

He squinted skyward, scrutinising the hovering grey clouds that were underscored by the low sun.

It was a canvas that did little to inspire.

Yet the vision it unexpectedly unveiled caused his heart to race and rendered him awe struck.

Utterly captivated by the airborne approach of the family of swans, Liam counted them in sheer excitement. There were nine in all. Now fully fledged. Mature and graceful, swooping beyond the tree line in a perfect single file formation.

Turning one hundred and eighty degrees, they veered their course and headed over the lake before commencing a silent descent.

Two parents and their seven young. Cygnets that had evolved into exact replicas of their ever-reliable guardians. With plumage of purest white, they represented all that Liam now aspired to. A symbolic inspiration that had guided him like a beacon for many weeks and months.

With rehearsed precision, each bird in turn landed smoothly on the surface of the lake, gave one braking flap of their mighty wings before assuming their inherent regal posture and gliding on the crystal film of water.

Once all had descended, the file of swans headed from the centre of the lake and steered a course toward their singular audience on the bank.

Liam watched in delighted disbelief.

Overwhelmed and inflated with pride at the natural ease with which the family moved as one. A beautiful and instinctive union that needed neither instruction nor effort.

The smile that had involuntarily broadened on Liam's face caused his features to wrinkle and catch tears of happiness. He crouched, watched, and waited as the family of birds came closer. Consumed by admiration, Liam chuckled to himself as one by one the birds left the water and paraded their exquisite regalia before him.

No more did the youngsters adorn the unkempt grey plumage of their formative weeks. They had been lovingly nurtured and confirmed their perfection to their eager spectator. Liam retained his position as his feathered friends moved into a close-knit group and began to preen.

Knowingly under scrutiny, they set about the task with enthusiasm as if to directly impress. Intermittently, one of the group would lift its head as if to acknowledge the presence of the special observer.

Or perhaps even, to offer their farewell.

The amusement continued for several minutes as the birds jostled for space and playfully snapped their beaks at one another.

Liam could sense a communication between himself and his glorious performers.

It was as though they had sensed his transformation over the past months.

Just as he had witnessed theirs.

Then, with cosmetic duties seemingly at and end for the time being, the mother offered a shrill command and led her young back to the water.

Their father watched with caution as his family left the shore.

Heading back for the centre of the lake, they presented one final bow. The swans swam a complete circle before heading for the far side, until they disappeared under the raking shadow of overhanging limbs.

With tears drying on his cheeks, Liam reluctantly turned his back on his personal piece of paradise. Perhaps for the last time.

A mind, heart and soul now fully sated by the spectacle.

The young man ventured through the tree line.

Back toward his own waiting family.

THIRTY-NINE

Liam did not feel that his sixteenth birthday was an occasion worthy of celebration. The twenty-eighth of March arrived too soon after the loss of his grandfather. The numbness experienced since returning to Talworth after the funeral had yet to dissipate.

He woke up in an empty house due the fact that his parents had arranged a company meeting in London and had left early. He ate breakfast alone whilst studying the note left by his mother that wished him many happy returns and that they would see him that night. He would open the card from his parents later.

The walk to school was endured without him even thinking of his supposedly special day. The only positive aspect to the itinerary was that as he walked through the school gates, the first person that Liam set eyes on was Carla Ferris, who had opted to make a reluctant return to her studies despite the very noticeable maternal bump.

'Well, well...look what the cat dragged in...'

She was evidently overjoyed to see her friend and hugged him closely as he patted her stomach.

'I don't think I'll be sitting my exams for obvious reasons, but I can't just give up school, can I? I'm only here for a month or two. Until the baby drops. Then I'll have to see what the future brings after that.'

Liam drew back and smiled warmly at her.

'You've made the right decision, Carla. Believe me. I'm glad you listened to the teachers.'

Carla's expression carried sincerity as she reduced her smile.

'I'm not really here because of the teachers, Warbs. Or my parents...although they have stopped being so angry with me at last. I'm here because somebody spoke sense. A good mate, in fact. You.'

Liam was taken aback at her revelation.

'It can't just have been me, Carla. You must have known yourself that trying to come back to school was the right thing to do for you. You'll soon catch up what you've missed.'

But Carla Ferris was adamant in her claims. Liam had spoken to her with compassion and clarity. He had made her believe in herself once again, at a time when she felt a complete loss of identity, ambition and focus for the future.

'Here you go Warbs. I didn't forget.'

She pulled a large blue envelope from her schoolbag and handed it to Liam whilst offering him a kiss on the cheek. The only birthday card that was likely to be received from St. Forsters. He opened it there and then, revealing the image of a teddy bear with a balloon.

The message was simple. A heartfelt thank you for his concern and attention. An expression of gratitude and appreciation of his presence at a vital time.

He had unwittingly been a stabilizing force in her very stormy world.

Liam was touched by her words. The lingering gaze they exchanged hinted at opportunities missed.

'Thank you, Carla. This means more than you can know.'

The two friends smiled warmly at one another before going their separate ways.

*****

Elson and Jonka eventually caught up with their one-time leader during lunchtime and offered their own form of formal birthday congratulations, but as is usually the case with all close male friendships, it was conveyed with minimal fuss and affection.

Liam enjoyed their company, but other matters pressed and served to distract him from the typical banter they would enjoy.

The school day played itself out without incident. The final bell of the afternoon came around quickly, with Liam's mood being of a more positive nature on leaving the premises than it was on arrival that morning.

However, it was during the walk home that his attention became firmly centred on the package given to him by his grandmother on the day of Fran's funeral.

He had complied with her wishes and not even been tempted to take a look inside until today. In truth, he had given the matter little thought whatsoever until departing the school building.

However, the potential content now intrigued him.

Instinct suggested that the parcel would have been of some personal relevance. Yet he had not even mentioned his birthday to either of his grandparents whilst staying at Clearlake. He had asked for nothing from them to commemorate the day.

Yet evidently, the mysterious package had been given for a specific purpose.

Liam entered the house, grabbed his parents' card from the kitchen table and went straight upstairs. Retrieving Carla's card from his bag, he housed it in pride of place on the cabinet next to his bed. The card from his mother and father sported a comical cartoon on the front and contained a cheque for two hundred pounds. A most welcome bounty as always.

Although he hadn't afforded much thought to what his grandmother had wrapped for him, his mind now raced with anticipation as he closed the bedroom door. He retrieved the bundle from the top of his wardrobe where it had been located and laid the present carefully on the duvet.

Pulling gently on the string, Liam then removed the outer brown paper to reveal a grey cardboard box with a lid. The quest into uncertainty continued as Liam's eyes widened at seeing the items inside.

One by one, as Liam slowly retrieved each memento, his emotions began stirring.

A birthday card sat on top. Peeling open the envelope, the front picture depicted a hand painted scenario, which looked uncannily like Summer Place. It was signed by Fran and Barbara and contained five, crisp twenty-pound notes which fluttered onto the bed as he read the scripture written in blue ink:

To our darling Liam – Happy Birthday Soldier!
Love from Grandma and Grandad Gould xxx

Liam propped the card next to those from Carla and his parents on his bedside chest of drawers before resuming his attention to the box of wonders. To his amused astonishment, the next item to be pulled out was the pair of work jeans that his grandmother had provided at Clearlake.

The flashback was intimate and pleasantly amusing.

He recalled how foolish he had felt on pulling them on for the first time. The jeans were still torn and stained, but as ever, freshly laundered. Back to the box. Underneath the jeans, almost inevitably, was the big woollen sweater that made him itch like crazy. It was bedraggled, well past its best, but also clean. He held it close and breathed in the scent of wash powder, as his mind travelled back in time.

Next out of the parcel was a black and white photograph in a wooden frame. It was of a handsome teenager. His hair was cropped tightly. He was decked out in what could have been his first army issue uniform.

The young man carried a stoic, determined expression as he stood rigidly to attention. In the background, a building adorned a large sign - Ottawa Armed Forces Recruitment Services.

Liam observed the proud adolescent in the still, who would one day go on to achieve his ambitions.

A vigorous youngster who would soon turn from a boy into a man.

He would also graduate from a private into a sergeant.

From a husband to a father.

And from a grandfather to a friend.

Liam stared into the picture, almost seeing himself behind the glass.

Even with such limited experience and tender years, Francis James Gould looked every inch a proud young man. It dawned on Liam at that moment how well his grandfather had aged. The taut, chiselled features and honed physique had hardly varied through the decades. With buttons on his uniform shining to match his boots, he looked to be the fighting machine of legend.

Liam placed the photo frame next to his birthday cards and delved back into the box. Next out was Fran's silver-plated cigar lighter. Liam thought back to the first time he saw it being used, as Fran sat cross-legged in the sunshine, waiting for his grandson to help him chop wood.

The episode raised a smirk of self-deprecation, yet that lighter was also symbolic of Fran's fight with his toughest opponent. An enemy that he ultimately failed to vanquish, despite years of hardened battle.

Another gem lay in the box.

Fran's copper bangle.

It looked to have been polished especially for the job. Liam thought of the distance travelled by such a treasured piece. Given to his grandfather by a dying friend; now passed downwards to a living grandson. The relevance of beholding such an artefact brought a lump to Liam's throat as he delicately slipped it onto his own wrist.

As he rolled up his sleeve to inspect the effect of the orange metal against his skin, Liam was forced to examine the remnants of his own self-induced persecution. The tint of the copper accentuated the crimson of the scars on his forearm. He looked beyond his bedroom window caressing the bangle, quietly considering lost loved ones.

And the absence of love he had held for himself for much of his sixteen years.

Fran could have taught Liam so much more. Even so, he had successfully instigated a thirst for change in his grandson.

Liam now had an undying will to learn about life and people. His relationship with Fran may have been brief, but it was time enough to influence the boy for the rest of his days.

Back to the box once again, Liam was surprised and immensely relieved to discover the sketches he had done whilst in Clearlake. Vivid memories on paper that he had forgotten to depart with.

The first was the drawing of the swans when they were still young and unkempt. The parents and their cygnets on the shore of the lake.

The scene was symbolic of the entire summer. The rapid and unnoticed passage of time that could never be reclaimed. The gradual change in the offspring and their dependency on parentage.

It brought to mind his initial reluctance to listen to sound advice. An obsession with misdemeanour and ignorance of proven standards. The will to inflict sufferance on others. Such a destructive mindset was so abusive of an intelligent brain and body.

Just one brief glimpse of that family on the lake was enough to eradicate any need to reflect on his previous self.

People were like swans. They should be treated as fragile beings and respected. They should be revered for their beauty and accommodated for their frailties.

Fran's wishes were now beginning to make sense. His desire for Liam to learn quickly; to change his unruly ways. To place an old head onto a young tearaway's shoulders was not an easy mission. But Fran had been successful in his endeavours.

The evolution in the teenager had been accomplished.

The second sketch was almost too difficult for Liam to acknowledge. The profile of an elegant female face, slender of feature and pure of skin. Not a perfect reproduction, but a pertinent impression of a girl that Liam would give anything to set eyes upon once again, if only for a second.

That heavenly second would maybe appease a lifetime of potential regret - maybe even unhealable heartbreak.

He turned over the piece of paper as if to omit her from his mind, but the image had been freshly ingrained once again.

Inside his conscience; behind his eyes. There was no chance of escape from the wondrous vision. The memories were both a blessing and a curse.

He had fallen in love with a girl he would never meet again.

Liam inspected the box for any remaining items. A humorous diversion ensued as he pulled out the devilishly gruesome caricatures of his grandparents. Drawn in anger by the artist. Witnessed in anger by the subjects.

Another photograph was in the box, this one in colour but not framed. Liam with his prize-winning fish at the riverbank. Fred had caught the moment superbly through the lens. How that day would end in such negativity.

The box was now empty aside from a small white envelope that lay in the bottom.

Liam became unexpectedly nervous as his shaking hand retrieved it and he studied his name on the outside.

Without hesitation, he split the seal and unfolded the single sheet of handwritten notepaper.

Taking a deep breath, he concentrated on the words.

To my dear grandson,
It pains me to think of you, reading this letter in such circumstances. This is of course, based on the selfish presumption that you will be somewhat upset at the news of my demise. I suppose that by now you know the history behind my illness. I hope you understand my reasoning for withholding my sufferance from you, indeed from all my close family. There's nothing anyone could have done but sympathise, and I'm far too old and stubborn to court pity!

I write this note to assure you of my love and hopes for you, Liam. Whilst having been a seemingly dormant aspect of your life for many years, I did nevertheless keep a distant eye on your upbringing and progress. I could see that you had slowly become lost and in need of guidance. My methods of education may have caused you concern at the time, but I can say hand on heart that inflicting fear was not the primary motive for my actions.

Let me compliment you, Liam. You're one hell of a quick learner. You left Summer Place a different person to when you arrived. I could see evidence of the change in you. You're a fine young man with an active mind and body. I think I did a reasonable job in the little time allowed!

In fact, you have the honour of being my last great victory! Please don't hold it against me.

In the box I have enclosed some gentle reminders of your stay with us. I hope that you will wear my bangle and your grandma claims that you were in head over heels in love with those denims! Try not to use the lighter too often - I can assure you that smoking is bad for your health!

Enjoy your continuing journey into undiscovered country and I hope you miss me every day of your life.
Because I know I'm missing you, soldier!
Do me proud with your endeavours.
Be brave...and behave!
Your ever-loving Grandpa
FJG

The tears dropped freely onto the paper, blotting some of the ink. With a writhing gut tormented by explosive grief, Liam deliberately packed the items back into the box and sat on the edge of the bed.

Regretful longing plagued his mind as he stared through the window once more to a lifeless sky littered with the last remnants of winter.

But the onset of spring was in evidence all around.

The future was brightening by the day.

FORTY

As a matter of priority, Liam's energies quickly began to concentrate on St Forsters and the impending examination period. It was on a sun-drenched morning in late April when Colin Smith called a meeting for all art students to discuss individual ideas for their exam submissions.

Around fifty pupils had gathered in the cramped art department awaiting words of wisdom from their mentor. With his customary half-smile, Mr. Smith took up his position at the front of the class and placed his hands in his pockets.

Not one for barking commands, he simply waited until silence gradually prevailed among the group.

Letting his eyes wander over the expectant throng, he watched their eager faces scan his un-readable expression, wondering what information was about to be revealed.

'You will have provision and materials to complete two finished pieces of work in the set period of eighteen hours. The theme of the work may be related, but each piece must be created via a different medium. Whether it be in oils, clay, watercolour, acrylic and so on. You will also be required to display any preparatory work done for the exam. Is there anybody out there that doesn't understand what I have just told you?'

The peace retained itself among the group until one inquisitive young man raised his hand.

'When is the exam date, sir?'

Mr. Smith smiled inwardly at the source of the query.

'Excellent question, Mister Warburton. It seems that you are the only one out of fifty students that needs to know such a minor detail! It is currently set for the third week in May - the Monday through to the Wednesday. How you apportion the eighteen hours is entirely up to you, but you will have to sign in and out of class as a time check.'

Liam countered again with curiosity.

'Are there any limits on ideas?'

Mr. Smith nodded his head and folded his arms, secretly overjoyed by Liam's renewed interest in his academic future.

'Again…it is entirely *your* choice. I intend to spend the next hour discussing your ideas with you. If we get the cogs turning today, you might just be ready in time!'

Liam's personal plan was already in place and had been so for several weeks.

There was little need for any discussion on his part.

As he immersed himself in consultation with the pupils, Colin Smith became distracted by the imminent departure of one particular youngster. He hurriedly made a move to stop the furtive exit.

'Erm...Liam. In a hurry to get somewhere, are we?'

The teenager stopped at the classroom door as the art teacher approached with not a little concern.

'No hurry, sir. No.'

'Don't you want to talk about what you're doing for the exam?'

'No need. I know what I'm doing, sir. I'm sorted.'

Colin Smith's initial concerns had now been eclipsed by pleasant surprise.

'Oh, really? Do tell.'

Liam had no hesitancy in relating his plans for the upcoming examination.

'A landscape in watercolour and a portrait in oils.'

The teacher nodded in silent relief.

'Yes, Liam. You do sound as if you're pretty much sorted.'

'Okay, sir. Can I go now?'

'Yes. Yes of course.'

Liam turned on his heel and opened the door.

Yet Colin Smith felt compelled to offer one last word.

'Mister Warburton...can I say just say something?'

A little bemused by the request, Liam turned to face his tutor once more.

'Yes, sir?'

The tone was whispered, but very assured.

'Thanks for coming back to me. I knew you would. I had every belief in you.'

Liam smiled, threw his bag over his shoulder, and strode confidently in the opposite direction along the corridor.

The teacher turned to the rest of the pupils, grinning from ear to ear.

He had always recognised the inner talents of Liam Warburton.

The real satisfaction came in knowing that Liam now recognised them too.

FORTY-ONE

Liam held the computerised piece of paper in his hands, which were shaking uncontrollably. He never suspected even twelve months ago that this moment would be so pivotal in his young life.

Exam results day for Year Eleven at St. Forsters was not an occasion any of his fellow pupils had relished.

Nervously, he scanned down the list of subjects and their affiliated grades.

Four B's and Four C'S.

Plus, a single grade A. For Art.

Inner euphoria began to build at that moment in the school hall. Reward for endeavour was not a sensation familiar to Liam Warburton - particularly when it came to his schooling.

Yet as he walked toward the exit door with his collection of passes, he suddenly felt able to conquer the world.

With dedication to his studies fully restored at the beginning of the year, his renewed commitment had been signified.

The thrill of achievement was better than the high attained from any drug. Liam had never experienced such self-belief in his life.

It was evidently on display as Jonka called to him across the room and walked over to meet his friend.

'Hey, man! Good news, yeah?'

Liam nodded and relayed his achievements.

'Jesus, Warbs! I only got four grades! And they were D's and E's! How d'ya fuckin' do it, man? Did ya cheat?'

Liam chuckled and pointed to the clock on the wall.

'Listen, Jonks. I've gotta get back to the supermarket. The boss had only let me have half an hour off and I've used that already.'

'Jesus, Warbs! You got a job, *too*? But its August!'

'Yeah. Only part time through the summer. But I'm hoping to hang onto it though for when I come back here in September.'

'You actually *want* to come back to this dump? And what the fuck you workin' for, man? No wonder we aint seen you all summer!'

Liam now laughed out loud as he began to walk through the doors of the hallway.

'I got the job for the money, Jonks! Why else? We still on for that celebration drink at your house tonight?'

'Yeah, man! My mum's doing a curry for us all. Bring some beer! About seven!'

Liam raised a thumb of acknowledgement and quickly made across the playground. He did not detect his secret observer covertly eyeing the departure from the second-floor landing of the main building.

Colin Smith watched Liam leave the school grounds. The teacher felt a sense of inner pride that didn't affect his professional position all too often. It was the satisfaction that only arises when youngsters not only acknowledge their individual capabilities, but also develop the enthusiasm to use them to the full.

Heading back to town, Liam looked at his results paper once again. The reality of the moment had still not yet registered.

Glancing up to cross the road, he recognised a familiar figure in the distance, but she was too far away to notice him.

Her attention was fully occupied by the baby girl that lay in the pram parked next to her. Liam noticed the expression of overwhelming maternal joy that Carla Ferris conveyed as she tended to the little one before moving onward.

Liam opted not to disturb the tender exchange between mother and daughter, instead viewing the scene from a respectable standpoint.

Carla looked radiant and happy as she navigated the street corner and finally disappeared.

It gave him genuine pleasure to see her so settled, having been fully aware of her severe misgivings regarding motherhood.

He made a silent pledge to catch up with her one day soon as he checked the time on his mobile phone and hurriedly headed back to work.

'You've been in that bathroom for nearly an hour! I didn't think you could get so dirty from drawing pictures all day! Do you want some supper or are you going out tonight?'

Emerging from his bedroom, Liam stood at the top of the stairs and dried his hair with a towel as he addressed his mother.

'What time is it now, Mum?'

'Half-past six.'

'No thanks. I'll grab some chips later. I'm supposed to be meeting the gang at the cinema at seven! I'm late already.'

Liam quickly dressed as the aroma of home cooking wafted through the house. Bounding down the stairway in almost one leap, he applied some gel to his hair and grabbed his jacket from the coat hook. His father followed him down, having replaced his staid business outfit with a leisurely track suit.

'How's school, Liam? Settling in again, alright?'

'Okay, Dad, yeah. Easy life, A-levels! No problem!'

Richard laughed as he took his seat at the dining table.

Stephanie repeated her offer.

'You sure you don't want some dinner, Liam. There's plenty!'

'No mum. I haven't got time. I've got to go *now*, or I'll miss the film!'

Stephanie placed herself opposite her husband and began to eat.

'Haven't got time to do anything much these days have you? Too busy socialising with your student friends. Who would have thought it?'

Liam entered the kitchen to bid his parents goodbye.

'I know, Mum. Your little boy's all grown up! Right...I'm off! Don't wait up. I've got a key!'

Liam kissed his mother on the cheek and made for the front door, checking his wallet for cash.

Stephanie interrupted his departure once again juggling her announcement with a mouthful of food as her voice echoed through into the hallway.

'Oh. Liam! By the way I nearly forgot. Liam! Someone telephoned for you while you were in the shower. I've left their number on the pad next to the phone. I presume they want you to ring back.'

Zipping up his jacket in the hallway, Liam quickly scanned the notepad on his way past.

'Don't recognise the number, Mum. Must be about tonight. I bet its Marcus, crying off because he's skint again! I don't know why he phoned the land line, though. He's got my mobile number.'

Intrigued, Stephanie had now left the dining table and moved to the lounge doorway to watch her son depart.

The smile on her face hinted at mischief as she folded her arms.

'Whoever said it was a *he*? You certainly kept *that* quiet, my lad!'

Liam was becoming a little embarrassed by the inquisitive expression on his mother's face.

'Kept *what* quiet, Mother?'

'You know…you…taking a girl out…to the pictures…tonight! A secret date, eh? Whatever next!'

He offered her a coy yet genuinely confused look but did not wish to play along with his mother's teasing. In fact, Liam was becoming rather frustrated by the seemingly pointless conversation and checked his watch.

'Look, Mum. I'm meeting the lads. I've got to go. So…who was it then?'

Stephanie chuckled to herself before replying.

'Sorry, who was what, dear?'

Liam was now losing patience. His mother was evidently enjoying her son's mild discomfort regarding the subject.

'Who was it that phoned me then?' he barked.

Stephanie held her hands aloft in feigned ignorance.

'*You* should know. *You* arranged the date, after all!'

Now bored by the charade, Liam undid the latch and pulled the front door open.

'I haven't time for this, Mum. I'll see you later. I bet you can't even remember her bloody name, can you?'

Liam stepped outside as his mother's voice carried after him.

'Of course, I can. I'm not old and senile just yet, you know! You'd better ring her back, though. It sounded very important. This Patricia doesn't seem like the kind of girl you'd want to keep waiting.'

Liam stopped dead in his tracks on the doorstep.

Without further thought, he re-entered the hallway and closed the door. He engaged with his mother's confused expression.

'Did you say…Patricia?'

'Yes. That's right. Are you okay, Liam? Did I do right by telling her you'd ring her back?'

'Yes. That's perfect, Mum. Thanks. I'll ring her now…thanks, Mum.'

Stephanie returned to the kitchen table to give her son some privacy.

After removing his jacket, Liam tentatively picked up the receiver and studiously dialled the unfamiliar number written on the notepad.

He suddenly felt his heart raging wildly as he listened to the number being transferred across the network and eventually connected.

His limbs rapidly began to feel heavy as they trembled, yet he was somehow floating on air.

As the ring tone sounded, heaven opened its gates to a young man who had once cherished so little in his life.

A young man who was now about to embrace the incredulous reunion with someone he secretly cherished more than life itself.

ACKNOWLEDGEMENTS

I wish to thank the following people for their invaluable expertise and
support in helping this book gain wings:
Samantha Thornton; Hannah Bliss; Charlotte Wilson; Robbie Wilson;
Carole Thornton, Chris Bliss; Charlotte Bliss; Jeanette Taylor Ford;
Sue Hayward; Ford Wood and last but certainly not least, David Slaney
for his superb cover design.
I couldn't have done it without any of you.
I am forever indebted.
RJT

Also Available on Amazon
by Richard John Thornton

DELIVER US FROM EVIL

AT HELL'S GATE

Printed in Great Britain
by Amazon

32803844R00191